DANTE

DANTE

GUY HALEY

BLACK LIBRARY

A BLACK LIBRARY PUBLICATION

First published in Great Britain in 2017 by
Black Library,
Games Workshop Ltd.,
Nottingham, NG7 2WS, UK.

10 9 8 7 6 5 4 3 2 1

Produced by Games Workshop in Nottingham.
Cover illustration by Akim Kaliberda.

See Black Library on the internet at

blacklibrary.com

Find out more about Games Workshop
and the world of Warhammer 40,000 at

games-workshop.com

Printed and bound in China.

It is the 41st millennium. For more than a hundred centuries the Emperor has sat immobile on the Golden Throne of Earth. He is the master of mankind by the will of the gods, and master of a million worlds by the might of his inexhaustible armies. He is a rotting carcass writhing invisibly with power from the Dark Age of Technology. He is the Carrion Lord of the Imperium for whom a thousand souls are sacrificed every day, so that he may never truly die.

Yet even in his deathless state, the Emperor continues his eternal vigilance. Mighty battlefleets cross the daemon-infested miasma of the warp, the only route between distant stars, their way lit by the Astronomican, the psychic manifestation of the Emperor's will. Vast armies give battle in his name on uncounted worlds. Greatest amongst his soldiers are the Adeptus Astartes, the Space Marines, bio-engineered super-warriors. Their comrades in arms are legion: the Astra Militarum and countless planetary defence forces, the ever-vigilant Inquisition and the tech-priests of the Adeptus Mechanicus to name only a few. But for all their multitudes, they are barely enough to hold off the ever-present threat from aliens, heretics, mutants – and worse.

To be a man in such times is to be one amongst untold billions. It is to live in the cruellest and most bloody regime imaginable. These are the tales of those times. Forget the power of technology and science, for so much has been forgotten, never to be re-learned. Forget the promise of progress and understanding, for in the grim dark future there is only war. There is no peace amongst the stars, only an eternity of carnage and slaughter, and the laughter of thirsting gods.

CHAPTER ONE

THE THRICE-BLESSED CHILD

452.M40
The Great Salt Waste
Baal Secundus
Baal System

A new life was beginning. Night was falling, and a boy and his father watched the skies.

The giant red orb of the sun passed behind the disc of Baal. First-night came to Baal Secundus with eclipse, Baal's shadow creeping over the Great Salt Waste of its second moon. Heat radiated rapidly through the thin atmosphere. The temperature dropped fast and the night wind blew hard, chilling the man and his son. The sand roamer behind them rocked in the breeze. The rusty springs of its suspension squealed in sympathy with the pained birth-cries coming from within.

The boy glanced back at the roamer. A rough ovoid of crude plates lifted high over the ground on six wheels, it was his home and refuge from the moon-world's killing landscapes. The open door cast a rhomboid of yellow light across the waste, softening the fractal harshness of the salt pan's surface. As if provoked by his gaze, the door banged shut, cutting off the warm light. The metal muffled the cries only a little.

The boy's father looked back also, then wrapped his arm tighter around his son, pulling him close.

'She will be fine,' said the man. 'Your mother is strong. Your brother will be here soon.' The boy was old enough to guess the words were intended to reassure his father, not he.

His father's body was ravaged by residual fallout from a war, twelve thousand years lost. Deep lines marked his cheeks. His lips were scabbed with plates of skin. Amid the stubble of his cheek, a trio of ulcers glistened, blood-red flowers blooming in a poison field. A thick mane of brown hair, shot with premature grey and coarsened by salt, framed his face. There were black gaps in his yellow smile. At a little over thirty standard years the man was old and regarded himself well past his prime. His goggles, a priceless family heirloom of age-yellowed, scratched plastek, rested on his forehead, exposing an area of paler skin around his eyes less damaged than the rest. For all the cruelties of the land and the hard life it had given him, in his perfect, amber eyes there dwelt humour and a tender love for his child. Privation was all he had ever known. His humanity had not suffered for it.

'Come away from the roamer, Luis,' the man said softly. His chapped hands adjusted the scarf around the boy's face, bringing it into a sharp triangle on the bridge of his nose. He smiled and touched his knuckle to his son's forehead. Long, dark robes swathed them head to foot. Although the sun killed slowly out there in the Great Salt Waste, the nearest mortis radzone was far away. They were blessedly free of the need to wear their rad suits.

'But da, mama–'

'Hush,' said the man, and he gripped his boy to him more tightly. 'Let the life-bringer do what she does. Your mother is safe in her hands, you'll see.'

A long, agonised moan came from the roamer to belie his words. The vehicle rocked hard, a sudden violence that subsided into ominous stillness. The wind soughed through the struts of the vehicle, setting the charms around the cab rattling. The boy's father had made them. There were strings of scrimshawed bones and chimes of wind-scoured glass of blue and turquoise, plucked from the buried ruins of forgotten lands. But the boy's favourites were two angels of metal scrap leaning forwards on the engine casing, frozen in the act of taking flight. From their outstretched arms, wings of blood-red ribbon snapped. In the growing dark they ceased to be familiar, becoming unnerving harbingers of terrible news – the very angels of death. The boy's fears for his mother grew.

'It will be fine, you'll see,' repeated his father. 'Come on, let's walk a little way.'

The boy was seven or thereabouts. Like his father, he had little idea of his true age. The seasons of a moon-world are complex and not easy to reconcile with the rhythms of Terra, a place far distant from their thoughts in any case. The home of the undying God-Emperor, Terra was to them a mythical world beyond conception. Nevertheless, their bodies remembered. Their unthinking genes had yet to throw off the stamp of their birthplace. Man was not made to survive on the Baalite trio. A genetic code forged over millions of years had had scant thousands to adapt to this hellish place, and frantically drove the creatures it made to reproduce before it was terminally compromised. Already the harsh environment had set its claws into the boy, eroding his features almost quicker than they could form. Life was short for the Baalites. They instinctively felt that it was not meant to be so and sorrowed, though they did not know why.

Their mortal shells yearned for the ease of a world that had ceased to exist millennia since. Old Earth was gone, and Terra as dry and dead as Baal Secundus. In those terrible times there were only deserts for men to inhabit. Deserts that had been made from paradises.

'Come away a little further,' said the man, when they had gone a way from the camp. 'We'll see them soon, up there, on Baal.'

'But we are not supposed to,' said the boy. He cast another glance backwards. His father gently but firmly pushed him on. Beyond their sand roamer were a score of similar vehicles. Some were bigger and some were smaller than their family home, but none greatly so, and they all followed the same basic pattern save the hulking salt hauler, in which no man lived. The orange light of fire scorpion lamps burned in the roamers' portholes and through cracks in their worn sides. They were the sole, lonely signs of life. Sometimes Luis felt his clan were the only people anywhere.

'I know you are not supposed to go too far, and you are wise to remind me,' said the man. 'But you are with me, and so you shall be safe.' The man squeezed the boy's shoulders. He took the boy further out from the camp. Plates of salt cracked under their feet. In every direction flat salt pan stretched away, a desiccated infinity as fractured as the skin of the man. During the day the sun streamed through clear skies stripped of protective ozone in the Long Ago Wars, as merciless to the land as it was to the flesh. At night the temperature plunged, and then the salt sucked greedily at the atmosphere's meagre moisture load. Complex hydrates formed in the wastes, as precious to the salt clans as the chemicals they scraped from the ground. The latter gave them wealth, the former water. Hard as it would be for an off-worlder to believe, theirs was a rich clan.

The cries had faded with distance, and so the man stopped his son with gentle hands. 'Here will do,' he said. He sat down with a satisfied sigh. Rest was a luxury he rarely enjoyed. 'Will you sit with me?' he said. The wind gusted harder, cooler with every second. It peppered the boy and his father with salty grit.

Luis looked out over the desert. Visibility was good. The giant red crescent of Baal proper poured sanguine light over their world. 'We can see for miles,' he said. 'Nothing approaches.' He looked up and searched the sky. The painful blue of the day was ceding the bowl of heaven to night. The sky was red, the stars were red. The broad slash of the Red Scar bled its ruddy light across the cosmos. 'No blood eagles fly. Fire scorpions are rare in the salt wastes.' He stamped. 'This ground is too salty to support trap-clams and too hard for catch spiders.' He looked at his father. 'I judge it safe. I will sit with you.'

The father blinked away grit from his eye, but did not put on his goggles. He grinned in delight at his son's answer. 'Soon you'll know more than I.'

'I already do,' said the boy confidently. The man laughed, openly, the kind of laughter than invites participation, but the boy did not join in. His appraisal of the deadly lands around had been a momentary distraction. Worry for his mother returned. Luis sat down and nestled into his father.

White streamers of salt snaked across the ground. Their hissing could not quite drown out the cries coming from their roamer. He watched it nervously. For all the pressure the world exerted on its inhabitants to mature quickly, he was still a boy. He needed his mother.

His father laughed. 'I will decide when you know more than I.' Following his son's eyes to their roamer, the man took his son's hand and pulled his attention away, directing it out to the horizon and the planet looming over it. 'Tonight is a good night, an auspicious night.' He folded his arms around the boy, feeling him shiver in the dropping temperature. They leaned into each other, seeking warmth.

'Why?'

'Watch!' said the man. He pointed to the brother planet, bringing his arm in line with his son's eyes. The shadow of Baal's own night crawled over the surface. It too was a world of deserts, red and vast, an all-encompassing landscape stretching from pole to pole. Mottled dun patches marked out mountains, blacker areas were depressions, modest spreads of frozen carbon and water capped the points of its axis, but no matter their hue all were various shades of red.

'The first wonder of tonight,' said the man. The dayside of Baal gave no hint that men lived there, but as night made its solemn procession across the surface, a single light blazed out from near the equator.

The boy had seen it on several occasions before, when the relative positions of Baal and Baal Secundus were favourable. His heart leapt every time.

'The Arx Angelicum! Fortress of Angels!' the boy said.

'The very same,' said his father. 'The great castle where the angels of light and blood live, those who bring the Emperor's judgement to all corners of the galaxy. Think, Luis, they are of Baal!' he said proudly. 'Why, there are even men there who might have come from our own tribe, once.'

'Would they know us?'

'No!' said the man with a smile. 'They have become mighty, risen past the concerns of mortal folk. They were chosen to become the sons of the God-Emperor, given great power and glory. They are the most wrathful of the Emperor's servants – the noblest, the purest, the best.' He whispered the truths of it into the boy's ear, his words displacing the cries from the roamer and the sinister hissing of the wind-blown salt. 'They are the lordliest of lords. The Emperor protects, the priests tell us in Selltown and Kemrender, but they,' he pointed again emphatically, '*they* are how He protects us and billions and billions more like us, all over the galaxy. But they would not know us, not as kin. They are given great lifespans, and the concerns of our lives are beneath them now.'

The boy looked up. Blood-red stars looked back.

'Are there really people there?'

'There are people everywhere!' said his father. 'On worlds around every star, worlds of every kind.'

'I have seen the fortress before,' said the boy, his wonder departing as quickly as it had come. Fear for his mother constricted his young heart.

'Have you seen this?' said his father knowingly. He directed his son's gaze to the farthest side of Baal, where night was deeply entrenched. Bright points moved across the world, some so close to one another they merged. Smaller lights twinkled as they ascended from the fortress on Baal.

'Stars,' said the boy. 'That is all.'

'Not so,' said the man. 'Stars cannot be so close to a world. Those are the great starships of the Blood Angels themselves.'

'Are they bigger than our roamer?' asked the boy.

The man laughed at his innocence. 'I would think so, my son. In those great void chariots the lords of Baal ride to war. You see a very special thing. Rogus saw them gathering last night. I thought you might like to see. Now, some will say the angels fly to war on wings of shining light, but I know that is not true. They fly in machines that vent fire, roaring louder than the thunder. Who can stand against such warriors?'

'No one,' said the boy, entranced again. 'There really are people out there, in the black?'

'Yes!' said the man.

'I would like to go there one day.' He turned around in his father's arms. 'Maybe I will one day. I could go to the brother planet and join the angels of blood. Would that not be a fine thing?'

The earnestness shining in the boy's face unnerved the man. Encouraging such an ambition had not been his intention. His scabbed brow lowered over his perfect eyes.

'More die in the attempt than get to join the angels,' he said. 'Only a very few make their way to the Place of Challenge at Angel's Fall, fewer still survive the challenges, fewer yet are chosen.' Reflexively, he hugged harder. Already he feared to lose his wife that night; the thought of losing his son as well terrified him. 'Better a life of hardship you know than the almost certain chance of doom. It is best to venerate the angels from afar.'

'Many people fail?' said the boy, refusing to be discouraged.

'Nearly all the people fail. Only the most exceptional survive to be chosen, and special as you are, chance will doom you before you have the opportunity to prove yourself.'

Luis was silent a moment. He craned his neck around to look at the lights over Baal. 'Nearly all, but not all. Someone has to become an angel.'

There was no arguing with this truism, and the man inwardly cursed his son's sharp mind. The coy edge of Baal Primus peeked around Baal, and the man seized the opportunity to change the subject.

'See! Here comes our moon's sister, Baalind,' said the man, using the local name for Baal's first moon. 'She is always trying but ever failing to catch us. Once the sisters of Baal were always in the sky together, glorying in their company for one another. Until the Long Ago War, when their falling out drove them apart and ruined both moons for the people.'

The boy knew the story very well, but loved to hear it. 'Why did they fight? Were they hungry?'

'No! In those days everyone had enough to eat and drink, enough metal to work and machines you could not imagine. They fought over gold and favour, for the love of Baal himself,' said the man. 'Baal made a gift to his little sister Baalind of a glorious necklace. It was so beautiful that his elder sister flew into a rage and attacked her. They say on the far side of Baalind there is a series of scars where our moon Baalfora tore the necklace free,' he said. 'But it burned her fingers, and she dropped it into the night, and the necklace fell into the Blood Sea,' he said, pointing at the Red Scar. 'And so the gift was lost, and the worlds were ruined. Both sisters were beautiful once. Their jealousies made them hags. There is a lesson in that. That is why we never fight in our families. Strife within family is death to us all. If we fight with ourselves, we cannot protect ourselves from what might come from without. Not until the Great Angel came to Baal did we find ourselves again, and learn this lesson properly.'

Luis thought in the deep, intense way of small boys. 'Maybe the stories are not true,' he said. 'Maybe home was always like this.'

The man hugged his son. 'An ignorant man says ignorant things. I hope I did not raise you to be ignorant. The stories are true. This world was once a beautiful place. This Great Salt Waste was once a sea, as wide a body of water as you can imagine, and many creatures lived in its depths. You have seen their bones. There is proof there.'

'I am sorry,' said the boy, worried he had annoyed his father. He was a good, kind man, but his temper was sharp and easily unleashed.

'No need to say sorry,' said the man, his tone softening. 'I correct you, not chastise. When you have seen all I have seen, you will understand what once happened here. The Great Angel made it better, though we still suffer for the sins of our forefathers. Even so, the Great Angel's sons love us of all people especially. This is what I am showing you – that they are out there, watching over us for the Emperor.'

The cries from the roamer were diminishing in frequency and intensity.

'We are fortunate tonight – a child born under the lights of the angels marshalling is destined for great things. So don't worry for your mother. This business of making children is fraught, but it will be right, you shall see. Your brother will be thrice-blessed.'

'Was I born on such a night?' asked Luis.

His father's pause was all the answer he needed. 'You have other blessings,' he said. 'But you are not marked for such things.'

'Father?' said the boy. He turned from the lights cutting their way across the sky.

'Yes, my son?' said the man. His pale eyes looked earnestly into those of his offspring.

'When I have a brother, will you still love me just as much?'

The man laughed and gave his boy a fierce squeeze. 'Love is a bottomless well, my lad. I'll love you both just the same. And if you ever feel yourself being jealous – and you will, for a new life needs much nurturing – then remember...' He leaned in close and whispered in the boy's ear. 'You were here first, and you and I had this time together. That'll always be yours.' He withdrew a touch. 'I'll love you so much no matter what, little one, for I am your father.'

The sky burst with light again as the sun drew past the edge of Baal. Firstnight ended. The sudden input of heat set the winds roaring across the plains, and the boy and man cast their long hoods over their heads and held each other, giggling for the thrill of being out in the scouring storm.

Abruptly it dropped. Luis' father shook out their cloaks. The sun set again as Baal Secundus – Baalfora – turned its face away from the light and the sun set a second time.

A sliver of Baal remained lit. That slice of Baal Primus inching around the mother world was bright still. For a rare moment all three worlds in the planetary subsystem lined up, and the aged sun kissed the foreheads of her sickly children one by one. The void chariots of the angels sailed through the sea of light and dark. Luis held his breath at the sight.

Then the sun was gone, and truenight draped its cloak over the Great Salt Waste. The wind dropped.

'Arreas! Arreas!' The shout had the father and son turn around. The life-bringer was framed in the light of the roamer's open door, her voice wavering on the dying wind.

Something in the woman's voice and manner had the boy's father stumble to his feet violently, spilling his son into the salt.

'Arreas! Come quickly!'

'Father?' said the boy. His eyes threatened tears. An indescribable dread had him. 'Father!'

But the man was running as fast as he could for the roamer and did not reply. The boy watched him recede from him forever, leaving him alone on the cooling salt.

CHAPTER TWO

THE GREAT DEVOURER

998.M41
Phodia City
Asphodex
Cryptus System

Other winds on other worlds blew harder than those on Baal. Fifteen hundred years later, the planet of Asphodex breathed its last violent breaths.

'Forward, to the walls! Let none pass! Here we shall make our stand!' roared Commander Dante. Gales screamed through the ruins of the world-city of Phodia, buffeting him with their ferocity. His men thundered past him into the wreckage of Port Helos. Ceramite slammed into crumbling walls as the survivors of the Second Company took up their firing positions. The tracks of battle tanks squealed as they passed under the port gate onto the landing fields.

It had been a hard battle, striking out from their strongpoint in the port to the Fabricator's Tower – one of many battles fought on the system's once populous worlds to activate the ancient device known as the Magnovitrion. A struggle undertaken in concert with beings Dante would ordinarily consider the most implacable foes, the cold, robotic necrons.

Against all the odds, they had been successful. The winds that howled through the ruins of the world-city of Phodia were born from the death of Aeros. An entire planet had been consumed by the necrons' ancient technology. Dante looked upwards through racing clouds. A new star outshone the baleful twin Cryptus suns as the system's gas giant burned to nothing. The blast of energy from Aeros had vaporised tyranid hive ships throughout the system, dealing Hive Fleet Leviathan a grievous blow. But the cost was high. Already ruined and overrun, the numerous worlds of Cryptus had shared in Aeros' death throes. Asphodex was protected by a thick atmosphere, but even so the shock wave hit like a hammer blow. The skies were in uproar, and the ground rumbled and swayed with aftershocks. Away in the city the gathering rush of buildings collapsing could be heard.

'General Dhrost!' voxed Dante, shouting against the wind. 'Do you live?' He watched the battle-scarred control centre with hopeful eyes. A pause had him fearing the worst.

'*Yes, commander, we yet live. You have returned to us.*' The Cadian general's steely voice betrayed no weariness or emotion.

'We depart together from this place. We have come to ensure no more brave warriors of the Imperium die in this endeavour. Prepare to evacuate your men.'

'*As you command, Lord Dante,*' came the crackling reply. Dhrost masked his surprise well, but Dante had been judging the minds of men for a millennium and a half, and he heard it. The Cadian had not expected to be saved. Many other Chapters would have deemed the risk too great and left the Astra Militarum to their fate.

The Blood Angels were not other Chapters.

'We shall bring our Stormravens and Thunderhawks down by the control centre.' Dante looked upwards again. The sky was free of flying tyranid creatures for the time being. Dhrost had made them a priority target during his initial defence, as had Dante when he arrived to relieve the Astra Militarum. What few remained had been cast from the air by racing upper-atmospheric hurricanes. Where monsters were absent, angels still flew. Through the burning remains of falling hive ships, blood-red gunships descended through the gales, slipping sideways in the sky as they fought to maintain their heading and evade the looped coils of blazing feeding tubes slithering groundwards between them. The brief, crackling burst of a datasquirt updated the command systems in Dante's armour.

'The first shall arrive in one minute, forty-six seconds. Thirty men to a ship. I have but seven craft remaining, so there will need to be several journeys. Choose your order of departure, general. I will leave no one behind.'

'*My lord Dante.*' Mephiston's dry, cold voice cut through the roar of the wind. The Chief Librarian held the further end of the line, and communicated by vox. '*The enemy stirs. The hive mind recoheres. They will come against us soon. Our respite will last only a few more minutes.*'

Dante pivoted on the broken rockcrete and ignited the jets of his jump pack, lofting himself high over the battlefield, his honour guard leaping skywards with him.

Towering manufactoria crowded Port Helos on all sides, ragged with battle damage. Fires sent swift streamers of smoke into the sky. Broken digestion tubes lay across leaning spires, as glistening and flaccid as entrails torn from a man's belly. Destruction's grey dust coated every surface, turning the city into a mournful monochrome broken by the bright chemical splashes of tyrannic fluids.

Outside the port, the broken bodies of weapons beasts formed an oozing carpet three metres deep covering every road and way of the Fabricae district. Shattered tank turrets protruded from the sea of flesh. These islands of plasteel, lapped by waves of bladed chitin, were the sole reminder of the Astra Militarum defence of Asphodex overwhelmed hours before the arrival of the Blood Angels. The Adeptus Astartes had been too late to save these bold men and women; the Chapter Master would let no more fall on his account.

Dante roared up a hundred metres, his battle-brothers becoming small red dots against the riven walls of the eastern landing fields.

The flaming moat of promethium that Dhrost had surrounded his last stand with had gone out, those few patches that remained guttering torn flags of fire that ran horizontal to the ground.

Adjusting his position, Dante leaned into the wind. It was a living thing, the fury of a star system reacting to infection, but it was too late. The Cryptus System was lost. Asphodex was a dead world. That men lived and breathed on it still was misleading; they were the last bacteria on a body already dead, and the agents of consumption had already devoured much. The other worlds of the system were similarly overrun.

To the west, the Archangel Terminators of the First Company formed a loose cordon along a barricade of shipping containers, knocked-out tanks, port loading vehicles and haulers, and the broke-backed, blackened remains of a surface-to-orbit hauler. Two demi-companies Dante had brought to Asphodex. Two demi-companies to stand against billions of monsters. A thin red line. He brought up the strategic level of his faceplate display. There were many mortis runes glowering at him from its forest of information. The death mask of Sanguinius concealed Dante's sorrow.

It was a similar situation elsewhere. Elements of the Second Company under their captain Aphael had been sent to Aeros. Gabriel Seth's Flesh Tearers fought on Lysios, while that part of the Blood Angels Seventh Company present in the Cryptus System had pressed outwards under Captain Phaeton to intercept and escort the small portion of the system's civilian populace who had managed to evacuate.

Switching his vox to the local relay, Dante contacted the *Blade of Vengeance*. The hubbub of a major ship at war filled his vox-beads, the sounds of cannons rumbling over shouted orders and the mindless confirmation responses of servitors.

'*My lord commander. You were successful. Sanguinius smiles on us.*'

'Captain Asante, what is the status of the flagship?' asked Dante as he bounded across the space port in long, powered jumps.

'*Good, my lord,*' said the Blood Angel fiercely. The feed was badly disrupted by the aftershocks of Aeros' destruction and Dante struggled to hear him. '*Minimal damage. We are clearing the rendezvous area of remaining hive ships. They are not putting up much resistance.*'

'Lord Bellerophon,' Dante said, switching his vox-feed to speak to his fleet commander, also aboard the *Blade of Vengeance.* 'The other forces throughout the system, how do they fare?'

'*My lord, it is good to hear you,*' said Bellerophon. '*I have good news. All elements report in. Seth withdraws from Lysios with the Adeptus Sororitas and remaining civilians. Captain Aphael and Lord Corbulo return from Aeros. Captain Phaeton made contact half an hour ago – he has taken refuge in the Castellan Belt and awaits your orders. Chaplain Arophan and the Death Company died fulfilling their duty. I am exloading a full report to you now.*'

'Do you have any sign of the necrons? They disappeared from the surface here.'

'*Their ships have gone, my lord,*' said Bellerophon. '*They faded out of visual contact and auspex before the shock wave hit.*'

'Was Corbulo successful?'

'*I regret not, my lord. The Satryx elixir was destroyed. I am sorry, my lord.*'

Dante let the play of information streaming down his faceplate distract him. Corbulo had been confident the elixir the Cryptosians used to survive the effects of the twin stars would alleviate the flaw, and perhaps offer a cure. He mastered his disappointment before he spoke again.

'Tell all elements to head to the fleet rendezvous over Asphodex. We shall make for thermal tunnel thirteen-alpha and depart this system as soon as able. Our retreat shall be undertaken in force. Prepare for the arrival of evacuated Astra Militarum personnel onto the *Blade of Vengeance,* many severely wounded. Have the warp engines blessed, and prepare for immediate translation once we are past the Aegis Diamondo – we must make all speed to Baal.'

'*As you will it, so shall it be done, commander.*'

Bellerophon cut the vox.

Dante leapt high and descended on roaring spikes of fire upon the northern part of the western defences, where Mephiston, Chief Librarian of the Blood Angels, and Epistolary Marcello held the line. Marcello radiated weariness, but Mephiston appeared unaffected by his travails. He was one of the few psykers Dante had encountered who could withstand the crushing presence of the hive mind.

The Lord of Death's hair fluttered in the poisonous wind. The psyker fought bareheaded, his solemn face framed by his psychic hood. His eyes glittered with the power of the warp, matching in coldness the shine of the rubies in the skulls crowning his hood's twin spines.

'Commander,' Mephiston greeted Dante as he touched down. The Chapter Master's honour guard landed with a series of metallic clanks, merging with Mephiston's own guardians to form a barrier of golden armour and white wings around them.

'The necrons have abandoned us, as we expected. We are perilously few to hold such a wide perimeter.'

'Hold we must,' said Dante. 'Ninety minutes, ·no more. I will not permit another death if it can be helped. We will evacuate the remainder of the Astra Militarum along with us or die in the attempt.'

Mephiston bowed his head. 'As you command, my lord. Death is my domain – I will gladly send more of the xenos into its embrace.'

'See to the defence here on the northern edge,' said Dante. 'Captain Karlaen holds the landing field. I shall take the south personally.' He gestured back to the Port Gate with the Axe Mortalis, where the Land Raider *Hammer of Angels* was manoeuvring to block the way.

'The mind of the Devourer is reeling from the destruction of its fleet, but it recovers. I sense its malevolence sharpening. We have a few minutes, no more,' Mephiston answered.

'Its thoughts clear and turn towards us,' said Marcellos, his voice thick with effort. 'It is angry.'

'No anger can match the rage of the Red Thirst,' said Dante confidently. 'We will keep them back. Stand ready. Blood and honour, Lord Librarian, Epistolary.'

Marcellos bowed his head in acknowledgement.

'The enemy may be numberless, Commander Dante,' said Mephiston, 'and we few, but we shall prevail.'

'Long enough to save the Astra Militarum – that is all that is required,' said Dante. He jetted skywards again. Surrounded by a flurry of white ceramite wings, he rocketed across the port's cracked landing apron to the southern gate. Great gaps had been clawed into the wall; the four-metre tall rockcrete face was pock-marked with bio-acid burns and studded with embedded flecks of bone and gristle. Three breaches had been opened in its length, hastily patched with twisted metal and lumps of masonry, but the alien dead were banked so high against the ramparts in ramps of bone and flesh that they robbed the wall of any efficacy.

There were only sufficient Blood Angels for one every ten yards of the wall. Little over one hundred sons of Sanguinius against an infinity of hate. Dante swore it would be enough.

The glaring red of tanks and Dreadnoughts marked the dull landing aprons like splashes of blood, bolstering weak points or arranged to cover the defended area with intersecting fields of fire should it be breached. Along the armoured ramparts of the control centre, blue-helmeted Devastators were taking up position. The glowing coils of their plasma cannons were green beacons in the last evening of the world. Some hundred yards back from the wall Assault Marines were stationed, their numbers whittled to less than a score, waiting to react to points of crisis. The last few hundred Imperial Guardsmen stood with them, the remaining handful of Astra Militarum tanks arrayed with their weapons facing outwards around the evacuation point near the control centre's armoured doors.

Dante had nothing but the highest respect for these mortal warriors. They had fought for days against a horrific foe. They were exhausted, terrified; beaten, by all rational appraisal. And yet still they fought on.

Dante came down on the gatehouse rampart. The plasteel gates had been torn free, the carnifexes that had done the work lying beneath them, still leaking stinking fluid into the dust. The bright crimson block of *Hammer of Angels* plugged the gap temporarily. There were four warriors to hold the gate alongside the tank, a combat division of Squad Vorlois. They went to their knees when their leader arrived among them.

'It is an honour to fight with you, my lord,' said Sergeant Vorlois.

'The honour is mine, sergeant.' Lifting his hands to bid them stand tall, Dante keyed his vox to speak to every warrior in the strike force.

'My brothers! I have asked much of you these last days, and I must ask again.' Dante turned to point at the battered control centre. Golden armour glinted. 'In the port are brave men who fought hard to save this world. They could not hope to succeed, but in their attempt they delayed Hive Fleet Leviathan, allowing us to strike. We have reduced the numbers of its monsters and deprived it of much biomass that it would otherwise have used against Baal itself. We could depart now, and leave these mortal men to their fate. They are mayfly creatures compared to we, the sons of Sanguinius. What matter that they die a few thousand days early?' He paused. 'These are sentiments some others might counsel, but not we! We are the Blood Angels, and I will not see lives discarded to appease cold logic.'

He swept his gaze over his warriors. Every helmet was turned in his direction.

'These men and women of the Astra Militarum have honoured us with their sacrifice. We speak of the Shield of Baal, those systems that stand guardian over our home. I say to you that the shield is not a thing of suns and planets, but a barrier of flesh and blood and will!' He shouted. 'These men, who fell in the millions outside these walls, whose mortal remains have been consumed by the xenos horror that dares feed upon this system, they are the true shields of Baal. We will not allow the last handful of them to die in pain and horror. Instead they shall ascend with us back into the void, and they shall be honoured in their turn. We shall repay their sacrifice with our own blood!' He raised the Axe Mortalis high and keyed its ancient rending field to life. Crackling blue lightning wreathed its brutal head. 'Brothers, will you fight with me one final time upon these blood-slick streets? Will you fight with me, not for glory or for Baal, but for common humanity and the lives of these worthy soldiers?'

'We will! We will! We will!' answered the Space Marines as one.

'For the Emperor and Sanguinius!' shouted Dante, sending his war-cry out through his vox-grille so that it rang from the wreckage of the port.

'For the Emperor and Sanguinius!' responded the Blood Angels.

Dante looked over his warriors. He could not have been prouder of them. Drawing strength from their determination, he turned to look out over the wasteland of dead beasts. The reflected light of fires danced across the death mask of Sanguinius, its mouth forever open in condemnation.

'*The pressure grows,*' voxed Mephiston. '*The hive mind's hunger can never be sated. We have its attention again. Beware.*'

'My lord, I have movement on my auspex,' said Vorlois.

Around a toppled statue a squirming disturbed the mounded alien dead. Broken purple-and-cream bodies were shouldered aside. A carnifex rose, screeching its hatred to the sky. Two of its arms were gone, yellowish ichor running from the sockets. Its carapace was scored with laser burns and mass-reactive impact craters, but it lived. It turned burning eyes upon the last outpost of mankind on Asphodex, and began a faltering advance.

Alarms chimed in Dante's helm.

'Multiple contacts, all directions,' said Vorlois. 'Squad! Stand ready!'

Boltguns were raised, energy weapons primed. Along the wall, the men of the Second and First Companies prepared for battle again. They were no less battered than their foe, honours and insignia obscured by carbon scoring and sticky alien fluids. The ugly, blistered lines of hardened shock gels marked out cracks in their adamantium battleplate. Many were missing parts of their wargear, or were injured. Vorlois' backpack leaked coolant fumes. Another in the squad fought with his left arm bared, his gauntlet and vambrace ripped away, the interface ports on his forearm clogged with coagulated blood. His hands gripped his bolter no less steadily.

The tyranids came tentatively at first, fragmented swarms of lesser weapons beasts emerging from the shattered Fabricae district, scurrying back and forwards mindlessly. Like a disrupted colony of ants, they reorganised themselves. Their random dashes became purposeful. Where leader beasts clawed their way out of the rubble or from under the heaped remains of the tyranid dead, the swarm coalesced all the quicker.

'Lord, I have auspex input from the fleet showing a massive movement of life signs converging on the port. All surviving xenos organisms in this sector are diverting themselves towards our position,' said Vorlois.

'*I feel great hatred,*' voxed Mephiston. '*We have wounded it. The hive mind means to annihilate us all.*'

'*The pressure is great,*' voxed Marcellos. '*We are under its eye.*'

'They are coming!' shouted a warrior down the wall. A single shot banged out, followed by the whooshing of the bolt's propellant charge igniting. An explosion and a screech sounded as the round found its mark, blasting apart a termagant skulking around a blackened tank hull.

The smoking remains of the creature fell to the ground. An all-encompassing hiss whispered out from the ruins, competing with the rush of the wind, and a thousand more weapons beasts rose up behind the corpse, flowed around the wreckage and bounded over the mat of corpses without impediment. They moved as one, switching direction with eerie simultaneity. As this brood leapt to the attack, so did many others break from cover and run towards the walls of Port Helos.

For the final time, the ruins of Phodia echoed to the gunfire of the Adeptus Astartes as the Blood Angels opened up with every weapon at their disposal.

Creatures boiled up seemingly from nowhere, converging on the Port Helos redoubt in scuttling hordes. The blazing suns of plasma cannons crackled overhead, blasting perfect round holes in the onrushing creatures that were quickly filled by more multi-limbed horrors. The creatures were mostly of the lesser sort, termagants, hormagaunts and their ilk, the majority of the larger weapons beasts and leader bio-constructs ruthlessly targeted and felled by the Space Marines in earlier assaults. There were still tyranid warriors present, but these higher species kept back, directing the onrushing wave of gaunts at the wall.

The creatures neared, a hundred yards and closing, rushing through the smouldering residues of the promethium moat towards the walls.

Dante dipped into the wider strategic overview of the theatre his sensorium offered him. Auspex-feeds from ground and orbit highlighted the streams of creatures coming at the port. The *Blade of Vengeance* moved to engage half-crippled hive ships before they could deploy yet more reinforcements, the flashes of its weapons showing as sheet lightning in the sky over Phodia. A system map showed him the blinking icons of Imperial ships as they converged, painfully slowly, on Asphodex.

A roaring announced the arrival of the first Stormraven. Dante risked a look behind him. Livery discoloured by multiple re-entries and combat, the Stormraven wavered in the wind, assault ramp opening before it hit the ground. Battered men and women ran from the building. Dhrost sent out the wounded and near-dead first. Exhausted medics and non-combatant medicae carried casualty biers up into the waiting craft's mouth. Dante's hearts swelled at their bravery as these hale men re-emerged to make way for more wounded. A blinking light in his helm signalled the Stormraven to take off. The instant it was away the second took its place, the third landing nearby alongside it, slotting itself neatly into the tight gap delineated by the Astra Militarum tanks. The fourth, waiting to land, hovered overhead, sending screaming missiles and lascannon blasts into the enemy.

Officers waved their men from the wrecked control centre as more ramps fell open.

Beyond the landing zone, Karlaen's Terminators opened fire at the enemy encroaching from the east. The sound of their guns was lost beneath the banging of bolters nearer to Dante and the cataclysmic booms of air displacement caused by the discharge of high-energy weapons as Devastator Squad Karos targeted those leader beasts foolish enough to show themselves.

The clacking of claw and hoof on alien bodies drew Dante's attention away from the evacuation. Outside the wall, the tyranids were coming into range of his perdition pistol. He dismissed the multiple overlays of runes and informational illuminations cluttering his vision. The wider battle would take care of itself. Now he had only time to fight.

The front ranks of the creatures were decimated by close-range bolt-fire, each Space Marine choosing his target and aiming carefully to conserve ammunition. There would be no more chances to resupply. *Hammer of Angels* carved deep and dripping furrows into the horde of creatures, slaying dozens with its lascannons and heavy bolters. The enemy exploded into collections of shattered exoskeleton. Strange organs burst in showers of colourful fluids as the bodies fell beneath the pounding hooves of the creatures behind, adding to the piles of the dead.

The Red Thirst stirred in Dante, feeding on his outrage at this affront to the Emperor. He envisaged himself abandoning reason, jetting from his position and crashing among the enemy to slay and slay until none were left. He could sense the bloodlust in his comrades, the desire to abandon their position and kill. He saw it in their posture, in the tightening of hands upon gun grips. Dante gritted his teeth against the urge to charge. Such abandon often served the Blood Angels well, the shock of their charge enough to carry the day, but giving in to anger would be disaster. Today was a day for the Angel's Graces, not the Warrior's Virtues. He repeated the calming mantra of the Solus Encarmine in his mind. Another image of his solitary warriors being dragged down to their deaths filled his thoughts. He held it there, pitting the reality loss of control would bring against the need to slay.

The gaunts approached his own position. His Sanguinary Guard readied their weapons. Bright flashes surrounded power swords and axes as motes of dust annihilated themselves on disruption fields.

The aliens raised fists bonded to lesser creatures. A storm of deadly quills spat from the symbiotic weapons. The enemy were close enough that Dante could see the peristaltic jerks of their weapons tubes, and the moist contractions of muzzle sphincters and exposed muscle fibres.

The Blood Angels switched their weapons to fully automatic fire as the gaunts came within leaping distance. The Sanguinary Guard levelled their wrists and opened fire with their Angelus gauntlets. Specialised rounds exploded among the gaunts, sending out clouds of flechettes, and a vast swathe of the onrushing creatures was turned into a gory mist. A final volley of lascannon beams and plasma discharge blasted those behind to pieces, and then they were too close.

'For Sanguinius!' Dante bellowed. A single shot from his perdition pistol turned a galloping termagant into atoms.

The gaunts hurled themselves at the Blood Angels, bounding up the heaps of corpses fronting the broken ramparts. Space Marines howled their anger as the first came over the wall. For a moment the warriors of the Emperor were swamped, the blood-red of their armour vanishing under a tide of dirty bone and purple, each Space Marine buried beneath a frenzied mass of slashing alien bio-weapons.

The slaughter began. The Blood Angels burst free, hewing limbs with combat blade and chainsword, smashing oversized alien skulls with point-blank bolt pistol shots, crushing throats in armoured gauntlets.

A hail of canid-sized attack beasts thundered into Dante and his honour guard, rocking him on his feet and obscuring his vision. With the practice of centuries, he dispatched them all, every move of his axe a paragon of efficiency. The Axe Mortalis' rending field crackled, shearing off heads and limbs in a blizzard of disintegrating molecules. Around him his Sanguinary Guard fought with skill almost the equal of his own. Though pressed close, they moved around each other with the fluidity of dancers. They ducked and wove past each other's weapons. Powered glaives, axes and swords were adroitly anticipated, the Blood Angels' evasions not once breaking the rhythms of their own strikes. Angelus bolters barked razored death. The smoking bodies of termagants fell around their feet with meaty thumps. Spilled viscera and the unpredictable roll of severed limbs made the footing unsteady.

Dante and his men found themselves climbing up over the level of the rampart on the bodies of dead creatures. The commander's perdition pistol took another, then another, blasting the creatures to greasy vapour. Other beings learned to run from the building roar of his melta pistol, but not the tyranids. They weren't mindless, as he had thought long ago, far from it. These were not individual beasts, but single cells of a greater beast. One might as well expect the shed skin cells of a man to feel fear.

'*My lord, the tyranids are overrunning our position. We cannot hold them here for long.*' Captain Karlaen's rich voice intruded over the racket of battle.

'Squad Forian, Squad Gerus reinforce,' said Dante, sending his reserve Assault Marines to bolster Karlaen's position. 'General Dhrost, how many more men have you in the centre?'

'*One hundred and eighteen, including myself,*' replied Dhrost.

Dante brought up another overlay, checking the status of his Stormravens. They were nearing the *Blade of Vengeance*. His pilots were skilled; it would take them only twenty minutes to drop off their passengers and return to the surface.

'Hold the wall! We fall back when the Stormravens return. Sanguinary Guard, disperse, reinforce where you see fit.'

His bodyguard split apart, leaping over the swarming gaunts. Where they landed, tyranids died, their blows often as not revealing an embattled brother.

For a moment, Dante had a clear view of the field. Karlaen's Terminators were ponderously retreating, faces to the enemy. Each step backwards was paid for by the tyranids with a toll of slaughtered horrors. The Blood Angels were inflicting great carnage. Where tyranids broke through the line they were met by the lasguns of the Astra Militarum and the punishment of heavy bolters. Leman Russ tanks hurled shells over Karlaen's line, gouging out divots from the tide of flesh. The Baal Predator *Sanguine Storm* washed promethium flame over gaunt broods that broke for the landing zone.

The psyker beasts the strike force had faced before were all gone, the bio-titans felled, the skies clear of winged tyranids, but still there were too many. The forces of the Imperium were dams of sand holding back the tide of the sea.

Dante was attacked again, and the first mortis rune of that final engagement chimed into red life on his faceplate. Brother Arames, of Squad Barosian. His name flared red and faded away. Dante's fury built. He fought and fought, the seconds becoming fleeting things. Were it not for the mission chrono running in the top right of his helm plate, he would have lost track of time. The Axe Mortalis was never still. His golden armour was smeared with the life fluids of extra-galactic monsters.

The screeching calls of larger bio-constructs sounded out over the endless swarms of gaunts. The creature he was fighting was obliterated, not by an Imperial weapon but by a storm of acid. Its cargo of attack grubs recognised friendly flesh and fell inert to the rampart, but the medium that propelled them was enough to kill Dante's opponent. He looked out from the port. Tyranid warriors had gathered in number, and were wading through their lesser kin.

'They mean to finish us!' he called. 'They see our victory is near!' He spoke fervently for the sake of his men, but his words were ashes in his mouth. He could see no true victory. All around him was a wrecked world, a valuable system of billions of people reduced to nothing in the course of days. Dante had seen too many planets laid to waste in his long life, the power of the Imperium

eroded system by system. If a man held a handful of sand and let
a single grain drop between his fingers once a year, still it would
empty in time. 'Fight them! Throw them back! There shall be no
triumph here for the Great Devourer! Let it open its mouth to feed
and we shall smash its teeth!'

His men fought harder. Seeing them hard-pressed on the walls,
the last Dreadnoughts of the strike force turned their attentions
from the landing fields and strode towards the ramparts.

A cry reached his ears. Sergeant Vorlois was staggering under
a hormagaunt, one of its long, scythe-like talons buried in the
weaker joint between his plastron and pauldron. Its slavering maw
snapped at his helm's muzzle. Dante advanced, sweeping aside
gaunts with his axe. A deathspitter shot splashed into the plascrete of the rampart, showering him with squirming grubs. Their
mouth parts gnawed fruitlessly on ceramite, their acid bodies
making it smoke.

He aimed at Vorlois and fired, making a shot that would have
confounded any other. In a welter of flailing limbs and bodies
where Vorlois wrestled and twisted, he hit the hormagaunt square
on. It exploded, leaving its twitching claw embedded in the sergeant's armour.

'Squad Vorlois, prepare to fall back. Squad Barosian, prepare to
fall back. Captain Karlaen, status report!'

'*We have ceded the barricades, my lord commander. By the Blood,
we are a wall that none shall pass.*'

'Hold in loose perimeter. Inner perimeter disperse more widely,
clear more space. We need more room for the transports to land!'

'*We will be spread thin,*' answered Karlaen.

'Speed is of the essence. Tanks prepare for extraction. We shall
evacuate the armour first. *Anvil of Baal* proceed to this point.' By
nerve-link, he thought a location into his armour's cogitator and
sent it to the force's second Land Raider.

Commander Dante ignited his jets and rose over the swarm of
tyranid attack beasts. He lined up his perdition pistol on one at
random. A squeeze of his trigger finger obliterated it. Superheated

steam roared out from the space the beast had occupied. Its brood brothers paid it no heed, but raced on, talons out to stab and rend. The tyranids poured over the wall like water. Behind them came larger creatures, nearly at the fortifications now. Further out, slower artillery beasts were ploughing through bodies. Once they were in range, their clawed subsidiary limbs slammed into the shattered pavements underneath to stabilise the giant living guns bonded to their backs. Larger and larger creatures were being drawn to the port from areas where they had not been extirpated. The Blood Angels were in danger of being overrun.

Salvation came from the sky. Missiles and battle cannon rounds slammed into the hordes assailing the space port in tight clusters, tearing huge holes in the tyranids all around the Imperial-held ground.

A pair of Thunderhawks banked round once, firing their weapons. A Thunderhawk transporter, the only one available to the task force, came after, escorted by Stormravens and Stormtalons.

'*My lord,* Red Doom *and* Carnelian Glory *inbound with evacuation group. Void war is under control. Captain Asante sent us to reinforce. Standing by for orders.*'

'Cleanse and land,' ordered Dante. 'Get the mortals off this world!'

'*Understood, my lord.*'

The Stormtalons broke off as the heavy transporter swung about and descended over the *Anvil of Baal.* Heavy clamps slammed into the tank's side. The transporter burned all engines and took off without landing, *Anvil of Baal*'s spinning tracks shedding body parts and debris. The Thunderhawks made another pass, then dropped in to land as the circle of tanks drew outwards.

The Stormtalons swept back and forth, blasting away tyranids in their hundreds. Missiles streaked out from Stormravens waiting to land, targeting leader beasts and the artillery arranging itself in the Fabricae district.

The pressure on the wall slackened.

'Fall back!' ordered Dante. He jetted backwards towards the inner perimeter. 'Abandon the wall before they recover!'

Still firing, his warriors leapt from the rampart, shooting back-wards before turning to run, their power armour lending them speed. Mephiston and Marcellos did not pause in their efforts, unleashing the dreadful blood magic of the Chapter upon the foe even as they cleaved at the enemy. The Sanguinary Guard leapt up and back, covering their infantry brothers where they could. One of Vorlois' men fell to a bio-blast as he turned to leave the walk-way over the gate. Another warrior was buried under a seething knot of hormagaunts. Though the foe were scoured away by bolt and flame, he did not rise again. The Stormtalons swept back and forth across the perimeter until their ammunition was exhausted, then turned and shot away into the sky. The first Thunderhawk, loaded with Militarum soldiers, lumbered up after them.

'*Hammer of Angels,* withdraw!' yelled Dante. 'Prepare for extraction!'

The *Hammer of Angels* jerked as its tracks engaged, crushing the bodies of dead tyranids to a paste. It was a plug in a dam; once removed tyranids burst through. The tank's guns obliterated hun-dreds, but the beasts were swift, thundering around and past it across the landing zone towards the newer, inner perimeter tak-ing shape about the Astra Militarum tanks. Brothers checked their flight, turned and, shoulder to shoulder, shot round after round into the aliens. Dante flew down and landed among them, his San-guinary Guard joining him once more. The second Thunderhawk was waiting for the last of the Astra Militarum to emerge. Two Stormravens cooled on the landing apron alongside it. Nearby were lines of black bodysacks, each stamped with the Chapter insignia.

'Squad Vorlois, Ancient Asdornae, Ancient Zorael, you are to leave,' ordered Dante. 'Epistolary Marcellos, go with them. Watch over the bodies of the fallen.'

He strode through furnace-hot engine backwash to the open mouth of one of the Stormravens. Imperial officers were embark-ing with stiff dignity. Dhrost came out first, his face composed. Showing none of the pain of his wounds or his defeat, he stood to one side as his men filed past.

'General, you must leave,' said Dante. 'My brothers shall evacuate as soon as you are away.' The frantic clatter of bolters accompanied his words. 'Go with honour.'

Dhrost walked halfway up the ramp and looked out over the devastated port. 'I did what I could,' he said. 'I leave three million dead men here. I pray it was enough.'

He saluted Dante and went aboard.

'Get the tank crews out, now!' shouted Dante. His warriors hammered on tank hulls, having to bodily drag out the Militarum crews from their vehicles. One by one, the guns fell silent, the tanks becoming little more than physical barriers.

Dante opened a vox-channel to the *Blade of Vengeance.* 'Asante, we are away from the wall. Commence bombardment of the city, five hundred-yard range around the port. Expedite the return of *Wings of Deliverance.* I need that transporter back *now.*' He cut the feed before he got an answer, knowing his orders would be obeyed without question.

Vorlois limped aboard the Thunderhawk, accompanied by the remainder of his men. Others hurried the bodies of the dead on board, watched over by Chaplain Ordamael. Dante cast a regretful look out into the seething mass of tyranids. There were a few bodies he would not be able to take home. The loss of gene-seed and wargear weighed heavy on his heart. Marcellos walked up the ramp without looking back, his pale face grey with the effort of his psychic battles.

The Dreadnoughts Asdornae and Zorael stepped back into the Stormravens' carrying claws.

'Get these ships off the ground! Return immediately,' said Dante.

Lance beams and macrocannon shells screamed through the atmosphere. Shocked air blasted out around pillars of light. Deafening blasts resounded around the crumbling city. Towers tumbled and more buildings, weakened by days of battle, collapsed around them.

There were ninety Space Marines left on the ground. Two more trips, if Dante was to extract the rest of his armour. As the three

Thunderhawks rose up into the sky flanked by Stormravens and Stormtalons, Dante rejoined the battle line.

The Thunderhawk transporter returned half an hour later, its escorts again peeling around to strafe the endless hordes. More ships were leaving the war in orbit. A trio of Stormhawks blazed overhead, the muddy crump of their munitions popping deep in the city. The Second and First Companies formed a line shoulder to shoulder around the tanks, so close that nothing could get through. Dante ordered his Stormravens to remain and keep back the larger beasts from the walls. *Wings of Deliverance* stooped low over *Hammer of Angels.* Beasts leapt at its sides as it rose up, *Hammer of Angels'* weapons still firing, turned around and roared out of sight.

'One more trip for the tanks!' said Dante, cleaving a tyranid warrior in two. There were several Rhino transports in the port, but he would have to abandon them. He would not leave the Predators.

Their cordon shrank, pressed back towards the mouth of the control centre. Two more of his warriors died before *Wings of Deliverance* returned, its metal hide steaming. *Sanguine Storm* and its sister *Desert Fury* rode out into the thick of the horde to allow the transporter to pluck them from the ground, the infantry line momentarily bowing out from the building entrance to protect them. The craft rose up, tilting itself from side to side to spill xeno-forms from its flight surfaces, then burned hard to get away, battling through the still-strong winds.

'*Report all primary armour assets extracted,*' voxed Karlaen.

'We are finished here!' replied Dante. 'All units, retreat to the control centre roof.'

Falling back by squad, the Blood Angels retreated inside. Karlaen's Terminators formed an impenetrable phalanx at the rear; the Stormravens came in to form a hollow triangle around the building, spitting fire into the foe. Thus protected, the Blood Angels sealed the gates and ascended the stairs.

A relentless booming echoed up the stairwell as the tyranids battered at the doors. They had a moment's respite. Dante stood aside to let his warriors run out onto the open roof of the control centre. The first of the Stormravens broke off and rose up to hover before the roof's low parapet. Its assault ramp slammed down onto the edge of the building, scraping the rockcrete white as the vehicle was buffeted by the gusting wind. Two below-strength squads thundered aboard, and it took off skywards. The Thunderhawks returned to take most of the rest of the force before the gates gave way. One perching itself on the control centre's tower, the other flying in circles around the building, both of them firing endlessly at the sea of creatures attacking the building. Karlaen and his men thumped up the stairs backwards, firing at the horrors chasing them. Dante ordered them away, blocking the exit to the roof himself as Karlaen and the battered Archangels made their way to the Thunderhawk crouching on the roof. Once full it took off and the second took its place, while Dante and his honour guard battled hissing bio-forms attempting to force the stairs. Pointed weapon forms clattered off ceramite. The sheer weight of the xenos numbers were forcing them back. The last pair of Stormravens abandoned their defence of the building and rose up.

'My lord, we are the last,' said Mephiston. 'We must leave.'

Dante looked at the press of creatures shoving and bristling before him. For every one his men cut down with their Angelus bolters, there seemed to be a dozen more. Dante hated them; he hated their endless hunger, their primal need to devour everything. They were utterly alien, inimical to all life. His fury rose in him, his lips peeling back from long fangs, twisting into a savage countenance at odds with the perfect outrage of the mask he wore. The pulse of his blood sang shrilly in his ears.

The engines of the Stormravens shrieked in the air.

'Now, my lord!' repeated Mephiston. He grabbed the Chapter Master by the arm and hauled him back. Eyes glowing, the Librarian cast a wall of force into the creatures filling the stairs, flinging them backwards.

'We leave! Now!' said Dante, shaking off his anger.

From Mephiston's back rose a pair of crimson wings. The Sanguinary Guard ignited their jump packs. With aliens snapping at
their heels, the last Blood Angels on Asphodex rose up into the
open bays of their transports. Bolt-rounds from the Stormravens
shepherded them all the way, bursting creatures that in their idiot
single-mindedness still leapt to snag the Space Marines from the
air only to plunge to their deaths on the rockcrete landing aprons
two hundred feet below.

Commander Dante stood at the lip of the ramp of the Stormraven. It rocked from side to side in the heavy winds, buffeted
further by the titanic overpressure unleashed by the magma cannon shells demolishing the city. He looked across a lost world.
Below he left sixteen ancient vehicles, a suit of irreplaceable Terminator armour and the bodies of six of his men and their gene-seed.
Under his perfect golden helm, his mouth twisted with inexpress-
ible fury.

'Asante, I am away from the planet. Send the tyranids one final
gift – level Phodia. Open every gun port. Empty the magazines. I
want nothing but the grit-filled flesh of their own kind left behind
for the Devourer to enjoy.'

The Stormraven rose up as the city erupted into a cataclysm of
fire. The light of it played over Sanguinius' perfect face until the
assault ramp hissed shut, and the Stormraven turned its prow
heavenwards.

CHAPTER THREE

THE DESERTS OF BAAL SECUNDUS

456.M40
The Great Salt Waste
Baal Secundus
Baal System

The night Luis' mother died was the last his father smiled. When they packed her and her stillborn son in the salt, something broke in Arreas. Luis sensed it go, a give of tension so slight it was naught but a whisper. Arreas was as wise and as kind to his son as he had ever been, but a stoniness came over him. Arreas no longer spoke of angels, nor did he show his son wonders, only how to survive and dig the salt.

Years passed one after another, the rolling of the sun over the ravaged face of Baalfora quickening as Luis aged. Grand Eclipses came and went, storms, raids by other clans. The work of staying alive filled every hour, only now Arreas did it without hope or joy. He lived to preserve his son's life, not his own. He saw nothing lovely in the world any more, and seemed impatient that Luis learn how to endure it so that he might leave it behind.

Whether Arreas' sorrow had any bearing on Luis' decision to attempt the trial is hard to say. Perhaps he would have gone if his mother had lived, perhaps not. His father warned him often enough that to attempt the trial was tantamount to a death sentence. Arreas, fearful of losing his last family, meant to frighten Luis, but all it did was stiffen the boy's resolve. By the time he was eleven years old, as the adepts might reckon it, the news came out that the heralds of the angels were abroad. A trial was imminent.

Luis kept nothing from his father, and told him his intention as soon as he was sure of his own resolution. It did not matter that the reaction he got was exactly as he'd expected; there was something honest and pure in Luis from the very beginning, and he did not wish to deceive his father.

He agonised for an age about how to tell Arreas. In the end, he blurted it out while his father prepared dinner in their cramped roamer.

'The sky chariots have been sighted. The heralds of the angels speak to the crowds in Kemrender and Selltown. The Time of Challenge is here. The angels will judge the worthy at High Summer.' Luis cringed at the pompous wording, delivered in his warbling boy's voice. The effect was altogether ridiculous.

'You can't do it,' said his father without drawing breath. He continued to methodically slice the scorpion biltong for their meal. 'I won't allow it. You're the only family I have left. Who will I leave the roamer to?' He glanced over his shoulder, those pale eyes pits of misery. 'Who will continue our line?'

This was the reaction Luis had anticipated, and he was prepared. 'Take another wife,' said Luis. 'Have more children. Da, I must do this.'

'You're too young. What do you know about wives?' said Arreas. He wiped the sweat from his forehead with his skinny arm. It was always oven-hot in the roamer, and he was tired. The sores on his cheek had blossomed into slow cancers. Death's bright fruiting, mottled red and purple. 'I'm too old. I've not got long. If we want to talk about wives, we should talk about yours. What about that?' he said. His levity forced. 'That Malina is nice. She's your age. I've seen her looking at you. She needs someone – they've four children in that family. She'll need somewhere to live. She could live here, with you. It's an arrangement that'll work for everyone.'

'It will not work for me. I will take no wife,' said Luis.

'Then you're being selfish,' said Arreas. 'Every boy that throws his life away for a dream of angelhood weakens the clan. You'd be an asset here, dead out there.'

'Not trying is selfish,' said Luis. His own temper responded to his father's. The change from boy to man had begun. He was getting bigger, more stubborn, swifter to fury. Twenty thousand years on Baal Secundus could not alter puberty's fundamental biology. His voice rose. Under the pattern of sunburn on his face, he flushed. 'If I stay here, I can help Malina maybe. If I become an angel, I can help everyone.'

Arreas set the knife down and bowed his head. 'If, if, if!' he said. 'You will die.' He turned around and leaned against the tiny kitchen work surface. 'What makes you so special? Why do you think you can do it?'

'Why don't you believe in me?' yelled Luis.

Arreas winced. Their voices carried. Their rows had become frequent. The others in the clan made jokes about it. 'Luis, you're small, you're not strong and you're young. But most of all, you're too kind. To be an angel, to fight those wars... What kind of men do you think make such warriors? You have your mother's heart – always you put others before yourself. Your mercy will kill you.'

'Kindness is no vice.'

His father shrugged. 'Not in a husband, but it is in a warrior.'

'Then I shall be stern yet merciful.'

Arreas sighed and took the knife up again. 'Maybe when you are a few years older. You can try the next trial. You'll be stronger then.'

'It will be too late.' With an effort of will beyond his years, Luis calmed himself. 'The trial happens once in a generation. I will be a man the next time it comes. I have to do it now, Da.'

For a moment Luis thought his father might relent. The hard set of his mouth softened and he regarded his son with tenderness.

'No,' said his father firmly, his frown returning. 'I can't lose you as well,' he added quietly. 'Now get ready, work starts soon.' He bundled up their lunch in cloth and stepped out into the dangerous morning, leaving the door to bang against the frame.

The best salts were deepest in the Great Salt Waste. The more easily accessible deposits had been dug up millennia ago, so the caravan of roamers veered away from the edges of the waste, heading to the very heart where the sun blasted the earth with unremitting wrath. They settled into a months-long routine of loading up the hauler with precious potassium nitrates and lithium salts, then making the long journey to Kemrender where they sold their cargo to the processors in their rusting factory fort, then heading back again. A profitable route, but far away from the city Angel's Fall and the Place of Choosing.

Every evening, Luis watched the sky nervously. Baal and its moons inched closer to the Duplus Lunaris that began High Summer. The time when Baalfora and Baalind edged out from the shelter of their brother to confront one another was coming. Each moon becoming completely visible to the other was the signal for the commencement of the trials.

Days turned to weeks. Baalind crept further out into the sky. Luis weighed his father's words; he was small, it was true, and undeveloped. But his body was changing quickly. He would be too old to be accepted if he waited, for the angels of blood took only boys with them into the sky, not men. He agonised on his decision, but made no further mention of it to his father. The boy and the man did not speak much; their relationship became tense, but such is the impact of adolescence. Arreas thought his son had yielded to his wishes, and slept sounder.

They were halfway to Kemrender when Luis left home for good.

The caravan route moved the closest it would get to Angel's Fall. The journey would be a long one across merciless salt pans, but some chance was better than no chance. Luis thought bitterly that it would serve his father right if he died because he had kept the easier road from him.

Such thoughts are unworthy of an angel, and Luis put them aside, praying to the Emperor and Sanguinius in the niche of the family shrine for forgiveness. For the last days, he was warm to his father, and Arreas' misery lifted a little.

As necessity and the tradition of such things dictated, Luis departed in the middle of the night.

Luis spent his last evening with the caravan in conversation with his father. He kept him up late purposefully, then waited for Arreas to fall asleep.

Luis crept out from under his bedclothes silently and pulled on his day clothes. Each movement of the roamer or jingle of a buckle made him stop, teeth clenched, but his father remained deeply asleep. His snores rumbled through the roamer. The tribe had been working all day at a rich deposit, and they were all exhausted. Nerves lent Luis energy. He hoisted his salt pack onto his back. Made of carefully hoarded leather to carry the big slabs of salt from the beds to the hauler, it made a fine haversack. Inside were his meagre belongings: as much water as he could carry, his rad suit, knives, rad-ticker, tinder stick, sleeping roll, water still and dried scorpion meat saved from weeks of meals. The water was the most important.

Moving carefully so as not to set the roamer rocking, he crept to the neatly arranged cupboards. Space in the roamer was limited. Everything had its place. He opened his father's strongbox, tensed and ready for the man to come awake in outrage, but he didn't even stir. From inside, Luis took one of three strings of lead coins. The guilt of this action bit at him deeply. He tried to drive it off by telling himself his father wouldn't need so much money with him gone. Nothing could be less true.

Luis paused by the door, taking one last look around the roamer's interior. It was cramped, barely enough room for two people. His bed curled around the rear wall of the driver's cabin, his father's at the back of the vehicle. Their sleeping places defined the whole of their lives. There was not enough space between for an adult to stand with their arms spread.

He looked at the man under the blanket for too long. Now he was on the edge of departure, he could not tear himself away.

'Goodbye, da,' he whispered to himself. He bowed to their household shrine. The alcove lamp had burned out, and the crude clay figures of the Emperor and Sanguinius looked on with quizzical expressions from the shadows. He took up his staff of rare wood, a gift from his mother and most prized possession.

As an afterthought, he unhooked his father's goggles from their peg and placed them around his neck.

For once, the door opened quietly. He pushed it to, and moved down the steps to the ground. The air was cool and crisp. He sneaked through the camp, heading for Orrini's roamer. He skirted around pools of fire and lamplight. A shout rang out from one roamer, and he froze, fearing detection, but the shout had not been for him. Laughter followed it, and he stole away.

The lights were off inside Orrini's roamer. Luis went to the dustbike fastened to the rear. He looked about himself. The bike was strapped high up. There was no quiet way to get it down; once it was off, he would have to flee immediately. Clenching his teeth, he undid one buckle. The roamer bounced on its suspension as the bike slipped. With tentative hands he released the second. The bike thumped to the ground. He froze, expecting shouts at any moment. None came.

Luis levered the bike up, got on, placed the staff across the handlebars and started the motor.

'Hey! Hey!' Orrini was on the way back to his roamer from a neighbour's, half drunk. 'Hey! Someone's stealing my ride!'

'Sorry, Orrini!' shouted Luis over his shoulder. He opened the throttle. The bike was made for a grown man, and the power of it was an unwelcome surprise that almost ended Luis' adventure as soon as it started. He slewed about as the duster shot out towards the edge of the camp. He had just wrestled it back under control when the shocked face of a sentry leapt out at him. Luis swore, swerved around him and then was away. Shouts and engine noise dwindled behind him. He was off before anyone could catch him. Sounds of pursuit petered out. Orrini's duster was the fastest in the clan, and he trusted no one would want to follow him out into the deep waste.

He drove by the light of Baal and Baalind until the camp was well behind him, then turned on the headlights. The lumens had cost Orrini a half-year's salt wage, bought from a technothurge in Kemrender, and cut a dazzling line across the flats.

Night beckoned. On the other side was his future.

The sun shone through Luis' eyelids, waking him from dreams of his mother.

He grumbled and flapped his arm across his face. He was lying on his soft bed. It was comfortable and he was tired. If he let himself sink into the yielding surface, he might sleep a little longer.

'Shut the door, da,' he mumbled.

He tasted salt on his lips. Wind caressed his skin.

Luis frowned. Through spread fingers he peered up. Blue sky shimmered in place of the roamer's ceiling. He lifted his head. With a start he remembered. The bike had struck something. He had come off.

Luis jerked fully awake. The ground he was on creaked ominously. He froze, and spread his weight as wide as he could.

Orrini's bike was disappearing into tarry mud under the salt crust. Only the rear wheel protruded over broken ground, and that was already sinking out of sight.

'Crack salt,' he whispered to himself. Under a thin crust of salt and sand, deep pools of mud large enough to swallow a roamer whole waited. He cursed his inattention. Normal salt pan and crack salt looked virtually the same, but they could be told apart. He had not noticed.

Fear sharpened his mind. He couldn't be too far from the edge, he thought. The bike would have broken through as soon as the crust grew thin enough. It should support his weight. With painful slowness, he crawled on his back, moving towards the tracks he had left in the waste, keeping clear of the hole the duster had made. As he moved, cracks spidered out from the hole, inching their way out towards him. He slowed, but the cracks came on. The ground creaked ominously and began to tilt. He flipped himself onto his front, and pushed hard. His foot broke the sand crust and his heart leapt, propelling him into a scrambling run to firmer ground. Behind him the crust broke into fragments that disappeared into the oily muck beneath. A foul, briny stink rose from the hole.

He was not safe yet. Luis slowed and unwrapped the fabric from one hand, exposing his fist to the poison sun. He rapped upon the salt with a knuckle, listening for the hollow tock that was the sole reliable telltale of crack salt. Carefully, with his ear hovering over the ground and his weight spread, he crept further away until his knocking returned a solid thump. He tentatively stood, and looked back.

The duster disappeared under the crust, slow, fat bubbles popping in the exposed mud. Already it was scabbing over, the mud turning from black to light grey under the heat of the sun. He cast up his hood to shade his face, his eyes fixed on the indentation of the crust where he had fallen.

One of his precious bottles of water had slid out of his pack. It lay on the crack salt, casting a long shadow dappled with broken light. His staff was a few yards from the edge.

Panic rising, he slipped off his backpack. The flap had come open. With mounting fear he went through its contents, lying them out on the bright pan so that he could see them. All was there, his rad suit, tools, scorpion biltong, water still, his precious handful of dried fruit, knife – all the things he had taken with him to survive. There were two water bottles of ancient glass scratched dull by long use. His third lay there on the crack salt.

He had calculated he would need one and a half bottles of water to cross the pan on the duster. Without the bike, even the extra he had taken would not sustain him all the way across, and he had lost a third of that. Beyond the dead sea was desert. Water was easier to find there, but still scarce. He thought through the scenarios. The worst case came to him most easily: him dying in the salt pan. The next worst case was his arrival at the edge of the Great Salt Waste, and him dying in the sand.

'Think!' he hissed angrily through his teeth. It was yet early, but already becoming hot. He weighed the warming bottles in his hands. They held his life in them. The white of the salt wastes went on to every horizon, inimical to all life. He imagined that expanse sucking the water from him as he dithered. There was not a single object anywhere to offer shade. His skin itched with dryness. At that moment he wished his clan would find him, and take him home. Whatever punishment they meted out, it would be better than death. He had made a dreadful mistake. He was going to die.

'Stop it!' he said, and hit his forehead hard with a bunched fist.

He breathed slowly through his nose and out through his mouth. Panic kills, his father had said hundreds of times to him. Think your way out of danger.

The bottle was out of reach. His staff was not. He lay down flat on the ground. Slowly, he crept out to the staff, and drew it to him with careful fingers.

The bottle was not much further. He moved towards it, and tried to hook it with his staff to roll it towards him. He succeeded only it bashing it through the crust, and it disappeared. Alarmed at the thinness of the crack salt, he retreated.

Luis looked up at the sun. He had to wait it out, travel at night. That was his only chance. Calmer now, he repacked his pack, removed his hood and took off his long, outer robe, exposing the lighter garments underneath. Unwrapped, his outer robe was a sheet three yards in area.

He took out three sections of tube from the edge of his pack, joined them together, and set the end in the salt. By draping one end of the robe over the pole, he made a low tent that would shelter him from the sun.

Hunkering down in the stuffy interior, he watched the robe ripple in the hot wind until he fell into a fitful sleep.

* * *

Luis awoke when the night wind came to snatch at his shelter. It was stronger than usual, and he was forced to wait it out. His eyes were gummy and mouth dry. He had not dared drink during the day, but while he waited he took a sip of the water. When the wind cooled and dropped he went out to urinate. He caught the stream in the evaporation bowl of his water still, and drank it all, grimacing at the taste. He could drink his own urine only twice before the poisons in it became too concentrated. After that he would have to distil it, if he could, and that meant losing a lot of it.

Setting his course by Baal and Baalind, Luis headed out across the salt. By day the Great Salt Waste was a searing pinkish white; by night it was stained red by the looming presence of Baal and the Red Scar. At those times every crevice in the pan was sharp with shadow, making the world look sick.

He paused when Baal was halfway across the sky and ate a single strip of biltong. The food woke his stomach, and it rumbled for more. He denied it. He finished his meal quickly. In a couple of hours, Baal would set, and real darkness would descend. That was the most dangerous time of the night, when catch spiders emerged from their holes to hunt. He could not afford to stop.

The red grew deeper as Baal sailed away. Baalind followed soon after her brother, and Luis' world became a ruby murk lit by the Red Scar and its sea of stars. When the pulsing glare of Cryptus came up, he had something to steer by and continued forwards confident of his course. Water was another matter. He drank his own urine again.

He trudged on, his feet crunching on the endless salt. Monotony dulled his senses. Out of a need for stimulation he took to counting his footsteps, and became dangerously absorbed by the task.

He didn't hear the skittering behind him until it was nearly too late. Part of the background of thumping heart, rushing blood, muttered counting and weary trudging, when noticed it leapt to the forefront of his attention.

He stopped. The noise stopped a moment later, a many-legged tread coming to a stealthy halt.

Gripping his staff, Luis turned about. He could see nothing. The night was deathly still. A black line separated the deep red of the sky from the dark rose of the salt. He peered into the ruddy gloom, practically blind.

A movement to his side caught his eye. Whirling around, he swung out with his staff, hitting a soft body. A blur shifted across the ground, and he struck again. A long limb caressed his knee, and he aimed blindly at a shifting mass by his feet. The catch spider yanked at his foot, pulling him backwards, and leapt at his chest. Luis brought his staff across his body, catching the thing's head as it protruded from the hooded integument of its thorax. Four tooth-tipped palps wiggled half an inch from his face, dripping acidic venom onto his cheek. Screaming with shock and pain, he thrust backwards, sending the catch spider off his body. He leapt up. The creature was on its back, coarse hairs rasping on the ground as it thrashed about, trying to right itself. Luis brought his staff down on the thing's segmented abdomen. The exoskeleton cracked and it thrashed harder. He brought his staff down again, then again, until the catch spider's belly was open to the air and its ten legs twitched inwards. Its complicated mouth let out a clicking rasp, and it lay still.

Luis breathed hard. Even so close, the catch spider's speckled white-and-red camouflage made it hard to see. He went around to the front and drove the tip of his staff into the armoured cavity where the head nestled, and pounded it to mush.

The salt around the spider's body was stained dark with fluid. Luis swallowed dryly at the sight of so much liquid going to waste. He could use none of the creature; unlike its scorpion cousins, every part of a catch spider was tainted by its poison. Shaking with adrenaline, he continued on his walk, ears straining for more pattering footsteps.

The days dragged by. The salt never ended. Luis distilled his urine during the day. The still was a cone of stiff canvas held up on wire legs, set over double bowls. His urine went into the central bowl where it evaporated, collected on the cone and trickled down the

canvas into the outer bowl. Every day his urine grew darker and
less in volume, until the outer bowl began to catch only a few drops.
At first he regretfully scraped away the thick paste left after distilla-
tion, unhappy to be wasting the resources trapped within. But as
the days passed and the amount of water he produced declined,
he became apathetic, performing his tasks out of ingrained habit.
He rationed his bottled water carefully, a few sips a day. He could
not save the water he shed as sweat, and nor could the still catch
all the vapour. Gradually, his water dwindled, until it ran out. His
urine ceased to come not long after.

Luis sat in the evening, looking into the outer bowl. A faint smear
of water was all that his still had produced while he slept in the
day. He stared at it; this was to be his last.

His dry tongue rasped on the plate when he licked the water away.

With heavy limbs he gathered his things, and stared out across
the waste. There was no end to the whiteness. The temperature
had been increasing steadily as High Summer approached. Haze
shimmered to the west, making the sinking red sun and the arc
of Baal jump and shiver.

His head had been throbbing for days. His lips were cracked and
his mouth was dry. He took out his thirst pebble from his robes
and placed it into his mouth. Sucking on the small stone produced
saliva, and though it could not help rehydrate his drying body, it
alleviated his thirst a little. He dragged his pack onto his back, as
great a burden as Baalfora herself, so it felt.

Setting his sights on the north, he began to walk again. He had
stopped resting during the day. The need to cover ground trumped
all other concerns. Night came and passed. Throughout he was
uncomfortably aware of his heart as it worked sluggishly in his
chest. His joints ached. When he blinked, his eyelids caught on
his sticky eyes.

He went on. He could not stop. In the day the sun pounded on
his head, adding a further beat to the throb of his headache and
pulse of his heart. His body was ruled by painful drums. His head
drooped, his feet dragged. Still he would not give up. Would the

lords of Baal stop here and die? No! He would prove his father wrong and become an angel.

So he told his heart, so he told his feet. They listened to him for a time, until the moment came when they rebelled. He lifted his foot and it did not move, and he toppled into the dry salt, landing on his back.

Luis drifted in and out of consciousness. The sky was halfway between day and night, and Baal was directly overhead. He stared at it blearily, looking for the lights his father showed him the day his mother died. Perhaps if he saw them, the angels might come, but he saw no lights.

'Emperor save me,' he said, his voice a husky whisper.

Luis fell unconscious, and he dreamt.

He stood on a field of rust-red sands. Time ran quickly, clouds raced overhead and two moons rose and sank above them. The sun arced through the sky so fast it left a trail.

Ahead of Luis an armoured figure of gold knelt. It had the shape of a man, but was far bigger. White wings of metal spread out from its back; a spiked halo of polished iron was set over its head. The armour was fashioned to look like a heavily muscled body. Long strips of parchment hung from its backpack and chest. Upon its shoulder pads were insignia of red and white. A sword as tall as an adult was belted at its waist, but upon the angel it did not seem too large. In one hand, it clasped a chalice.

Luis approached. Its bowed head came up to his shoulders. It remained motionless.

Sorely afraid, Luis reached out to touch the angel. His fingers caressed smooth, golden armour.

The face lifted. The helm was made in the likeness of a beautiful man with long waves of hair. Tears of gold were frozen on its cheeks. Slowly, the being got to its feet. Luis stepped back, craning his neck to look into expressionless glass eyes.

The silent figure lifted a hand to point. The landscape shifted, becoming the salt of Baalfora's wastes. Fifty yards away a dark shape lay huddled. Was this his own body he looked at?

It stared at him, its outstretched hand a command to live. Its metal wings began to beat, and it rose from the ground. The appearance of armour was lost; metal curves became muscle, cast hair growing blond and waving in the stir of air. The tears melted to water and began to run. A true angel looked down on Luis with sorrowful compassion, before flying away.

'Wait!' he cried. 'Take me with you!'

Luis was awakened by the clap of huge wings. With the last of his strength, he rolled onto his stomach and began to crawl. He sobbed dryly with the effort of keeping his head off the ground, but he had to see.

He spied the dark shape not far off.

Hope lent him one last surge of strength, enough to get him to the figure on the salt.

A body, long dead, skin cured deep reddish brown by the salt and sun. The gossamer remains of spider silk fluttered away from the body as Luis clambered over it. He half embraced the hard, dead corpse and reached for the backpack. His fingers trembled on leather made unyielding as iron by years of exposure.

Inside were a number of items, any of which he would have coveted only a week ago. He closed his eyes in thanks when four bottles slipped out and clinked on the ground. They had been sealed with wax from salt ant nests. All were full of water.

The Emperor alone knew how long the water had been there waiting for him. He offered a silent prayer and opened one, still lying atop the bony corpse.

Before he drank he scratched up a small handful of gritty salt and put it in his mouth. It burned him, but he must take it first or he would vomit the water back.

When he poured the blood-warm water into his mouth, it was as if the oceans returned to Baalfora, sluicing over the wasteland his mouth had become and down into his stomach. One small mouthful was a deluge. He forced himself to stop after that, to let his body absorb it slowly.

Over the course of the next few hours, hidden from the sun by his hood, he drank the rest of the bottle, then slept. He awoke feeling better, and by the time evening came he was well enough to stand again. Thirst gripped him still, but he was no longer dying. His pack was light, he discovered, and he found that he had dropped a good deal of his gear. After some time in decision, he set off down his trail to collect it all, leaving his staff speared into the ground by the corpse as a marker. Fortunately, his supplies had fallen in a line no more than a couple of miles in length, and he recovered everything except one empty bottle.

He stripped the corpse. It was shrivelled, but male and perhaps not much older than he. Could it have been that this boy was trying what he was, only to die here, miles from Angel's Fall? There were further spider signs on the body, a double puncture in the leg. The wound was difficult to find in the stone-hard skin of the boy, but clearly seen in the cloth. There had been food in the pack; this was deceptively well preserved. When he tried it, Luis found it tougher than rocks and saltier than the ground, so he discarded it. Luis filled the corpse's pack with some of the dead boy's clothes. By then it was night-time. Luis looked away to the north. There was a dark smudge on the horizon that had not been there before. He sagged with relief. That was the line of the ancient shore. If he were careful with this unexpected bounty of water, he might make it to the desert.

He should start out now.

He looked back at this unnamed boy who had died so he might live. The Emperor had decreed it to be so, Luis was sure, but to leave him out in the open like that seemed disrespectful.

Using his staff to make a shallow scrape in the ground, Luis interred the corpse as best he could, then knelt and offered a lengthy prayer to the Lord of Mankind for His infinite mercy. The Emperor protects, the saying went, but sometimes He sacrificed one to save another.

'May the God-Emperor find your soul and guide it to the safety of His eternal light,' said Luis. His throat was raw, but he would live. 'I thank you for your sacrifice.'

He set out while Baal was large on the horizon. Two days later he reached the edge of the Great Salt Waste.

CHAPTER FOUR

THE MOUNTAINS OF BAAL SECUNDUS

456.M40
Heavenwall Mountains
Baal Secundus
Baal System

Soon after Luis' world acquired the black line on the horizon, the ground rose from flat salt pan to craggy rocks sculpted into fantastical form. For a day Luis picked his way through stone of fluid shape, coated in sparkling salt, and came to a platform of pocked stone. Cliffs of a different sort rose up ahead, their lower portions weathered into fluid shapes, the upper jagged, and he stepped from sea to land. Though this ancient shore was coated with a fine sift of wind-blown salt, softening the edge of the coast, there was no question that the Great Salt Waste had ended.

Mountains rose high behind.

Luis checked his supplies. There was half a bottle of water left. In need of more, he set out into the crags in search of a spring. He'd been in the desert and craglands often enough to know what he was looking for: darker dirt where water seeped up from deep underground. It was always best to check round the bases of cliffs, where there were cracks and faults the water could travel to the surface. Sometimes there were plants marking the spot. The best part of a morning he spent on his search, going deeper into the maze of ravines and gullies leading away from the waste. It was blessedly cool surrounded by stone, although being a native of the wide-open, he felt the first stirrings of claustrophobia.

Eventually he happened upon a natural bowl cut out of the land. Though it was surrounded by cliffs, they were far enough apart to let the sun shine down. He never thought he would miss the sun, but a day in shadow had him yearning for a clear view of the sky. A stepped channel led up through a gap deeper into the hills. In better times, a waterfall had carved out this hollow. At the bottom of the plunge pool water lingered still. A cluster of water leaves stood invitingly around sand darkened by moisture, their immature leaves held tight to woody stems and thick with cruel thorns. The mature, outer leaves were sacrificial. Thornless and fat with moisture, they had evolved to tempt animals to eat them and spread the seedpods dangling from their tips.

Luis cut the seeds away from the leaves and crunched on them. Water leaves were bitter. After a week in the salt with little food and water, they tasted like the nectar the angels supposedly drank.

Luis dug. Dark sand turned moist, then wet. When he was a foot down, water ran in an eager rivulet to fill the hole. Luis rushed to catch it in his bottle.

'Lookee here, a little salty out of the ocean.'

Luis whirled around. Standing in the entrance to the bowl were two boys. They were scrawny things, dressed strangely to his eyes. They wore belts hanging with the tools of survival, and upon their backs they carried bulky, square packs. Over their shoulders they had long poles of bleached bone.

Luis dropped his bottle and came up, his staff held defensively in front of him. The boys were older and bigger than him, the talker especially. The second was patchily bald with alopecia, but he was stocky and looked strong. Luis affected nonchalance to conceal his alarm. 'Hello,' he said.

'What ocean?' said the second boy.

The boy made an exaggerated expression of stupidity at Luis, exposing black teeth, and walked into the bowl. 'Salt waste was an ocean, stupid, before the Long Ago War. All water, see, went with the bombs and the rads and all that.' He put his pack down. His poles made a musical clatter when he dropped them. He stretched luxuriously, glad to be free of his burden. 'Only salt now. How do you not know that, Daneill? Even the salty knows that, and he's not very clever. I can tell.'

The first boy grinned infectiously. The stockier boy scowled at his companion.

'I am clever. I know how to live out there, for a start. I found this water,' said Luis.

'Water,' said the second newcomer. 'Give.' He set his pack and poles down, and took out a bottle.

'Help yourself, if you're thirsty,' said Luis amicably.

'What you going to do if we took it? Don't need your permission,' said the stocky boy. He purposefully knocked Luis with his shoulder as he came past.

'Leave it, eh? Don't know nothing about him yet,' said the first boy. He settled himself into a crouch on a rock near Luis, all elbows and knees. 'No need to threaten him. Where you headed, little salty?'

Luis evaded his question. 'We're salt roamers – we dig at the flats and take what we find to Selltown on the north reaches, or take it to Kemrender. Kemrender was where my clan was headed. I was going to go to Selltown myself – you can get anywhere from Selltown – but decided the straight course was best.'

'Ah, but the straight course where?' said the elder boy, seizing on Luis' words. 'Angel's Fall?' he said slyly. 'Going for the trial?'

'What if I am?' said Luis.

'Hss!' said the elder boy, flapping his hand. 'Listen to you, all full of yourself. Can you fight though? Can you kill? Ain't no good to the angels if you can't.'

Luis' ears coloured. 'I killed my first man when I was ten. A band of nomads attacked our caravan when we were heavy with salt – not just the white kind, but heavy chlorides and potassium salts. Lots of it, good money.' He realised he was babbling and reined his tongue in. Why was it suddenly so important he impress these boys? 'I was on the spring gun on my da's roamer. A nomad on a duster is hard to hit, but I got a shot off and zing!' said Luis. 'Dead. Got him right in the centre of his chest. Red blood all over the white.' He didn't mention the late-night horror that had followed the elation, or the shame he had felt at ending a life.

'Is that so?' said the elder boy. 'Well, well,' he said, crawling over the boulder until he was so close his rotten breath choked Luis. 'You are so brave. Tell me, how are you going to cross the canyon lands? How you going to get up the Heavenwall?'

'How are you?' said Luis a little petulantly. He was beyond his clan's habitual grounds. The canyons were exotic to him. He sensed a trap in the boy's words. Mockery awaited him.

'I think he's going to walk,' said the first boy to the second.

'Gonna walk,' said Daneill. His laughter was rough and unpleasant. He shook his head over the little pool of brown water.

'You ain't going to make it on foot, stupid salty. The deserts all round here are hot with old rads. Where they ain't the lands are full of scorpions bigger than clan tents, and no water but the thirsty kind. Need something with a little zip to get over.' He patted the bundle on his back. 'Angel's wings, salty. If you want to get to Angel's Fall from here, you got to fly!'

'Yeah, fly,' said the other boy. He laughed again as he screwed the cap back onto his bottle.

'You don't know much, don't know about the wings,' said the boy with black teeth. 'You're not a good candidate. Don't know why you bother.'

'I got this far,' said Luis. 'I can get there.'

'Not without wings,' said the boy.

'Maybe we should kill him now,' said Daneill with sudden menace. 'Save ourselves the competition.'

The posture of the boys changed. They looked at Luis with

calculating eyes. Luis' heart froze. This was what he had feared. He gripped his staff more tightly.

They stared at one another, weighing their capabilities against each other's. Luis tensed. Then the first boy burst out laughing, his stocky companion joining in. 'Had you going there. Thinks we were going to kill him, eh, eh?' said the boy.

Luis watched them cackle. He did not relax. Had he appeared a little weaker they would have killed him. He was sure of it. They might still.

'The name's Florian,' said the black-toothed elder, patting his chest. 'This stumpy patch-hair is Daneill.'

Daneill gave him a filthy look accompanied by a nod that might have been an attempt at friendliness.

Pretty names for ugly souls, thought Luis.

'Don't say much, do you?' said Florian.

'So?'

'Tell us your name,' he said.

'Luis.'

This information brought more howls of laughter from the boys.

'What's so funny?' said Luis.

'Luis? What kind of stupid name is that? That's a child's name!' said Florian. Daneill hooted with laughter. 'Don't you get angel names in your clan?'

'We do. We just don't use them in public, that's all. It's private, for family,' said Luis.

'Kresking funny salties, ain't you?' mocked Florian. 'Are you going to tell us what it is then? You'll have to use your angel name if you're gonna be an angel.'

'No,' said Luis. 'I won't.'

Florian's smile became dangerously fixed. 'Suit yourself.' Florian looked to Daneill. 'What do you reckon, let him travel with us awhile?'

'Don't see why,' said Daneill. 'He's not gonna be able to fly, is he? He ain't got no wings.'

'Three sets of eyes is better than one, that's why,' said Florian.

'So what if he can't fly? We get to Angel's Leap, we can just leave him to find his own way.'

Daneill shrugged, already losing interest in the conversation.

'You can come with us to Angel's Leap by the Wind River,' said Florian. 'Then we're going to jump off and fly all the way to Angel's Fall. After that, you're on your own. What do you say? We can watch each other's backs. Not everyone out here is so friendly as us.'

Luis considered the offer. If he accepted, they might kill him in his sleep. If he refused, they could chase him down. They knew these lands better than he did. If they were true, they could get him to Angel's Fall faster, wings or not. That was attractive, but in the end he said yes because he was tired of being alone.

'All right then. You have a deal. We work together, we have a better chance.'

They grasped hands. Daneill laughed. 'Scrawny salty like you, you haven't got a chance no matter what.'

Florian frowned and threw a pebble at his friend's head. 'Shut it, Daneill. He's with us now. Brothers, just like the angels,' he said to Luis, holding his hand tighter.

'Brothers,' said Luis warily.

The way to the Wind River took them high into the mountains of Baalfora. Florian led the way confidently; Daneill brought up the rear. Having the stocky boy behind made Luis uncomfortable. Every time he looked back, Daneill was staring at him balefully.

They rested halfway through the morning, having already ascended a few thousand feet. Luis was fit from a life of hardship, but such slopes were new to him, and his feet and legs ached, pains the other two did not seem to be suffering. Daneill pointedly sat away from Luis when they rested, and Florian joined him. The two shared a meal and a muttered conversation. Luis didn't catch the content, but from the dark looks Daneill cast his way and the angry tone of Florian's remarks it was evident to him that Daneill was not happy with Luis' inclusion in their party. Luis did not wish to provoke him and so watched from the corner of his eye while he worked on a strip of biltong and pretended to be absorbed by the view. The colour of the salt seemed much purer from the mountainside, shockingly white, barely tinted by the red sun, and dead flat. The whiteness stretched as far as he could see. He tried to imagine it covered in water, but failed. The most water he had ever seen had been a small pool. He had no internal reference for oceans, coloured by the sky as the stories told, and found the idea hard to believe.

Florian stood from his crouch and came over. Luis tensed a little. Florian saw.

'Hey, I ain't come to stick you, salty.' He squatted by Luis. Florian never sat, but crouched with his skinny arms draped over his legs.

'Why you going then, to the trial?' said Florian. He didn't wait for an answer. Having accepted Luis, he had revealed a certain volubility. 'Daneill there, he wants to be a warrior and fight for the God-Emperor. Never thinks on nothing but fighting, that one. I gotta go.' He pulled aside the neck of his dirty shirt, revealing an ulcerated mass near his armpit. 'This flesh eater is gonna kill me soon. Better I chance it going to the angels than dying in three passes of Baal. So, you a fighter like Daneill, or a selfish kreck like me?'

Luis looked up at the sky where Baal floated, diaphanously in the full light of the sun. 'I want to do something with my life. Not just fight... I mean, obviously we'll have to fight. But I want to help people – that's what the angels do. I want to protect them. I don't know.' He dropped his head, finding it hard to express himself. He expected Florian to mock him, but was surprised.

'I get that, I do. It's hard to watch people die, all cancered by the sun and the rad, or dying from thirst, killed in a feud... Baalfora's got fifty ways to kill you before breakfast – she's a bitch. It'd be a fine thing to be able to do something about that. First though, I gotta not die from skin rot.' He gave a dark chuckle and grasped Luis' shoulder. 'Hey,' he said, looking at his bag. 'You got a ticker in there?'

'Yeah, I have.' Luis followed Florian's gaze to his open backpack. The dull iron corner of his rad counter stuck out from the bag.

Florian pulled it out. It was a simple thing, a metal box with a round circle of holes punched in one end, an unshielded needle and an unsteady arc painted in thick white and red. There were no numbers on the gauge.

'Now that is a stroke of luck!' said Florian. 'We couldn't get one before we left. Patches of these mountains are hot with old rad. We were thinking we'd have to climb all the way to Angel's Leap in our suits, and that would be nasty work.' He slapped Luis on the shoulder. 'Hey! Daneill! He's got a ticker!'

Daneill gave a sour look and grunted.

'Ah, he's a miserable kreck!' said Florian. 'I'm beginning to like you, Luis. You're a good find.'

Not long after, Luis' ticker began a tentative tock-tock-tocking that increased in urgency and volume. He took it out of his bag, and released the needle from the catch. Within one hundred yards of first sounding it was buzzing hard, and the needle twitched up towards the red portion of its range.

'We need to put our rad suits on,' said Luis, holding up the ticker to the others.

'Well then,' said Florian. He dropped his poles and pack, and fished about for his rad suit. 'Fifty weeks' worth of work in these,' he said. 'Had to steal them, didn't we? Our clan don't give out the suits to challenge hopefuls to lose in the desert.' He shook his head. 'Good job I'm sneaky.'

Daneill produced a similar outfit of heavy rubberised canvas, gloves and boot coverings. A tight hood went over his head, his eyes protected by meshed cages of fine lead wire. They were remarkably similar to Luis' own, traded from the manufacturers of Selltown. The tech clans there exacted a heavy price for the garments, knowing full well no man could survive on Baal Secundus without them.

All their suits were heavily patched. Luis hated the feel and the chemical stink of the treated cloth. His field of vision was reduced to nothing, and he began to sweat.

His backpacks were at least lighter. Daneill and Florian got their much bigger packs on and picked up their curved bone poles.

'Lead on,' said Florian, his voice muffled.

With the ticker in one hand and his staff in the other, Luis motioned upwards on a line oblique to their previous path. 'That way,' he said.

They struggled on in their thick suits. Luis didn't want to think how much moisture he was losing. Wherever there seemed to be an easier path, the ticker buzzed angrily, the needle wedging itself into the danger zone, and they were forced to take more difficult routes. Luis thought bad things about the ticker's machine-spirit, but dared not voice them for fear of offending it.

The rad zone lasted for several hundred yards of punishing climb. The sun was shining on them the whole way. His body was slick with sweat and his throat tight with thirst. He became dizzy, but they could not stop.

As the climb became unbearable, the sun crested its noon and went to the other side of the Heavenwall Mountains, bringing them welcome rest from its heat. As the day became cooler and the shadows reddened, the ticker's rattling became a regular tocking. The needle twitched by fits and starts away from the red. Soon it was bumping only sporadically up from the bottom of the white, and the ticks became quieter, then stilled.

Luis led them on a hundred yards further until he was sure the needle would not spring back into action.

They were on a steep slope of wind-smoothed rock. A few more degrees of gradient and it would be impassable without ropes. He braced his feet awkwardly and tore his hood from his head. He sighed with pleasure as the gathering night wind chilled his damp face.

'The rads are gone. We're safe here,' he called. The others came nearer.

'Looks like there's a cave ahead,' Florian said. 'We can make camp there.' He nodded at a break in the rock face. 'We should stop for the night.'

* * *

The cave was a fault in the rock widened by erosion. They had to stoop to get in, but once inside the ceiling rose high enough so that they could stand, before doubling back down. Thirty paces from the edge, the weight of the stone pressed the cave down to little more than a few feet, although the crack continued back into the darkness of the mountain. Sand covered the floor.

'This is good!' said Florian. He ran his hands over the stone as he walked towards the back. He dropped his things, ducked down and peered into the narrowing tail of the cave.

'What's back there?' said Daneill. He stood near the entrance. 'I don't like it. It's too deep. Could be anything back there.'

'There's nothing! Comes down together not far back, I reckon.' Florian sat on a boulder and began to tug off his rad suit with his back to the crack.

Daneill still did not set down his pack and poles. 'I wish we had something to make a fire. It's getting cold.'

'Too cold, frightened of a crack in the rock – what kind of angel are you going to make?' said Florian. He folded up his rad suit. The boys had no knowledge of the need to decontaminate their gear, and no way to do it if they had, and so he simply jammed it back into his pack. 'This is the best campsite we've found for ages. You'll see.'

Luis put down his bags. 'You're probably right. I'm exhausted. We need to rest.'

'What do you know about anything?' said Daneill.

'He knows enough to have a ticker when we don't!' snapped Florian. 'Will you just give it a rest?'

Daneill's eyes widened, followed by his mouth. He took a step back. 'Florian!' he whispered.

'Don't start!' said Florian. 'Can't you just...' The look on Daneill's face stopped him. The older boy turned to look into the back of the cave. Glinting there in the subterranean dark were three clusters of four eyes.

'Fire scorpion!' yelled Daneill. He stumbled backwards, cracking his head on the cave mouth. Luis snatched up his staff as Florian screamed.

The scorpion lunged out of the dark.

The fire scorpion of Baal Secundus had little in common with the scorpions of Terra, but enough resemblance to warrant the name. Cousin to the catch spiders of the salt wastes, it had a similar flat, oval body but was much bigger. Six of its ten limbs were legs, the foremost pair having evolved into giant crushing pincers. Like the spiders', its body was divided into three flat segments covered by natural, banded armour and its head was protected by a peaked cowl coming off its exoskeleton. The mouth had multiple, toothed palps. Luis cursed their laxness; they should have been more careful.

The scorpion seized Florian's foot in one huge claw. Florian responded by kicking it repeatedly in the face, forcing the head and its deadly mouth back into the chitinous hood. Hissing angrily, it heaved itself out of the crack fully into the cave, and the tail came up and over its back. Florian screamed again.

'Stay away from the tail!' shouted Luis.

It was at the rear where the scorpions' anatomy diverged most significantly from the spiders'. The scorpions' rearmost limbs had fused, and turned up and backwards into a long, jointed tail. The feet had become a hollow gland fronted with an orifice closed by barbed hairs that locked together. The tail swayed back and forth. Chemical brume boiled from the tip.

Luis made to help. Daneill grabbed his arm.

'Let it get him! We can run. We can't stop that – it'll kill you. It'll kill us all!'

'You leave if you want,' said Luis harshly, 'but you'll be no worthy angel.' He threw off Daneill's arm.

Florian scrabbled for a rock with his hand while continuing to kick at the scorpion's face.

The scorpion drew back its tail. The gland oscillated rapidly side to side. Within, thick vestibules opened, mixing volatile chemicals in the chamber behind the hair-locked plates. The scorpion's characteristic bubbling screech, caused by the building exothermic reaction, filled the cave.

'Florian!' shouted Luis. He charged at the scorpion, knocking its bulbous fire gland aside as it opened, spraying a sheet of stinking, flaming liquid across the cave. Florian yelped as fire landed on his arm. Luis caught the tail under the fire gland with his staff and yanked it back, dragging it towards the ground. The scorpion hissed and pulled back, rotating towards Luis, dragging Florian with it. Smothering his burning sleeve with sand, Florian snatched up a rock and raised it over his head in both hands and started to pound at the claw.

Luis was dragged back and forth by the whipping tail. Chitin cracked on the claw. The scorpion shrieked. Luis leaned back with all his weight as the fire gland made its song, yanking it vertical. The chemical fire jetted out and hit the ceiling, spread out in a circle, and rained down all over the cave, setting Luis' cloak on fire. The confined space was choked with reeking fumes.

'Let! Go! Of! Me!' shouted Florian, driving the rock through the claw's armour and into the soft muscle beneath. The scorpion keened and released him. He scrambled to his feet. Trailing its smashed claw, the scorpion turned to snap at Luis with the other, but Daneill came in, yelling an incomprehensible cry, and drove his knife into the joints on the tail. The scorpion whipped its tail back, snapping the knife off near the hilt. Luis was sent tumbling to the floor. Cornered and injured, the scorpion skittered around and dived back into the crack.

The three boys lay gasping in the cave, chemical fire burning out around them.

'We were lucky it was a juvenile. It must have moulted recently, or you'd never have cracked its claw like that,' said Luis. He held out his hand to Florian.

'You came back for me. You could have run,' he said, taking the hand.

'I would never run,' said Luis, and hauled Florian to his feet. He could feel Daneill glaring at him.

'A bigger one would have killed us all,' said Florian. 'You were brave to tackle it.'

'Brothers, you said. At least until we get to Angel's Leap and the

Wind River,' said Luis. 'I stand by my promises.' He looked back at the crack. 'We can't stay here.'

They climbed as far as they could. Firstnight lasted an hour at that time, giving them half an hour of extra daylight when it finished. Truenight came soon after, forcing them to halt. The chill of night came on, and they huddled together for warmth under Baal's cold stare.

They took it in turns to watch for the fire scorpion, although in truth none of them slept. Every noise had them staring into the night. When dawn came they greeted it with ecstatic whoops.

'We gotta go up,' Florian explained. 'Cross the mountains. The Wind River is a long way on the other side. This bit is going to be hard.'

Following Florian, they climbed high, up so far the Great Salt Waste was just a blur. The mountains reared higher, their faces steep as walls. Florian took them on a narrow trail that dropped precipitously to the lower slopes. They stood on a knife-edge, the radzone and scorpion cave far below them. Luis' breath failed to nourish his lungs, and the cold burned at his throat. Daneill had it worse, stumbling so much Luis had to help him walk.

The path joined a ruinous road, its surface worn away and buttress walls fallen down. The air grew thinner. Daneill became confused. Luis felt dizzy.

'We're nearly there,' said Florian, pointing upwards.

At the mountain's shoulder a wide pass split one peak from another. The heights stood imperiously, impossibly high, their heads white with ancient snow, and yet on one of them the remains of an ancient building could be seen.

They reached the mouth of the pass, a wide vale between the peaks.

The boys climbed on a few more hours. The air was so dry the insides of their noses crackled and their tongues stuck to their mouths. When they finally stopped, they were exhausted. Daneill cried out in his sleep.

Luis awoke feeling sick and exhausted, but forced himself up all the same. He looked forward to descending.

He stood to rearrange his clothes for the day's trek, but stopped dead. Florian and Daneill were nowhere to be seen. Florian's gear was where he'd stacked it the night before. Daneill's outer robes looked like they had been abandoned, but his pack and wing spars were gone.

'Florian? Daneill?' he called.

'...eill, ...eill, ...eill,' the mountains responded.

The silence of the mountains pressed down on him. Cliffs of sheer red stone walled him in. The floor of the valley was a jumble of giant rocks through which the faintest of trails ran. The wind drew sorrowful notes from the landscape. He couldn't remember a time when he had felt so alone.

There was shout from ahead, upslope. Wrapping his outer robe as he ran, he stumbled upwards. The air at that altitude was rarefied and he could manage no more than a jog.

Florian was shouting. 'Daneill! Stop! Stop!'

The slope of the pass ended in a brow. They had ascended many such the day before, expecting each one to be the last and the pass to begin its downward path. Every time they had been disappointed. This one, however, proved to be the summit. Luis crested it, and looked down onto the pass as it rapidly widened, forcing the mountains apart as it headed away to far deserts.

'Daneill!' Florian shouted. His voice was weak in the attenuate air. A moment's searching revealed two figures a few hundred yards down slope, struggling in the lee of a mighty boulder. The air was so clear, only the boys gave the landscape scale. Without them, Luis could never have guessed the boulder's true size.

He set off running, eyes fixed on them. Daneill and Florian were fighting. Daneill was carrying his pack and was weak from mountain sickness, but Florian had been burned and was exhausted. Daneill's strength won out, and he shoved the other boy to the ground. Taking one of his wing spars he hit Florian hard on the head. Luis ran harder.

Luis reached Florian, gasping for air that could not satisfy his body.

'Stop him!' said Florian from the ground, where he nursed his bloodied face. 'The mountain sickness is clouding his mind. He's going to drink it!'

Luis' face displayed his confusion.

'Thirstwater!' said Florian. 'Go!'

The pass shelved off to the east there, and Daneill was making his way down the slope. Luis ran after him, but he could not catch him. He reached the top of a slope to see Daneill making his way towards a sparkling pool of water bubbling up from a spring in the stone. Luis' blood ran cold.

'Daneill! Daneill! Stop!'

The stocky boy gave him a stare as hateful as it was bleary, and continued down to the water, where he dropped his pack and poles, still smeared with Florian's blood. Luis ran after him, reaching him just as he neared the edge. He grabbed Daneill's arm and pulled him back from the pool. 'Don't drink it!'

'What?' he said. Daneill's manner was confused. His voice slurred, and his actions were slow and exaggerated. 'I'm thirsty, salty. Let me be.'

Daneill was still strong, and he was older than Luis. He swung a rock into Luis' wrist. Luis released his arm with a cry, and before he could stop him, Daneill was reaching for the water. Luis grabbed his foot, receiving a kick in the face that sent stars rocketing across his vision.

Daneill plunged his hands into the thirstwater and sucked greedily from cupped palms. He made three swift gulps, then stopped. He spat, raised his face up and looked at Luis in horrified realisation.

'Help me!' he said.

By then, it was too late.

'Daneill!' Florian cried, hobbling down the slope.

Luis scrambled away from Daneill's outstretched hand. Florian gave an anguished shout. Luis grabbed him to stop him aiding his friend, and with a snarl Florian fell on Luis, punching and kicking him. Luis grappled with the plainsman, locking out his arm and pitching the boy face first into the dust.

'Stay away from it. Don't get any of it on you!'

'Floriaaaaaaan...' The name trailed off to an agonised rasp. Daneill's mouth gaped, showing his tongue shrivelling to a black nub in his mouth.

Daneill walked three steps, scarecrow stiff, legs kicking out as his tendons dried. His mouth worked, trying to suck air in to speak, but his lungs were gone, and his lips smacked together even as they dried and pulled back from his teeth. Hollows appeared in his cheeks, and his eyelids drew back from eyes that rolled in terror. His limbs contorted into painful shapes as his tendons drew tighter than gun springs. His fingers jabbed out at unnatural angles, the sharp cracks of snapping bone echoing around the pool.

Daneill's moistureless corpse crackled like a fire as his tissues shrank and split. His body shuddered as his spine curved, and his skin turned black. Finally his eyes, freakishly moist in his desiccated face, shrivelled up to nothing in his skull. A hideous clicking emanated from a throat now little wider than his spine.

'You know what it is, right? You know what it will do to you if it gets on you.'

Florian choked and spat helplessly into the rocky ground. 'In our clan they say it was a weapon, that it's alive, breeds, creeps around looking for people to kill. They say it was thirstwater drank the oceans dry and made the wastes. I know what it is. Now get off me!'

Luis stepped back, releasing his hold on Florian's arm. The older boy snatched his hand back and stood, looking helplessly at the mess of sinew and bone trapped in tight yellow skin. Daneill's lipless smile bared teeth made huge by gum recession.

The water swirled, a vortex that sucked itself away into the fractured stone of the pass. Its passing left no moisture, as if it had never been.

Florian crouched with his head in his hands, sobbing. After a time he stopped. His breath still hitching, he scrambled angrily to

Daneill's pack and poles. He snatched them up, marched to Luis and threw them at his feet in a fury.

'Looks like you found yourself some wings,' he said, his voice brimming with anger. 'You're coming with me, salty, all the way.'

CHAPTER FIVE

THE SANGUINOR

998.M41
Asphodex Low Anchor
Cryptus System

The relentless firing of macrocannons ceased as Dante's Storm-hawk approached the *Blade of Vengeance*. The port battery fell silent first, to allow past the ships fleeing Asphodex. The *Sanguine Shadow* went by quickly, towards the giant flank shield halfway to the stern where the hangar decks sheltered. As soon as the last ships had pierced the field holding back the landing bay's atmosphere, the guns arrayed along the battle-barge resumed their devastation of the planet below.

The *Sanguine Shadow* touched down next to its sisters. Hardened deposits of alien fluids clogged the landing claws' workings, causing them to squeal in complaint as they took the load of the craft. The blood-red of the hull was marred with dark scars and acid burns. In places the ceramite armour plating was pocked through to the plasteel airframe beneath. Forge-servitors rushed forwards, esoteric scrubbing gear plugged into their multi-sockets, to cleanse the craft of xenos fouling. They moved with uncharacteristic swiftness, impelled perhaps by some sympathy of machine for machine. The Stormraven's spirit was in no mood for patience.

73

The assault ramp slammed down as brutally as if the craft had landed in a combat zone, and Dante strode out.

Chapter equerries awaited their masters at the back of the deck, all in red. Those whose masters had perished wore black crosses sewn upon their breasts, and skull amulets of polished basalt around their necks. Along the wall, three-tiered corpse biers held the bodies of Dante's brothers in arms, stacked and waiting to be borne away to the apothecarion. The blood thralls of the Chapter were stoic men, as emotionless in their way as their lords, but they wept silent tears, all of them, for the Blood Angels who had fallen. Chaplain Ordamael went from corpse to corpse, offering praise for the deeds of the dead and thanks for the return of their gene-seed, chanting servitors trailing in his wake. Sanguinary Priests gave the bodies cursory examinations, checking for progenoid damage. Techmarines from the Armoury removed wargear, their blood thralls reverently swaddling it in crimson sheets.

Dante's equerry waited for him along with the rest of the servants. No official rank was his, but his peers stood behind him, never to the front. Arafeo stepped towards Dante, his face solemn, though his eyes could not hide his delight that his master had survived.

Arafeo was old by mortal standards and his movements showed his pain. Dante could scarce believe it; in what seemed to him like months, his young servant had transformed into an old man and would soon die. Arafeo was the sixty-seventh equerry to serve Dante. He would not be the last.

'My lord, it is good to see you returned to the *Blade of Vengeance* safely,' said Arafeo. He held out a goblet of wine in a trembling hand. Dante shook his head. Without comment, Arafeo withdrew the drink.

Sanguinius' blank, outraged face, worn always over Dante's own, turned to regard the dead Blood Angels with eyes of crimson glass.

'Too many did not return. This may be regarded as a victory by the High Lords, but not by me – its price was too high. Attend to me later, Arafeo. The day's work is not yet done. I must oversee the return of my brothers from the surface.'

Dante's equerry bowed and withdrew. The other equerries greeted their own lords and enquired after their needs, offered refreshment in the form of wine and scented cloths to wipe clean sweaty faces freed from helmets after days of fighting. The newly masterless went to stand beside their dead lords in silent vigil, their moods sombre. More than a few of them would take their own lives later that night, such was the bond between the blood thrall equerries and their masters.

'Karlaen!' Dante called. The first captain lumbered over from his conference with others of his Archangels. His helmet had been removed, and this was towed behind him upon a suspensor sled by his body servant. Under the arching crag of his Terminator armour's cowl, Karlaen's grimy face was white, as if peering from a cave. His blue eyes gleamed, and the muscles in his cheek were tight. Dante recognised the signs of the thirst easily enough, the overwhelming passion of Sanguinius. Most of his men would be suffering from it after so hard a battle. He would discover soon enough who had been unable to resist and gone recklessly to their deaths, and who had fallen further and succumbed to the Black Rage.

'How many of our Archangels are gone?'

'Seven,' said Karlaen. 'Brothers Morfeus, Cortizae, Mestus, Brahe, Zostane, Daniaeus and Brother-Sergeant Salazari. I have twelve wounded. Twelve Terminator suits are heavily damaged, and most have suffered some injury. All but one was recovered from the battlefield, thank Sanguinius, but I will not be able to offer full deployment for several weeks.'

'Give a more exact answer than several weeks, first captain,' said Dante. 'These times call for better than generalities. I need precision.'

'I regret I cannot, lord commander.' Karlaen shuddered, his suit exaggerating the movement. The Red Thirst nipped at his humours, making him tense. 'Not until Lord Incarael takes the wargear into the Armoury.'

Dante searched the face of his heir apparent carefully. Six first

captains had come and gone in his one thousand-year reign. Two
had been lost to the ravages of the Black Rage. Karlaen exhibited
no signs of that, thankfully. The commander's own thirst lapped
around the edges of his consciousness, aroused by the war against
the tyranids. But his fury was tempered by crushing ennui, for
Dante had waged many wars of every kind, and the thirst was
background to them all. The anger he experienced most keenly
was of a more human, mundane kind: that another world of the
Imperium had been lost, and another light in the sky put out.

'My lord?' asked Karlaen, when Dante said nothing.

'Give me a full report as soon as you are able. Go, rest. We shall
convene as soon as Aphael and Phaeton return to the fleet.'

Karlaen inclined his head gratefully. 'It would be good to be out
of this war suit, commander.' He paused. 'You must take time for
yourself, my lord. This has been a hard fight.'

'I will rest soon enough,' said Dante. 'I wish to see the others and
take stock of our casualties.'

'My lord,' said Karlaen. Dante sensed that he wished to say more,
but had the good sense not to trouble his leader when he needed
to grieve.

Flanked by his bodyguards, Dante walked across to the dock-
ing slot at the aft of the deck. There was one either side, so that
a ship could land and take off again without changing direction.
The grand space clamoured with activity. The tech-priests of the
Armoury went among the battered ships, directing great gangs of
blood thralls and servitors who dragged on chains attached to the
block and tackles of cranes. By sheer muscle power alone, they
lifted and manoeuvred Stormravens and Stormtalons onto sleds.
These ran on rails so that the craft might be dragged easily into
the maintenance bays set into the starboard side of the deck. The
hangar deck ran through the *Blade of Vengeance,* just aft of amid-
ships and directly above the larger space of the embarkation deck
in the ship's ventral spine. The hangar was protected by the projecting flank shields of the craft, while its position allowed the easy
transfer of flight craft between the hangar and the embarkation

deck via huge lift platforms. The maintenance bays connected the port and starboard sides of the hangar deck together, allowing repair crews easy access to both sides, while their blast shutters provided rapid means of isolating one side from the other.

The stink of oil, promethium and engine exhaust coated the back of his throat. The peppery, gunpowder smell of hard vacuum clung to the returning ships. Underlying the mixed smell of space and hydrocarbons was the tang of blood. Dante was aware of it above all else, though it made up but a part of the bouquet of the hangar deck. Every other Blood Angel would be the same. A dark impulse to feed shifted in his subconscious. The lord commander quashed it. He kept his thirst trapped in the cage of his noble soul. His control over it was total, but he could not shut it from his awareness, and it pricked at him as a thorn that could not ever be removed.

The smell of blood grew stronger as he passed a crowd of Astra Militarum troopers sat together in silence. There were a few hundred of them, of all ranks and regiments. From half a dozen worlds, they had forged a new fellowship by dint of survival, and shared it in exhaustion. When they saw him approaching, they nudged each other and stirred themselves and made the sign of the aquila. When he looked at them they called out for his blessing.

Dante kept his eyes from their wounds, swallowed back the excess saliva gathering in his throat and spoke to them. 'Be still and rest. You have fought and won a great victory today. Heroes such as you will be lauded for all time. We of the Chapter owe you a blood debt for your efforts.'

They gave their thanks. The lines of fear smoothed from their faces. They sat a little straighter. One of the officers got to his feet, and then another, and then all their hundreds stood as one. The wounded called out to be lifted to their feet. When all stood, they saluted in their various fashions, united further in their worship of this living icon.

'All praise Lord Commander Dante! Saviour of Asphodex! The hallowed angel!' one shouted.

'All praise, all praise, all praise!' the others responded. Their lusty shouts were but a minor chord in the clashing symphony of the deck.

Dante was a modest man. He disliked the veneration given him, and the stories that had grown around his deeds, but he understood their utility and stood tall while they chanted his name. 'Silence now. Be still,' he said. He touched the shoulder of a blood thrall marked with the prime helix of the apothecarion.

'Where is Dhrost? I do not see him.'

'In the apothecarion, my lord,' said the thrall. His eyes averted from Sanguinius' golden mask, he kept on binding the wounds of the man he tended. 'He is under the care of the Sanguinary Priests.'

'How serious are his wounds?'

'He will recover fully, my lord. He will fight again.'

'Those are good tidings. He is of a rare sort much needed in these times. These men,' he said. 'Once their hurts are seen to, see they are found accommodation and refreshment. They should not be left here to sit and ruminate upon their losses. They are heroes and should be treated as such. This is my command. See it is acted upon.' He was irritated that it had not been done already, that he must order it. Designed and launched in mightier days, the battle-barges of the Space Marines had ample space for thousands, and were never full. There was no cause other than thoughtlessness to keep the men sitting in the hangar.

'Of course, my lord,' said the thrall.

Dante turned to address the men. 'When the fleet is under way, you will be feasted by the Blood Angels, in honour of your courage. You will be taken from this place shortly. Rest. You are safe.'

Dante ignored the men's entreaties to lay hands upon them, and continued towards the rear hangar slot.

Stormravens flew in and out of the hangar deck, atmospheric integrity fields shimmering around their prows as they entered the ship. These were the stragglers, units sent on missions elsewhere on Asphodex or delayed by attack and mechanical problems. Not one was undamaged. From every craft the battered remnants of his strike force emerged, carrying the wounded, the dead and salvaged wargear. Sanguinary Priests came out with their reductor capsules extended, a sign they were full of the progenoids of the dead. Some of the ships touched down, disgorged their cargoes and took off again immediately, hurrying to save brothers left behind. He watched Techmarines board one ship, off to retrieve the Chapter's precious technology from the teeth of the enemy. From another serfs dragged several large pallets under the watchful eyes of senior Armoury blood thralls. Upon them were drop pod cogitator units. The craft were easily produced and regarded as disposable; their machine-spirits were not.

At the furthest end of the aft hangar slot, tall angelic statues were moulded into the walls. Armourglass bay windows filled the spaces between their outstretched wings and arms that protruded into the void. Dante entered the small space encompassed by glass and looked down upon the ruin of Asphodex. Knowing their master's moods well, his Sanguinary Guard kept a respectful distance.

The ship shook with the discharge of bombardment cannons, sending withering salvoes of lava bombs into the surface of Asphodex. Dante had ordered Bellerophon to empty the ship's magazines, and the Lord of the Heaven Gate was cleaving to his command. Asphodex's surface was buckling under the strain, a deep fissure opening in its crust. As tectonic plates unknitted, the glow of the world's secret fire was exposed. The *Blade of Vengeance* lacked the power to enact *Exterminatus* on the planet, but Dante would scour it with flame, leaving little for the tyranids to feast upon. Where it had not collapsed entirely, the world-city of Phodia was a raging inferno, its thoroughfares traced in flame.

Across the orange burn of world-death, organic silhouettes floated, for around Asphodex swam a shoal of corpses. The giant voidbeasts were dead, their heavy, crustacean shells cracked. Globular clouds of frozen fluids and chunks of flesh surrounded each with its own swarm of gory satellites. The frozen particulates of vented atmosphere masked the dull, clotted red of the Red Scar.

A few of the ship-beasts remained alive. The *Blade of Vengeance*'s escorts darted among them, finishing off those that were wounded with volleys of torpedoes. Flights of Stormhawks and Thunder-hawks raced alongside their mothership, destroying ship-to-ship infiltration organisms and the directional bladders of fragmentation mines, laid like so many eggs by the xenos.

The liveliest enemy ships listed drunkenly, feeble tentacles flicking at the coldness of space without purpose. The coordination the fleets had possessed was gone. Chaos filled the absence. They were easy prey, and the guns of the Blood Angels had a surfeit of targets.

Lesser minds would see this as a triumph, but it would only be a matter of time before the ship-beasts reorganised as the swarms on the surface had. The fleet was enormous, divided into several armadas attacking each of Cryptus' worlds. Hundreds of thousands of them had been destroyed. Too many remained, and this was but one splinter of Hive Fleet Leviathan, itself a smaller part of the greater tyranid whole. They had done no more than lop off a fingertip.

Dante dwelled on his disquiet alone.

How many more worlds would he watch die? Privately, he saw this latest tyrannic war as unwinnable. No effort was great enough. Every victory against them had been won at enormous cost, and those victories were isolated instances in long lists of defeats. Who could defy the tyranids if the Imperium did not? Not the eldar, nor the upstart tau. The former were divided, the latter's empire too small. Neither were sufficiently numerous. The orks would rage against the Devourer, but be consumed by the voidspawn as methodically as caprids strip a meadow and turn it to a wasteland. None of the galaxy's other myriad races were great enough to stand against them.

If they were all to come together, they would last a little longer. Dante could not envisage unity among humanity. An alliance between species strong enough to overwhelm the Great Devourer was an impossibility.

Dante lacked Sanguinius' gift of foresight, but he could imagine a galaxy scoured of biological life easily enough, the bones of civilisations picked over by necron dynasties and other abiotic beings. Even they would not survive, but dwindle and die in the ruins. Looking out over the shattered mess of the tyranid fleet, he found it all too easy to envisage the same scene played out over the skies of Terra – a final defiance before inevitable consumption. Corbulo knew. The Sanguinary Priest had the prophetic sight. He had become withdrawn of late, and haunted looking. Dante could imagine the end. He was sure Corbulo had seen it.

For all his early life, Dante had been taught to mistrust the alien. It was true the least offensive xenos harboured a deep perfidy. Lenience towards xenos species bought a bounty of betrayal. But in all his long years, he had never truly hated them, not as some of his brothers did. Non-humans strove only to survive as mankind strove. Dante had gleaned enough of the galaxy's history to know that more often than not, folly and hubris had undone the great civilisations of the past, humanity's first stellar empire included, and not external threat.

Mankind had more in common with other sentient species than the adepts of Terra would admit. He supposed that was why aliens were so easy to hate. Not for him. Besides the treacheries and atrocities he had witnessed by xenos hand, he had seen nobility, honour and mercy. Twice recently, he had been forced to fight alongside the necrons against the tyranids. On neither occasion had these most arrogant of aliens betrayed the alliance. Flashes of the virtues and the graces were in all living things.

In the tyranids, he had finally found something to hate, and powerfully. His loathing for them was the strongest emotion outside of the thirst he had felt for centuries. There could be no accommodation with the tyranids, only war. They had no redeeming features. When he had seen them as beasts, he had regarded them as a problem. When he had learned of the existence of the hive mind, he had come to view them as an existential threat. Now that mind was proving to be as vindictive as the cruellest man, he had grown to despise it.

Victory might be possible, in the end, but what then? The forces of the Imperium would be so depleted as to fall easy prey to the Great Enemy, or to be overwhelmed by orks, or cast down by the metal overlords of the necron dynasties who would, he had no doubt, turn on them after any ultimate triumph.

As he looked down upon the boiling hell of Asphodex, Dante was seeing a foretaste of the end. Weariness sank deep into him, and he was glad of the support of his armour.

He turned from the window and looked out at his Chapter and their servants, already preparing for fresh conflict. They were so few, and growing fewer.

I have failed them, he thought. This is the beginning of defeat.

The losses of the Blood Angels would be great. He did not have to see the casualty reports – the broken bodies carried by grief-stricken brothers from the Stormravens told him all he needed to know. A dread crept along his limbs, bringing with it a weakness. There would not be enough of them left to defend Baal. The Chapter would be finally destroyed.

Disturbed by his fatalism, he closed his eyes.

Lord Sanguinius, he prayed. *Forgive me. I am old, and the toil of conflict has worn my soul thin, although my body remains strong. I will never falter. I will never retreat. I will never give in. If I cannot ensure a better future for humanity, then I will see it has a glorious end, defiant to the last. Forgive me my moments of doubt. Lend me the strength to overcome them.*

Can he hear me? Dante thought. Is the brightest son of the Emperor somewhere now, watching me?

Sanguinius was dead ten thousand years before Dante had been born. He had prayed to him since before he had become a Space Marine. The primarch had never answered, but Sanguinius was not a god. Sometimes it was hard to remember that. At times, the words of the Adeptus Ministorum sounded true.

As if in answer to his doleful thoughts, a blaze of light shone from the centre of the deck. A wind blew in all directions. Guns were raised. Tocsins blared. Machine voices warned of intrusion, and that the deck defences were now online.

Dante's hand gripped the handle of the perdition pistol. His guard had their angelus gauntlets pointed at the epicentre of the radiance, staring into the light unflinchingly.

The light faded to reveal a golden figure, its armour almost the twin of Dante's, standing at the centre of the hangar deck.

'The Sanguinor!' boomed Chaplain Ordamael from the far side of the deck. 'The Sanguinor is here!'

The activity in the hangar ceased all at once. Armour clanged on the deck plating as Blood Angels dropped to their knees and bowed their heads, their servants knelt beside them like children kneeling by their fathers at prayer, hands clasped so tightly their knuckles whitened.

Dante did not kneel. The Sanguinor stared at him. Broad wings of white ceramite spread either side of a face that resembled the one Dante wore. But whereas Sanguinius' face bore an expression of anger on Dante's helm, his mouth wide in a silent war-cry, the rendition on the Sanguinor's was troubled, with tears of gold rolling down its cheek.

It was a mask Dante had seen many times before.

Deliberately, the Sanguinor strode across the deck towards Dante. His Sanguinary Guard moved aside. They would not have stood in the way of the Sanguinor had Dante ordered them to.

The Sanguinor came to a halt before the commander. The face of Sanguinius looked into the face of Sanguinius. A sensation of wrongness took hold of Dante. He felt presumptuous, standing before this avatar of their primarch, wearing his face. He rarely removed the mask in public nowadays. Let the men of the Imperium take heart from the sight of Sanguinius' golden face, he thought; he had come to terms with the effect the mask had on others, even if it had at first disquieted him. Warriors responded to the visage of the primarch. Sanguinius' face and Dante's deeds had become indivisible, welded together in the crucible of legend. So be it.

But there was a reason for concealing his own face that went beyond pragmatism. As the years had coursed by, Dante had aged. He was old, and he looked it.

He only reluctantly revealed his face, though he was honest enough to see his motives had as much to do with pride. Many of the younger Chapter members had never seen him without his helm. To them, his was the face of Sanguinius, as the face of death was the face of the Chaplaincy.

Standing before the Sanguinor so masked lacked humility.

He hesitated, torn between the needs of preserving his own legend and acknowledging his individuality. His men had their heads bowed. None of them were looking at him.

Sudden determination moved his hands to his helmet. He disengaged its seals and removed the death mask of Sanguinius smoothly and quickly, exposing his face to the Sanguinor.

A distorted version of Dante was reflected in the burnished chest armour of the Sanguinor. Dante knew it well. His golden hair had turned as white as the Sanguinor's wings. The skins of ancient Space Marines became thick, seamed with shallow wrinkles akin to the cracks in leather. Dante had gone beyond that. Deep wrinkles covered his face, sharpening the fine bone structure of his gene-father to the point of brittleness. His eyes remained pale amber and clear as the morning, the same as his long-dead birth father's eyes, but they were sunk into their sockets. The skin about his neck had begun to gather the first signs of loose folds.

Without the medium of helm lenses, the Sanguinor appeared unbearably bright. Light shone from every surface of its armour. Once, an inquisitor had challenged Dante as to the true nature of the Sanguinor. Dante had replied the Sanguinor could be nothing other than pure. He had come face to face with the being on many occasions. Always, he had felt close to his gene-father in its presence, and comforted by his love for his sons. Almost like Sanguinius himself were there.

The Sanguinor stared down at him. Dante was diminished by its gaze.

'Why have you come, my lord?' Dante said, bowing his head. 'Have I failed? Have you come to condemn me for this defeat?'

The Sanguinor stared back at him in silence. In one hand it held its chalice, but it did not offer it to Dante's lips. Its sword was in its hand, but it did not seek for Dante's neck. If it were there to weigh Dante's actions, it had not determined its judgement.

'Are these events the will of our primarch? Is his hand at work here?'

There were no words. The Sanguinor was ever silent.

Dante dropped his voice to a whisper. 'Is there hope? Can Baal be saved?'

Dante expected no reply. There was not a single record of the Sanguinor ever speaking. The presence of the Sanguinor seemed to swell, and fill his vision with its purity and its light. Ferocious in battle, a great peace surrounded it now, and it settled on Dante like a blessing.

'There is yet hope,' said the Sanguinor.

With a rush of air, it vanished. Amazed voices rose up all over the hangar.

'It spoke! The Sanguinor spoke!' voices called.

Dante replaced his mask with shaking hands. Ordamael came rushing to him, his black boots ringing off the deck.

'What did it say? Never before has the Sanguinor said a single word. What did it say to you?' he said. In his excitement, he grasped Dante's pauldron.

'It said, there is yet hope,' he whispered. He gripped Ordamael's arm, then turned to face the wider room. 'That there is yet hope!' shouted Dante. His rich voice, unchanged by age, boomed from his helm, and he invested it with the confidence his warriors expected. 'The Sanguinor has spoken. We shall prevail!'

His warriors cheered. The blood thralls broke into song at seeing so holy a sight.

Dante could not share their optimism, not in his heart of hearts. He watched them a moment, proud and sad, and turned back to the window, ignoring the rush of questions Ordamael bombarded him with. Disappointed, the Chaplain saluted and left him alone.

Outside of the windows, Asphodex was still dying, a spark to light a conflagration that would consume the galaxy.

CHAPTER SIX

ANGEL'S LEAP

456.M40
Heavenwall Mountains
Baal Secundus
Baal System

The pass continued down the mountains, out into fresh deserts of grey sand studded with thorny trees. Columns of dust hung over caravans of nomad vehicles in the distance. Dominating the plain were the remains of a vast city, the spires at its centre still tall twelve thousand years after the rest had been cast down in nuclear fire.

'The Ghost Lands,' said Luis. 'The cities of the dead!' The scope of the ruins was hard to fully grasp. Even though much of it had been covered over by shifting dunes, the city was many times the size of Kemrender or even Selltown.

'That means we're nearly there,' said Florian without expression. He bade Luis turn to the east again to follow a trail that went up and down the mountainsides. They followed this for two days until it joined with a road paved with pitted rockcrete patched with cobbles. More trails wended their way up to meet the road on long flights of stairs, and they began to pass other travellers. Merchants led long trains of chained pack slaves by, angrily shoving them aside. Lone pilgrims were friendlier. They talked with these people, some of them families.

'We're going to see the leap,' one boy said as his parents smiled indulgently. 'Are you going to jump?'

Florian laughed and ruffled his hair.

The father was delighted that his son had been paid attention to by potential aspirants. 'Sanguinius' blessings upon you, my boys!' he called after them, and gave them a bottle of precious water.

Florian waved cheerily back at them. Luis was gladdened to see the plainsman return to himself. Other families gave them food and shared news of lands far distant. Their eyes shone at the prospect of breaking bread with the boys, that they might eat with future angels.

Tinkers and itinerant craftsmen solicited them for trade until they saw the boys had nothing they could offer, and moved on. 'We go to the trial,' Luis said, to those who approached them, and they shook their heads and shouted, 'Good luck!' and went on their way. There were men of more unsavoury aspect moving through the growing traffic, too; whether the boys' own travel-worn look protected them, or their sacred quest to reach the trial, Luis could not say. These lands, and their customs, were foreign to him.

Before long they met other youths like themselves. Boys of their age, sometimes younger, but none with beards, the last marker of manhood. Many carried the packs and bone tubes of the angel's wings. Others, some of them savage in appearance, seemed just as confused by the devices as Luis had been.

The tubes were surprisingly light, and Luis quickly learnt from Florian how to carry them the most efficient way: resting on his shoulders, with his right hand draped over the edge to steady them. Several times Luis had a look through the pack, but could make no sense of what he was supposed to do with the broad spreads of membranous leather and their thongs and tying points.

The road was wide and well maintained; the slopes became stairways. Wells were set every ten miles, open to use by all. Inscriptions in the high tongue proclaimed them the gifts of the lords of Baal. Thirst ceased to trouble them.

'Baal Secundus,' said Florian, laboriously reading one such inscription, ignoring the angry jostling of the men behind him. 'What's that?'

'That's here,' said Luis, fighting to fill his bottles amid the jostling travellers. 'It's the angels' name for Baalfora. Baalind is Baal Primus.'

'What's Baal then?' said Florian.

Luis pulled a face. 'That's just Baal, yes?' A rough hand grabbed at him and pulled him away from the well. 'Watch it!' he said. A man with a rad-scarred face jabbered at him in a dialect Luis couldn't understand. 'Let's move on. I don't like it here,' said Luis.

The stairs steepened, winding their way back up into the mountains, narrowing and crushing the people together. They saw more and more youths making their way to the Angel's Leap. A few nods of acknowledgement were the friendliest signs that passed between them. They were rivals, and at times the looks they received were openly hostile.

At a point higher than any the boys had yet ascended, the stairs reached the end of their climb, abruptly switching downwards over a sharp ridge into a hanging valley. To the east rose an enormous, bare-shouldered mountain composed of unnaturally smooth sandstone that looked impossible to climb. Streaks of snow marked its lofty head like clawed scars. Florian drew Luis' attention to a flash of gold on the peak.

'The High Statue,' he said. 'The angels mark the place Sanguinius was said to have landed after his first flight. Here, at Angel's Leap, he trusted his wings for the first time and took to the air. This is holy ground, my friend. Can you believe it?'

The valley was crowded with a city-sized camp of people. Tents and stalls spread colours across the dull stone. Massive pens held food animals. There were no vehicles; all of the teeming masses had come on foot to witness the would-be aspirants take their flight of faith.

To the west, the valley ended dramatically over a giant canyon, the far side tinted yellow by the dusty distance. On the very brink of the valley rose a tall pinnacle of black rock, thrust out from the red stone as violently as a sword through flesh. It leaned out precariously, westwards over the canyon.

Luis' heart flipped at the sight. Crowds of youths clustered around its base, tiny as salt mites. At its tip figures flexed wings and leapt. Flocks of what looked like birds but which had to be boys like himself circled on the thermals. A few dived down into the canyon, and soared away. Others alighted, coming from the opposite direction along the currents of the Wind River.

'From that column Sanguinius first flew,' said Florian. His eyes gleamed.

'Is this the only way?' Luis said weakly.

'Not the only way, but the quickest. It's days on foot to Angel's Fall from here through the mountains, the Cracked Lands and worse. You can do it in ten hours if you fly. People from the deserts and the mountains see the leap as a test of manhood, and my father said that the angels look favourably on those who make their way to Angel's Fall by the Wind River. The river is dangerous, and blood eagles haunt its side valleys, but if you pass them all, you're on the way to being chosen. It's practically part of the trial. You're lucky you met me,' said Florian. Then, the cheer drained from his voice, and he mumbled. 'You're lucky Daneill died. You'd have no wings otherwise.'

Luis could only nod in response, too numb to offer words of comfort to his friend. His mouth was dry, and not just from the altitude. The floor of the canyon wasn't visible from where they were. It must have been a drop of five thousand feet at least. On the edge of hearing a rushing, booming noise impinged on the sounds of hawkers and entertainers below.

'That's the Wind River,' said Florian.

'I've never flown before,' said Luis. The thought sickened as much as it exhilarated him.

'Then you better learn quick,' said Florian. He laughed and

punched Luis in the shoulder. 'Don't worry. Messengers come this way from out of the Ghost Lands to Angel's Fall all the time. Most of them don't die.'

They went lower, watching as more figures jumped from the pinnacle. 'Some of them are leaving now, but there will be a race,' Florian explained. 'Whoever wins that is sure to be chosen, or so they say.' He asked around to ensure they knew the day it would occur.

'We're leaving tomorrow,' he said after one conversation. 'We're just in time. The race will begin in the morning.'

As they descended, the camp seemed to grow in size. More people were arriving, coming down the narrow stairs into the valley in a long stream. Tents and awnings were anchored over ancient dry stone wall bases. Luis hadn't expected this, but the Trial was evidently good business. Men and women sold water and salt, food of all types, even fresh vegetables grown in far-off geodesic domes, to the crowds. A good many of these people proved to be the parents of potential aspirants.

Florian looked longingly at the wares on display as they pushed their way through the throngs. When Luis produced his stack of lead coins, his eyes bulged.

'You could have bought your own wings with that! I was wrong about you, salty. You're full of surprises.'

'Never judge a man by his outer being, that's what they say,' said Luis, and bought them hot food and water.

'It's true,' smiled Florian round a mouthful of food.

There was a carnival air to the camp at Angel's Leap. Shawms and windpipers played late into the night. The shouts of competing preachers extolling the virtues of the angels and the Emperor echoed from the mountains, intermingling with the cries of hucksters selling relics, or tonics to aid those undertaking the trial, or promising the best vantage points for the great departure. Bookkeepers took bets on favoured members of various clans.

Florian and Luis joined the other youths around the base of the spire, away from the press of adults and the haze of dung-fire smoke. Overspill from the Wind River raced between the rocks, stirring up dust devils that spooked the more suspicious among them. The main current roared on down the canyon in endless exhalation.

A trickle of the youths wended their way upwards, determined to leave before the others. All strategies, thought Luis. He doubted getting out early mattered. He doubted winning the so-called race mattered. The angels weren't likely to choose on that basis alone. He questioned the wisdom of flying by night, even though Florian maintained certain clans preferred it.

The food was plentiful, the water welcome; a feast it seemed after days of short meals. They spoke a little about the coming day. Florian explained how the wings worked.

'Your arms go into the loops. I'll show you how. Your feet into the stirrups. It's not hard, you just got to feel the wind. Push back with your feet – it bends the wing struts, makes you soar up. Relax your feet, the opposite. Dip your arms to turn. Don't try to flap like a bird, it don't work. You'll get it.' He left unsaid that if Luis didn't get it, he would die.

Luis tried his best to remember, but the more he concentrated on what Florian said, the more important details seemed to slip from his mind. Florian talked about stalling, that if he fell, he had to get his arms out straight, make sure he was the right way up. Luis was sure he hadn't understood properly. He was half terrified, half excited that soon he might fly like the blessed Sanguinius.

They ate more. Drank more water than they strictly needed, feeling wicked for their profligacy. Baalind tracked across the sky, Baal was nowhere to be seen.

Florian fell asleep. Though Luis tried to follow him, he could not. All night he lay awake, listening to the noise in the camp quieten as Baalind sailed by and people went to their beds. The canyon roared at Firstnight, the Wind River quickening with the nightwind, dying back when truenight fell, but never ceasing, like the wailing of the mothers soon to lose their sons.

Eventually, he fell asleep.

* * *

Florian woke Luis. The sky blushed decorously with dawn. A clamour of cymbals and harsh clarions greeted the new day. Priests shouted hoarse praises to the Emperor of Man, thanking Him for allowing the sun to return. The wind blew as it had for thousands of years, weaker slightly in the morning, but rising as the sun warmed the deserts that fed it.

'You all right?'

'I didn't think I'd sleep at all,' said Luis. He yawned, then he remembered what he was to do today. His stomach turned queasy as adrenaline burned tiredness from him.

'Breakfast?' said Florian.

Luis looked at the remnants of their supper. 'I don't feel like eating,' he said.

'Neither do I,' said Florian. 'Come on. Better sooner than later.'

'We should leave our gear. I won't need it again.'

'You will,' said Florian. 'You'll need water and food if you crash and survive, and you'll need money if you're turned away from the Place of Trials at Angel's Fall. Leave what you can't carry, that's all. You don't know what will come in useful.'

Luis agreed to the sense of this, so he abandoned only some of their gear. He left behind Daneill's clothes and those he had taken from the corpse. He took two full bottles of water, and left the rest. He felt a pang of regret as he lay his staff down, but he could not possibly carry that. He touched it gently to feel the grain of the wood one last time.

Once they were behind him, a weight lifted from him, as if he were laying his old life to rest.

A long, winding stair went up to the pinnacle of Angel's Leap. Many of the youths had roused themselves already and thronged the way. Knots of parents packed the base of the stairs, expressions prideful yet pale with fear for their sons who passed by, their wing poles over their shoulders and packs on their backs. The stone spine was black and glassy, the steps carved into it slippery and their edges still sharp from their carving, though it had been done unimaginably far back in time. More than once a boy slipped, caught and hauled back from his death by the arms of his fellows. Those who fell onto the steps cut themselves, sometimes badly. From time to time aggressive youths would shove their way up, glowering at any who delayed them, but Florian and Luis went patiently, not disturbing the flow.

The climb was slow. At the top, the boys had to assemble their angel's wings and don them, and this caused frequent halts. The line of youths snaked out across the valley as the line backed up. The camp roused itself and the noise rose, becoming feverish with excitement. Turn by turn Florian and Luis walked around the spine of rock. Sometimes the steps were cut into the body of the stone, so that there was a low ceiling overhead, sometimes they would ride out over natural protuberances. A frieze wound its way around the wall of the stair. Millennia of trailing hands and harsh winds had worn the carvings to vague shapes. Only one faceless figure, that of Sanguinius, stood out by dint of his wings and frequent appearances.

The drop grew. Luis saw people gathering around the canyon edge, cheering every time a boy launched himself from the pinnacle. His heart hammered with nerves. The height terrified him, even with the rock beneath his feet. The wind seemed to want him, plucking at his clothes mischievously. The roar of it through the canyon grew louder and louder the further out they went on the jutting pinnacle until Florian had to shout into Luis' ear.

The pinnacle leaned out over the canyon, and soon Luis had his first look down into its depths.

The floor was lost in shadow, the sun shining so rarely upon it that dirty ice lurked between the talus slopes cloaking the lower reaches. At the very bottom an orange river flowed, threadlike and insignificant within the valley it had made. This was the first river Luis had ever seen. The wonder of it was overshadowed by the terror of the drop, much as the river was overshadowed by the scale of its canyon. His stomach flipped, his head swam. He fought the sudden, terrifying urge to throw himself off there and then. Clammy sweat beaded his forehead under his scarves.

Florian steadied him. 'Careful, salty. You don't want to fall without your wings.'

Desperately, Luis fumbled his father's goggles on. They were so old and scratched as to be practically impossible to see through, and the yellow tint to the aged plastek made the world unreal. He found this helped. His heart steadied. He had to bury his fear. He could not fail now.

Noon came and went. As they got higher, the view of the boys flying away improved. They fell so fast that they streaked across the eye, arms outstretched, whooping madly. When they hit the river of wind, they were snatched away. More than a few misjudged the speed of the current, and were rushed to their deaths against the cliffs. Luis distracted himself from the buffeting wind and horrendous fall by examining the flyers, gauging what technique was successful and what was not, the set of their feet and arms, the way they moved their bodies to fly out to the centre of the canyon. The boldest boys snatched themselves up before they hit the torrent of air, rising on the treacherous eddies coming off the Wind River to swoop over the crowds before diving into the canyon and racing off towards their destiny.

The shadows lengthened. The pinnacle narrowed. The turns of the stair came more frequently, and became sharper. Manoeuvring the bone poles around the corners became difficult. The whole line of boys was halted as one youth fell screaming past the crowds at the base, his half-assembled wings furled round him. Fear became so constant that Luis ignored it. By the time they reached the last turn his heart beat slowly. Dread was as normal as breathing. He could cope with that.

The top of the pinnacle was a level platform twenty yards across. If he could have stood in the middle, then Luis would have felt safe, but the pinnacle was crowded with boys attempting to assemble their wings. Arguments broke out as poles were laid over one another, or a boy felt his space to be violated in some other way. Luis and Florian waited for room to be available, hurrying over as soon as a boy had his wings on his back and moved to the canyon edge. He spread his wings without hesitation and leapt. Others stared down for many seconds before jumping, seized with terror at what they must do.

'Watch me,' urged Florian. He set down his wing spars and pulled out the leather panels from his backpack. With deft twists, he set the poles into each other, making a pair of long, curved spars which were hinged by thongs in the centre. He had two shorter poles and one long straight one left over. He set them to one side. The longer pair he put side by side, outstretched, and began to lace the leather onto the wing bones. 'These spars are made from blood hawk wing fingers – very light,' he explained. 'Follow the knots I'm making. It goes on easy once you know how. These grooves take the thongs, stops them from coming loose. Make sure they're tight. If they come undone in flight...' He grinned his black-toothed grin. 'You don't need me to explain it to you.'

Florian worked quickly, assembling the wings faster than many of the others. Once complete, he reversed his backpack, so that the chest straps were at the rear. These, Luis saw, formed the anchorage for the wings. He laced the panels together, tying them to the bones, then began to lace the edges of the wings to each other, testing them for tension and strength. 'These laces and leather panels might look flimsy, but they all work together,' Florian explained. 'The tension has to be right, though.'

Then, with the remaining poles, he made a sort of tail. The short poles made up either side, the last long pole connecting the tail to the wings.

'There, all done.' He folded it up and moved it over. 'Now let's do yours.'

A shadow fell over them. 'Don't you know what you're doing?' asked an incredulous voice.

'I do. Leave us be,' said Florian.

'Not wise to speak to me so,' said the boy. He was bigger than anyone else on the platform and unusually well muscled. Other boys with the same clan marks were putting his wings together for him. 'Who are you to speak to me in such a way?'

'Flat Desert clan,' said Florian. 'I'll talk to you how I please.' He continued lacing up Luis' wings.

'What about the scrawny one?' said the other boy. He had an arrogant manner, though there was good humour hiding behind it.

'I am of the Salt Waste roamers, Irkuk's clan,' said Luis.

The boy snorted. 'A salty in the mountains! So you made it this far? Impressive. Not like you salties to take the quick road. Well done. You're too little though – the angels will never take you.'

The boys accompanying him finished his wings. The big youth checked them over, grunting in annoyance when he found a loose thong. When he was satisfied, his followers assisted him in strapping on his wings, and he spread them wide. 'I am Lorenz, of the Clan Ash. Do I not look like an angel already?'

His toadies laughed, and quickened their efforts to climb into their own wings.

'This goes here, and there. Tie it like this,' said Florian. Luis moved around his own spread wings. He knocked a spar, raising laughter from the assembled boys.

'Don't say that this little salt chipper has never been on wings, that he has never flown before!' said Lorenz.

Luis' expression revealed the truth. Under the peeling skin of his sunburn, his cheeks burned.

'Then he is gonna die, eh?' Lorenz stepped back to the edge of the platform and crossed his arms over his chest, furling his wings about himself. 'For you, my friend, this is going to be a big leap of faith.'

He fell backwards, uttering a long drawn-out scream. Luis leapt up with a gasp. All the boys moved closer to the edge.

The flyer swooped upwards at great speed, borne aloft on the vertical winds created where the river hit the pinnacle. Steadying himself on the currents, he darted back and forth overhead in a near hover, laughing at his own skill.

'See you in Angel's Fall, if you make it!'

He dived down to the canyon in a long, graceful swoop, and was borne away by the Wind River.

'He's a cocky one.' Florian pointed at the wings. 'We're finished. It's our turn.'

Lorenz's friends turned to their own fates now their leader was gone, leaving Florian to help Luis into his wings. His hands gripped straps sewn to reinforced panels. His feet were set into loops attached to the tail bones. Florian told him to spread his arms, and he laced the wings into place.

'What about you?' asked Luis.

'There's a way to do it yourself. I'll be fine. Remember, push back with your feet to flex the spine and change the shape of the wings. Dip your arms to turn. Don't, for the love of the Great Angel, try to flap your arms. You glide, you got that? No flapping! If you stall, get your arms out, face down. Stay on your front.'

Florian opened Daneill's pack on Luis' front and loaded it with food and water. The last item that went in was a water bottle plugged with a clay cap, from which protruded a hollow bone. 'Drink from this when you need. You will get thirsty. Don't be tempted to stop –you won't be able to get airborne again. If you need to piss, do it in your pants. Now, are you ready?' Florian slapped him in the chest, exposing his black teeth.

Luis nodded mutely. His heart in his mouth, he approached the edge of the pinnacle platform. The edge was smooth and treacherous. The movement of his feet was restricted by his wing rig, and he nearly fell when he spread his wings and the wind caught them. He tottered. Lorenz's last couple of cronies tittered. Their contempt steadied him. At his feet the world opened. The crowds were watching him. He was not a frightened boy to them; he was a lone silhouette on the edge, an angel in the making.

'When you're ready,' said Florian.

'No point delaying,' said Luis. But he couldn't jump. He thought it several times, his muscles tensed, but something in his limbs rebelled and rooted him into place, five thousand feet above the rusty river.

'Get on with it!' shouted someone behind him.

'Go on, Luis,' said Florian. 'Jump!'

A scream of defiance built in Luis' throat. He couldn't keep it in, and it burst from him. Once it was out, he had no choice but to go.

It was easier than he had expected.

He fell like a stone. He was still yelling, but the wind snatched the sound away from him. It tugged mercilessly at his spread wings, threatened to rip his father's goggles from his face. The edge of the canyon rushed at him, the crowd going from a single mass to individuals.

Why aren't I flying? Why aren't I flying? he thought in a panic.

Though his mind became blank, his body was not ready to die. His feet kicked back. The spine pole connecting wings to tail flexed. Leather thongs running from the tail spars strained, pulling at the ends of the wings and bending them. The wings filled out. He angled his arms upwards, though to do so was like trying to lift the world. Suddenly, he was ripped up out of his dive. Wobbling madly, he drove straight at the crowd on the edge of the cliff. Their cheers turned to panic, and they ran back from the edge. In the nick of time, Luis tilted his arms and went rushing away towards the centre of the canyon. There the main stream of the river of wind grabbed him hard, threatening to turn his graceful bank into a deadly tumble. He managed to correct himself, and he was away, chasing after other winged boys at a hundred miles an hour. The roar of the wind dropped as he matched its speed.

He strained his neck to look behind him and got a brief view of the hanging valley, but the motion upset his flight, and he faced resolutely forwards after that.

For an hour, he flew rigid and scared. After a while he detected differing notes to the wind's song, strange slappings where it encountered bluffs or shoulders in the rock, hooting where it passed through storm-worn arches. These sounds affected the invisible flow of the air, and he learnt quickly what they meant. The wind gave the air a sense of solidity, so much so that Luis could fool himself he was not high above killing stone, but sliding belly first down a sand dune. He began to experiment, twitching his arms and feet, sending himself into wide curves, or up and down.

As his experiments became bolder, he discovered that if he were to dive quickly then climb smoothly, he could increase his speed, or that if he rose up high he would slow so that it seemed he hung there, the world spread out beneath his belly. Once he almost stalled himself doing this, but Florian's instructions ran through his mind, and he recovered. Soon he was overtaking other boys, or chasing them down the quickest streams of air.

He was flying, like an angel. He laughed at the joy of it. Even if he were turned away by the angels, at least he would have the memory of this to take to his grave.

Minutes of joy turned to hours of tedium. Keeping his arms and legs braced made them ache. He could not relax, and slowly but surely the discomfort became tortuous. Performing turns and dives alleviated the ache, but at the cost of tiring his limbs further. Soon his muscles sang with agony. The day crawled by. Thirst bothered him. He found he could not reach the bottle on his chest without sending himself into a dangerous dive. He snatched a sip or two, but large, refreshing gulps remained tantalisingly out of reach.

The canyon curved off its northern path, turning to the north east. The wind currents became erratic as they encountered the turn, breaking into choppy vortices reflected back off the cliffs. For a few moments Luis' pains were forgotten as he fought his way through. A pair of boys ahead got into trouble, tossed up and down until they were pushed into a long glide yards above the canyon floor. They were forced down and landed awkwardly.

The wind buffeted him, and he dropped lower and lower. He feared the same fate awaited him. With a final effort, he pushed the leading edge of his wings upwards. They juddered along his arms, the leather flapping. Then he punched through the turbulence, leaving the grounded boys far behind. For the next half an hour he expended much effort in regaining height, and remained wary of the lower reaches for the remainder of his journey.

The mountains on the eastern side of the Wind River diminished and became hills; those on the other stayed tall, but turned suddenly west to march into the desert, leaving high table lands behind them. The canyon's eastern edge softened and dropped. The west remained a mighty cliff, topped by a plateau riven with gullies.

The day had been old when Luis departed, and the sky darkened. Deep red evening light turned the land to blood. The Wind River weakened. Luis slowed. He risked looking back. A train of winged boys stretched away into the canyon. Florian could have been any one of them.

Thin screams had him looking forwards once again. For a second he thought that some of the youths had turned on their fellows, for the canyon ahead was full of black, wheeling shapes diving at each other. Then he saw through the failing light that some were men, and some were birds.

'Blood eagles!' he said. A flock of the giant raptors was plunging from on high, stooping on the fragile angel's wings and sending boys spiralling to their deaths. They left the meat for later, smashing passing youths out of the sky in their frenzy to take advantage of this seasonal glut.

Helplessly, Luis drew closer to the aerial brawl. The raucous screeching of blood eagles and the screams of dying youths rent the air. The birds were everywhere. Their graceful bodies were bigger than grown men. Four powerful talons sprouted from their feet, and these were but the least of their armoury. The majority of their heads were dominated by huge beaks, long as swords. The lower portions fitted into a slot in the upper, snug as the blades of shears. They were blunt tools, for crushing bone, and weighty because of it. Long, wattled crests the colour of blood sprouting from the back of their skulls counterbalanced these brutal natural weapons. Though their beaks made them appear ungainly, they were nimble flyers, and far more agile than the gliding boys. The blood eagles powered themselves upwards with beats of broad wings, turned and fell again, wings bent, claws outstretched, pouncing on the steady flight of youths. For every ten youths felled, only one or two were making their escape.

Luis was horrified. To die here, a victim of mere chance...

'Emperor, if you truly do watch over us all, aid me now,' said Luis.

He forced his angel's wings into a sharp bow, and by leaning towards the cliffs went into a steep turn. He flipped his wings up, catching the wind directly. The Wind River blasted him sideways. His speed increased; he turned into a long spiral, wheeling around and around upwards, and although the river carried him towards the massacre, by the time he was near the eagles he had gained three hundred feet in altitude. Levelling out, he half folded his wings behind him like the eagles did and pointed himself at the ground. He dropped, meteor fast, and hurtled into the middle of the attack.

Eagles with limp bodies in their talons rushed by. He jinked to avoid a bird tearing at a wing rig. Another boy fell screaming past him. The ground raced at him.

A screech came from behind. An eagle was on his tail. Flicking out one wing, Luis swerved violently to the left, then the right, risking a stall. His flight was slowed by evasion, and the eagle shot past him, screaming angrily. Luis waited for it to spread its wings, braking over the muddy trickle of the river, then spread his own and set them level.

He sped past the enraged raptor, skimming the canyon floor.

He rolled a little from side to side, searching the sky through the dirty yellow of his goggles. There were no more eagles. He looked back. The eagle chasing him was shrinking rapidly behind. Several of the birds appeared to have abandoned their hunt and were circling to the ground, to tear at the dead and wounded with their beaks.

Ahead the canyon was turning into a broad valley. Evidence of a much bigger river marked the floor. The worn remains of walls emerged from the dunes along the ancient banks. The orange river he had followed from Angel's Fall was pathetic in the bed, and was becoming thinner and thinner as it sank into the sand.

The wind was dying, spreading out as the canyon relaxed its grip. Luis needed to gain height before he lost forward momentum. All of the boys who had passed the eagles' gauntlet had lost height and were attempting to do the same. He looked enviously up at the black specks of those who had managed the feat. He ignored the boys who crashed into the sand and shouted for help.

If he could keep going until Firstnight abated and the rush of the nightwind came, he might gain altitude. Luis forced the wings into a sharp curve with his aching legs. He aimed arms numbed by lack of movement skywards. The wings lifted him up, but his speed died. He was going to stall. He pitched forwards, and he gained speed again, but lost height. Four times he tried this, moving in a series of sharp swoops closer to the ground. By now he'd come some miles from the eagle's attack.

One last attempt saw him fly fifty yards up. There, his wings failed to catch the wind when he dipped down. He went hurtling at the ground. At the last moment, he pulled up into a deliberate stall, braking enough that he hit the ground with merely bruising force. His wing spars shattered around him, tangling him in leather and straps as he rolled over and over violently along the dune-choked riverbed.

Groaning, he pulled himself into a sitting position and shed the wings with the help of his knife.

Boys sped through the sky, their whoops distorted by their speed. Wretchedly, Luis pulled out his bottle and drank greedily of his water. Once his thirst was slaked, his failure hit him.

He had no idea where he was. Switching his pack to his back, he stood, oriented himself with the line of youths winging their way eastwards and began to follow.

Firstnight ended. The nightwind blew, ten minutes too late to help him. Truenight fell. Luis continued his trek by the light of Baal and Baalind. The river of water died pathetically, sinking into the sand and leaving a series of brackish pools behind, until these too disappeared and the ancient riverbed continued dry as old bones. The Wind River lost its force, its constant blow turning fitful, then dispersing, until it had blended itself with the slackening night-wind of Baalfora. The valley sides receded further. The western mountains were a line as brown as old blood; the eastern range dwindled to nothing, surrendering to the dunes.

On Luis plodded. It was too dark to see the flyers passing, and he kept his head down, doggedly placing one aching leg in front of another. He missed his staff.

Day dawned. Luis continued. A flash caught his attention far away. He strained his eyes and lifted his goggles.

Away on the horizon a forbidding cliff raised itself out of the desert, soaring to a thousand feet high from nothing. The rock-face was in isolation from other such features, the hill it fronted sloping back and down almost as sheerly as the cliff. Before this anomalous mount was the titanic statue of an armoured angel facing the sky. His wings and arms were spread, a sword in one hand, a chalice in another.

In permanent exultation, Sanguinius greeted the morning sun. A dim smear of brown blocks crowded his feet.

Luis staggered forwards a couple of steps, then sank to his knees laughing. He was looking at the city of Angel's Fall.

CHAPTER SEVEN

ANGEL'S FALL

456.M40
Angel's Fall
Planetary Capital
Baal Secundus
Baal System

Hundreds of people waited in queues for the gates to open. Luis joined them before dawn. For three hours, he crept forwards. The bells of the city's many cathedrals rang out in great cacophony every hour, calling out brazen songs to the Lord of Mankind and His most perfect son while His subjects shuffled in the dirt to be first to market. At the gates Luis was asked what his reasons for being at Angel's Fall were. When he said he was there for the trials, the officials on the gate nodded as if that were the only answer they expected and pointed down the main street.

'The feet of Sanguinius. There you will find the selection ground, the Place of Choosing. May the Emperor bless you in your endeavour.' The blessing was heartfelt. Luis could only stare back as the men wished him well, his mouth open. Clear as day, they wore the winged blood drop of the Blood Angels on their shoulders. He gaped so long that the officials' demeanour changed, and they shooed Luis out of the shade of the gate and into the city.

'*Deus Imperator regnum imperpetua!* Praise the Emperor! Beware the heretic! Fear freedom of thought, for the unfettered mind is the pathfinder of heresy!' A line of dirty men in torn robes trotted past, roped together at the neck, left hands on the left shoulder of the man in front. The leader rang a bell as he shouted out his homilies. Luis stared at this filthy procession, recoiling as one man raised his head; he had his lips and eyelids neatly sewn shut.

Angel's Fall was nothing like he expected, bigger and filthier than both Kemrender and Selltown. Both towns, huge to him, were revealed as the dusty villages they were. Luis had never seen so many people. They crammed the streets of Angel's Fall from side to side. The stink of so many bodies together made him dizzy. And there were more than Baalites there; citizens of many worlds came on pilgrimage to the place where the most blessed of the Emperor's sons had fallen from the sky.

Rarely, a landing ship would thunder towards the city's modest port. Later he would learn that only the most devout and important off-worlders were permitted to set foot on the planet, and then only within the confines of Angel's Fall. As a consequence, he saw displays of wealth in the city that staggered him. Men and women in fine clothes, their bodies unmarked by rad burns and fat with easy living. It was his first inkling how poor a world Baal Secundus truly was.

Sanguinius spread his bronze wings over the wretched poverty of the town, his beatific face turned away from the squalor towards the flawless blue of the heavens, as if he found his own people distasteful. The statue was immense, five hundred feet high, its wingspan almost as broad. As the sun rolled around its track, Sanguinius' wings shadowed the town like a sundial. The shade was welcome, even if the Great Angel's magnificence made Luis feel pathetic and powerless.

He tarried awhile on the main street, suddenly sheepish about going to the Place of Choosing. He was unworthy, he was sure. He bought food he had no appetite to eat, and dawdled by stalls of goods so long their irate keepers moved him along.

The push of the crowd drew him eventually to the square. He emerged from a warren of buildings into an unexpected plaza paved with hard Baalite granite glass and surrounded by stern buildings of stone and rockcrete. In the very centre was a massive, two-tiered podium of white, veined marble, a stone not found on Baal or its moons. The first tier made a balcony fenced by an ornate balustrade, interrupted by a broad staircase that led to a pair of massive bronze doors set into the second tier. The winged blood drop of the angels was cast into the doors. Upon the flat roof of the upper tier, the demigod perched on the tips of his toes, forever trapped in the act of taking flight. Overwhelmed by the sight of Sanguinius so close, Luis fell to his knees and mumbled a prayer, shamed at his presumption of coming here to serve him. Others, more jaded than he, banged into his back as he knelt. He did not care. Several minutes went by before he dared stand and look upon the Great Angel again.

Everything else in Angel's Fall was caked in a layer of dust. The animal smells of dung and richer stink of human ordure clung to its streets, but the monument and its statue were pristine. Hideous amalgams of man and machine moved over it, constantly mopping away the sands of Baalfora's deserts as soon as they settled with gallons of precious water. The washers were followed by polishers, whose hands had been replaced with soft buffing tools. Around the base was an artful garden watered by the constant stream sluiced over the stone. The brilliant greens, reds and yellows of the flowers were strange and somewhat frightening to Luis' eyes.

About the garden gathered hundreds of boys. Different hues of skin and build, wearing clan marks ranging from the discreet to the bizarre. Most Luis did not recognise, but for all their diversity the majority were united in their disbelief at the city.

Hesitantly, Luis went to join them.

Among the boys Luis found sleeker youths for whom the city held no novelty. They were better fed and not so scarred by radiation and scouring sun. These were natives of Angel's Fall. They had not endured what he had, and yet they were to be accorded the same chance as Luis. He saw this as a gross injustice. His fists clenched involuntarily. He wanted to hit them, to punch them in their perfect faces. His sudden anger surprised him. He turned away from these boys, seeking out others more like him. No matter how hard he looked, he found no others of the Salt Roamer clans.

Wiry arms wrapped around him. Luis let out a sharp cry, drawing nervous laughter from the crowd. He turned around, ready to rebuke whoever had the presumption to grab him. He was on edge now, a greater terror than he had felt at any time of his journey fuelling his temper.

'Get off!' he snarled, throwing off the arms and whirling around.

'Luis! It's me!' Florian's black-toothed smile and reeking breath greeted him.

'Florian?' said Luis.

Florian embraced him in a fierce hug. 'I thought you were dead. I thought the blood eagles got you.'

'They nearly did,' said Luis.

'Your first flight, and you made it through! It was his first flight!' Florian said to the nearest boy. The boy raised his eyebrows to express his disinterest and looked away.

Lorenz, the large boy from Angel's Leap, shoved his way through the crowd after Florian.

'So, you are also alive. I am impressed. You are in time for the choosing.'

'When?'

'Today, tomorrow. All week. There are young clansmen coming in from all over Baalfora still,' said Florian. 'Today is the first pick.'

'They will take five hundred to the Place of Trials,' said Lorenz. 'Only one hundred will be taken to Baal. Only fifty will be chosen from the hundred.'

'Imagine failing now,' said Florian. 'Imagine that.'

Lorenz shrugged. 'Better here than on Baal, perhaps. Those not selected here will at least live.'

'They kill those that fail?' said Florian.

'We do not know,' said Lorenz. 'But at least those who fail here go home. No ever one returns from Baal.'

'Then I will not fail,' said Luis.

Lorenz gave him a wry smile.

They joined Lorenz's following of boys, reduced to three by the brutal flight. All of them were less arrogant than before, and grudgingly welcomed Florian and Luis.

At noon, the sun was directly behind Sanguinius. The front of the statue was cast into shadow, and a glorious halo erupted around his head.

At the precise moment the sun wreathed Sanguinius' face in fire, the bronze doors on the podium opened and a clarion fanfare of exquisite purity sounded. From out of the monument came a score of men in red robes, their faces hidden in hoods. They chanted benedictions in the high off-world tongue, swinging censers that billowed clouds of scented smoke as they walked around the platform, taking up position every five yards. Once they were all in place their singing stopped, and they cast back their hoods showing faces free of flaws.

'The Blood Angels!' said Florian in awe. The whole square was packed with boys and others who had come to look upon their lords. Silence fell on them, and they knelt in knots, until the whole square was on their knees on the hard stone.

'Those aren't the Blood Angels,' breathed Lorenz as others came from the podium interior. 'They are.'

The first men out had been tall and heavily muscled, the most perfect examples of humanity Luis had ever seen. They were nothing compared to their masters.

There were but the two of them. One was armoured in bone-white armour and blood-red robes, a velvet sack at his waist and a bulky device wrapped around his right gauntlet. The other was a giant in grim black battleplate decorated with bones, skulls and other signifiers of mortality. Luis was confused by their colours, wondering why they did not wear red as the legends said. They were armed as well as armoured. The skull-masked warrior carried a long staff topped with a winged skull; the one in white armour had a long, toothed sword at his side. Both wore pistols snug in holsters. Pistols. They were pistols, thought Luis, though they were as big as the boys' torsos. The warriors were at least seven feet tall, and their armour made them even bigger. The metal of their boots rang on the stone, and their battleplate hummed with the activities of mysterious spirits. Rubies carved into blood drops hung from their weapons, glittering in the sun and clinking in the silence of the square.

The Blood Angels stopped at the top of the stairs. Humming skulls swooped out over the crowd, artificial eyes winking in their sockets. A pair of cyber-cherubim flew behind, trailing a rippling silk flag emblazoned with the Chapter's heraldry. They settled between the feet of Sanguinius, draping the flag down over the open doorway.

Both warriors kept their helms on. The black-armoured warrior stayed back. The one in white and red stepped forwards to deliver the message of the angels.

'I am Brother Araezon,' he said, his voice carried to the back of the assembly by arcane means. Youths of more primitive clans started in fright. The voice was so clear, so perfect, many others among the crowd begged for forgiveness, or cried unashamedly. 'I am the Sanguinary Priest of the Redeemers, the Tenth Company of the Blood Angels, Adeptus Astartes Chapter. I am the surgeon to the recruits of our order.'

'I am Brother Malafael,' said the black warrior, and his voice was as sonorous as a funeral bell. 'Chaplain-Recruiter of the Tenth Company. It is we who will judge you worthy or not of proceeding from this Place of Choosing to the Place of Trials. There you shall be tested by our captain. Most of you shall be found wanting.'

They swept the crowd of dirty, malnourished boys with their helm lenses. Araezon's eyes rested on Luis a moment. Luis held the unblinking gaze despite the pressure of his regard. There was no expression to be read, but Luis felt contempt and pity, and a fierce, unattainable pride.

'The path to elevation is arduous and fraught with peril,' said Araezon. He spoke fairly, with an eloquence rare in the desert clans. 'Of the many hundreds of you we choose, only a handful will be suitable in mind, soul and body to join our ranks. A number of you that fail will die. Those of you who succeed will be pledged to a life of service to the Emperor, and in that service you too shall die. Yours will be a life of constant war and hardship, with no satisfaction but that of war, and no rest but that of death. There will be no love but that of your brothers, no family, nothing to pass on to future generations save the stories of your deeds and service to humanity preserved in our Chapter records, and from those too you shall eventually fade. You will pass from the knowing of your clans – they will not learn if their sons dwell among the angels or have died in the attempt. Life on Baal Secundus is hard, we know this well, but it is life. To become an angel of death is to embrace death – it is to become death.'

He paused and looked over the kneeling crowd again. 'Look you upon the visage of my Brother-Chaplain. This death's head is the future for you all, whichever path is chosen. We shall offer you a final choice, to be assured of the place of your death. Many of you have suffered long journeys to come here, have staked everything on the possibility of joining our brotherhood. Nevertheless, there is time to change your minds. Those of you who are wavering now should turn away and leave. Choose life over death, however short and cruel that life will be, and none shall judge you poorly. Those who do not, and who are chosen by my brother and I here, your life shall no longer be your own. That is the covenant we make between us. There can be no breaking it once it has been entered into. So then, speak! Who will leave?' called Araezon.

Falteringly, a boy got to his feet. Head bowed, he pushed his way from the square, a ripple of turning heads following him.

Where one had gone, others followed, breaking from the crowd in shameful silence. Scornful whispers hissed after them.

'Do not judge, lest ye yourselves be judged!' shouted Malafael, and his voice was stern. It too was amplified by some means, and boomed off every surface, startling the crowd. Youth and adult onlooker alike begged for forgiveness. The black angel swept his staff of office around at shoulder height. His huge shoulder pads shifted to accommodate the movement, growling softly, as if alive. 'In acknowledging a lack of courage can be found courage. Some of these boys will be your future leaders, your husbands, the fathers of your children. By fulfilling that role, they are the future of the Blood Angels too, for their sons will come here one day, and lo, they shall look upon the face of our lord Sanguinius, and they shall know no fear. For a man to acknowledge the true measure of his worth, no matter how paltry, is a moment of holy revelation. Do not scorn them!'

The crowd quieted. Luis looked around quickly; perhaps fifty or so boys from the hundreds who had originally gathered there had gone.

'I ask again, who shall leave?' Araezon shouted. No one else moved. 'Very well, you who remain have consented to be tested. Your life now belongs to us. Begin!' he declaimed, lifting his hand and letting it fall.

Half the red-robed thralls came down from the podium, and went among the crowds. They selected boys, pulled them to their feet and led them trembling to the feet of the Blood Angels. The bravest of them shook in fear, the weakest wept uncontrollably to be so close to such godly power. The Sanguinary Priest took out a device from his belt, put it near the boys, then consulted it. The white angel spoke to each of them, too silently to be heard, and pulled aside items of clothing on some to perform physical examinations. Malafael gave his opinion with a tiny nod or shake of his head. The boys were led to one of three groups in front of the statue's garden. From these areas the crowds were pushed back to make space for the growing selection groups.

This went on for some time. The crowd shrank; the three groups of boys grew.

Luis' turn came. He was grabbed and taken up the steps. Araezon stood over him, taller than the statue itself, so it seemed. He had a strange odour about him, a mix of machine oils, perfume and a sweet, coppery scent Luis could not place. Araezon's device was laden with needles that pierced Luis' skin when pressed against it. The boy gritted his teeth against the pain. Araezon smiled.

'You bear the testing well.' The device made a musical note. A green light shone from its insides. Luis could not keep his eyes from the wonders of the angels. Technology on Baal Secundus was rugged, most of it battered, all the parts and materials for it scavenged from rad-wasted cities and endlessly recycled. He had never seen such elegant machines.

Araezon tugged aside Luis' shirt, exposing the sores on his chest.

'Some contamination, nothing too extreme,' Araezon said to a thrall working by him. The man scribbled notes onto a long roll of parchment spilling over a portable writing desk strapped to his chest. 'Tell me, what is your name?'

'Luis, my lord,' said Luis. Appalled at how meek he sounded, he stood taller and said again with greater force, 'Luis, my lord.'

'You appear frightened, Luis.'

'I am frightened, my lord.'

'And honest, an admirable quality,' said Araezon. His voice was kindly, if harshened by his armoured suit's emitter, but his aspect was warlike. His armour hummed. A blow from the sword at his side would turn Luis into scraps of flesh. 'Why, if you are frightened, did you not turn away and go back to your people?'

'Because fear is nothing,' said Luis as defiantly as he dared. 'I have been frightened many times. Fear is to be ignored and overcome.'

'Tell me, why have you come?' asked Araezon. 'Do you wish to fight, to win glory? Do you wish to live forever?'

'No, my lord. No man lives forever, not even an angel. I wish to serve. I want to serve the Emperor, and through Him I will serve mankind.'

Araezon gave Luis a long, appraising look.

'Luis... Luis. That is a boy's name. You are of the clans that do not use their angel names in the day-to-day speech?'

'No, my lord. I mean, yes, my lord.'

Araezon made a noise that might have been a laugh. 'I understand. You will have to reveal it, if you are to be chosen.'

Luis kept his eyes on Araezon, but watched Malafael from the
corner of his eye.

'Go on then, boy, tell him,' growled Malafael. 'Tell him your angel
name.'

Luis hesitated. Nobody but family knew a person's angel name
in his clan. They were precious words, kept safe from the searing
sun and corrosive salt, pure things in an impure world. Luis had
voiced it a handful of times in his entire life.

'It is... My name is Dante,' he said, the word strange on his own
lips.

'Your opinion of Dante, brother?' asked Araezon of Malafael.

The black angel nodded.

'Group Areosto,' said the priest to the thralls. They led him away
and sat him with other boys he did not know. In time, Florian was
brought, breaking into a huge, black grin as he was led to Luis'
side. Lorenz joined them too.

Their group was smaller than the others. Luis fretted over whether
this was good or bad. The day dragged on. They were offered neither food nor drink, but were forced to rely on what little they
had. A boy in their group fainted from the heat. He was dragged
from their group into another. It was the first sign of the winnowing that was to come.

The last boy was tested and taken to the middle group.

'The initial testing is done! Prepare now for our judgement of the
First Winnowing,' said Araezon. 'Group Kaifus, you are not com-
patible with our gifts. No matter your personal qualities, you are
not fit to serve with us and can never be. Go from this place and
live out your lives among your people. Leave with honour, but do
not attempt the choosing again.' The red-robed thralls got the boys
to their feet and led them from the square.

'Group Hadrianus, your talents are insufficient to allow admit-
tance to our brotherhood, but you are suitable to join us as blood
thralls. You are exceptional youths, with the qualities needed to

be leaders among your people, and so you must decide whether to come with us or return home. If you choose to serve, many of you will attend upon the angels of death as equerries, and you may reach high office among the servants of our Chapter. Be not sorrowed, for but a few shall be angels, and we do you a great honour. Make your choice.' The second group were roused. Faced with the stars or the desert, most chose the stars, and those so electing were also led from the square.

That left the third group, the smallest at around five hundred youths. Luis' heart was in his mouth. He knew what was coming, but he could not believe it until he had heard it from the Blood Angel's own lips.

'Group Areosto, you shall be further tested. You have been selected as potential recruits. You are now aspirants to the Blood Angels Chapter of the Adeptus Astartes.'

They did not dare cheer or speak. Lorenz nodded, as if he were a sagacious elder with the right to agree to an angel's words. Florian grinned madly.

Luis' heart pounded. He did not smile. He had no illusions about what lay ahead.

CHAPTER EIGHT

DANTE DISARMED

998.M41

Asphodex High Anchor

Cryptus System

The lavateserium blasted Dante's armour and weapons from every side with jets of boiling water. The smell of xenos blood filtered through the open vents of his breathing mask. The scent revolted Dante, and he shut the mask, switching to his battleplate's internal oxygen supply. Water ran over his eye-lenses. The drumming of droplets on the gold reminded him of the first time he had seen rain. There were many things he could no longer recall – Space Marine or not, there is only so much a human mind can hold. But some things he could never forget. He remembered standing on brilliant yellow mosses under the open sky as a torrential downpour soaked his combat fatigues and battered his skin. He held his mouth open, letting the warm water fill it. The ghost of a smile haunted his lips as he remembered his Scout sergeant, Gallileon, hauling them all out of the rain and calling them a great many names angels should not know. All the gifts of the Emperor, the might of his comrades and teachers, the power of technology he had witnessed – it was all nothing compared to the sight of water falling freely from the sky. He could still not credit the miracle of oceans and rain.

The smile faded. The others in his training group were dead, the last slain hundreds of years ago. Memories were precious things that bound people together. No one shared his any more.

The lavateserium played quiet notes. The water shut off, the final drops plinking on the metal decking. Swirls of filthy water drained away. A broad-sweep decontamination laser played over the armour, flash-drying the water and killing everything on the surface. Superheated steam burst all over him. He could not feel the scalding heat. The rapid increase in temperature registered as a brief flicker on the faceplate read-outs of his sensorium. The door opened onto his armourium.

The cleaning was not complete. The decontamination was ineffectual, a ritual that had lost all practical use with time. The armour was still filthy. Alien fluids were caked in every crevice, gumming up the ribbing of the flexible joints, encrusted in the sculpted musculature of his torso. The jewels that studded his plates were rimmed with gore. But the wash was a start on the slow road to purity.

He stepped out. The door closed, shutting away the utilitarian machinery of the lavateserium, and leaving him surrounded by beauty.

Dante's personal armourium was a haven of peace. Lit in the soft warm glow of a thousand red candles, it was gently perfumed by the scents of wax, fragrant oils, lapping powder, the dry smell of active stasis fields and rare incenses. The velvety quiet that accompanies candlelight draped itself over everything. In the many angles and nooks, rich shadows embraced warm light. At forty yards long and fifteen wide, the armourium was among the larger of his chambers. Art and war were equal parts of the Blood Angels' character. Everything they had was glorious in decoration. The high roof was supported by vaulting whose perfect simplicity revealed the complex mathematics that went into its construction. Glass-fronted recesses set between carved figures of angels held dozens of different weapons. Dante was expert in the use of all of them, and trained regularly with every kind, though he rarely used anything but the perdition pistol and the Axe Mortalis. Bronze doors sealed away external noise. The beat of the *Blade of Vengeance*'s cannons was a heartbeat rumble, easily ignored.

Dante could not deny a weary sigh as he stepped onto the runner carpeting the stone floor the length of the gallery.

Arafeo waited there, half a dozen hooded blood thralls in the shadows behind him to attend to Dante's disarmament.

'We are ready, my lord,' said Arafeo, his voice cracked with age. 'I have had a meal brought to your chambers and drawn your bath.'

'Thank you,' said Dante, and meant it. If there was one thing Dante wished to do more than anything else, it was to bathe.

He walked the long gallery to the empty case where he kept his battleplate. His attendants came to him without speaking. Three of them took the Axe Mortalis from his right hand and set it into its stand. Two others unplugged the perdition pistol's power feeds, and he relinquished it gladly. His fingers cracked as he uncurled them; he had been clutching it for so many days they had moulded themselves to its grip. Flakes of alien vitae fell upon the rich carpet.

He reached the armour case and caressed its touch pad. The red light over the glass door clunked from red to green. The door opened with the pronounced whoosh of pressure equalisation. Candles fluttered in the sudden, brief gust. The arming stand moved out from the case on its armature with a long, solemn whine. It stopped, and spread its clamps. Dante turned around and reversed his battleplate into it. Soft-tipped claws gripped his jump pack. He raised his arms, and other clamps took his elbows. Rests ran out under his forearms to support the weight. Grips closed around the back plates of his greaves.

He blinked away the last few datascreeds still crowding his faceplate display, then shut down the reactor of his armour. Power cut from its supplemental musculature, it sagged heavily, pressing down on his shoulders. The neural spikes that linked his nervous system to the battleplate withdrew and he gasped at the cold, sharp pain.

Arafeo beckoned attendants forwards. They brought wheeled tables topped by slabs of exotic stone. Tools gleamed on one. Whispering the rites of disarming, they began to take Dante's golden battleplate off. Dante allowed his eyes to close. Under his breath, he spoke the rite of disarming with his attendants.

'The battle is done,' they said, 'though war never ends. Brief rest for the warrior, service for the wargear. Praise the machine-spirits that guard us in battle.'

Sanguinius' death mask came off first. Of all the pieces of his suit, this was the greatest burden, though not the heaviest. As it was pulled off his head, he felt Sanguinius' presence go with it. It was a mental trick. If Sanguinius lingered anywhere it was not in the mortal world. His legacy, however, was more potent than ever.

The softseal about the neck was taken away next. The material peeled from him like a sticky kiss, releasing the humid air trapped between his battleplate and arming suit. He wrinkled his nose at his own stink, brewed in his armour by days of hard battle. The scent of angels was no more pleasant than that of other men, and possessed of harsh, chemical notes besides – volatile by-products of his enhanced biology expressed through his sweat that no amount of perfume could mask.

The servants worked quickly. With many hands and specialist tools they removed his armour far faster than he could have alone. Once his power cabling was all disconnected and the armour's plastron removed, he was near free. The blood thralls moved onto his legs, whispering their hushed praises to the armour's machine-spirits as they worked. Once the front plates of his cuisses were removed he did not wait for his greaves to be taken apart, but stepped out to stand in his close fitting bodysuit. The tables were covered in armour components. A Space Marine might remove his armour himself if need be, but total disassembly was the proper way to treat such sacred gear. Without cleansing, testing and servicing between campaigns, its machine-spirit would grow sick.

In contrast to the gilded, decorated exterior of the armour, the short-sleeved bodysuit was plain and practical. Two of his servants unsealed it from around his neck. It adhered to him by a layer of grimy sweat and came away from his skin wetly, snagging on the metal of his neural interface ports. He stepped forwards again to free himself from the clinging, rubbery fabric of the suit completely, leaving his naked skin to cool in the ship's air.

Dante turned back. His armour had been taken apart. His jump pack hung trailing cables from the stand's claw. Blood thralls were wrapping other components in clean cloths of red silk, bowing, and withdrawing.

As soon as he was done in his quarters, his servants would emerge from their alcoves and take away his wargear to the workrooms hidden behind the armourium's ornate walls. There they would clean arms and armour fastidiously, repair them and bring them back to their stands. When he returned, his weapons would gleam, and his armour would be assembled upon its stand in isolate purity. One war washed away by diligent hands, the weapons would be ready to be employed in another. The only stains left would be those upon his soul.

He reflected that the last time he would undergo this ritual would come soon. But not yet, not yet. Not while the candle of one human soul burned in the galaxy would he rest. He had sworn that long ago, and Dante was no oathbreaker.

He walked the length of the gallery naked. Embedded servitor wardens drew open the armoured doors to his bathhouse. Dante passed into an antechamber decorated floor to ceiling with mosaics of dark red, gold and white tesserae. Standing in the centre of the room, he allowed his servants to wipe the worst of his battle sweat away with warm cloths, and went into his calderum. For half an hour he sat in heat high enough to bake an unaltered human, letting scented steam soothe his aching muscles. From there he stepped into a cubicle, where hundreds of litres of iced water were dumped on his head and gurgled away through ornamental drains. Skin tingling, he passed into the colonnaded main bath. Large enough to swim in, the bath was milky white with restorative minerals. Fine art beautified the walls and ceiling.

He descended its fan of steps, allowing the water's blood-warmth to embrace him, and sank up to his neck.

He closed his eyes and breathed deeply. The rumble of the ship's weaponry matched the run of his pulse. He sank into a meditative state. He wished he were able to take to his sarcophagus in the Hall of Making, and sink into the long rest. This yearning went with him as he drifted into a torpor that was halfway between sleep and death.

'My lord?' Arafeo was standing by the edge of the pool. The white water still rippled with the regular thump of the bombardment cannons. The Long Rest of Baal was a distant dream. Mortal concerns never ceased.

'I have slept?' Dante said. The water had dropped a fraction of a degree in temperature. He had been idle longer than he intended.

'Only for two hours, my lord. Captain Aphael is en route to the fleet. We have word from Captain Phaeton also. He has engaged a fragment of the splinter, but does not anticipate much delay. He should be with us presently.'

'Why was I not woken?' said Dante.

Arafeo looked his lord in the eye, an action that had taken him half a century to dare to attempt. He was one of the few Dante allowed to see his unshielded face. They were both old men, in their way.

'Because I would not allow them to,' said Arafeo. 'You exhaust yourself, my lord. You must rest.'

'I thank you for your concern, but I am needed more than I need rest,' said Dante. He pushed himself up out of the bath with his powerful arms, and got out of the water. The hairs on his arms were a pale white gold, still fine. His muscles rippled under skin only now losing the tautness of youth.

'My lord commander, if I might be so bold as to say, if you destroy yourself for want of rest, those needs will go unfulfilled.'

Arafeo's hands were twisted with arthritis, like roots, and shook as he held out Dante's towel. Dante's eyes rested on them. Arafeo looked away, ashamed at his feebleness. *If only he knew we share the same worries,* thought Dante.

'I should rest, and you should rest,' said Dante.

The man kept his trembling arms outstretched.

'How can I rest when you will not?'

'You are not I. Different fates are ours,' said Dante.

'Your responsibility is by far the graver, my lord. If I had passed my tests at the Place of Choosing, then perhaps my burden would be similar, but I did not. I am a thrall, not an angel. But we all must serve the Emperor in our own way, and I shall help you carry your burden in whatever small way I can.'

'I promise, after the meeting of the Red Council, I shall rest.'

Mollified, Arafeo nodded.

Dante took the towel. Arafeo bowed and went to fetch Dante's goblet from a side table. He was getting slow. The tremble in his limbs grew more pronounced when he was tired, and Arafeo was tiring more readily with every day.

One thousand five hundred years of grinding war versus eighty years of humble service, but they were both servants. If given the choice, Dante wondered, would I exchange places with my equerry? Not willingly, he answered himself. But if forced to, I would not rue the change. Service is service. All have a part to play, he told himself. Arafeo is right in that.

His servant's humility humbled him. 'Arafeo,' he said gently. 'You have done enough for me today. Thank you for shielding me from my own labours awhile. It is appreciated. Rest now, I command it. I can pour my own wine.'

The wine salver rattled as Arafeo set it down. He bowed his head unhappily. He did not want to be dismissed, nor did he want to be seen as old.

Save the man's pains or save his pride. Every decision Dante had to make in these black times, from the most inconsequential to those that could topple the Imperium, was a choice between two evils. Good had leached from the galaxy. He was weary of decision. Not a flicker of this was displayed on his face, still inhumanly beautiful despite his age.

'As you wish, lord commander,' said Arafeo quietly. He departed reluctantly.

Dante went to the table and drank the wine. He felt bad for Arafeo, and annoyed that he had to order him away for his own good. He had to be careful that that irritation did not transfer itself to Arafeo himself. It was not his servant's fault he had aged.

The food Arafeo had laid out for him had grown cold, and though finely prepared, had the taste and consistency of ashes in his mouth. He ate it anyway, relishing his first solid sustenance in days.

He chewed slowly, washing his meal down with frequent gulps of wine. His digestion took longer to reaccustom itself to eating with the close of every campaign. While he ate, he told himself that the food satisfied him, that it was enough. He ignored the other appetite gnawing at his stomach and his soul, the hunger that filled his dreams with the bright lustre of blood. The lure of the Red Thirst was potent. It was a yearning best resisted, for though the thirst was quenched for a while, it was an addiction that grew stronger for being fed.

The desire to drink living vitae tormented all those of Sanguinius' line, and he was so old. He denied that he needed it. He refused to acknowledge his cravings. He would not listen to his body, which told him in its aches and fatigue that if he were to drain just one mortal, his strength would return and his spirits rise.

Dante would not. He had not consumed living blood since the war on Ereus. Since then he had refused to put his own comfort before the lives of others. There was a way out of this weakness that had come to wear him down, but he refused to take it.

He was an angel, not a monster.

Half an hour later he left the bath and went into the armourium. His armour had been meticulously cleaned and replaced. It looked like a museum piece behind the glass.

He stared through the glass, his lined face superimposed over Sanguinius' ageless mask of gold. The two were a near match, for Dante had taken after his sire closely during the Blood Change. He blinked as Sanguinius' golden mask never could. The primarch's mouth remained open in a howl of righteous fury. It was such a shame, Dante thought, that this most thoughtful and dutiful of the Emperor's sons should be remembered by this image of wrath. There were thousands of representations of Sanguinius throughout the Blood Angels fleet and their fortress-monastery on Baal, but this was the one most knew, a roaring fury descending from the heavens to mete out death and spill blood.

If only there were space for his gene-father's gentler nature to be celebrated. If only there were not such an endless need for battle.

If Dante could have any wish granted, he would have chosen to be made obsolete by peace, to become a museum piece himself. He wished this not only for the sake of others, but also for himself. With peace would come rest from his labours.

Peace would never come. War was without end. The only rest he would ever know would be death. That was how Araezon had said it, all those years ago. That was what the Sanguinary Priests still said at the Time of Choosing. How bitter it was that he should come to know this better than any other.

His finger caressed the touch pad. The case opened and his servants emerged from the shadows.

He must become his lord Sanguinius once again.

CHAPTER NINE

THE PLACE OF CHOOSING

456.M40
Angel's Fall
Planetary Capital
Baal Secundus
Baal System

Nine days of games followed the First Winnowing. Under the shadow of Sanguinius the aspirants competed in simple athletic contests, as were practised among the clans of the Blood at tribal moots – running, leaping, the hurling of shot-stones and rope disc, and wrestling bouts to the point of submission. Malafael and Araezon spoke to individuals among the aspirants, dismissing some out of hand, giving others the choice to return home or become blood thralls. Victory in the games was not the signifier for selection the boys thought it at first, and they came to see that everything they did was observed closely, even how they accepted defeat or celebrated wins. For those who were consulted and not dismissed, Araezon's servants took copious notes. Whether for good or ill was concealed from the boys.

Large crowds came to watch the games. A carnival atmosphere took over Angel's Fall. The aspirants could only watch the food stalls and performers with envious eyes. They were kept separate from the people of Baal by a fenced stockade.

Although the aspirants thought these gentle contests the whole
of the challenge, they were but the beginning of the selection process. The ninth day came to an end. The tribes whose sons had
triumphed were honoured by the Blood Angels, to the delight
of the crowds, and presented with totem-trophies of rare wood.
There were none of the Salt Clans there, not that it mattered. Luis,
smaller and less physically able than many of the other hopefuls,
won nothing. Lorenz took several plaudits. Even Florian won a
carved victory stave for his people.

When the Second Winnowing came, Luis braced himself for
rejection, but Malafael passed him by without a word.

There were two hundred and forty-seven aspirants remaining
from the five hundred first chosen.

On the tenth morning their belongings were taken away. They
were taken into a well-made building by the blood thralls. It was
plain of decoration, save a single iteration of the winged blood
drop of the Chapter over its solitary door. What was remarkable
was the smoothness of its construction. There were no seams in its
walls, the whole thing seemingly cast in a single piece from liquid
stone. There were no air bubbles to pock the surface. It was perfect and flawless in a way nothing on Baal Secundus was.

Their hair was shaved. They were stripped, made to wash and
provided with loose trousers and tunics of smooth material that
felt obscenely comfortable. After they were uniformed, small packs
with water and rations were handed out. Their questions went
unanswered. Through silent crowds they were led through the city.
The gates shut behind them with a boom. Angel's Fall was quiet.
Pennants snapped in the hot breeze. Sanguinius stared upwards,
searching for a heaven that could not be found on Baal Secundus.

For nine more days they were led through merciless heat and
freezing night without rest. Malafael and Araezon were nowhere to
be seen. They were guided by quiet men who, although they wore
the flowing garb of Baalforian nomads, wore badges that marked
them as servants of the Blood Angels.

The march was the first part of their real trials. The water they were given was insufficient for the trek. Several boys, weakened by their journey and the exertions of the games, died of exhaustion or dehydration. The corpses were abandoned without comment by the adults, and the aspirants taken deeper into the desert. Luis hoarded his water carefully.

Many days later a curved scarp of rock a mile across broke the monotony of red dunes. Through the shimmer of heat, Luis spied walls of close-fitted stone growing from shock-riven cliffs, turrets every hundred yards. Barracks, eating halls and the like, he assumed.

'This is your destination,' said one of the sombre thralls. 'Now your true test begins.'

They arrived at an entrance at the base of the cliffs, tired and desperately thirsty. More blood thralls opened gates to admit the aspirants to a tunnel running under the scarp. After the merciless sun, the square-cut tunnel was blessedly cool, but too soon it opened into an interior shielded from the wind where the sun glared from a floor of sharp white sand. A furnace heat welcomed them. From the wavering of the air, Araezon and Malafael emerged, the vents on their armour sending out their own oily curls of rippling air.

'This is the Place of Challenge,' Malafael explained. 'In the wars before the foundation of the Imperium, this crater was blasted from the ground by a weapon of unimaginable power. Though potent, that long-forgotten weapon is nothing compared to the might of a single Imperial Space Marine. Here we shall begin forging you into the greatest warriors in this galaxy. Most of you will fail. These men who guard this place,' he swept up his staff to encompass the sentries standing on the walls of the crater, 'did so. Those who are deemed unsuitable at this stage can never leave. They guard this fortress against those who would learn its secrets. Live or die, for nearly all of you, this will be the last place you see.' Malafael regarded them all, his red eye-lenses sinister in the death's head helm. 'We shall meet your fellow aspirants.'

A murmur went through the youths.

'I thought we were it,' said Florian tensely.

'More youths, more competition,' said Lorenz.

They looked around for others, but saw no one. Malafael pointed to the sky.

'They come from above!' he said.

The aspirants looked skywards, squinting into the light of the sun, shading their eyes with their hands. From out of the sun six chariots of the angels descended on pillars of fire, blasting up curls of dust from the ground. The youths feared the machines, and had one broken his ground and run, more would have followed. But no one moved.

The craft touched down on broad metal feet, landing in a perfect line. They were bigger than most buildings in Angel's Fall, bristling with weapons. Their colours were brighter than any Luis had seen. Their fronts resembled a jutting chin and they had about them an air of predatory menace, as if alive.

Ramps lowered. From the first another Chaplain appeared, leading a group of youths. From the second came a second Sanguinary Priest and more youths. Then others, led by Space Marines in the red armour of line troopers, came out from the remainder of the sky chariots.

'These aspirants accompanying Chaplain Laestides and Sanguinary Priest Rugon are of Baal Primus, which you know as Baalind,' said Malafael. 'They are different to you, but as worthy of the honour of selection as you are. It would be easy for us to pit one set against the other, but the Blood Angels do not do things the easy way, only the best way. Brothers, bring them forward!'

The foreigners were brought from the line of voidships by Laestides and Rugon, and arrayed in ranks facing the youths from Baal Secundus. Though they wore the same uniforms as the aspirants of Baal Secundus, they were alien-looking, physically different: taller, paler and their clan marks outrageous in colour and form.

'These aspirants were winnowed as you were, through gene-scan and contest. Before you continue your trial, the groups will be mingled,' said Araezon. 'You will work with these aspirants and come to love them. As a Blood Angel, you will love your brothers above all others. These bonds will last for centuries. A Chapter of Space Marines is not an army. It is a brotherhood. Without these ties, we would fall. With them, we are strong enough to defeat enemies that outnumber us many thousands of times over.'

Luis feared his small band of Lorenz and Florian would be broken up, but the mingling was not undertaken randomly. The little tangles of friendship that had formed among the aspirants were respected, and were joined with similar groups from the other moon to form small cohorts.

Joining Luis, Lorenz and Florian were three aspirants from Baal Primus – Ereos, Duvallai and Ristan. Despite their odd appearance and thick dialect, the newcomers too had the custom of angels' names, given to honour the primarch who had ruled the planetary system in the distant past. They greeted each other cautiously, struggling with the pronunciation and cadence of each other's speech. Of the Baal Secundus three, Luis made the greatest efforts at friendship.

'If we don't work together,' he explained to a surly Lorenz later that night in the barracks, 'we will fail. The angels told us themselves – they are a brotherhood. We have to accept them, and they us, or we will be rejected.'

'I don't care,' said Lorenz petulantly. 'I am the strongest fighter. I will succeed.'

'Listen to him!' said Florian. 'Go on, make friends with them.' He nodded to the other side of the barracks room where the other three of their group sat on their beds.

Rolling his eyes and throwing aside his blanket, Lorenz got up and crossed the room.

'He's worse than a child,' muttered Florian.

'He'll learn,' said Luis. 'We'll make him, or we'll die.'

Luis' ordeal began in earnest. He and the others were tested in every conceivable way. They were deprived of sleep, made to run in blistering heat and in the near-total dark of nights when Baal and Baalind did not shine. Their endurance, intelligence and strength were subjected to all manner of tests. They would wake after limited sleep to find the arena of the crater filled by a maze, or an assault course, or a variety of puzzles they must solve in groups, many deadly. Tests of stamina followed combat drill, and battles that began as mock combats often turned deadly.

From time to time the Chaplains Malafael and Laestides would walk among them. The aspirants grew to fear the touch of the Chaplains' winged staffs on their shoulders, for those indicated so were taken away and not seen again. There were deaths. All of them were retested over and over by Rugon, Araezon and their mysterious machines, and others also removed as a result. The numbers dwindled from five hundred boys to four hundred, then three hundred.

As the days marched on, Luis became stronger and fitter. He was taught to wield a staff, then a wooden sword and shield. He was given a powerful spring gun like those used by the tribes of the Blood, but far better made. They were tested endlessly on all forms of combat. Those who did not learn quickly did not get the chance to learn any more. Judgement came without warning, and was final. 'The tap of my crozius cannot be withdrawn!' said Malafael. 'He who feels its touch will not ascend to Baal. Fight for your place, or you will fail!'

As the final hurdle approached, their dread of failure grew, until it towered over them as surely as a mountain. Failure became everything, greater than death. The trials became harder. They were sent out to survive in the desert, taken far away and told to find their way back. They were pitted against captive fire scorpions, asked to make leaps across deep ravines, forced to run miles through the hottest part of the day. Their lessons in melee became deadlier. The wooden weapons became steel. In their desperation for success they took risks. They fought without mercy. More of them died.

Nine long Baal Secundus weeks went by. As Baal waxed to his fullest for the ninth time, the surviving combatants – Luis could no longer consider them competitors – were called into the training ground at the centre of the Place of Challenge.

Araezon, Malafael, Laestides and Rugon stood upon the stone podium that watched over the main ground. With them was a fifth Blood Angel of high rank. His blood-red armour was heavy with ornamentation. Inset skulls stared out from his greaves. The plates of his suit were edged with gold, and his helmet too was golden and circled with a laurel wreath. Upon his helmet's brow a ruby skull glinted. A white cloak covered his left pauldron. His right hand gripped the hilt of his sword, whose scabbard was encrusted with skulls. Everywhere Luis looked on the figures were skulls and other iconography of death.

It was Laestides who spoke, his hard, judgemental voice blasting from the amplifiers set into his skull helm.

'Aspirants to the Chapter! This is the Master of Recruits, Captain Verono of the Tenth Company, known as the Redeemers. Throughout these trials he has been watching you. You should consider yourselves worthy indeed that you now look upon him! It is into this company that you will be inducted, and where you will be trained, should you prove worthy. The Final Choosing approaches. Verono will have ultimate say over who will be selected, and who will not. Fear him. Respect him. He is a mighty warrior. To some of you he will become as a father. Heed his words!'

Verono unclasped his hand from his sword hilt. His helm moved from left to right, scanning the crowd of boys standing to attention. His green helm lenses sparkled in Baal's fierce sun.

'You are the chosen of Baal!' he said. His voice had a mellifluous quality that the harsh electronic projection of his helm could not destroy. 'Tomorrow is the penultimate test, and then will come the Final Choosing. Tomorrow we will test your mettle as warriors. You shall face your greatest challenge. Rest well. You will need all your strengths – mental, emotional and physical – to accomplish what we shall demand of you.'

'What does that mean?' said Lorenz uneasily from the corner of his mouth.

'It means there's going to be a battle,' said Luis.

Verono speared them with his gaze. When he spoke again, Luis felt his words were directed at him. 'Tomorrow is the Trial of War.'

Morning stole in through the slit windows of the barracks to find the aspirants hollow-eyed and quiet. They rose from their simple cots and readied themselves according to their character. The more aggressive stared others down, behaved angrily towards aspirants outside their subgroup. Luis saw through their posturing to the fear beneath. The quieter of them would not look up. A few shook visibly with fear. Luis and his comrades spoke little.

Blood thrall guardians came into the dormitory. The groups were merged into six larger formations, eighteen aspirants in each. They were guided to the Place of Challenge's refectory, one of the facility's larger buildings, and given a large breakfast. Ration packs and water were handed to them. Then on to the armoury. Every boy was told to fetch a spring gun from the racks and was given a combat knife as long as his forearm.

Outside, the groups were gathered beneath the scrutiny of the five Blood Angels officers and assigned numbers. As they were given, Araezon inscribed the numbers into potsherds. When he was done, the Sanguinary Priest removed his gauntlet to reveal a perfect hand. It was the first time they had seen the angels' skin, and Luis was fixated by it. With a pearl-handled knife he cut his palm and dripped his blood onto each sherd.

'The blood of Sanguinius guide your fate!' he proclaimed. A blood thrall gathered up the pieces and placed them reverently into a large pot of simple design. There was nothing remarkable about the pot, but the angels and their servants treated it with utmost respect, bowing to it every time they turned to face it or away from it.

'This vessel belonged to the tribe of Blood who adopted our lord Sanguinius,' explained Araezon. 'It is nine thousand years old. The sherds upon which your groups' numbers are written were gathered from the ruins of the cities that once stood proud and beautiful upon this moon, Baal and Baal Primus. From ruin comes the promise of the future. The drawing of these sherds shall determine the participants in each contest.'

'Draw the first two,' commanded Verono.

The pot's neck was too narrow to accommodate a Space Marine's arm, so the potsherds were pulled by a blood thrall. He prayed as he put his hand within, and handed the two pieces of pottery with great reverence to Verono.

'Primus and quintus!' said Verono. He dropped the sherds upon the stone dais and ground them to dust under his boot heel. 'You have the honour of the Battle of the Morning. You shall compete first.'

In total silence, the first two groups were led away, neither side looking at the other. The remaining four groups were taken to the edge of the Place of Challenge, and bade sit in the shade of the wall. The Space Marines conferred on the dais, then left the training grounds for the reinforced building they dwelt within. Unlike the shaped stone of the rest of the Place of Challenge, their keep was made of seamless, grey plascrete studded with dishes, antennae and other unfathomable items. Shortly after the Space Marines entered it, a crowd of devices flew silently up from the roof and headed out into the desert. Dust trails, the telltale sign of vehicles moving across the sands, rose into the sky to the east.

Silence fell. The tarpaulins covering the angels' sky chariots rippled in the desert wind.

'I wish it was us out there first,' muttered Ereos.

'Why be in a hurry?' said Lorenz with a grin. 'It's a lovely morning.'

Luis thought Lorenz's bravado thin. He avoided being drawn into their conversation, but stared fixedly at the ground. He gathered up handfuls of the fine dust and let it trickle through his fingers, making small, perfect cones in the sand.

'I would prefer to have this over and done with,' said Ristan.

'Quiet there,' said one of the blood thralls watching over them. 'You are not permitted to speak. You will have time to discuss whatever you wish before the trial begins. For now, cease talking.

Think. Meditate on the honour given you, and pray that you are successful.'

Three hours went. Luis had made a field of sand cones. The inner gates of the wall tunnel swung inwards. The blood thralls escorted a battered, bloody group back within. Half of them were wounded, some absent. They were grim, but victorious.

Another group of blood thralls followed, escorting the second group. Only seven remained of the eighteen; all had their heads bowed. The aspirants watched the first two groups in silence. They were taken into the low medicae building abutting the inner wall not far from the barracks.

Another half an hour went. The angels came out from their building, and went to the dais. The boys were taken to stand before them. Again, two groups were chosen by lot.

'Tertius and Quartus!' proclaimed Verono. 'For you is the Battle of Noon. Fight well, and you shall draw the eye of the greatest son of the Emperor.'

'Just our luck,' breathed Florian anxiously. 'We're going last.'

Again, Luis' group was taken to the shade of the wall. The Space Marines withdrew. This time, the aspirants knew for certain who they would be fighting, and had to sit in close proximity to the youths they would soon have to kill. Luis watched them watching him. He knew them all well. He had completed exercises with them, sparred with them, joked with them. He had expected this to happen, and had kept his distance, but others had formed fast friendships across the groups. These aspirants were grey with dread.

Two more hours. The groups returned, similarly depleted, though the numbers lost on either side were more even.

The ritual of the potsherds was repeated, though all knew the result.

'Sextus and Secundus!' said Verono. 'You are honoured to fight the Battle of Evening.'

'At least it'll be cooler,' said Lorenz under his breath.

It was their turn to be taken out of the gate into the wider desert, and loaded into vehicles. Their unpadded seats were sticky with blood, its metallic reek even more disturbing than the feel of it on their fingers. Luis sat opposite Florian, who stared at him, his face white.

Not all of the boys had killed before the trials. Rivalry between the Baalite clans led to war from time to time, and there was the ever-present threat of the Dispossessed, those bands of exiles, renegades and malcontents that preyed on others, but the tribes of the Blood relied on each other for survival, and the boys were young. They had all been in danger. They had all fought against the best efforts of their home to kill them, but to end another's life was a step many had not taken. Luis considered himself lucky that he had, and his stomach still churned. He had the urgent need to urinate. Upon the sand of the training grounds he had managed to contain his emotion, to stay calm. But the walls were coming down, and he felt nauseous.

Time in the back of the stuffy transport went too quickly. As if in a dream Luis found himself standing in the desert several miles from the Place of Challenge. Between a lacework of crossed tyre tracks, the ground was dark with trails of spilt blood. Luis followed them with his eyes to a humpbacked rock outcropping riven with cracks. It could have been a mile or five miles long. A dead flat plain of packed sand surrounded it, reducing the island in scale to an unguessable size. Homesickness ambushed him; the place reminded Luis of the Great Salt Waste.

Verono approached them. His means of coming to the place were mysterious. Luis wondered if he were safe out there. No one of the Blood travelled alone if possible. Then his stressed mind conjured up the ridiculous thought of all the aspirants assaulting the captain. They would bounce off and be crushed, was his conclusion. Then it didn't seem so dangerous for Verono to be alone. There was nothing on Baal that could harm one such as he.

'There you will fight, the Island of First Blooding,' said Verono. His armour purred as he pointed a vitae-red finger to the outcrop. 'This was an island in a great lake once. You would be well to see it as an island, with no way off. For an island it is, surrounded by a sea of death. If you leave its environs before the trial is done, you shall be killed.'

He gestured at a line of blood thralls bearing solid-shot weapons. They were few, one every half-mile, but the desert was free of cover of any kind, and Luis thought it certain they were excellent shots.

'And well so,' went on Verono, 'for disgrace shall be heaped upon the name of the one who flees. Do not assume safety upon the island. At either end is a fort. In each fort is a skull. The goal of this contest is simple. You must take the other group's skull and bring it to your fort, if you can. You will be watched. Your behaviour will dictate who will proceed to the Final Choosing.' He let his arm drop and spoke more quietly. 'Victory is not all. We do not look for ferocity. Brotherhood, honour, humility, mercy, restraint and intelligence we prize above all other qualities. But make no mistake, if you do not kill, you will die.

'The contest will last ninety minutes. You will have twenty minutes to appoint your leaders and devise a strategy. Decisiveness is the forerunner of success. You must move quickly, or you will fail.' He turned to Luis' group. 'Group Secundus, you will take the western fort. Group Sextus, the eastern. A red flare will signal the beginning, a second the end. When the second is fired, all of you will drop your weapons immediately. Anyone who fights on will be killed by me, personally.' He towered over them all. Luis imagined the captain's armoured hands crushing his skull.

'Do you understand?' said Verono.

'Yes, my lord!' the boys shouted in unison.

'Good. Sanguinius guide you. Now go!'

Group Sextus contained a youth name Barrazael from Baal Primus. He was huge, the biggest in the two groups. He glared at Luis a second, eyes narrowed, before he held up his hand to gesture to his colleagues. They ran in close formation for the island.

Luis broke into a run. Lorenz, Florian, Ereos and Ristan followed to catch up to him. Duvallai was engaged in fierce debate with a boy named Michaelo, and sprinted hard to join the others.

'They've chosen their leader already,' said Florian. 'It'll put them ahead, won't it?'

'Barrazael is a fierce kreck,' said Lorenz. 'The others are frightened of him, but he doesn't think well.'

'Fear is a good motivator,' said Luis. They were running and talking easily, despite the heavy spring guns they carried across their chests. Weeks of hard training and good food had improved their physiques. 'And we're all afraid.'

No one disagreed with that.

'Well, I'll be backing you for leader,' said Lorenz. Luis gave him a quizzical look. 'Come on, Luis,' said Lorenz. 'You're the smartest out of us, even if you aren't the biggest.'

'That he ain't!' chuckled Florian.

Duvallai joined them. The rest of the group was straggling out behind. It didn't look good – Barrazael's warriors seemed far more cohesive as a group. 'Michaelo is going to put himself forward as leader,' Duvallai said in his thick Priman accent.

'Well I'm backing Luis,' said Lorenz accusingly.

'Me too!' said Duvallai indignantly.

'I didn't ask for this,' said Luis.

'Then who were you going to back?' said Lorenz. 'You can't hang back all the time. We know you, waiting for everyone else to mess it up before coming forward and telling us all how we should have been doing it. Not this time, my friend. We haven't got time for the famous Luis patience. Sometimes, you have to step up and take the responsibility of action.'

'I'm patient?' said Luis.

'More so than me,' said Lorenz.

'Half the others are for Michaelo,' said Duvallai.

'We'll see who's in charge,' said Lorenz.

They reached the island. The rock was worn smooth, the channels through it carved into fluted shapes by prehistoric waves. They leapt from the flatness of the packed sand and onto the stone, bounding from outcrop to outcrop as they moved up to the fort.

Florian was first up, well used to such terrain. Luis arrived not far behind. The rock spread out, its surface pitted and cracked, a wart on the smooth skin of the desert. A sole bleeding tree grew from a crevice a few hundred yards away, its limbs bent sideways in the direction of the prevailing wind. Far off, the surface of a broad expanse of water shattered the sun into orange razors: one of Baalfora's remaining stretches of toxic sea.

The fort looked like something a child would build had he time and resources for such folly. There was a wall a little over five feet high, twenty feet a side. In its modest courtyard a small tower, ten feet tall, stood over the wall. Atop a rusty pole an ancient skull had been placed. Once, it had been stained green, but the dye had rubbed off most of it, showing dirty brown through the washed-out tint. It was missing its lower jaw and most of its upper teeth. The few remaining shone in the sun like jewels.

There were bloodstains everywhere from the earlier contests.

'Kreck!' said Florian and pointed at a figure watching from the low summit of the island. 'They've got a scout up already.'

'We should do the same,' said Luis. 'We need to look this place over, see how defensible it is and put together a plan. And we need to be quick.' He looked at the sun, descending on the final leg of the day's journey. Other boys were joining them – all looked at Luis. 'Florian, you're quick.'

Florian nodded and made to run for the summit.

'Stop!' said Michaelo, running up. 'Who are you to give orders? We should choose a leader first.'

'We've chosen,' said Lorenz, standing in front of Luis, his meaty arms folded.

'Luis has got the mind for it,' said Florian.

'He's clever, so am I. If you were clever, Florian, you'd follow me.'

'We don't have time for this!' said Ristan.

'We don't, so choose,' said Laziel, one of Michaelo's closest friends.

'Just let me do it. We don't want to lose,' said Michaelo.

'You're going to get us killed,' said Lorenz.

'And you're wasting time!' said Laziel, squaring off to Lorenz.

'Let him,' said Luis. He nodded up. A motionless black shape hovered over the group. 'They're watching. Michaelo wants to do it, so let him.'

'Bad idea,' said Lorenz.

'Not as bad as arguing until the others come charging over here, kill half of us and take our skull,' said Luis. 'Go on, Michaelo. What are your orders?'

Michaelo blinked several times. He had not expected to be given command so easily. 'We should defend. Stop them taking our skull. That way we'll win.'

'Wow, you're a real strategist,' said Lorenz sarcastically.

'We have to take their skull,' said Luis.

'We'll force a stalemate,' said Michaelo. 'That's what we'll do. Barrazael's strong, and his group is tight-knit. We don't have time to beat that. We'll hold them off until time is called.'

'Barrazael's overconfident and too aggressive,' said Luis. 'He'll throw everything he has at this fort. That's his weakness.'

'Yes!' said Michaelo, seeing agreement where there was none. 'That is why we should prepare to throw them back.'

'So,' said Luis, looking at the fort. 'You think we should all try to cram ourselves into that?' he said.

'There's no space,' said Lorenz, smiling unpleasantly.

'He'll hang back, fire his spears upwards and...' Luis mimed the falling of spears into a packed fort. 'He will not miss.'

'It'll work!' said Michaelo.

'Maybe you'll listen to this,' said Luis, walking towards Michaelo. The other boy bristled at Luis' confidence. 'You hold this fort with eleven of us. I'll take seven up ahead and take the fort from Barrazael's men while you hold them off here.'

'What if he does the same?' said Michaelo.

Luis shook his head. 'He won't. He's too arrogant. Their scout has already seen us arguing, and that will make Barrazael more reckless. He'll attack with everything, take our skull, then retreat back to his fort to defend it. We can sneak through these channels and arrive unseen. Speaking of scouts, maybe we need one? Like I was saying,' said Luis mildly.

A flare shot upwards over the transport's position, trailing red smoke.

'The signal. The game has begun. What do you say, Michaelo? We're losing time,' said Luis.

Michaelo's face darkened. 'Do what you like. We're staying here.'

Luis shrugged. 'Who's with me to take the skull?' All the aspirants from his barracks group put up their hands. Luis chose another, Kalael, to supplement his core group. 'I'd take you all, but we don't want to leave the commander short-handed.'

Michaelo spat on the rock.

His men made to move out. Luis caught Florian by the arm. 'Get up on the rocks. Let them see you. Let them get close, then allow them to chase you. We'll head north around the island, lead them to the south.'

Florian nodded. 'Got it,' he said, and scrambled away over the rocks.

Luis looked back at the fort. Michaelo's men were bickering over who got which spot.

'Come on,' said Luis.

Lorenz shook his head grimly.

They disappeared into the maze of the rock, jogging through the channels. Luis didn't think Barrazael would use them; he was too straightforward. In all their tests, brute strength had been his first and last position. Luis halted his men every so often, listened carefully and popped his head out of the cracks. Seeing no one, he would proceed.

The sound of distant shouts stopped them. Luis looked out. On the ridge of the island, Florian was sprinting. He waited. Fourteen of Barrazael's warriors chased after him. Florian was far enough ahead to avoid the spears thrown out by the spring guns.

'Fourteen,' he said to his men. 'That means he's left four in the fort.'

'We knew you'd be right,' said Ristan.

'We've not won yet,' said Luis. 'Come on.'

They ran down an open tube worn from the rock in wetter eras.

Its lips curved together to almost touch, leaving a stripe of sunlight to mark the centre. They were heading diagonally across the island. Luis took them into a narrower crevice, switching back and forth, coming nearer and nearer to the enemy fort. From the direction of their fort came a distant yelling.

'It's begun. The guards in the other fort will be distracted,' said Luis. 'Quickly now.' He split his group into two, putting Lorenz in charge of one. Leading the second group himself, he went around the island, emerging from a crack within spear-shot of the walls. The gulley was shallow, lower on the desert side, and they had to lie against the stone to avoid being seen.

'Wait,' said Luis. He eased his head up. Four sentries stood vigilantly around the walls. A sharp whistle sounded from the other side. Three of the aspirants rushed over to look. The fourth hesitated.

'Now!' he whispered.

Luis leapt out of the crack and ran for the wall. The boy remaining on their side of the fort aimed and shot in a panic as he saw Luis coming, missing him. Ristan shot from behind Luis, his spring gun punching a spear through the boy's shoulder. Squealing, the boy fell from sight. Ereos ran up to the wall with Luis. They slammed into the crumbling masonry.

'Boost me over,' said Luis.

Ereos laced his fingers together. Luis stepped into them and Ereos half threw him over the wall. Luis vaulted it easily, scrambling onto the firing step set around the inside of the fortification. The injured sentry was lying on the floor, half unconscious from pain. There was no one in the tower. Only their skull kept sightless watch over the rocky island. The other sentries were on the far wall, hidden by the tower, shouting excitedly as they fought against Lorenz, what they thought to be a token force.

Luis looked from the gate to the tower and back. Silently, he slipped across the small courtyard. While the other three sentries were busy exchanging volleys of spears with the aspirants outside, he undid the simple bar holding the gate shut.

Ereos and Ristan came through, spring guns loaded. They aimed them at the boys. Luis whistled.

'Surrender!' he said. 'Hand over your skull and no harm will come to you.'

One boy whirled around, gun ready to fire. Ristan put a spear through his heart.

The others put their weapons down and held up their hands.

'We should kill them all,' said Ristan.

'We should be merciful,' said Luis.

Lorenz, Duvallai and Kalael came through the opened gate. Lorenz grinned widely and slapped Luis on the back before heading up the tower to get the skull from its pole. This was red, but otherwise similar in age and condition to the green. The bone felt rough and warm in his hands. Luis wondered who he had been.

'Take their guns and load them,' said Luis. 'Tie them up. Lorenz, get the door off its hinges.'

'Why?' said Ereos. 'We should just hold it.'

'We'll be outnumbered if they come back. We need to make them angry, take them off guard.'

'Right you are,' said Lorenz. The hinges were simply made, and it was the work of minutes to bash out the pins and throw them down. Meanwhile, the others ripped strips from the clothes of their prisoners and bound them hand and foot.

The captured boys glared angrily at Luis' men.

'Now what, Luis?' asked Lorenz. 'They might have our totem.'

'Ristan, hide this in the maze, in case they take the fort back,' said Luis, pushing the skull into Ristan's hands. 'The rest of us are going to wait.'

'In the fort?' said Ereos. 'We took the gate down!'

'Only some of us in the fort,' said Luis. 'Wait and see.'

Ten minutes later Barrazael's men came running from the direction of the western fort whooping in triumph. One of them carried the green-stained skull victoriously in his hands. Several were wounded, and three had not come back. Luis watched them unobserved.

'Get back into the fort! Take up your stations,' said Barrazael triumphantly. 'They'll try to get back at us.'

'That's if they dare!' laughed one of the boys.

Luis noted only half of them had reloaded their guns in their haste to be away. He smiled to himself.

The war party slowed. 'The gates!' cried one.

A good third of them instinctively ran for the fort.

'Stop!' shouted Barrazael, realising too late he was looking at a trap.

Luis stood from his hiding place and aimed his gun at Barrazael's chest.

'Surrender and give me the skull.'

Barrazael didn't even pause to consider Luis' command.

'Ambush!' he roared. His war party turned and charged. Luis fired his gun, impaling one boy through the stomach. The others faltered.

'There's only one! He's only got one shot!' urged Barrazael.

'Wrong,' said Luis, dropping his gun and retrieving the other from where it leaned against the rock by his legs.

His warriors rose up from their hiding places, surrounding the group. In the fort, Ereos and Ristan emerged.

'Now surrender,' said Luis.

Barrazael's face went bright red. 'Attack!' he spat.

Luis dropped him with his second spear. Half of Barrazael's remaining aspirants milled about. The others attacked ferociously. One leapt at Luis, and both of them fell to the ground. The boy was called Garviel. Luis had trained with him several times over the month. They had got on fine. That didn't stop Garviel from trying to kill him.

Garviel got onto Luis' chest, hands locked about his throat. Luis bucked and kicked, but Garviel was much heavier than he. He spread both arms, barely resisting the instinctive but useless urge to claw at Garviel's hands. His left hand found a rock. The rock met Garviel's temple with a horrible hollow sound. Garviel made a strangled noise, but his hands remained tight around Luis' throat.

Black blurred Luis' vision. He smacked again and again, until Garviel fell sideways off him.

Choking, Luis got onto his hands and knees. His throat was swollen and he could barely breathe.

'Luis!' Lorenz dropped into the crevasse. He hauled the smaller boy up. 'Are you all right?'

Luis nodded. Lorenz waved the green skull in Luis' face.

'Our skull! We've won!' Not waiting for Luis to recover, he hauled him out onto the surface of the rock. Seven boys lay dead on the stone, their blood running into the gaps. Ereos was among them. Ristan and Laziel covered the survivors of Barrazael's band.

'We did it!' said Lorenz. 'Both skulls! All thanks to you, we have a chance of being angels!'

Luis nodded wordlessly. His ears filled with a buzzing noise. His vision sparkled. The stench of blood filled his nostrils. Lorenz and Kalael hoisted him onto their shoulders. They were all shouting his name, 'Dante! Dante!' But he took no joy in their victory.

His eyes remained locked on the dead.

No victory was worth this price.

CHAPTER TEN

THE PLACE OF CHALLENGE

456.M40
The Place of Challenge
Baal Secundus
Baal System

Nine days of recuperation, fasting and meditation followed the Trial of War, all undertaken in isolation, before the last aspirants were gathered together for the Final Choosing. One hundred and eight had gone into the Trial of War. Seventy-two remained. Tension was heavy around these boys who had been asked to kill each other and now had to meekly wait side by side. Triumph among the victors had given way to introspection. Luis was glad he could not see the faces of the Blood Angels beneath their helmets. If he saw looks of pleasure or of pride, he thought he could not stand it. Always they had been angels to him, protectors of Baal, the pinnacle of human development. The trial had been a hard reminder of their full name.

The great door of the keep opened, revealing a vestibule walled by another large gate. A smaller door was open within the second gate. Luis could see little beyond it, and the keep remained mysterious.

The Blood Angels came and went into the group, silently and

solemnly touching boys on the arm and beckoning for them to follow. He had no reason to expect the Space Marines would take pleasure in the killing, but the suspicion was bad enough. He sat on the sand in front of the angels' keep, his arms locked around his knees, the faces of the boys whose deaths he had been responsible for drifting across his vision. They weren't raiders, or people he had to kill; they were people he knew, killed because they were in the way of his personal desire. He could pretend he did it in order to serve the Emperor, but in reality they were dead because he wanted to be a Blood Angel. They were Barrazael, Garviel, Darrevael, Cosimo, Ludovic and others dead by his hand or by his orders, which was just as bad. And now they were nothing.

He burrowed his face deeper between his knees as their names echoed around his head.

One after another the boys were taken from the group and led through the great door into the angels' keep. No indication was given if the aspirants taken within were chosen or not. Luis supposed he would not see some of them ever again. They were told to be silent, to make no farewells. The unfairness of that chafed at Luis as his friends were stripped away. Ristan went first. Lorenz was called an hour later. He stood and strode out without looking back. A few went hesitantly. Florian followed Lorenz's example until he reached the door. He smiled sadly back at Luis, and lingered so long Araezon took his arm and led him within.

Luis' turn was a long time coming. Name after name was called. The group dwindled. The aspirants were blank-faced, burned out with exhaustion and dogged by trauma. Maybe this would be the final hurdle he would fall at. Not cruel enough to bear the murder of his comrades easily, he would be driven out.

He would not be sorry if that were so. He could not fight for monsters. Shadows lengthened. The light inside the keep did not have to fight so hard against the sun, and the room inside revealed itself by degree. He saw only white walls. Baal was coming up. Perhaps this was the last time he would see it. The moon's presence calmed him, and by the time he was finally called, when eight boys remained, he rose up by Malafael and walked into the keep with a steady heart. The Chaplain went behind him, leaving Luis painfully aware that the black angel could destroy him without difficulty. Still, he made himself stop, and the Chaplain halted behind him. He craned his neck to see past the looming, skull-encrusted majesty of the Chaplain – one last glimpse at the heavens before he entered an unfamiliar world. Baal filled the circular patch of sky over the Place of Challenge. At the fullest part of its waist gleamed the fortress-monastery of the Blood Angels. In moments, he would know if he was to go to dwell there, or remain on Baal Secundus forever.

Malafael pushed him inside.

The barracks and fortifications of the Place of Challenge were built of mud-brick and stone. They were the same as all the other buildings Luis had been inside: small windows to keep out the heat and dust, hot and dusty just the same.

The keep was different, as finely made as the building they had been taken into at the Place of Choosing, from the marvellous seamless stone of the Imperium. Harsh, artificial light glared from strip lumens. A strange taste filled his mouth, and the machines that infested the keep's innards buzzed annoyingly.

Malafael took him to another door leading deeper into the keep. The temperature dropped, and Luis shivered.

'I believe this is yours,' said Malafael. He took a staff from an attendant blood thrall and handed it to Luis.

The wood was remarkably familiar, rough towards the end, smooth where his hands had polished the grain away.

'This is my staff!' he exclaimed. 'How? I left it behind. This is impossible!'

'You will learn that many things are possible,' said Malafael. 'Does it not please you to have it back?'

Luis weighed it in his hands. It was undeniably his lost staff. It occurred to him then that they had been watching him all along.

'May I keep it?' he asked.

'If you wish,' said Malafael. 'Though you may be about to die. I gave it to you because I thought you might wish for a familiar weapon.'

The toothed doors slid apart.

'A weapon?' said Luis.

'One last test awaits.' Malafael directed Luis into the next room. It was much larger than the others and lit with a deep red light. Aside from a few unadorned conduits, the rockcrete was bare. In the middle of the floor stood Florian, staff up and ready to fight. His teeth were gritted, all his muscles tense.

Luis' heart fell. 'Florian?'

Florian's fierce expression flickered from anguish to determination and back.

'I'm sorry. They said I had to fight you for my chance.'

'What is this?' demanded Luis.

'Your final test,' said Malafael in his grating, machine-modulated voice. 'I would give you a speech to set you on your way, but I'll wager you are tired of those after these long weeks. Your friend has it right. You must kill him, or he you. One and only one place on Baal is at stake here. What are you waiting for?' said Malafael to Luis. His voice took on a fierce goading edge. 'Only one stands in your way! Kill your opponent and earn the freedom of the skies!'

'Kill him?' said Luis weakly.

'You are to become a warrior, are you not?'

Both of them hesitated. Florian, close to tears, gave in first.

'I'm sorry,' he whispered, and drove at Luis with his staff with a cry halfway between a battle-shout and a scream of despair.

Luis shifted back to evade the blow. The staff hummed past his face, the violence of it hot in the air.

He pivoted and met Florian's staff with his own. They clacked sharply. They moved together, intimate as dancers, the ends of their staffs rattling off each other in a frenzied percussion to their steps.

Luis cracked Florian's shin. The other boy suppressed a cry and smashed back so hard his staff burst through Luis' defence and knocked him on the forehead. The blow was comparatively light, but Luis saw stars. He staggered back, bringing up his weapon in time to deflect Florian's other blows. Florian had expended a lot of energy quickly, knowing he had to overpower Luis. It was never going to work. Luis had become by far the better fighter.

Florian's blocks grew wilder. The opening was there. Luis took it. He ran his staff up the inside of Florian's as hard as he could, crashing it into his wrist. With a high yelp, Florian released his weapon from his injured hand. Luis whirled around, stepping out from Florian and letting his hands slide to the end of the staff. Florian's one-handed parry was clumsy. Luis' staff hit Florian's elbow. The sound of the bone breaking was similar to the knock of the wood on wood.

Florian went pale with agony and stumbled, his staff falling from his fingers. Luis drove his weapon into Florian's face, breaking his black teeth, then spun it around to bring the other end hard into his sternum. The air whooshed from Florian's lungs in a spray of bloody spittle. He stumbled forwards, mouth gaping for air that he could not draw into his body.

Luis circled his friend. Florian was on his knees coughing a stream of bloody saliva, and cradling his broken elbow.

'Now finish him!' urged Malafael savagely.

Luis' hands tightened on his staff. A few blows, then over. He would win. He would have everything he had striven for. He would be an angel, able to do so much, to serve the Emperor. He would be a hero. His father would be wrong.

What kind of hero kills his friend?

'Why are you hesitating?' roared Malafael. 'Your position in the Chapter hangs in the balance! Strike!'

Luis looked at the wood, the gift from his mother. Suddenly it felt unclean in his hands, tainted by his consideration of the Chaplain's demand.

'I will not slay him,' he said quietly.

'What did you say?' asked the Chaplain.

'I said I would not slay him!' Luis shouted in sudden fury.

'You would throw away your chance to become a servant of the Emperor, a Space Marine, one of the greatest warriors in the galaxy for the sake of him?' scoffed the Chaplain. 'You are a fool, and not worthy of the gifts we would bestow. Kill him!'

'No.' Luis cast his staff away. It clattered into the corner. He stood tall. 'For him I would abandon anything. He helped me when I needed help. He befriended me when I had no friends. He guided me when he could have left me. I will not repay his kindness with treachery. If that means I am not worthy, I do not care. Kill me. I will not serve masters who demand the blood of my brother.'

Malafael leaned closer. Luis took a step back from his grinning skull face. 'What of glory and of power?' he whispered, his voice hissing through the vox-grille. 'Surely a fair price for such things is one life?'

'I did not come here for glory or for power. I came to serve,' said Luis calmly. He felt cheated, after everything he had undergone, all he had suffered, all he had hoped. He was angriest most of all at himself, for he had been a whisker away from spilling his friend's brains upon the floor for his own gain. He hid it all and faced his death with dignity. 'I will have no part of evil.'

The Chaplain's posture changed. He rested his weapon's head upon the floor and crossed his hands upon its pommel.

'Then you have passed.'

'What?' said Luis. Florian looked up dazedly.

'There are many tests in the Final Choosing, for each aspirant is different. This one was selected for you. Among ourselves we call this the Test of Horus. Do you know why? Do you know who Horus was?'

'He was a devil, a monster who fought the Emperor for control of the heavens,' said Luis.

'You are almost correct. Aeons ago, there was a great war, where angel fought against angel. Our lord Sanguinius was but one of twenty sons of the Emperor. These warriors were invested with the powers of ancient technology and prosecuted a Great Crusade, reuniting the worlds of humanity for the first time in thousands of years. But the favoured son of the Emperor, the Warmaster Horus, grew bitter and turned on his father, destroying the work of the Emperor ere it had been completed. Half of his brothers joined him in treachery. Our lord did not, but stood to the end against Horus, whom he had once loved. This test is named for him because it is a test of loyalty and brotherhood. We wish to see how well your principles endure when you are ordered by a mightier being to commit atrocity, and you held fast to your morals.'

Luis was aghast. 'But... But, the Trial of Blood. That is the same. You told us to kill, and we killed. Here you ask me to kill, and hope I do not. Are you hypocrites as well as torturers?'

'You ask questions now, defiant ones at that,' said Malafael after a moment's pause. 'You are unusual. I should cast you out for your impudence, Luis Dante.' He stared down. 'But something stays me, and I will answer your question. On occasion, as a brother of the Blood Angels, you will have to do things that might otherwise appal you. This test is a measure of your moral compass. Will it always point true to the ideals of our lord, or can it be wavered? There are lines, boy, that should never be crossed. To kill rebellious soldiers who fight because they have no choice is a regrettable evil that should tear at you if you are ever required to do it. The slaughter of the innocent to stop the machinations of the guilty must some-times be undertaken. But to revel in slaughter for slaughter's sake is forbidden, and to turn upon a brother for personal glory or gain is the first step on the path to damnation. Temptation, above all else, is the hardest test for a Space Marine to bear. Offered such great power, what man would not waver in his devotion to the true Lord of Mankind. Do you see?'

Luis looked down at Florian. Emotions of the most powerful sort warred in him.

'You seem to be an intelligent boy. You will therefore have noticed we did not split the groups you had formed yourselves,' explained the Chaplain. 'We asked you to fight against those who you had but fleeting loyalty to, not against those whom you held in genuine affection. You must forgive us for the artifice of these tests.' A note of regret crept into Malafael's voice. 'If this universe were fairer, then such cruelty would be unnecessary, but believe me when I say the universe you shall discover is not fair, and it is not kind. These petty horrors help humanity, in the end.'

'But... then... this is a test for one,' said Luis.

'It was a test for you, not for Florian.'

Florian sobbed and sank low to the floor.

'You have passed. Your comrade here could not. Either you killed him and spent your days reflecting on your actions as a guardian of the Place of Challenge, or you spared him and joined us. He cannot join us.'

'Why?' Florian cried. 'Why did you do this to me?'

Malafael turned his skull face to the beaten boy. 'Because we had to. You are but one of trillions of men. All have their purpose. You have served yours. This is a time of all-out war. You are privileged to have found such meaningful service.' Malafael turned back to Luis. 'The other aspirants face tests of their own. Every one is different. Protestations of service often mask a desire for power in the cunning. This is why your test took the form it did.'

'He will die. He is sick,' said Luis.

'This is true. I am sorry. It was his determination to seek out a place with us for survival's sake that made him an unsuitable candidate. Your friend has many qualities, but the desire to live he has exhibited would endanger his brothers should it come to the fore again. Self-sacrifice is important in our Chapter. So I have judged, and my judgement is irrevocable.'

'Florian, I...'

Florian turned his face down. Blood, snot and tears mixed freely and ran onto the floor. 'It's true. What he says is true! I came here to live. You know that.'

'But Florian, you are a good person. You are my friend. You are worthy!'

'I say not,' said Malafael.

'Go, Luis. Leave me,' said Florian. 'I am sorry. I would have killed you. I... I could never have passed the test.'

'He is my brother,' said Luis.

'And that is why he lives for now.' Malafael extended his open hand to Luis. 'He will live what little life he has in sacred duty, as important as yours in its way, and his sacrifices will be less. If you could see his life and yours laid side by side from beginning to end, you would envy him. You have been chosen for great and onerous duty. Do you accept? Are you willing to become a Blood Angel? If you have doubts, best unburden yourself and I shall end your suffering.' His armoured fist creaked as he gripped his crozius and lifted it from the floor.

Luis looked again at Florian. The other boy pulled himself into a painful crouch, smiled through his broken black teeth and nodded encouragingly. 'Go. Do what you can. Serve the Emperor.'

The black-clad hand of Malafael waited unwaveringly. The Space Marine was as still as a statue. Luis reached up and grasped the armoured hand. The metal was warm as living flesh, and vibrated slightly with the workings of hidden machinery. Malafael folded his fingers around Luis' hand, engulfing it completely.

'I accept,' said Luis. 'I will become an angel and serve the Emperor.'

CHAPTER ELEVEN

THE RED COUNCIL

998.M41
Asphodex High Anchor
Cryptus System

There were twenty-five chairs in the Chamber of the Red Council aboard the *Blade of Vengeance.* The total number required, should the entire council be gathered together at once. There were times when there were fewer than twenty-five members, but there had never been an occasion when there were more. At its fullest, the Red Council was made up of all ten company captains, and those captains with offices beyond company command, the Keeper of the Heavengate and the Warden of the Gates. Further seats were reserved for the Master of the Blade, the Exalted Herald of Sanguinius, the Sanguinary High Priest, the Chief Librarian, the High Chaplain and the Reclusiarch of the Lost. The remainder were drawn variously from captains assigned to command the mightier ships – always Blood Angels themselves – and whichever of the Chapter ancients remained lucid enough to pass on their wisdom. History had witnessed few occasions when all the Red Council had gathered together aboard one battle-barge, few even when all were present together on Baal, but there was a replica of this room on board the *Bloodcaller,* the Blood Angels' other battle-barge, itself a copy of the chamber on Baal. The symbolism of what the council represented, and who was entitled to sit upon it, was more important than its actual membership. In practice the Blood Angels' war council comprised whoever was available to represent the various sub-orders of the Chapter on any given campaign.

Filling much of the room beneath an armoured dome was a table, round so that the voice of every man might be heard. Though the throne of the Chapter Master was larger than the rest, it was not so grand as to set him apart. As with all the effects of the Chapter, the room was richly decorated, luxurious by the standards of the age. Banners hung around the wall. Bowls of loose rubies were set into the surface of the table before every chair, each gem a perfect blood drop marked at the atomic scale with the name of a lost brother. From the apex of the dome a huge, simple flag depended, bearing the Chapter badge of winged blood drop, black on red. Finely made rugs covered the floor. The paving they hid was also masterfully wrought: red-veined black stone cut into triangles and squares, arranged into complex geometries.

For the moment, the Chamber of the Red Council was quiet as the grave, lit with thick, bloody light that blurred the outlines of its fixtures. There was not a soul inside. It was the chamber of a stilled heart, red and black and lifeless.

The noise of steel on steel penetrated the gloom. The scrape of a key as long as an arm entering a lock designed to hold shut not just doors of earthly plasteel, but the gates of reality. Intersecting psychic null fields ensured no psyker or sorcerer could scry what went on within the chamber.

A stuttering whine followed. With an audible boom, the gates cracked open, polluting the red purity of the chamber's illumination with yellow lumen glow.

The gates yawned wider and wider with a building creak. Beyond, in the outer vestibule, waited the council.

Present were Commander Dante; Chaplain Ordamael, speaking for the Chaplaincy; Sanguinary High Priest Corbulo; company captains Karlaen, Aphael and Phaeton, of the First, Second and

Seventh Company respectively; Brother Bellerophon, the current Keeper of the Heaven Gate; Captain Asante of the *Blade of Vengeance;* Techmarine Muziel, speaking for the Armoury; and Chief Librarian Mephiston. Attending as honoured guest was Master Gabriel Seth of the Flesh Tearers, whose own brotherhood had fought so hard in the Cryptus campaign alongside its father Chapter. In the shadows of these inhuman heroes came Sister Superior Amity Hope of the Order of the Sacred Rose, her battered power armour porcelain-delicate next to that of the giant Space Marines. General Dhrost of Cadia walked by her side. For all his rank and experience, in his uniform he looked like a prematurely aged scholum boy.

Dante entered first, his battleplate shining with red and golden highlights in the mixed light. All the Adeptus Astartes were armed and armoured as if for battle. This was a council of war.

Flights of herald cherubs swooped under the door lintel and into the room, singing out the names of those in attendance. Vat-made seraphs trailed censers that filled the air with smoke. Servo-skulls examined every nook and cranny for threats while servitor-recorders, brains stripped to the barest language processing and movement functions, clumped into position where they would record the proceedings.

'Draw back the shutters!' commanded Dante.

The Chamber of the Red Council boomed again to the activation of giant gears. A tremendous groaning reverberated throughout. Armaplas shutters the size of city gates drew back into their housings either side of exquisite traceries, revealing the domed roof to be a wide cupola breaking out from the greater body of the ship's command spire.

One of the shutters caught and juddered as it opened, snagged by battle damage. The tyranids had assailed the battle-barge in great numbers. It had emerged triumphant. Gears ground until they bit. The penetration spines of slaughtered voidbeasts sheared off and floated away into the mess of debris crowding the fleet.

The *Blade of Vengeance*'s dorsal aspect angled towards the planet, affording a view of its battered surface. More yellow light flooded in to compete with the blood-red glow of the chamber's lamps. Fire still raged on Asphodex.

Dante marched to his throne. The others stood behind their seats, waiting for the commander to sit. Once he had, they sat as one. All but Dante and Ordamael removed their helmets, exposing faces that bore the genetic stamp of Sanguinius, all handsome beneath their networks of scars and the thickening effects of age.

Blood thralls moved into the room silently, bearing steaming salvers of scented water. They ritually washed the lips and gauntlets of their masters, and laid fine white linen over their left arms. Other servants followed, carrying ewers of wine and silver goblets chased with rubies and gold. The Blood Angels believed in beauty in all things. Beauty also comes from excellence, and the servants worked flawlessly, their procession around the table and ministrations to their masters well choreographed. When they set the metal bases of the goblets on the stone, they made no noise. Dhrost and Amity Hope were provided with drinking vessels suited to mortals, and their own small ewer of wine. They would not care for the Blood Angels' drink.

Dante waited for the sacred ablutions to finish. A senior Chapter servant brought him a silver basin where lay thirty-four rubies. Stones bearing the names of the newly dead. Dante picked them out and let them run through his fingers into the bowl before him.

'Let them be remembered,' Dante said.

The senior servant bowed. The blood thralls filed out.

'We speak with truth on our lips,' Dante intoned.

'No blood shall stain our words,' the Space Marines responded. 'Rage shall not colour our judgement.'

'The Emperor shall judge our words,' said Amity Hope. Her armour was scratched down to silver ceramite. Only traces of its white paint remained, and the bare metal was scorched with acid burns. She was exhausted, but defiance burned in her eyes.

The sons of Sanguinius bowed their heads in silent communion with the spirit of their father. Amity sought out Dhrost's hand and clasped it while she recited holy psalms. Falteringly at first, he joined in. When all lifted their heads again, their attitudes had changed, becoming relaxed. They shifted in their seats and took their wine. Dante drew in the scent of his through his mask's filters. A fine vintage from the Chapter's oasis gardens, subtly spiced and flavoured with blood. His mouth watered, but he did not wish to remove his mask and reveal his aged face to his warriors. Furthermore, even the small amounts of dead blood mixed into the Blood Angels' wine had of late fired his thirst to intolerable heights, and he had come to eschew its drinking altogether except for the most sacred rituals, for fear of what might follow. He pushed the drink aside.

Mephiston picked up his goblet. Leaving the table, he went to stand by the armourglass windows, apart as always, staring through the dome at the dying planet.

'The tyranids have suffered a blow. We cannot call it a victory,' said Dante. 'In depriving the hive fleets of biomass to replenish their armies, we have borne witness to the destruction of a productive and populous Imperial system. I did not come here to utilise the Kryptmann strategy, and yet we leave a devastated system in our wake. No choice has been given us, and our empire suffers. This is my interpretation of the events here. I will have no one refer to victory at Cryptus. Is that clear?'

His officers murmured their assent.

'Captain Phaeton. You will address the council first. Tell us how many civilians were saved.'

Phaeton was younger than the other captains, his pristine face unmarked by scars, and his hair still Sanguinius' golden colour. He was the image of an angel encased in ceramite.

'Some two million, my lord. There were more. Several of the evacuation craft were destroyed before we could reach them.'

'Two million from a population of billions,' emphasised Dante. 'More of them will die. I have looked over the provisioning of these ships. It is inadequate. Starvation will set in soon. They must be taken to other systems as soon as we are through the Aegis Diamondo, or the blood we spilt in saving them will be wasted.'

General Dhrost spoke up. 'I cannot speak on behalf of Cadia, but we shall do what we can to take some of them in.'

'Cadia is a long way from here,' said Karlaen. 'And threatened by the Eye.'

'It is clear they do not have enough food for all of them to travel all the way, but we shall do what we can,' said Dhrost. 'Cadia is safer than many other worlds.'

Karlaen shrugged. 'Maybe.'

'Most will have to be settled nearer,' said Dante. 'Preferably away from the line of tyranid incursion.'

'Who will take them in?' said Karlaen. 'Charity is not a word many Imperial commanders are familiar with. Those close to the invasion will refuse to burden their planets with extra mouths, those further away will not see the urgency.'

'Dhrost will take them away from the front. You intend to return to Cadia?'

'I do, my lord.'

'And you will do this duty in our name?'

'I shall,' said Dhrost. 'But your word will sway other systems better than mine, my lord. A personal communication from you will aid us.'

'Time grows short,' said Dante. 'I cannot speak with every Imperial commander.'

'Of course not,' said Dhrost humbly.

'I shall provide you with a letter of demand. Many of the worlds beyond the Red Scar will petition us for aid once the tyranids are through. I will make it clear our aid is contingent on their mercy. Bellerophon,' said Dante.

'My lord,' replied the Master of the Fleets, an old warrior whose golden hair was grizzled with streaks of grey.

'Contact the Logisticiam on Baal. See how many we might take across the three worlds. I shall leave it to you and Lord Adanicio to work out the details. Perhaps there are some within the survivors who might be taken as aspirants. We must accelerate our recruitment process.'

'As soon as we are free of the warp shadow, it shall be done, my lord,' said Bellerophon.

'We shall turn our attention to the defence of our home. Satys has fallen, Vitria and now the Cryptus System. The shield of Baal is buckling. The Oculus Stars have almost certainly been over-run.' Dante gestured a hololith of the Red Scar into being over the table. The scarlet veil that gave the region its name was pierced by graphical representations of the questing tendrils of Leviathan in half a dozen places. Scores of star systems were contained within. Those to the galactic south of Cryptus had their names greyed out.

'Cryptus was the last bastion system between the tyranids and Baal,' said Dante. 'The Red Wilderness is to one side, interstellar deeps to the other. There are few places the enemy can go. These were the positions of the Leviathan swarms before we entered the warp shadow.' Dante set a chronograph into action. The ghostly limbs of the hive fleets began to move sinuously. Every inhabited system they crossed blinked twice and went dark. 'This is their pro-jected position now,' he said, freezing the movement. He restarted the sequence. 'And this is where I project the tyranids will have reached within the next month.' The tyranid fleets, spread like the arms of some great cephalopod, converged into a dagger tip half a light year across aimed directly at the Blood Angels' home sys-tem. Baal blinked. 'Our future hangs in the balance.'

'If I may petition you, lord commander. We could concentrate our efforts on the guiding minds of the ships, the norncraft and their queens, as we depart,' said Dhrost. 'If we might dismantle their command network, it shall afford you more time to reinforce Baal.'

Phaeton and Aphael shared a worried look.

'Speak!' said Dante to his brothers, holding up his hand. 'While Dhrost is here, he is to be accorded the same rights as a member of our Chapter. Let the record state that the Red Council will speak freely.'

'We have accounted for eighty per cent of the norn, brood and hive ships seen in the system, general,' said Aphael. 'As per stand-ard engagement strategy when making war upon the tyranids.'

'The hive fleet recovers quickly. How?' said Dhrost.

'We lack sufficient intelligence to say exactly, general, but we are certain that adaptive evolution among the tyranid swarm has made the previous strategy unworkable. It appears the tyranids have found a means to counter our destruction of their largest vessels,' said Phaeton.

'Theories?' said Dante. He toyed with the bowl full of rubies set into the desk before him. The glassy rattle of them against each other was supposed to aid meditation.

'I have two,' said Phaeton. 'The first is that the hive mind has devised a way of exerting its will over a larger area, with fewer intermediary vessels required as nodes in its neural network. If this is true, it may be used to our advantage. If we were to commit to multiple strikes across a broad front of several infested systems, the operation of the hive mind might be greatly disrupted. By extending its range, the hive mind has increased its vulnerability.'

'Provide the second theory,' said Dante.

'They have evolved a way of spreading their neural network more widely across a given area, making it harder to disrupt,' said Phaeton. 'The larger ships are no longer the only nexus points for the broader synaptic web of the fleets.'

Karlaen slammed his goblet onto the table with a growl. 'You mean that shooting the big ones will no longer work, brother-captain. Speak plainly, Phaeton.'

'In fleet actions, yes, brother, that is the case,' said Phaeton. 'Shooting the big ones will no longer work.'

'We have yet to witness this change in the ground swarms,' said Aphael. 'Can we expect it? Engaging swarms that remain coherent even when deprived of their leader beasts will be difficult.'

'That will not happen for a while. Unlike the ships, the smaller organisms are not large enough to carry psychic nexuses,' said Corbulo. 'Instead we have seen the ships produce increasingly larger numbers of the warrior strain. According to the latest information I have from the rest of the Imperium, they remain the smallest species to be fully linked with the hive mind, and capable of projecting its influence.'

'Can we add to this knowledge ourselves?' asked Dante. 'What has Cryptus taught us?'

Corbulo leaned forwards and tapped on the table once. 'My main concerns are elsewhere. This xenology is not my area of expertise, but it is self-evident to say that their voidcraft are sufficiently large to allow a number of specialisations to be contained within one body, whereas the same cannot be said of the ground beasts. However, I would not rule out change. Successive tyranid incursions show a growing number of organisms tailored to exploiting the weaknesses of this galaxy's races – the toxicrenes and psyker beasts among the more recent – and to countering its own shortcomings in the face of our weaponry. We have been exploiting one weakness. The hive mind will compensate for it, of that we can be sure.'

'At the same time, we are witnessing a drop in speciation among the ships,' said Phaeton. 'I suspect owing to our targeting of their command-and-control vessels. As a result, it is becoming harder to accurately target nexus ships.'

'They employ camouflage,' said Ordamael scornfully. No Space Marine would ever hide his colours.

'Yes, and it is very effective,' said Phaeton.

'Then if they are hiding the higher nodes, we must devise means of telling the ships that contain them apart as a matter of priority,' said Dante.

'I have had our auspexes recalibrated many times, my lord,' said Bellerophon. 'We are no closer to being able to successfully scan the tyranid ships. We can locate the mechanisms they contain, if mechanisms we can call them, but accurately deducing their function still eludes us. This problem continues to vex other armed forces elsewhere in the Imperium.'

'Mephiston,' Dante called over his shoulder. 'Can you provide me with better news? You are among the few psykers capable of withstanding the roar of the hive mind. What do you see?'

Mephiston turned from the spectacle of the burning world. 'Psychic means could be employed to divine upon which ship the

higher nexuses reside, lord commander, if indeed we are witnessing something as simple as camouflage. But it will take time in
every battle, and will draw my Librarians from their combat duties.
Our astropaths and other mystics cannot withstand the mind-
scream of the Great Devourer. I am sure you will tell us all that
time is the one currency we have little left to spend.'

'Not the only one,' said Dante. 'Blood, metal – we run short of
all the coin of war, my brothers.' He dropped the last ruby into
the bowl. 'I have studied the reports of other Chapters and battle
groups combating Leviathan. Other splinters do not evince the
same level of accelerated evolution. The splinters continue into
the Imperium elsewhere. Baal is but one system in their path, but
it has become clear to me that the hive mind is actively seeking
our destruction.'

'Is such a thing possible?' said Aphael.

'The evidence is there to see,' said Dante. 'We are the primary
military asset of the Imperium in this part of the segmentum. We
must blunt the attack on Baal for the sake of the wider Imperium.
When we are victorious, we might aid other forces elsewhere. We
are reorganised, ready to depart this doomed place.'

Bellerophon nodded an affirmation. 'It is so. The fleet awaits
your command, my lord.'

'We return to the home world. Today.' Dante raised his
golden-masked face and surveyed his commanders. 'Have no
doubt, this will be a difficult war. Our Chapter is at little over
three-quarters full strength owing to our recent losses here and at
Armageddon. We may make up some of our numbers by elevating
those neophytes who are ready. If the implantation of their cara-
paces takes quickly we might bring our strength back to four-fifths
within a month. But though we are depleted, we shall not stand
alone.'

'You shall not,' said Seth. 'The Flesh Tearers are yours to command, my lord.'

'You have our everlasting thanks, Chapter Master. Seth is not the
only one to pledge aid. Before we entered the shadow of the hive

mind, I received replies to messages I sent to the Angels Numinous, Angels Sanguine, Flesh Eaters, Exsanguinators, Blood Drinkers and Angels Encarmine. All will send warriors to Baal's defence. Although some can spare only a few, the Blood Drinkers are sending four full companies and the Angels Encarmine are gathering at Chapter strength. Others of our bloodline have not responded yet, but with Sanguinius' grace we shall have news of them soon. The Blood Templars, Carmine Swords, Charnel Guard, Brothers of the Red...' He reeled off the names of a score of Chapters. 'I calculate a certainty of five thousand Adeptus Astartes to defend Baal, and perhaps as many as fifteen thousand, should they respect their oaths of blood and fellowship as scions of the Great Angel.'

'That is not all of them,' said Aphael cautiously.

'I contacted the Lamenters. They responded unfavourably. If they were of a mind to obey our call, they are too depleted to help us,' said Dante. 'It is a sign of the bond between the Chapters of the Blood that they are the only ones to say no. While such brotherhood persists, we might prevail.'

'I did not refer to the Lamenters,' said Aphael.

Dante turned Sanguinius' frozen expression of rage upon his second captain. 'I will not contact the Angels Vermillion. You know my feelings on that matter.'

'They are close! Why not?' said Aphael.

'Enough!' said Dante. His voice rose only a little, but it rang from the crystal dome. The others waited quietly; Dante's temper was infrequently roused, but when a rage came on him, it was terrible to behold. 'I have received word from the Knights of Blood. They too will come.'

'Renegades,' said Karlaen. 'You court disaster speaking with them.'

'I did not contact them. Their aid is unasked for. They offer their help freely. We are in no position to say no.'

'They are renegades by the Ordo Astartes' order alone,' said Corbulo. 'Victims of the Inquisition's politics.'

'They have just cause in declaring the Knights renegade,' said Phaeton. 'They are savages. Renowned for their brutality to foe

and friend alike. We have an ample quotient of savages already.'
He eyed Seth meaningfully.

'They are raw in their anger, it is true,' said Corbulo. 'But they fight
for the Imperium despite their persecution. They have ceased to
fight alongside others to prevent... unfortunate incidents.'

'Is it persecution?' said Phaeton. He was guarding his words carefully. They could not openly mention the flaw in front of Dhrost
or Sister Amity Hope.

'Their path could have been ours, if we had been less fortunate,'
said Seth.

'Maybe it still should be,' said Phaeton coldly.

'I should call you out for those words. I have had enough of your
petty slights, captain,' said Seth. His anger spiked suddenly, and spittle flew from his lips. 'I lost two hundred battle-brothers fighting for
your cause. Perhaps I should have followed the Lamenters' lead.'

'So we see your true character emerge,' said Phaeton.

'If you saw my true character, brother, it would be the last thing
you saw.'

Phaeton half rose, hand going to the hilt of his sword. Seth stood,
a feral expression narrowing his eyes.

'Gabriel, please!' Dante said. 'Captain Phaeton, hold your tongue.
It is known to me that not all of the council regard our rapproche-
ment with the Flesh Tearers favourably. Put those feelings behind
you. By their sacrifice and their nobility the Flesh Tearers have
redeemed themselves five times over, whatever the excesses of
their past. I so decree. I will brook no more dissent!'

Seth bared his teeth, showing his long canines, but relented.

'The more warriors we have, the more likely we are to succeed,'
said Karlaen. 'We are in a situation where honour must bend
to mathematics, Brother-Captain Phaeton. The savagery of the
Knights of Blood will be welcome in defence of Baal, and I for
one have only the greatest respect for Seth and his Flesh Tearers.'

'Provided their savagery is unleashed only on the enemy. But if
we are willing to deal with necrons, then we should overlook any
fault on the part of our brothers-in-the-blood,' said Aphael.

Dante silently dared Aphael to mention the Angels Vermillion again. The second captain was one of the most vocal of their supporters. Dante was grateful he did not. Aphael did not know what High Chaplain Hereon had discovered in their fortress-monastery five centuries ago. He prayed all at the table would remain ignorant of that horror.

'We face a stark choice,' said Dante. 'In the galactic south, the Ordo Xenos under the guidance of Inquisitor Kryptmann is employing a scorched earth policy, laying waste to swathes of worlds to halt the xenos advance. This strategy is not working.' The cartolith zoomed out, depicting the estimated location of the main mass of Leviathan coming up from below the galactic plane, enclosing the heart of the galaxy in its immense talons.

'The Adeptus Terra have sanctioned *Augetem Ultima* across the Red Scar – they will build a wall of bodies to exhaust the fleet, despite the questionable wisdom of providing the tyranids with an endless supply of fresh meat. Cryptus was the first test of that strategy, and it has failed. Without the light of the Astronomicon to guide them, the reinforcements promised to General Dhrost here could not arrive. We can safely assume the same will occur in the systems beyond Cryptus and the Oculus Stars, and that whatever resistance can be mustered in the shieldworlds will quickly collapse. The tyranids may be slowed, but without constant redeployment, impossible through the shadow in the warp, these efforts are doomed to failure. We have seen here, this week, what we as Space Marines might achieve if we choose to lend our might to these system fortifications. The question I have been debating these last hours is therefore this: do we fight the tyranids system by system, or do we marshal the full strength of the Blood Angels and our successors, and make a stand at Baal?'

Dante stood. The cartolith made a dizzying zoom into the Blood Angels' home worlds. 'I fear the first strategy will lead to our slow erosion. As here, we will not stop the tyranids, only slow them, and so our eventual destruction will be inevitable. Contrarily, if we do not attack where we might, we risk allowing Leviathan access to resources that will speed its growth exponentially. Either strategy has its merits – both are risky. I have therefore determined a third way.' He waved his hand. The cartolith zoomed back out. 'We shall gather the majority of our warriors at Baal. I shall request that the masters of the fleet-based Chapters assign portions of their strength to mobile strike groups. These will stand ready to deal pinpoint blows to the hive fleets.'

'How will limited strikes slow them, my lord, when outright war has not?' asked Aphael.

'Missions will be carefully determined. The removal of norncraft clusters, considered reinforcement of Astra Militarum army groups, bolstering the Imperial fleet. Exterminatus, if need be. Diversion, distraction and disruption. We cannot accomplish more. While these actions are ongoing, we and the successors shall fortify Baal and its moons. We shall meet the aliens at the edge of the Baal System in full fleet array, and attempt to split them. By slowing their planetfall we can hope to deal with them piecemeal. The strategy was attempted here by General Dhrost, and would have succeeded but for want of more men. Our armouries are fully stocked. Billions of bolt shells await their targets. The Sanguinor itself told us that there is hope. The Sanguinor spoke!' he said emphatically. 'Hope is only candle flame – it must be fanned by action into a blaze.'

Dante looked around the table of solemn faces. 'We have blunted their attack here, at Cryptus, but this manner of victory will not be sufficient at Baal. Leviathan has to be crushed. What I suggest has only a slim chance of success. This decision is too great to be made by me alone. I ask the representatives of the council for their opinion. Do we stand on Baal in the manner I propose, do we split ourselves among the shieldworlds, or do we consider the unthinkable and flee?'

'Flee?' said Ordamael. 'Never! It is agreed. We shall stand. I speak for the Chaplaincy. The commander's strategy is sound. Sanguinius' wings shield us in these desperate hours.'

'I second Ordamael's approval,' said Corbulo. 'The Sanguinary Priests will stand by Commander Dante's plan.'

'Brother-captains?' asked Dante. 'Gabriel?'

'I stand where you stand, lord commander,' said Seth. 'There is no need to ask. I am yours to command – by the Blood I swear it so.' He slammed his fist into his battle-scarred plastron.

Karlaen looked to the second and seventh captains, and to Bellerophon and Asante. They nodded. 'We of the captaincy agree,' said Karlaen.

'And what do you think, Dhrost?'

The general's steely eyes glinted with emotion. 'I lost three million men on Asphodex. I owe my life to your intervention. If you are to concentrate your forces on Baal, billions more will perish, but I do not believe you have another choice. If the Imperial Navy can bring its transports through to the shieldworlds, your presence will have minimal positive effect. If they cannot – and we all agree this is likely – your presence will strengthen the hearts of every woman and man under arms, you will slaughter the xenos by the million... and then you will fall, to the last man. There is no other choice. Thousands of Space Marines together can succeed where hundreds will not. I condemn worlds to their deaths in saying this, but you must do what you suggest.'

'Sister Amity?'

'I go where the Emperor sends me, my lord. You are the sons of the Emperor's most holy offspring, the Great Angel. Sanguinius' soul works through you, and the Emperor works through him. If you have decided to fight for your home, that is what the Emperor demands, and you cannot deny His will.'

Dante inclined his head in respect. The Adepta Sororitas and Adeptus Astartes did not always see eye to eye on the matter of the Emperor's divinity, but he respected their prowess in battle.

'I thank you for your advice, my brothers, my guests. Make all ships ready for immediate departure. Once we are through the Aegis Diamondo, we will make all speed for Baal.'

'By Sanguinius' blood, so be it,' the Blood Angels and Seth responded.

Behind his golden mask, Dante worried. In the face of such single-minded destruction, hope could not be enough.

CHAPTER TWELVE

SECOND BIRTH

456.M40
Baal Secundus to Baal transfer
Baal System

The sky chariot shook. The vibrations were so intense Luis' vision blurred. Metal creaked from every quarter, punctuated by hollow bangs. The roar of the engines hurt his ears. The aspirants gripped their passenger restraint cages for dear life. Malafael and Rugon flew with them, and their comportment could not have been more different. They stood away from the few seats in the sky chariot – Thunderhawk, Luis corrected himself – chatting with one another. Their conversation was inaudible, either lost to the roar of the jets or projected helm to helm, but he could see they were talking, completely at ease. They were unaffected by the great pressure that pushed at Luis as the craft accelerated out of Baal Secundus' reach. His weight increased, until he was crushed by his own body, pinned to his seat. Black spots whirled around his vision.

He made himself examine his surroundings, to immerse himself in its detail, where he could hide from fear. The black spots became a tunnel. He could not breathe. Something huge and malevolent was pressing the air from his chest.

The Blood Angels swayed with the jolting movement of the

gunship; their feet were unmoving, locked to the deck by their armour somehow. Luis moved his eyes painfully around the compartment, searching for other things to occupy his mind. There were a handful of seats in the ship, and although all of them had the massive restraint cradles like the one he was clinging to, he thought that the Space Marines rarely used them. There were only nine seats, but space within the hold for twenty, maybe thirty of the giant armoured warriors if they stood shoulder to shoulder. While he thought, he calmed his breathing. Watch, he told himself. Do not fear. To his left, Lorenz had his eyes screwed shut. Ristan muttered prayers under his breath. There were nine aspirants in their ship, one for each seat. Sixty-three had been chosen. Others rode in other ships. Six ships all told. Two moons, one planet. These facts kept him calm as he felt consciousness slip away. He could not prevent the final closure of the black tunnel crowding his vision, and he passed out.

He was unconscious only for moments. The pressure ceased. Aside from a faint tremor in the craft, it now ran silent. He was as light as air and a little queasy for it. He lifted his arm and marvelled at the weightless sensation. The other boys were laughing and flapping their hands around. Malafael turned from his conversation. His vox-grille clicked on.

'Be calm, aspirants. We are outside the gravity well you have known your entire lives. This sensation will shortly cease.'

'We are in the void!' said Lorenz.

'You are in the void,' said Malafael indulgently. 'Enjoy the novelty of it. Quietly.' His vox clicked off, and he turned back to his private conversation with the Sanguinary Priest.

Unable to contain their excitement, the successful aspirants talked in whispers for the two hours of weightlessness, smiling as they let their arms float around their heads, until, without warning, a loud rumble shook the cabin and Luis experienced the pressure again.

'*We are entering the Arx Angelicum approach vector, my lords,*' said a voice over the craft's internal vox. '*Aspirants, prepare yourselves.*'

'If you thought the ride up hard on your bones,' said Rugon, his smile audible in his words. 'Then you will think this a nightmare. I advise you to hold on tight.'

Luis' stomach flipped. More noises sounded outside. The ship tilted and he lifted, banging himself against the restraint cage.

'Grip your cages!' said Malafael. 'Your bruises will be lessened. Keep your mouths shut, or you might bite off your tongues.'

Atmospheric re-entry began with a quiet rumble, and built quickly to a roaring that transcended all noise Luis had heard before. The ship's internal temperature rose rapidly. It bounced with such violence Luis thought the craft would land and open to reveal the shaken-apart remains of the new recruits. He screwed his eyes closed, teeth gritted, praying to the Emperor and Sanguinius for salvation.

As soon as it started, it was done. The Thunderhawk levelled out. Whining noises came from outside, and the engine sound changed. The Space Marines' boots clunked as they disengaged, and they walked forwards to the massive assault ramp.

'Nearly there,' said Malafael. At least, that's what Luis thought he said; his ears were screeching from the punishment meted out to his hearing.

They were over another world, flying down to Baal itself. Luis yearned to see, but the ship's armour permitted no windows other than the canopy over the cockpit. To the fore of the cabin a grainy flat pict screen blinked into life, too small for him to see much detail, but he caught a view of dunes rushing past before Malafael leaned in close to it and obscured it completely.

The Thunderhawk slowed and banked around. Mechanisms whined within its metal skin. Three closely spaced clanks banged sharply through the deck.

'We arrive,' said Malafael. 'Prepare yourselves. This is your last day as mortals.'

True to its name, the ship emitted a riotous thunder of engine noise and slowed further. There was a series of delicate shifts, then a soft bang as it touched down and sank into its landing hydraulics. The engines screamed higher, then spooled down and shut off.

'Stand!' commanded Malafael in the sudden quiet. The restraint cages disengaged and lifted up. The boys rose stiffly. Luis felt heavier than he had on Baalfora, feeble even. Moving was an effort, though again the Blood Angels behaved as if nothing had changed. Rugon punched a massive red button on the wall, and the ship's front ramp whirred down, letting in a soft light.

'Exit the craft, and see your new home.'

Luis exited into a plain hangar that stretched away out of sight, full of ships bristling with weapons. The air was cool and smelt of oils, and he shivered. Again he was subjected to terrifying noise as the other ships landed and the rest of the aspirants came out of their craft, blinking dazedly. Laestides and Araezon herded them together under Verono's stern gaze.

In the centre of the hangar, back from the landing pads, forty-five Space Marines waited for them, stood in smart ranks, each warrior's armour different in its exquisite decoration.

'Our brothers come to meet you, five from each company, save the tenth,' said Rugon. 'Come, you have laboured long. There will be no more delay. Your elevation to an adept of the stars begins now.'

The Space Marines turned, marching into two long files with a space between them. Malafael directed the aspirants into the gap. Luis glanced nervously at the giants. They formed two walls like waves of blood. He couldn't see how he would ever be able to call these demigods brother.

'We go!' said Verono.

The Space Marines marched.

A confusion of sights greeted Luis. The aspirants were led down staircases from the hangars. These were immense in size and highly ornate, their balustrades mounted with decorated metal lamps of complicated, exquisite design. Their walls made curving friezes of the Blood Angels at war, carved from the living rock. The width of the stairs was enough to accommodate the whole party with ease.

They passed into a huge space, open to the sky. Luis gaped at it, breathing alien air for the first time. The heavens of Baal were a similar blue to home, but tinted with a delicate yellow. The court-yard, although the name barely did it justice, was bounded on all sides by walls higher than cliffs. Statues of angels hundreds of feet tall played host to bastions bristling with weapons. Around their feet were many tiers of stepped fields, green with growing things. The weighty smell of rich soils came off them. A high tower reached arrogantly for space on one side. Servitors clumped about, tending to the plants. Brothers in blood-red day robes stopped to watch the new recruits being marched by, hiding their faces in their hoods. The courtyard was a mile wide at least. The figures on the far side of its worn, hexagonal flagstones were tiny against the monumen-tal effigies defending it, like salt ants infesting a roamer.

They were over the courtyard quickly, the Space Marines set-ting a fast pace, and taken onto another stair that led upwards again. A vaulted hall of black stone opened up. The far side was a bank of enormous windows. The middle panes were clear, and outside Luis saw a landscape of dunes that faded into the dusty yellow sky, already tinting pink as the red sun of Baal neared the end of its path. The panes around the window edges were stained and assembled into images of Sanguinius. Sanguinius was every-where, looking down from niches, held aloft in flight by cunningly wrought pillars of rock, standing with his sword held high and wings spread. He was depicted at peace, at war, in flight, at his crafts, raising up the tribes of the Blood, but whatever he was doing, his expression was tinged with an ineffable sorrow that pierced Luis' soul.

No explanation was given to the purposes of the rooms and spaces they were taken through. They went across the aisle of a huge hall. Luis caught a glimpse of a giant statue of Sanguinius made of gold. He was unarmoured, his weapons sheathed, his wings furled. He was looking down, his right hand out and open, blessing his children.

Like all the other wondrous sights, it went by, replaced by more and more. A black iron gate was drawn back. The Space Marines formed two lines either side of it. The aspirants were taken inside a small chapel. A single light shaft pierced the thick outer walls of the fortress-monastery. A rose window was at the far end, thirty yards away. The walls were carved from the black stone and inlaid with precious minerals. Space Marine armour was rendered in deep red carnelian; eye-lenses were emeralds. Gold and silver adorned everything. The aspirants had never seen such riches and skill on display. Everything about the monastery seemed designed to cow them, and although they were the best either moon had to offer, they were afraid.

'This is the Chapel of Vigilance in the Basilica Sanguinarum,' said Malafael. 'In here you will meditate for three days and three nights. Think upon your fate. Draw inspiration from the artworks around you.' He held up his hand. 'But you may not move from your position, you may not speak, and you must not sleep. Any aspirant who fails this test will be removed. Do I make myself clear?'

The aspirants were too wise to speak, but Luis' chest clenched. How many more tests must they undergo? He was already weary from the trials and his journeys. Such a vigil would be all too easy to fail.

'There is one final test after this. Be assured your trials are nearly over,' said Malafael, anticipating the aspirants' fears. 'First, you will eat, and you may see to your ablutions. You will be given robes fit for your vigil. Ready yourselves, and be warned – many fail here at the Winnowing of Weariness.'

Three times the sun arced through the heavens, its shaft of light moving like a searchbeam over the polished black floor of the Chapel of Vigilance. The aspirants, dressed in simple shifts of pure white, were untroubled by the lack of food and water. All of them had experienced worse privation in their lives. Sleep was another matter. It beckoned them all. The final weeks of the challenge had been hard, and they were exhausted before they arrived upon Baal.

Luis compensated through meditation, focusing his attention on detail as he had on the Thunderhawk. But fear is easier to banish than sleep, and he sank into a deep pit of tiredness he could not escape. At the end of the second day he felt better than expected, but come morning of the third day he was beyond tired. From the corner of his eyes he saw black shapes skittering across the floor, running like vermin over the limbs of his fellow aspirants. The youths sat cross-legged in rows, facing towards the rose window at the top of its deep shaft. Luis let it captivate him. How strange the light was there, and how different the air to breathe. There was no glass in the window's elegant traceries, and the scents of this alien world were free to blow in and beguile him. Dust and more dust, the dryness of it less than the extremes of the Great Salt Waste, but deeper somehow. Baal had never known oceans. Its aridity was inherent.

Incense wafted in through the open ironwork of the chapel gate. Two sentries in full plate remained at guard there. Every five hours or so, the Space Marines gathered for convocation in the basilica. He could understand little of what they said, for the native speech of Baal's moons had diverged from the High Gothic, but he caught enough to be surprised at what he heard. What he took for sermons were not. The Chaplains exhorted their brothers to deep thought, and restraint against thirst, and considered action. Though they asked for His guidance, they did not praise the Emperor as a god, but spoke to Him as a leader, and when they turned to Sanguinius, it was not as a saint but as a much-missed father. Services came and went through the vigil, setting a rhythm that would later dictate the days of Luis' life forever.

By the end of the third day, he could barely keep his head up. Aspirants began to fall asleep. It had seemed until that point that all of them would pass the test, but once one drifted away, others followed. As each one fell asleep, whether they toppled from their sitting position or their heads drooped to their chests, they were dragged out by the sentries. They awoke, and pleaded to be given another chance. One tried to fight against the hands pulling him from his fellows, and screamed out his anguish. The Blood Angels were unmoved, and took him away with the rest. The boys were never seen again. Not until years later did Luis learn their fate.

The booming voices of the Chaplains and the beautiful hymns of the brothers seemed not to cease now with the close of each service, but continue on, becoming ever more elaborate. Such sweet music filled Luis' ears that he began to cry. Despite the tears brimming in his eyes, they were intolerably dry and scratchy. They gained weight, until they seemed to be shutters of lead that had to be bodily held up, and he was so tired, and the muscles that held them back so puny. His limbs hurt from inactivity. His circulation was pinched off and his feet cold from the stone. His fingers twitched, and an unpleasant tingling troubled his nerves.

He felt light, lighter than he had in the void. His spirit seemed tethered to his body by the weakest tissue, and threatened to tear free at any moment. His head nodded, and the gathering disassociation of sleep poured into his mind, thick as mud under crack salt. The chapel retreated. The sense of his corporeal being dissolved. Images whirled through his consciousness, so lucid that he mistook them for reality. He was back on Baal Secundus. His father and mother looked at him, the wind tugging at their clothes.

'Father!' he said. His father stared back at him angrily, his arm tightening around his wife's shoulders. Luis' mother smiled and nodded encouragingly.

'You are an angel, my son,' she said, though her lips did not move. 'Spread your wings and fly.'

There was a flash of light on golden armour in the sky behind her.

The music swelled and swelled, the sound of the heavens. Surely the voice of the Emperor could not be so sweet.

A hand touched his shoulder, and he jerked fully awake again. He had failed, he was sure. But instead of the red-armoured sentries, the golden angel was in front of him. He filled the room with his presence, but no other saw him. The golden angel shook his head and rested a hard armoured hand on his shoulder. Strength flowed from it into Luis. He smiled.

'Thank you,' he said.

'Aspirant,' said a gruff, vox-moderated voice.

Luis blinked in confusion. The golden angel was gone. An angel of death stood in his place, his helm a grinning, bone-white death's head.

'The vigil is over,' said Malafael. 'Get up, Luis Dante.'

Around him dazed boys were being helped to their feet by blood thralls. Sanguinary Priests stood about the room overseeing their efforts. A number of boys had gone.

'Fifty-seven of you remain,' said Malafael. 'It is time. The Ritual of Insanginuation begins.'

At the centre of a chanting procession they were taken through the cathedral. Luis walked light-headed. The world had taken on an unreal cast. The statues of angels had become living creatures trapped in stone that moved with liquid menace, threatening to break free from their imprisonment at any moment. The green eye-lenses of his potential brothers hid secrets he no longer wished to share. He could not understand the words the Blood Angels sang. The incense fumes stung his eyes and hurt his throat. He swayed on his feet, pins and needles raging through his limbs. Firm hands steadied him. He looked up to meet the fanatical eyes of a blood thrall. He sang into Luis' face, his breath cloyed with wine and spices. Lorenz walked by him stiffly, his reddened eyes directed ahead. Two gateways of black stone, barely distinguishable from the carved walls, creaked open. Lines of power-armoured warriors marched from both, joining the throng. The Chaplains were shouting, the Sanguinary Priests too. Warriors touched his shoulder. Blood thralls held him up. They were singing, all of them, joyful songs that promised battle.

The assembly gathered around the statue of Sanguinius. The primarch's sorrowful face swam in and out of focus.

Rugon and Araezon were there among other Sanguinary Priests. They ascended part way up steps leading to a great altar at Sanguinius' feet. They gathered around one of their number whose armour was more heavily modified than the other priests. The blood thralls fussed over the right arms of the priests, removing armour plates to expose smooth, flawless skin. Blue veins pulsed under its translucent perfection. The blood-hued crags of armoured Space Marines crowded the aspirants, jostling each other, seemingly without the controlled order they had previously exhibited.

A bell tolled. The assembly fell silent, and the High Priest spoke.

'Aspirants, I am Dereveo, Sanguinary High Priest of the Blood Angels. This is the last of your tests. Soon you will sleep. If you awaken, you will be of our number. It is time for you to look upon the faces of those you would call brother.'

The Space Marines reached up to their helmets. Helmet seals hissed as they were disengaged, so insistent and disorienting Luis woozily expected a plague of serpents to crawl over his feet. Beneath every war mask was a face of unbelievable beauty, so similar to the visage of holy Sanguinius that they could have been blood relatives. He looked around himself. More perfect faces emerged. Some were older than others in a way that was hard to define. The perfection of some was marred by injury, but under the marks of war and the years all shared a look. They were brothers in more than name.

Dereveo was older than some; his golden hair had turned silver, and was worn unusually long. He smiled at the recruits. His teeth were even and white. His eye teeth were unnaturally long: a predator's fangs.

'To be a Blood Angel is to embrace blood and death. To be a Blood Angel is to thirst for blood and death.'

A pair of blood thralls brought forwards a wooden reliquary. From this, Dereveo took out a huge cup, its bowl cast from gold in the semblance of a skull. He handled it reverently and lifted it above his head.

'This is the Red Grail. In this vessel, the blood of the lord Sanguinius was caught.' He lowered it. A circle of Sanguinary Priests crowded around the cup and extended their right forearms. Each produced a tiny, razor-sharp knife, and opened an artery. Blood splashed into the bowl in spurting starts, before their enhanced bodies quickly staunched the flow.

'Always we have used the blood of our father to activate the sacred gene-seed you will soon be implanted with. After our father was murdered at the hands of the arch-traitor, his blood was taken from this cup and injected into the veins of our Sanguinary Priests. Each one of us entrusted with this most holy duty is a living host for the blood and spirit of our gene-lord.'

A second circle of priests crowded the cup. They too slit their wrists and allowed their life fluid to patter into the grail. The hot, coppery smell of blood was everywhere. The Blood Angels changed upon experiencing the scent, morphing from angels to monsters. Though their faces remained perfect, their eyes dilated, their skin reddened and their fangs grew longer, extruding from gums and pricking at lower lips.

'Each one of you will be invested with the gifts of the change, granted to this Chapter by the Emperor Himself in ages past. You will be infused with the blood of Sanguinius, and his seed will take root in your organs and alter you, making you more than a man.'

The third and final group of Sanguinary Priests added their vitae to the cup. Dereveo took a tiny crystal phial from a cushion held by a thrall and opened it. He let a single drop of clear liquid fall into the blood. He stoppered the phial. The blood smoked.

'First, you shall drink, and by this act take your first step to becoming a champion of the Emperor of Mankind.'

A boy was grabbed by a Blood Angel whose face had twisted into that of a grinning fiend. He was half coaxed, half dragged to the steps. The grail was lowered to his lips.

'Drink! Drink and know the last satisfying of your thirst,' commanded Dereveo. 'From this day forth, it shall never be slaked.'

The boy took a sip, and spluttered. More blood was forced down his throat. He came away gasping, his lips coated red.

'More! Bring them all!' commanded Dereveo. The Blood Angels shouted out encouragement rowdily. Their civilised airs were torn away.

Luis took the blood like all the rest. It slid down his throat, sensuously thick but repellent. When it hit his stomach it curdled,

and he feared he would vomit up the sacred life-stuff of the Great
Angel. His vision, already made hyper-real by sleeplessness, distorted further. A red stain tinted his sight. He gasped, and a trickle
of blood dribbled from his mouth onto his chin. He wiped it off,
smearing the sleeves of his robe.

'The change will be upon you. Some of you will not be able to
withstand it, and will die.' The High Priest's voice slowed. 'Those
that live will experience a life of war!'

'War! War! War!' chanted the Blood Angels. 'For the Emperor!
For Sanguinius!'

A drip of red fell into Luis' soul, spreading ripples across a thickening pond of vitae. His eyes rolled up into the back of his head,
and he collapsed.

War. War beat out its drum across the void. From one side of the
galaxy to the other, the sons of the Emperor fought each other.
Luis witnessed the heartbreaking spectacle of warriors meant to
ensure mankind's survival tearing each other to pieces while dark
gods laughed.

He fell through the sky, a burning portent of better times.

He crawled from the wreckage of a wrecked suspension pod
onto the surface of a blasted world, his child's mind full of bewil-
derment and fear. Young wings twitched on his back.

He wrestled a titanic being in the sky, whose radiated fury threatened to eclipse all reason.

He was the lord of hosts, and the galaxy shouted his name in
approbation.

The desert stretched before him. The fate of his people sorrowed
him.

His true father stood before him, radiant in His majesty.

A dark face snarled out its hate as it drove down at him with a
weapon cloaked in diabolical power.

Signus. Ultramar. Melchior. Kayvas. Murder. Names of worlds
he had never visited whirled through his mind. The memories
of Sanguinius flooded into him, bound up with his genetic code,

suffusing themselves into the meat of his body. He wrestled daemons, for he knew them for what they were. He battled traitors he
had once loved. Rage and sorrow fought their own battles in his
heart. He nursed suspicions that his father had known, all along,
and grew introverted and bitter.

And yet he could not speak of these things, for he was the Great
Angel, the most perfect and most beloved of the Emperor's unruly
sons. His sorrow went unvoiced. And always the rage, the terrible
desire to kill and slay at the edge of his consciousness which he
dared not reveal to any being. He looked to his brother Angron, and
feared what he might become. He turned away, but the anger never
left him. In his soul, mercy and violence hung in precarious balance.

Sanguinius became Luis, and Luis became Sanguinius. His existence, so much lesser than the primarch's, was subsumed and
fragmented. For a time, Luis ceased to be, and he was plunged
into the awful life of a demigod. His ordeal went on forever, a
string of waking nightmares that came at him in no logical order,
assailing him with fresh horrors. The sainted Sanguinius' life was
one of despair, and despair awakened in Luis' breast in response.

Finally, finally, he was at the end. The red of his own blood
obscured his vision. The face of Horus stared down at him in
triumph, but it was not Horus who regarded him through his
brother's eyes, but something far older and far worse. His wings
were broken. His body shattered. Pain and sorrow were all that
remained to him.

The vision rippled. Luis was aware of himself again. He was sinking through a thick ocean of blood, down and down, pushed at
by the pulsing current of a titanic, dying strength. The beat of a
giant heart, Sanguinius' heart. It pulsed slowly, rippling the seas
of vitae into galaxy-engulfing vortices. The pulse slowed further.
Then it stopped. The ocean of blood stilled, and Luis sank away.

Gentle dark enwrapped him.

The pulse started again, weaker, doubled. Two hearts pulsed.

Luis was no more.

* * *

He awoke trapped and thrashing. The space he occupied was tilted off vertical and barely larger than his body, and full of liquid tainted red by bloody fragments. A dim light shone through the murk. His limbs were enmeshed in strings of cables. Embedded needles tore free, stinging him as he flailed. On his face was a mask of some kind, and in panic he tore it off and screamed. Liquid flooded his lungs. He was drowning, and he fought against it with furious might, hammering against an unyielding surface, not realising that he was not dying, but breathing freely.

Mechanical noises sounded beneath his feet. The liquid gurgled and the level dropped. His eyes were uncovered. The light came from a tiny round window in front of him. Outside, shapes obscured by streaks of gore moved. Peeping chimes sang urgently around him. Blinking the thick liquid from his eyes, he tore at the pads on his chest and the needles piercing his arms and thighs, and roared like a beast. Memories of betrayal and death tormented him, and all around was blood and more blood.

Locks disengaged. Light cracked around the wall in front of him. Warning tocsins blaring nasally, the wall lifted, revealing itself to be a lid, and the space he occupied a sarcophagus of ribbed metal. The coffin tilted upright. Hands reached for him. He batted at them and snarled. His teeth were sharp and pierced his lips. The hands slipped on his skin.

In a flood of bloodied amniotic medium, he fell forwards onto a shining floor of basalt. Tormented faces screamed in his mind. A great claw descended towards his wings and broke them. Sorrow filled his heart. He knelt there on all fours, panting, as the woes of another's life tortured him. Red tinged his vision. An unquenchable thirst gripped him. All sensation had been replaced by pain. He no longer knew who he was.

'This one fought all the way through the transformation,' a vox-moderated voice said. 'Another for the tower.'

'Or a warrior of fated promise,' said another. A hand rested gently on his shoulder. His head snapped round, teeth bared. The hand remained in place. 'Brother Dante. Brother Dante, can you hear me?'

For a moment the hand withdrew a fraction, the owner alarmed at the savagery of his charge.

Dante. An angel's name. Dante.

The red mist receded. The last recollections of Sanguinius flickered from his mind. He was in a low-ceilinged hall, full of sarcophagi. Up and down the row, servitors and transhuman giants worked, hauling naked, massively muscled warriors screaming into the world.

He looked down at his hands and arms. They were enormous, swollen with ropes of muscle. Not his hands. Once he recognised that they were different, he remembered who he was.

'I... am... Luis,' he panted.

'You are Dante now,' said the voice. Dante blinked. A Space Marine in a white-and-red surgical suit bent down to him. 'I am Brother Araezon. Do you remember me?'

'Dante,' he said. 'You are Sanguinary Priest to the Tenth Company.'

'And you are now a member of that company, and a neophyte to our Chapter.' Araezon's angelic face softened with relief. 'You are aspirant no more!'

'Arise, neophyte,' growled the vox-voice. Chaplain-Recruiter Malafael reached out an armoured hand. Unlike the others in the chamber, he was fully armoured and masked.

Dante took his hand and rose. He felt strong, and massive. When he stood, he could look Malafael straight in his eye-lenses. He held up his hands in wonder.

'What has happened to me?' he said.

'You have spent a year in the Hall of Sarcophagi undergoing the Blood Change,' said Araezon. 'After you fell asleep, you were implanted with the sacred seed of our lord, the Great Angel, activated with the infusion of his precious blood. You have passed your final test, and been granted the blessings of the Emperor's knowledge. You are a Blood Angel.'

Others were coming out of their sarcophagi, smeared in jelly and blood. A tide of slick fluid rose over the floor.

He saw a half-familiar face. 'Lorenz?' said Dante. He could barely believe what he saw. Lorenz had changed almost beyond recognition. He was as tall as the other brothers, fully mature. Not a man, but more than a man, hugely muscled, his face so broad and heavy it pushed at the furthest definition of human. Yet at the same time it was radiantly handsome, stamped with the sharp beauty of Sanguinius. Strangest of all, underneath these changes, Dante could still see his friend.

'Come, neophyte,' said Araezon. 'Come and see.'

'Yes, my lord,' said Dante, and was shocked at the bass rumble of his voice. He swallowed. The internal make-up of his throat felt different.

Araezon laughed. 'You may call me brother, neophyte, as I shall call you, once your period in the Scout Company is done.' He took Dante's hand and led him towards the far wall. The screams and shouts of second birth echoed through the chamber, but Araezon's calm voice cut through it.

Against the wall was set a large mirror in a wheeled frame. Dante saw Araezon approach with a stranger. It took a moment for him to realise the powerful creature he saw was himself. The blemishes of life on Baal had gone. His skin was alabaster smooth, and pale as if it had never felt the touch of the sun. His face was no longer his own, but a blend of Luis' and Sanguinius'. Araezon released his hand and Dante stood in front of the reflection in silent amazement. Only his eyes remained unchanged in appearance: pale amber, his father's eyes. But they looked out from the face of an angel.

He would learn in later life that not all Space Marines were made this way. Outside of the bloodline of Sanguinius, such rapid maturation processes were unused, the specialised organs that made a Space Marine implanted gradually over a period that stretched into years. Not so for the Blood Angels. All the organ seeds were put in at the same time, save the last.

'I am an angel?'

'Almost,' said Malafael. 'Years of training await you. If you survive that, you will be implanted with the black carapace. That final gift is what truly defines us. It is into the carapace that the interface ports are set. Without it, our battleplate is useless.'

Lorenz was led to his side, then another new brother. They were silent, too awed to talk.

A frantic thundering came from one of the sarcophagi. Alarms rang, and Malafael grunted and half ran towards the sound. Dante saw now that there were bodies on the floor, three of them, draped in blood-red sheets.

Malafael stopped by a sarcophagus. It began to open, but the lid was bashed aside and sent skidding across the floor. The brother within burst out, lines and wires ripping from his skin. With clawed hands he flew into one of the servitors tending to his awakening. With inhuman strength he wrenched the cyborg's head back, and buried his long fangs into the wizened grey flesh of his throat.

Malafael raised his boltgun and fired. The boom as it detonated made the newly formed Blood Angels flinch. The crazed neophyte fell to the floor, headless.

'The process does not always work,' said Araezon sadly. 'You have had your first glimpse of a beautiful but savage world. Come. You must eat. You have been sustained by complex philtres for the last year, but your body requires meat and wine.'

The dead neophyte was covered over. A blood thrall, tiny now, led them from the hall.

Dante could not keep his eyes from the man's neck, where the skin throbbed to the pulse of his heart.

The pained cacophony of rebirth followed them, resounding throughout the fortress-monastery, and continued long into the night.

CHAPTER THIRTEEN

FIVE GRACES

457.M40
The Arx Angelicum
Baal
Baal System

Dante woke from horrifying dreams to hard artificial light. He blinked away visions of twisted masks, and groaned. His eyes opened upon a maze of pipework and conduits. Lumen balls of long, stiff pipe mounts hummed in square formation. The small windows of the barracks were red and dull.

Dante's mouth was dry and tasted of metal. His forearm slid from his forehead. He blinked and wiped at an itchy crust on his face. His fingers came away powdered with gritty blood. He had bitten his arm in his nightmares. Clusters of paired holes, scabbed over already, marred his newly perfect skin.

'Still night,' groaned Lorenz. He rolled over on his cot, bare feet slapping the cold floor.

Dante sat up. His awakening yesterday, and the lavish feast that had followed, seemed like a dream.

A clarion fanfare rang through the bare dormitory.

'Neophytes!' A familiar voice boomed at them. 'You will rise. You will dress. Your training begins today. Wait at the table to break your fast.'

'Captain Verono,' said Ristan.

'He's our lord now,' said Dante. 'I suppose it will be him that trains us.'

'What do you know about it?' said a queasy looking neophyte. He staggered past with a couple of others to the plasteel ablutorials sticking out from the wall and was noisily sick.

'I'm so damn thirsty,' said Lorenz.

'There's water,' said Ristan, rubbing at his eyes and pointing to a large glass sphere embedded in another wall.

'It's not just thirsty – it's more like hungry and thirsty at the same time...' Lorenz's eyes lost focus.

'It could be worse – you could be them,' said Duvallai, walking by. He pointed at the sick neophytes. The sharp smell of vomit spoiled the air.

'Can we smell better, or does that really stink?' said Dante, wrinkling his nose. He could taste the neophyte's meal in the scent, though it did not make him nauseous as he might expect. He got up and went for water. His body was strange to him; its proportions threw him off, and although he felt inherently more graceful than he had been, he kept misjudging where his limbs were and smacking into things. The damage to the objects was significantly greater than any he did to himself. He barked his shin on a cot, bending its frame and sending it scraping across the floor. A bruise flowered on his skin and faded just as quickly. He spent a minute dumbly staring at it, until Laziel slapped him on the back.

'Are you going to move or stay standing there?' he said peevishly. Dante's anger rose shockingly fast. He brought it under control and stood out of the way.

'My thanks... brother,' mumbled Laziel, abashed at his tone. 'I'm desperate for something to drink.'

Dante went with him to the water orb. One hemisphere bulged out of the wall, the other went into the rock. He laid his hands on the cool surface. The glass was flawless. Amazement at the smooth beauty of the vessel and the amount of water it held pushed his other thoughts away.

'There must be two hundred gallons of water in here,' he said.

'More, I reckon. I've never seen so much clean water in one place,' said Laziel. He opened the tap, filling a silver cup to the brim. Shining bubbles swam up the glass ball. He drank and gasped appreciatively. 'Sweet, too.' He took another three cups, gulping each faster than the one before. He stopped halfway down the third with a frown, and walked away.

Dante understood Laziel's actions soon enough. No amount of water could quench his thirst. Each drink he took worsened the sensation, and he left troubled and still thirsty, his belly stretched taut with water. A line of other Scouts waited behind him, all of them complaining of thirst.

In a locker bearing his Scout number, Dante found a set of loose-fitting fatigues in blood-red. The neophytes dressed, and in ones and twos they took their seats at the barracks' refectory tables.

Of the hundreds of youths who had set out to take part in the trial on both moons, forty-eight had made it through to the very end. Their conversation died on their lips. Their first day as angels, and they had no idea what was expected of them.

'What now?' whispered one of them.

'It's not like wisdom has landed on our shoulders,' said Duvallai. 'What are we supposed to do?'

They looked at one another. Lorenz grinned at Dante. 'Funny, isn't it? We're in the heaven of the Blood Angels!'

The doors banged open. 'I fail to see the humour in your situation, neophyte,' said Araezon as he strode inside. He wore his day robes. Blood thralls followed in a double line, pushing carts stacked with covered plates. 'You have won a great honour. We will see if you are worthy of keeping it. If you are incapable of understanding that, perhaps you are not worthy.'

Lorenz's face fell. 'Sorry, my lord.'

Araezon stopped at the head of the table. 'You will be taken to your first training session shortly. First, you must eat. When you have passed the first stages of training, you will be allowed to join the other neophytes and the rest of the Chapter in the Great Hall. Before that, you will take your meals in here.'

'There are others?' asked someone.

Araezon gave him a hard stare. 'Of course there are. They proceed through their training. You are at the primary stage. Eventually, you shall pass this and advance to the secondary. After that, you will be inducted as Scouts into the Tenth Company, and serve the Chapter on the field.'

The blood thralls put bowls in front of them. Cautiously, the boys removed the covers and sniffed suspiciously.

'What by Terra is this?' said Duvallai. A number of others shared his frown, but others looked at the slop before them with relish. The bowl was filled with thick blood. Dante poked at the hunks of raw meat bobbing in it with his finger.

'Blood gruel,' said Araezon. 'Your bodies are still changing. This food contains the necessary nutrient balance, along with certain preparations, to make sure that your Emperor's gifts finish their maturation processes.'

'What animal is it from?' asked Ristan.

Araezon ignored him. 'Who here vomited this morning?'

The neophytes who had been ill tentatively raised their hands. It was comical. They had the bodies of demigods, but the mannerisms of boys.

'See me after you have eaten. I shall test you all again later today. Do not be concerned. It is a matter of chemical imbalance and is easily rectified. Now eat,' said Araezon.

Dante bent his head close to the gruel and breathed in deeply. Flashes of insight sparkled in his mind's eye. Things that grew that yearned for the earth, animals taken from their flock. The ecstatic face of a man bled white. He shook his head. Some boys pushed away the food. Dante would have been one of them, but the smell of blood fired his appetite so that it exceeded his revulsion, and before he knew it he was spooning the raw mix into his mouth with his fingers. His thirst burned his gullet, then quickly subsided as the first cold blood and meat hit his stomach. He turned to Lorenz, his mouth full and his face smeared with blood.

'My thirst is gone,' he whispered. Other neophytes remarked on the same thing, and on how good the food tasted, and the barracks filled with their chatter. The acoustics in the room were terrible, muffling some sounds and turning others painfully sharp.

Araezon surveyed the neophytes. 'You are performing satisfactorily. Eat. Then we shall begin your training.'

After they broke their fast, Araezon led them in a period of meditation designed to balance the working of their new bodies, so he said. Not long after that, a wheeled servitor came to the barracks and commanded monotonously that the neophytes follow. The cyborg set off at a fast pace, and the neophytes ran to keep up with it in a column four abreast. The halls and passageways of the fortress-monastery seemed endless, honeycombing the rock curving round the great central space. Although it was spotlessly clean, lavishly decorated and in fine repair throughout, much of it appeared deserted except for the odd blood thrall or man-machine. Dante wondered what kind of place it was, how it was built and how extensive were its halls. Lorenz had other matters on his mind.

'What do you suppose our first training will be?' said Lorenz. 'Swords? Guns? Maybe they'll teach us how to fly!'

Dante shook his head. 'It'll be nowhere near so exciting. This is going to take years.'

'You're a pessimist, you know that?' grumbled Lorenz.

Dante proved to be right. They entered a large hall. The servitor halted suddenly, the neophytes right behind it running into its back. Lights snapped on, revealing yet another massive hall, this one full of rows of workbenches and tools and objects covered in dust sheets.

The column broke up in confusion, the young Space Marines wandering around the place.

'What's this?' said Ristan. He picked up a pot from a bench. 'Where are the weapons? These are paintbrushes!'

'Is this the Armoury?' someone else said. 'Are you malfunctioning?' he said loudly and slowly to the servitor.

The servitor spun around to face the youth. 'This is your destination,' it said in its dead voice. 'This is not the Armoury.'

It reversed and turned, and rolled out of the room at the same
pace it had led them there, 'scattering neophytes.

'Are we here alone?' said Laziel.

'What are we supposed to do?' said a neophyte called Arvin.

At the far end of the room, a figure jerked into life. The young
Space Marines' attention went to the movement instantly, like a
flock of hunting raptors catching sight of prey. A battered-looking
servitor limped up the room. The left arm, shoulder and left half
of its face had been replaced by machinery, as had most of its legs.
Although the workmanship of its decoration was astounding, the
mechanicals must have been poorly made or worn, because it
lurched unsteadily towards them.

'Great, another servitor,' said Ristan.

The machine-man's remaining eye burned.

'That's not a servitor,' said Dante.

'Your young friend is correct!' barked the ruined man. 'I am
Brother Cafael, Master of Artistry.' He clanked closer.

'Artistry? We were supposed to be warriors!' said Laziel, holding
up the paintbrush. 'How am I supposed to defend the Imperium
with this?' A nervous laugh rippled through the neophytes.

Cafael increased his pace and came to a stop before Laziel. He
stared at the neophyte long and hard. Laziel waved the paintbrush at him.

Too quickly to see, Cafael swung out his arm and sent the young
Space Marine sprawling to the ground.

'I have served the Chapter for six hundred years,' said Cafael.
'Ninety years ago, I was crippled. I am no more fit for combat duty.
Do not underestimate me because of my infirmity. I may be half
a man, but I am twice the warrior you are.'

He held out his organic arm to Laziel and hauled him back up.
Laziel bobbed his head apologetically.

Cafael swivelled and addressed the room. 'There are many battles you must fight as Blood Angels. None are as hard as the one

you will fight with yourself. You will have noticed the great thirst that you feel.'

The scattered neophytes nodded.

'In a circle! Comport yourselves like warriors, not a rabble!' shouted Cafael. The neophytes quickly rearranged themselves. 'The thirst will abate as you adjust to your change. But it will return throughout your lives, and when it does it can overthrow sanity. Here I will teach you the Five Angelic Graces, so that you might learn to control the thirst, which we name as red, and to avoid its worse twin, the rage, which we name as black.'

Cafael fixed them all with his ferocious stare.

'These urges derive from the passions of Sanguinius. We are fortunate to feel such emotion, for we harness it for the purposes of our art and our warmaking. But there is danger in it. Sanguinius was made to be perfect. We are made in his image, but alas, we are not perfect, and such great passions as he bore overfill the human soul so that reason spills out. A man cannot bear easily the choler of a demigod. For though the gifts given you are many and varied in their wondrousness, great power brings evil with it in many forms. As you learn to control your gifts, you must learn to control your passions, the red and the black, and direct them to your will, lest they supplant it.'

His revelation stunned the neophytes into silence.

'You will learn more of the Red Thirst and Black Rage in time, how they affect you and where they come from. For now, let it be known that they exist, and that you must oppose them through the Five Graces of our Chapter. Your first lesson is their names,' he said gruffly. 'They are thus: Focus, Humility, Mercy, Restraint and the last and greatest of all, Forgiveness.'

'Are these a warrior's traits, my lord?' said Lorenz. Dante nudged him hard, but Lorenz blocked his elbow.

'There are the Warrior's Virtues, as there are the Angel's Graces. You will learn both, in time,' said Cafael. 'With me, you shall focus on the graces. Ask me not of the virtues again today.'

'Why should we forgive our enemies? The creatures that prey

on the Imperium deserve neither forgiveness nor mercy,' said
Arvin.

Cafael turned a metal-toothed smile on Arvin. His face was like
a ruined cathedral, a glorious building shattered by war that preserved some vestige of its beauty, but those metal teeth tipped the
balance in favour of hideousness.

'You will fight and kill men and women. You will slaughter whole
worlds at the command of our Chapter Master, and you will do
so willingly. You may come to wish to kill everything you see, in
the end. You must learn when to stay your hand. But you are right,
my boy. No one who defies the Emperor of Mankind deserves our
forgiveness!' he said.

'Then I ask you again, why should we forgive our enemies?'

Cafael made a dismissive noise. 'You are callow, and arrogant with youth. You see with certainty the answer to the wrong
question. Forgiveness is not for our enemies. Forgiveness is for
ourselves,' he said. 'You will have seen the great artworks of our
home and the fine decorations lavished upon the wargear of our
brothers.' Cafael raised his voice and held up his hand to indi-
cate the carved ceiling, the frescoes around the walls. 'All of this
was done not by our thralls, but by we brothers. Through the calm
practice of the arts, you shall master your passions and yoke them
to good. Then you shall be able to master the galaxy.

'Make no error, the education you shall receive will broaden
your minds in every direction. Deep understanding of history and
mathematics, and many other subjects will be yours. The arts of
war your other instructors will teach you will save your lives, and
the lives of thousands of others. But the arts I shall impart will save
your souls. The precision of engineering, the application of paint,
the striking of the sculptor's hammer, the wielding of the calligraphy pen – through these and more shall you defy the monsters
that dwell within you. You look like Blood Angels, but you are yet
boys given the power of gods. Without the Five Angelic Graces, the
gifts the Emperor has given you will be useless. You will not learn
to use them, and the power of our lord's anger will overwhelm you.

These lessons are as important, if not more so, than the combat doctrine you will be asked to absorb. Is that clear?'

The neophytes nodded and said yes.

'Good. Firstly, you must learn how to live in splendour as Sanguinius decreed, for all beauty was precious to him. Under my supervision you shall outfit your barracks and make it a place fit for angels to dwell. Now choose a bench. And choose carefully – it will be yours for the next five years. The first lessons are always the hardest. Fail them, and you will fail all.'

The boys chose desks randomly. None of them had anything to recommend them over the others.

Cafael waited for them to be ready.

'We begin,' he said, and took up a paintbrush.

Days turned to weeks, and weeks to months. Combat instruction began four weeks after their lessons in artistry. Dante absorbed everything eagerly, but his favourite lessons were those under Cafael. He took deep joy in the creation of beautiful objects. The lessons were formal to begin with, but as their expanded minds mastered new skills quickly, they were soon given free rein to create whatever they wanted. They were not yet permitted to modify their uniform or gear, but their barracks was gradually transformed. Painted panels covered over the pipework. The walls were hidden behind murals and stucco work. There was no plan behind the works, and they clashed in style and skill. But the drabness of their new home was replaced by a crude approximation of the fortress-monastery's splendour.

Remembering the angels his father had created for the family roamer, Dante decided to make something similar. The golden angel who had come to him in the desert provided him with a model, and he set to work. Unlike his father, he had access to all the tools of a metallurgist, and his plans grew in ambition. He sketched for days, until he grew despondent and set his book down.

'Neophyte Dante!'

Dante looked up. He had become so mired in self-reflection that Cafael had come up on him unawares.

Cafael spoke over the clatter of tools in the workroom. 'Why do you sit inactive?'

'I plan a statue to honour my father, but as I draw, I realise that the work will far surpass his own, and this seems arrogant, as if I would deliberately belittle him.'

'You cannot belittle Sanguinius,' said Cafael.

'I meant my other father.'

'You have grown beyond him and all other mortals,' said Cafael.

'It does not mean I love him less,' said Dante.

'You must put him from your mind.' Cafael rested his calloused hand on Dante's shoulder. 'You have a new father now. The memory of your life before will fade in time.'

'Will I forget?'

'Some do. Some forget everything. Some remember. If you held your father in such high regard, you will never forget him entirely.'

'Do you remember?' asked Dante.

Cafael's face softened to near humanity. 'No, neophyte. I can recall nothing from before my insanguination. I do not remember remembering. To my mind, I have always been a Blood Angel. Now, let's have a look at your sketches. You are to attempt a bronze?'

'Yes, my lord. It seemed fitting, although I would like to make the wings from ribbon, if I can get it to look right. That's what my da... my father used. When I was a child, I used to like the way they fluttered in the wind. It would be good to capture that somehow.'

Cafael picked up Dante's sketchpad. On the first leaf were many studies of detail for the statue's hands, executed in soft charcoal. He made approving noises. 'These are very good. You have a natural talent that your training here will only bring out.' He turned over another page. 'This face for example is...' He frowned, the skin of his forehead puckering oddly where it joined the metal of his augmetics. He flicked the pages over quickly. He held the pad out suddenly. On the page was a full sketch of the angelic warrior Dante had seen. It wasn't the statue he planned to make, but a drawing of how Dante remembered him. From there he had meant to work up a treatment for his bronze.

'Who is this? Where did you see him?' said Cafael urgently.

'My lord, have I done something wrong?'

'Where did you see him?' repeated Cafael.

Dante paled at Cafael's tone. 'In the desert, on the way to Angel's Fall on Baal Secundus. Why? Who is he?'

Cafael looked around to see if any of the others had noticed or were listening. Seeing they were not, he leaned in close. 'Follow me. Immediately.'

The Citadel Reclusiam perched upon the rim of the Arx Angelicum, six-sided and massive, its walls carved into louring skulls that looked in all directions over the desert but one. From the sixth side the soaring Tower of Amareo sprang to spear the sky, the stone flower of its machicolated top sprouting from the peak and laying its shadow across the world like a sword blade.

Dante was taken to the Citadel Reclusiam by blood thralls in black, whose faces were tattooed with the Chaplaincy's death's head. He asked them repeatedly where he was being taken as they took stair after stair up through the Arx Murus. One grew tired of his demands and opened his mouth to show the stub of his severed tongue. After that, Dante asked no more. He was taken across a drawbridge of bright steel that projected from the mouth of one of the citadel skulls. Once within, he was sequestered in a cell whose outer wall was open to the desert.

Dante sat on the edge, marvelling at the size and scale of the Arx. It was a fortress carved from a hollow mountain, the black rock of its flanks planed smooth, studded with weapons batteries, hangar slots, windows and soaring statuary. Lesser peaks around the Arx were remade into redoubts topped with immense defence lasers. The soapy film of void shields encased the whole, dividing it from the deserts. Through the faint purple sheen of the field, Dante looked out over dunes that went on forever under the afternoon sun. He searched the sky for home, but Baal Secundus had not risen. This made him profoundly sad, and he sat and let his legs dangle from the edge. He looked between his knees at a drop a thousand feet high, and he felt nothing. No sense of fear, no terror of the urge to jump. It was a height, a measurable vertical distance, that was all.

He occupied his mind with a thorough survey of the Arx Angelicum. For a while, he derived pleasure from the hot wind blowing over the desert. The void shield tainted it with its strange scent, but allowed it through. Its touch reminded him that Baal truly shared kinship with his sisters.

The door peeped and yawned open. Dante's improved eyes adjusted instantly to the darkness of the interior. Malafael filled the entrance. The Chaplains – and they were numerous – never removed their armour in sight of their battle-brothers, but the suit of each was highly individual. By their wargear were they recognisable.

'Brother-neophyte, come to me,' said Malafael.

Dante went before him and fell to his knees.

'Tell me what you told Cafael, Dante.'

'I told him of the golden warrior I saw on Baal Secundus, my lord.' He related the story of how an angel had saved him from dying of thirst, and how he had seen him again during the Winnowing of Weariness.

'Is that all?'

'Yes!' said Dante.

'Dante, you have no reason to fear to speak your heart and mind to me, if you are telling the truth.'

'I am, my lord!' Dante lifted his eyes. The Chaplain rested a heavy gauntlet upon his head.

'I believe you. Stand, and come with me.' Dante followed the huge figure of the armoured Chaplain through the high spaces of the Reclusiam's heart. A large cross-shaped chamber rose to the top of the citadel. The four ends terminated on the inner face of a skull. The carving inside was as accomplished as on the outer surfaces, and the stone had been cut to a shell so thin it was partly translucent. At the very centre was a large altar under a baldacchino a hundred feet high. Another Chaplain walked by, trailed by servitors pumping out scented smoke from chimneys embedded in their backs. Otherwise, the giant space was empty.

'Do you recall that I was forced to execute one of the neophytes in the Hall of Sarcophagi?' said Malafael, his voice echoing around the Reclusiam.

'Yes, my lord,' said Dante.

'And has Cafael impressed upon you the peril of succumbing to the passions of our lord, the Great Angel?'

'Yes, my lord.'

'That boy I killed had fallen into the Black Rage while he changed. It can happen to any of us, at any time, as soon as the gene-seed is implanted. There are triggers of course, and it can be avoided. That is why we teach you the graces and the arts. But the rage cannot be held off forever. Not by anyone, only forestalled.'

'I understand, my lord.'

'I was close to executing you,' said Malafael bluntly.

'Why?'

'Throughout the process of insanguination, you raged and thrashed in your sarcophagus. You shouted out the names of ancient monsters and heroes.' He laughed gruffly. 'Such was your might, you scored the inner lid of the device with your bare hands.'

'I remember none of this.'

'You would not. You were deep in the blood fever. Some of my order thought you would emerge a monster. Others maintained you would be a warrior of great importance. But you emerged perfect. No aspirant in our records has suffered so much as you and emerged alive, let alone sane.'

'And what did you decide, my lord? I do not feel special.'

'You are wise not to think you are someone of import, neophyte. For all I knew at the time, your swift descent into madness was certain. But now I am not so sure. Here.'

He led Dante to a wall into which was set a gleaming brass representation of the golden warrior.

'It is him!' said Dante.

'And you have never seen this image before your vision in the desert?'

'No, my lord, I swear. I saw statues of angels at Selltown and in Kemrender. Nothing like this. Who is he?'

'It,' said Malafael, breathing a deep sigh, 'is the Sanguinor. No one truly knows who or what it is, only that at times of peril it comes to aid the Chapter. So dire are the circumstances under which it appears there are few witnesses. Throughout our nine-millennia history, it has appeared only so many times as to half fill a slender codex. Each appearance is recorded. Now, the question your revelation poses is, should we include another entry in the record?'

Malafael stared down at Dante.

'I believe what I saw,' said Dante.

Malafael regarded him a moment longer. 'There is something else I wish to show you.'

They went to the side of the great altar. In a niche in the side was a tall brass cylinder worked with marvellous fretwork of beasts and angels intertwined, hunting one another through the foliage of an alien forest. 'This is the Reliquary of Amit, forged by the founder of the Flesh Tearers, one of Sanguinius' most favoured sons. Our brotherhood extends beyond this Chapter, remember that. All of Sanguinius' descendants are close.'

'It is beautiful,' said Dante.

'Study hard, and you might craft the like. However, it is but a housing for the greater glory within.'

The Chaplain lifted the *crux terminatus* badge hanging on a chain around his neck, and pressed it to a lock-stud hidden in the fretwork. The flicker of an energy field played over the reliquary as it shut off. A soft illumination shone through the holes in the metal, and the doors opened silently. Floating in a stasis field was an enormous feather, as long as Dante's leg.

'This is one of the pinions of our lord Sanguinius. It was dropped into the stasis field as it was activated. It has, in effect, been falling for nine and a half thousand years. It is said that as long as it remains suspended and touches not the unclean floor, the sons of the Great Angel shall never fail. See here these flecks of blood, red as the day they were spilled?' He pointed. 'That is his blood, the same blood that now flows in your veins. It is immeasurably precious. There are only two sources of our father's blood that have not been adulterated by inclusion in the living vessels of the Sanguinary Priests. That contained in the Blood Ruby of the lord commander's mask, and that upon this feather here.'

'It is enormous.'

'This is one of the smaller ones, a secondary from his left wing. Sanguinius was a towering figure. I have visited the mausoleum of Roboute Guilliman on Macragge, where the body of the Ultramarines primarch sits in stasis. The primarchs are past our understanding, Dante, as far beyond us as you are beyond the boy you were. They were beings beyond mortal comprehension, and they had many gifts.' He regarded Dante again. 'Among our lord's abilities was the power of foresight, inherited from his own father, the Emperor, Lord of Mankind. The size of our Librarium attests to our primarch's psychic might, for we are shaped by him as much as we were by our birth fathers. His second sight exhibits itself sometimes in our ranks, even in those who are not in other ways considered to be psychic. So tell me, have you had any other visions, Dante?'

Dante hesitated. 'There are the dreams, my lord, of strange battles,' he offered.

'We all share those, the death pangs of Sanguinius and fragments of his recollections. You will grow used to them, or they will destroy you. I speak of foretelling only. Do you have dreams that come to pass? Or waking visions like the one of the Sanguinor?'

'None, my lord.'

'There is nothing more you can tell me of the encounter with the Sanguinor?'

Dante shook his head. 'It seemed... sad. And caring.'

'There are certain writings in the Scrolls of Sanguinius...' Malafael trailed off into reflection.

'What does it mean?'

Malafael took in another deep breath, and his voice quickened. 'It means, neophyte, that I shall be keeping an even closer watch on you. Have you told anyone of this?'

'No,' said Dante.

'Good. I forbid you to speak of it with anyone else. Such knowledge would be dangerous, in the wrong hands. Now you are dismissed. May the Blood flow vital in your veins.'

'But, my lord–'

Malafael cut him off with a chop of his hand. 'No more questions. Be content with what I have told you, and that you have laid eyes upon one of our most holy relics. To ask too much suggests a lack of humility. Pray that tendency does not undo you. Now return to your lessons.'

CHAPTER FOURTEEN

FIRST COMMAND

467.M40

Ash Wastes

Rora

Eudymimous System

Dante pushed the bike as hard as he dared, sending it hurtling over the ash plains of Rora. Dust hung on the air behind him, showing his position as clearly as a banner, but the time for discretion had gone.

He gunned the engine, sending the bike up the side of an ash dune. His breathing mask made a warning chime; its filters were beginning to clog. He glanced at the combat bike's rune display in case the engine intakes were suffering the same. Dante seemed to spend all the time he wasn't fighting on Rora cleaning air filters, reciting prayers to the machine-spirit of his mount. Thankfully, today it was breathing clearly.

He half jumped the ridge at the top of the dune. The wheels spun on the slipface of the dune, the vehicle skiing down the loose ash. He checked a skid, dropped gears and accelerated as he hit the bottom. Waves of ash slumped behind him, burying his tracks.

Lorenz was on lookout by the abandoned pumping station, Dante's keen Space Marine eyes picking out his camouflaged position from hundreds of yards away.

He pushed the combat bike hard up the slope. The ground around the station was firmer, and his mount growled with pleasure as it surged to the base of the pumping tower. Dante brought it to a halt by his friend and shut off the engine.

'You're late,' said Lorenz, slipping his magnoculars back into their case.

Dante dusted ash off the combat bike's faring. Its red livery was covered in a thin layer of grey. 'I had company,' he said. He got off the combat bike and genuflected in thanks to the machine. 'Ork scouts.'

'Were you followed?' said Lorenz. The bike's engine ticked as it cooled. Loose plates of rusted metal banged forlornly on the pumping tower.

'They'll be here soon,' said Dante. 'We don't have much time.' He grabbed the combat bike's handlebars and pushed it past the tower towards the station interior. The strength gifted him by the Emperor's arts astounded him still. Massive with armour plates and an enormous engine, the bike weighed nigh on a ton, but he could move it without difficulty.

Water had once been pumped up from the aquifers of the hills by the station. They had been sucked dry millennia ago, their replenishment ceasing as Rora made its sure and sorry progression from living planet to Imperial hive world. The vast reservoir tanks that surrounded it had collapsed, leaving faint ring-shaped outlines in the sand. The control complex was barely more sound: it was choked with fine ash, jagged holes corroded into its sides. In empty, crumbling machine halls the Scouts camped, their bikes and bivouacs out of sight of prying xenos eyes.

There were two squads. Sixteen neophytes and two brother-sergeants to guide them through the last stage of their training. Sergeant Gallileon was the senior, a warrior with half a millennium's experience in training Scouts. He was a grizzled man with a biting sense of humour, his angelic face scarred by centuries of battle. Sergeant Arael was his second in this campaign, young enough to remember the trials of Scouthood and quick to form bonds with his charges as a consequence.

Gallileon seemed to sense Dante before he saw him. He was explaining something to five of Dante's comrades, sketching in the grey dust burying the floor, but he stood as soon as Dante came into the room, and beckoned to him.

Dante had liked walking through the Scouts barracks as they made their way to the hangars of the Arx Angelicum a few weeks before. The unassigned neophytes looked on jealously, a feeling Dante was glad not to have to endure any more. The younger Scouts had years before they would come anywhere near a battlefield. Dante and his intake were near the end of their journey. All they lacked was the black carapace and the power armour to go with it. The full panoply of war would soon be theirs. Over all things, Dante yearned for a jump pack, to fly like a true angel. He tingled with anticipation thinking of it. But this deployment had been the longest and most gruelling yet, and Dante had come to miss the spartan comforts of the training halls.

'Dante,' said Gallileon. 'What news from Captain Rodrigo?' The sergeant led the Scout into an adjoining room, far enough from the others that they could not eavesdrop.

'The orks are moving on the primary hive, brother-sergeant,' said Dante quietly, aware of his brothers' enhanced hearing. 'The lord captain asks that we rejoin the main force. This is to be the final blow. Our covert operations are to end immediately, and we are free to abandon vox silence.' He withdrew a message tube from his combat webbing and handed it to his superior. 'It's all in there.'

'He told you all this?'

'Yes, brother-sergeant.'

'Hmm,' said Gallileon, opening the tube and removing the scroll inside. He read the contents with one glance, and rolled it up again. 'Well, that's it, all as you said.'

'There's more, brother-sergeant. The area around Rodrigo's forward post was swarming with ork outriders. I was seen.'

Gallileon cocked an eyebrow. 'Unavoidable, I suppose?'

Dante nodded. Gallileon's gaze bored into him, releasing Dante's excuses. 'This time, yes, brother-sergeant. I had to ride for my life. I lost them, but they will have picked up my trail.'

Gallileon was displeased. 'Be more careful in future. Tell me at least that you exacted a heavy soul tally from them.'

'Four dead, at least,' said Dante.

Gallileon placed a hand on Dante's shoulder and guided him back into the main hall. Murmured conversations ceased. All eyes went to Dante and Gallileon.

'Scouts of the Tenth Company!' shouted Gallileon. 'Prepare for battle. The orks are approaching our position, and we must fight free of them. We have been ordered to rejoin the strike group. Today we shall destroy the ork threat. Soon we will depart and return to Baal.'

The Scouts smiled. They were tired of food that tasted of ash. They were tired of hiding for days at a time. Each and every one of them had dreamed of war's glory. The campaign had been a taste of its tedium. They began to talk excitedly.

'Silence now!' Gallileon scowled. 'There is more I must say. For many of you, this is to be your last mission under my tutelage. If you survive this, you shall be ready to wear the blessed battleplate that is every full brother's right and burden. You will be neophytes no more, but warriors of the stars. You shall be the angels of the Emperor, and every man shall fear and love you. I can teach you no more.'

The Scouts' eyes gleamed with excitement and they started speaking again. Gallileon held up his hands, palms down, to quieten them. 'That is if you can shut up for five minutes! You have to survive first. More importantly, you have to impress me. That is the harder task. Dante, give the order of battle.'

Dante's eyes widened in surprise. 'Sergeant?'

'Yes, Dante, I want you to present a plan of attack. You do realise that part of my role is to assess what function you might fill in our Chapter when your training is complete. I'm testing my opinion of you right now. I suggest you hurry, or you'll find yourself guarding munitions trains for the next hundred years.'

Dante cleared his throat. Ristan smirked at him when Gallileon wasn't looking. Lorenz nodded encouragingly. 'Ork outriders are inbound. We've been ordered to regroup with Captain Rodrigo and the Ironhelms, but we're going to have to fight our way through. Mount up?' suggested Dante.

Gallileon looked at him incredulously.

'Sergeant?' asked Dante.

'That is an edification? You will never be more than a line warrior with powers of leadership like that! I am not often mistaken, but it looks like I have misjudged you.'

Dante flushed red. 'I... I'm sorry. It's my first one. I–'

Gallileon shut his eyes and pressed his fingers to his temples. 'By the powers of foresight my gene bond with our sire Sanguinius grants me, I predict you will...' He screwed up his face. 'Be a woeful officer, neophyte. Pitiful.'

The Scouts laughed.

'Well, I don't know what I am supposed to say!' snapped Dante, now deeply embarrassed. He could deliver plans – he had done so before – but Gallileon made him bashful, so anxious of making a mistake he could do nothing but. 'Ork speed cultists usually attack en masse, screens of bikes in front of light transports. Their weaponry is heavier than ours. Attacking them front-on would be counterproductive. We should divide ourselves into a number of groups – maybe three, try to split them up. If we stationed a small squad in the pumping tower with sniper rifles and set a field of cluster mines about the base, we could cut them apart before they can reorganise themselves. We'd avoid fighting them all at once, where they're strongest and...' Dante slowed down. Gallileon was watching him carefully.

'And?' said the sergeant.

'We can scatter them and ride through. We can't kill them all.'

Gallileon nodded and pointed at Dante. 'Now that, young warriors, is a proper plan. Get to it. Brother-Sergeant Arael, if you'd be so good as to assign groups.'

Arael nodded and waved his Scouts to him.

'Be confident, young blood,' said Gallileon. 'You are a Space Marine, the chosen of the Emperor of Terra. Feel it when you speak.' He slapped Dante hard on his pauldron. 'Now ready yourself for combat.'

Lorenz scanned the horizon, intent on the blur where Rora's grey deserts met its blank sky.

'He is in love with those magnoculars, I think,' said Ristan *sotto voce*. The others in the squad laughed.

'Shut up, Scout,' growled Gallileon. 'Let him perform his task. The Emperor has a use for good eyes, and none for a jester.'

The Scouts laughed harder for that.

'They are coming,' said Lorenz. 'Dust plumes on the horizon.'

'Numbers, boy!' said Gallileon gruffly. 'Always give as much information as you can. Information can mean the difference between victory and death.'

'A hundred, maybe. Not a lot, but not a little.'

'Now he sounds like an ork.'

'I'll not say "shut up" again, Neophyte Ristan,' said Gallileon. 'Next time I shall shut you up. You will find it hard to exercise your wit with a broken jaw.'

'Sorry, sergeant.'

'Well then?' asked Gallileon of Dante. 'Stop looking so surprised. It is your plan.'

Dante nodded and activated the vox-set attached to his ear. 'Diversion group two, are you ready?'

'*Affirmative,*' voxed their leader, a Scout called Giacomus from Baal Primus. Dante and he had been in different training cohorts, and he was only just beginning to get to know him.

'Sergeant Arael?'

'*We can see them, Scout Dante,*' said Arael. '*Lorenz guesses right. We count seventy-two attack bikes, and twenty ork warriors in three transports.*' As part of the equipment they had to monitor the Scouts, Gallileon and Arael had complete control over the neophytes' vox-sets. They could hear everything the younger

Space Marines said at all times, if they wished. '*What are your orders?*'

Dante hesitated. They'd all run command-and-control exercises, but he had never been given command in a combat situation. 'Maintain silence until they close? Open fire at medium range, to make sure of high kill ratio? As soon as they see you they'll come for you... We need to split them up – get them angry so they won't notice they're dying. Sergeant?'

Gallileon crossed his arms and shrugged. 'That is not my problem to solve.'

'*You are the one giving the orders this afternoon, Scout,*' voxed Arael. '*But you know, if they were bad, Brother Gallileon or I would let you know. A word of advice – stop phrasing commands as questions. The Blood Angels do not operate as a committee. Arael out.*'

Gallileon sat across his bike, his arms crossed, staring at Dante. 'Sergeant?'

Gallileon goggled his eyes at Dante. 'Neophyte?' he mimicked Dante's voice. 'So, do you think we have all day here?'

'No. Sergeant,' said Dante. 'Let's ride up the ridge, close formation. Revane, keep on the inside of the formation. Stand ready to fire your grenade launcher when I order.'

'Yes, Dante,' said Revane.

'Let us keep it slow, lure them in. We should split them closer to the tower than further out.'

'Why?' challenged Gallileon.

'Greater concentration will provide a more target-rich environment for our snipers, sergeant, and they are more likely to ride straight onto the mines.'

Gallileon nodded approvingly. 'It sounds like you have learnt something after all. Well then, what are you waiting for? You heard him, Scouts. Move out!'

Engines coughed into life and roared out white exhaust.

Dante led the way towards the approaching dust cloud, feeling proud yet nervous to be put at the head of the group. The bikes fanned out around him, Revane and his heavier weapon protected by the rest. Gallileon rode beside him, scrutinising his every move.

'Make some dust of our own – get their attention and bring them in.' Dante glanced to the far side of the pumping station. Four hundred yards away, their brothers rode out away from them.

Skidding his bike purposefully from side to side, Dante sent up a cloud of dust. His comrades copied him, and soon a column of it was lifting skywards.

'*You have their attention,*' voxed Arael. '*Half have broken off. They are coming towards your position.*'

'Everyone, forward half a mile, double back. Goad them into the chase. Group two, prepare your envelopment.'

The other group of Scout bikers accelerated obliquely towards the ork outriders. The orks saw them late, making them peel further away from the main line of the ork reconnaissance group's advance.

Dante's group moved forwards, approaching the wall of ash and oily smoke thrown up by the orks' half-tracked bikes. Dante got a fleeting glimpse of silhouettes in the smoke. Huge, brutish creatures hunkered over the handlebars of crude machines.

'Fire!' he ordered.

Boltguns mounted on the bike fairings chattered, sending streams of bolt-rounds at the foe. The magnesium line of tracer rounds flared bright in the choking air. Orks exploded, bikes detonated. The orks fired back, but their weapons, though powerful, were shorter ranged than the Space Marines' boltguns. Overpowered for their bikes' small mass, the ork guns sent their vehicles slewing about, and their rounds went whining past. The battlefield was a roaring confusion of engine noise and airborne particles. Dante stole glances left and right. His squad mates maintained perfect formation. Then the orks drew near, and their guns came into effective range.

Despite the unbalancing effect of the guns on the bikes, and the orks' natural inclination to fire without aiming, the sheer number of bullets the xenos' weapons put out meant some were bound to hit. Heavy slugs smacked off Dante's bike's bulletproof tyres and rang off the shield. His comrades ducked low, using their bikes' considerable armour to shelter behind. Phaerist spat a guttural, nomad's oath as a round nicked his shoulder, but none of the Scouts fell.

The bikes roared past one another, like feral world warriors jousting on horseback. Dante ducked a swing from a madly grinning ork, its long tongue lolling from its mouth.

'Spread!' ordered Dante. The combat bikes opened up their formation. Heavier ork vehicles were coming towards the Scouts, a pair of heavily armed halftracks flanking a stripped-down transport crammed with whooping greenskins. Revane's grenade launcher huffed twice, blasting a crater in the dust. The second smashed straight into the halftrack, reducing its driver to paste and blasting off its front wheel. The contraption snagged on the wreck of its front portion and flipped, becoming a tumbling ball of scrap and fire. Bolt-rounds punched orks from their handrails on the transport.

'About!' ordered Dante. In unison, the bikers braked, slammed their left feet down and turned sharply about, back towards the pumping station. They accelerated, gunning down the orks that had charged past them from behind, killing a dozen and causing them to scatter. Dante's squad rushed through.

'*That should have made them sufficiently annoyed,*' voxed Gallileon.

'To the tower, round and back!' voxed Dante.

They sped towards the pumping station, now a dark shape behind wreaths of sand and ash. Orks fired indiscriminately at them.

Air cracked over Dante's head, just audible through the rumble of engines and guns. Arael's men had opened fire. Dante risked a look back. Orks were tumbling from their machines, neat holes punched in their manic faces.

The pump station came close.

'Single file!' he ordered.

The bikes closed up, rushing one after the other along a narrow predefined path back to the station. The orks maintained a wide formation, gaining as the Scout bikers decelerated to fall into single file.

The ground bucked as the orks rode over the cluster mines the Scouts had planted around the tower. Dante's squad jinked and wove through the minefield, the neophytes relying on their superlative memories to guide them through safely. The orks had no such chance. The brighter of them tried to follow the path described by the Scout bikes, but most ended in fiery ruin.

The Scouts roared past the station's buried reservoir tanks, and arced around the back. Giacomus' bike group arrived a moment later. The Scout units crossed paths, blasting apart the few pursuing orks who had made it through the minefield. Lorenz whooped with laughter. Dante smiled. The plan, his plan, had worked.

They emerged around the front to find the ash dunes dotted with smoking bikes and dead orks. The survivors were retreating at speed, falling from their saddles as Arael's snipers calmly picked them off.

Dante slowed and stopped, scanning the area for threats. Gallileon rode up beside him.

'Arael! Get your Scouts down and mounted. We are moving on the front!' bellowed Gallileon.

The Scouts in the tower broke down their sniper rifles quickly and rappelled to the desert floor. Moments later, the first of them came roaring out of the pumping station on their bikes, joining Gallileon's squad.

Gallileon waited for both units to assemble, then nodded at Dante.

Not bad, Dante, he signed with one hand. Not bad at all.

The roar of battle reached the Scouts long before they crested the rise overlooking the plain: the thunderous reports of whirlwind rockets; the buzz-saw rattle of Baal-pattern Predators' guns; the rippling, popping bang of exploding mass-reactive shells intermingled with the gruff chatter of ork stubbers and the weird singing of their energy weapons. A flight of Stormtalons rushed over the Scout bikes, tipping their wings in salute. They disappeared over the brow of a hill, which the Scouts summited shortly afterwards.

Gallileon brought them to a halt at the top, Arael pulling up beside him. He shut off his engine, and the Scouts followed suit. A long, shallow declivity swept down to a plain of baked mud, so similar to parts of Baal Secundus that Dante could almost believe they were home. In the far distance the hollowed-out bulk of Rora's Hive Quintus smoked. It was devoid of life now, and had been burning for three years. The air smelt of burned oil and blood. Dante's eye-teeth twitched in his gums at the scent, and he had to swallow away a flood of saliva.

Tanks billowing oily smoke dotted the hillside. The corpses of orks lay thick in clusters where smaller parts of the greater battle had been fought and decided, their apish limbs entangled. The fight had started on the hill before moving to the plain. A wedge of Blood Angels were driving deep into a sea of orks. The gunships unleashed streaking missiles at an ork heavy tank, destroying it in a spectacular mushroom of fire.

Gallileon made a disapproving noise in his throat.

'The position does not look good,' said Dante.

'It is not. You witness the effects of the rage of our lord, the greatest of angels. Look upon it. Ask yourselves, my Scouts, are you ready to control such fury and bend it to your will?'

'They are in the grip of the thirst?' said Dante.

Gallileon nodded. 'Our brothers are outnumbered, and close to being overwhelmed. They have felt the thirst call, and have answered.'

'They may lose because of it,' said Lorenz.

'It may seem so,' said Gallileon. 'But at times such as these, the thirst can be our greatest weapon. They shall prevail.' He pulled up his breathing mask and spat gritty saliva into the dust.

'Surely it will not be enough,' said Dante. 'They will be slaughtered.' The line of red was very thin, and the orks near numberless.

'Have faith, young one,' said Arael. 'For wonders grace the sky.'

The younger sergeant pointed to a golden figure streaking through the heavens. The figure wore a jump pack fashioned in the shape of spread white wings, a sword held out in front of it that glittered with the blue fire of a disruption field. It dropped like a hawk into a mass of orks. The Scouts held their breath, for the aliens piled onto it in their multitudes.

A second later, the figure exploded out of the melee, leaving a crowd of dead orks behind.

Dante gasped and leaned forwards, squinting. At that distance his enhanced vision gave him but the fleetest glimpse of the warrior's mask, but he knew it.

'Who is that warrior? I did not know any of the guard had come with us,' said Ristan.

'Not joking now, Ristan?' said Gallileon. 'That is no ordinary brother – that is the Sanguinor, the Herald of Sanguinius, the true angel. It appears when the sons of the Great Angel are sore beset, coming from nowhere, departing as mysteriously. The situation is dire indeed if we witness its presence.'

'The Sanguinor's real?' said the Scout Lethael. 'I thought it was a metaphor, Sanguinius looking over us from beyond the grave.'

Gallileon would ordinarily greet such an utterance with a blistering remark, but he stared out over the battlefield, watching the lord of the hosts do its bloody work. 'No, Scout, it is real enough. You will find there is a lot that is strange and terrible in this universe. The Sanguinor is one of those things. Be glad it is on our side.'

Gallileon turned his engine on. 'Our brothers need our help as much as they need the Sanguinor. We are going into the thick of battle. Follow me. Do exactly what I say, and you will make it out alive today. Hit-and-run, short bursts, strafe the edge of the foe. Draw some off if we can, but do not engage in melee, no matter how strongly Sanguinius' blood calls for you to fight close. You will slay many of them in your fury, but you will be swamped and cut down. This light armour is not good for protracted hand-to-hand combat against the likes of orks.'

The Scouts readied themselves for the ride onto the plain, but

Dante stayed rooted to the spot, watching the flashing of gold as the Sanguinor swooped low to strike at the orks.

'Dante! Do not let success go to your head. Move out!'

'Sergeant, I have seen it before,' he said, pitching his voice so that the sergeant alone could hear him.

'What?'

'The Sanguinor. I've seen it before.'

'I do not recall reports of a manifestation from any of your engagements. What's this, your twenty-third?'

Dante nodded.

'It does not show up just like that, Scout,' he said, snapping his fingers. 'This is a great wonder you bear witness to, not a commonplace happenstance.'

'No, sergeant, before. I mean I saw it before I was chosen. On Baal Secundus. I was dying of... lack of water.' He couldn't bring himself to use the word thirst any more for something so prosaic. 'On the way to Angel's Fall. It appeared in a vision, and pointed the way to water.'

'You are serious?' said Gallileon. He looked at Dante with new eyes.

Dante nodded. 'I do not lie. I swear it by the Blood.'

The sergeant shrugged uneasily and looked around to see if they were overheard. The other Scouts continued to prepare, too excited to pay attention to the conversation. 'If that is true, then it means something. Best speak with the Chaplains. See what they have to say. It is their task to divine the meaning of such mysteries, not mine, thank Sanguinius.'

'I have spoken with them. I was told not to speak of it.'

'Then you have already said too much. The Chaplains do not make such bans lightly.' He became thoughtful, and looked out over the maelstrom engulfing the plain. 'None of that will matter one drop of blood if we lose this battle. Ready your steeds!' Gallileon shouted. 'The orks die today!'

He twisted his throttle, making his bike roar off, drawing his chainsword as he sped at the foe.

Gallileon leading the way, the Scout squads thundered down the hillside into the raging battle.

CHAPTER FIFTEEN

DUTY'S BURDEN

998.M41

Interplanetary space, en route to the Aegis Diamondo
Cryptus System

Ordamael finished his reading and snapped shut the *Book of Sanguinius,* the volume that contained the most profound epithets of
their primarch. Music, beautiful but dolorous, played from behind
the fretted screens either side of Sanguinius' statue.

He rejoined his Chaplain brothers and Dante took the podium.
Rows of brothers in their full wargear, repaired and repainted after
the events of Cryptus, looked up to him. Dhrost and Amity Hope
were small figures at the front. The broad space before the podium
was occupied by dozens of biers. On each one was the corpse of a
fallen brother, shrouded in tight winding sheets from head to foot.
Their necks were covered with white bandages pinned in place
with gold blood-drop badges, covering the wounds where their
progenoids had been excised. They lay like the ancient mummies
of Old Earth, awaiting a resurrection that could not come. They
were each as dead as their progenitor.

Though every Space Marine in the strike force was present, Flesh
Tearer and Blood Angel, along with all the mortal humans they
had rescued and all the blood thralls not on duty, the chapel was

only half full. Dante had never seen it fully occupied, not even back in his earliest days when the Chapter was mightier. Every turn he took in the ship confronted him with another truth of the failing Imperium. The days of the Legions were so immeasurably distant he could not imagine seeing the room full. In those days the assembled Chapters would have filled the hall fifty times over; there would not have been enough space on the *Blade of Vengeance* to accommodate them. He wondered fleetingly if the ship remembered those times, and if under the surging violence of its machine-spirit it regretted their passing.

His thoughts remained his own. Not one trace of his exhaustion or his doubt entered his voice. Sanguinius' mask amplified his words to fill the chapel in a way his warriors could not.

'Brothers, brave soldiers of the Imperium. Sisters of the Ministorum orders. We ask you here today to share in our grief at the loss of so many brave souls. Yet do not despair! By their efforts, the progress of the Hive Fleet Leviathan has been slowed, and it might yet be turned away from Baal. We shall never relent in our defiance, not until every last drop of Sanguinius' blood has been spilt from our veins.' He looked down at the list of names before him. The tragedy of the losses at Cryptus gnawed at him. He was empty inside, tired beyond comprehension. War no longer fired his soul. If he could, he would lay down his burden and depart into the trackless wastes of the galaxy, but he could not.

'We remember Brother-Sergeant Pharael,' he intoned. 'Sergeant of Squad Pharael, Tactical Squad, Second Battle Company. Hero of the Dirian Purge, master sculptor, beloved by his brothers, respected by his captain. Slain upon Aeros securing our victory. Brother Pharael.' He held out a hand to the first corpse. Blood thrall bier bearers went to the slab Pharael rested on, and lifted the board bearing his corpse high onto their shoulders.

The names were in no order, the intention not to raise the deeds of any brother over another. They were equal in death by dint of dying. Differences in rank no longer mattered.

'Brother Moriar, Specialist Weapons for Squad Arias, Tactical

Squad, Second Battle Company. A fine shot, and calmer of machine-spirits. Accomplished poet. Brother Moriar.' Again he lifted his hand. Four more blood thralls came forwards and lifted up the corpse.

The list went on and on. Slowly but surely the chapel emptied of the dead, and a small weight was added to Dante's burden.

He came to the name of Ancient Cassor, slain on Asphodex fighting alongside Karlaen. Dante's memory was no longer perfect; there is only so much information a man can hold in his mind, enhanced or not. But he could recall the loss of every man he had ever fought alongside, their triumphs and failures, their habits, their faces and their prowess. How many Cassors had he known? Cassor was the name of the Dreadnought. Kezellon had been his original name, unbeaten until cut down by the eldar. There was another Cassor obliterated by the daemon Skarbrand at Pandemonium. He remembered both men, their lives separated by a hundred years. Four more warriors named Cassor he could bring to mind that he had known personally. Their deeds ran into each other, preserved in Dante's recollections. Then there was the Cassor who had given his name to the machine when first it was activated. There were others in the records. It was of no consequence. The Blood was all, Sanguinius' sacred vitae, and it had been spilt in tragic abundance.

'Ancient Cassor of the Death Company, who died his second death in the service of the Emperor. Ancient Cassor, who was Kezellon before his first death. Sergeant in the Second Company in life. Sword champion. Thereafter in his first death, the fury of the Blooded. Many foes fell to his blade. Now he is Cassor no more, and he is Kezellon again in the second death. May his deeds be remembered under both his names.' The corpse he gestured to was smaller than the others. Dante remembered his first death well. The captain had been cut in half and left to die. Sheer will kept him alive long enough to be interred in the Dreadnought. 'He died his second death honourably,' said Dante. His departure from the ritual made the Chaplains and Sanguinary Priests look to him in curiosity. 'He was defiant to the end, as we shall all be.' He pulled himself back, before he could reveal the true nature of his feelings.

The body was taken away. The next name awaited his utterance. Many others followed.

When the last of the names were spoken and the bodies taken away, Dante bid his guests goodbye, and went with his captains and his priests of red and black to lay his men to temporary rest.

Marmoreal silences greeted the Blood Angels as they entered the Sepulchre of the Fallen. Marble shelves waited for the bodies of the dead, to carry them home to Baal where they would be interred with the heroes of the ancestors. That could be decades hence, and the Sepulchre of the Fallen was chilled to a hundred degrees below zero to preserve their mortal remains for their burial.

Carbon mists curled around their feet. The party did not have far to go down the shelves. The catacombs were mostly empty. The *Blade of Vengeance* had been at home often in Dante's reign, for Baal had been threatened several times. The shelves stretched off in frozen quietude, with spaces for more bodies than there were Space Marines in the entire Chapter.

Dante waited in silence as the warriors were laid into their niches. Ordamael and Corbulo carried out their brief ceremonies over each one, whispering words into ears that could not hear them. The bodies were sealed beside heavy glass screens that fogged immediately.

Frost spidered the gold of Dante's armour by the time they had finished. Ice cracked from the joints as he moved.

'It is done, my lord,' said Ordamael.

Dante nodded in acknowledgement. He did not have the heart to say more.

They approached the Aegis Diamondo not long after. Dante took to the command deck of the *Blade of Vengeance* as the wall of ice and rock approached. Asante and Bellerophon directed the efforts of the ship and armada. Most of the other officers had dispersed among the fleet to their own vessels and companies, leaving Dante to contemplate the barrier with Corbulo and Mephiston.

The area was free of tyranid vessels. Occasional activity around the gunnery stations preceded the thrum of energy discharge or the muted rumble of a solitary cannon, barely audible over the constant vibration of the ship as it pushed its way through the void. Weapons fire grew rarer, and eventually stopped.

The Aegis Diamondo was a field of ice that filled the ship's oculus and displays, an uncountable number of objects tinted a rose pink by the light of the Red Scar. The ices were compressed to unimaginable density by temperatures that, somehow, exceeded absolute zero. It was a total barrier to Imperial shipping. Anything that attempted passage was frozen out of existence. The Aegis' presence forced a risky in-system warp exit. The resources of the Cryptus System had been so vast that the inevitable losses had been regarded as acceptable. It had been hoped that it would provide an uncrossable barrier to the tyranids. The deployment of any military force to Cryptus at all evidenced unusual foresight on the part of the High Lords.

The Aegis had not stopped the tyranids, nor had the military. Cryptus was dead, locked into its frozen tomb as Dante's warriors were preserved in the sepulchre.

Planetoids of superfluids and exotic ices resolved themselves from the mass of objects. According to Dhrost the hive fleet had passed through, freezing over with a protective sheath of ice and emerging alive despite its organic nature.

If the likes of the Aegis cannot halt the tyranid advance, nothing can stop them, Dante thought, but kept his misgivings to himself.

'How was it possible, my lords, that the tyranids breached the Aegis?' he asked instead.

Corbulo answered first. 'The physical explanation is thermal regulation of the tyranid vessels, but their output would have to be equal to that of a dwarf star. Vessels warmed by fusion reactors have frozen solid, killing every soul on board. The tyranids do not appear to produce their energy this way. Mere biochemistry could not have warmed them enough. They are dormant as they travel across interstellar space, where the temperature is low but still greater than that of the Aegis. My opinion is that they should never have woken from their hibernation after passing the Aegis. There is no physical explanation for what they accomplished.'

'The metaphysical explanation, my Lord of Death?' asked Dante of Mephiston.

'The whole of the Red Scar is shot through with anomalous phenomena, my lord. There is the touch of the warp upon the Aegis especially. Weak, but enough to pervert the natural order of the material realm. Perhaps the shadow of the hive mind afforded some additional protection. Its blanketing of the warp may have divorced the Aegis from whatever cools it so, allowing them passage.'

'That makes some sense,' said Corbulo. 'Testing of the regions they breached would have to be undertaken to prove your hypothesis.'

'Such work is for the adepts of the Adeptus Mechanicus, not for we Blood Angels,' said Mephiston. 'The Aegis did not stop them. We must find another way. That is all we need to know.'

'My brothers,' Asante said to them from the command podium. 'We approach the thermal tunnels.'

'All ships prepare to follow these exact coordinates,' said Bellerophon, voxing the captains of the fleet.

For a while the fleet slowed, rearranging itself from broad battle formation into a column headed by the Blood Angels with the Flesh Tearers as rearguard. The Aegis was now directly before them, a boundless field of eerily still objects. It looked like the messy space of objects that mark the borders of most star systems, but Dante could feel the supernatural chill of it through the warding of the ship's shields and hull. Asante ordered the hololith lit. A cartolith of the passages through the Aegis showed, dull orange on blue-white. There the rules of reality held sway, and the void was the temperature it should be.

'Helm, engage on my mark,' said Asante.

The *Blade of Vengeance* slid like a dagger into the field, moving past giant rocks and balls of dirty ice. The thermal passage looked like every other part of the Aegis. One mistake would see them all frozen for eternity. The temperature of the command deck fell. Clouds of steam issued from every unshielded mouth. Dante's cooling systems reduced their efforts, allowing the reactor strapped to his back to warm him, but it was a feeble heat, as if someone were holding a warm coal a foot away from his naked back on a winter's night. Warning runes blinked on his faceplate display; temperatures tumbled away. The ship's ventilation system roared as it pumped warm air onto the command deck, but it could not lift the chill.

An equilibrium was struck. The ship laboured hard to keep its fragile occupants alive in the face of this cosmic anomaly. The unnatural cold reached out to kill them. Without the thermal tunnel, death would have been inevitable.

Asante ordered the ship to accelerate.

'What is your estimation for emergence, Brother-Captain Asante?' asked Dante.

'We will be through in nine hours, my lord commander,' he said.

'Inform me when we break out of the system,' he said, and departed the command deck. He had promised Arafeo that he would sleep, so sleep he would.

Dante slept little away from Baal. There was always too much to do, too many decisions that had to be taken, and the actions of his underlings to be overseen and reversed if necessary. Thousands of souls looked to him for guidance. Billions more depended on his protection. His Space Marine's physiology kept him alert. Sleep did little for him. Only with respite in the Hall of Sarcophagi could he restore his soul.

Ultimately he was human, and needed to sleep, else he would never have agreed to Arafeo's request. When the message came he was twitching on his ornate bed, enmeshed in dreams awash with blood. Armies of Traitor legionaries marched across the faces of burning worlds. The Traitor primarchs led their twisted Legions upon the path of blood, and the screams of trillions of human beings shook the fabric of reality.

The universe rippled. Hosts of daemons poured from bleeding cuts in the sky. Brazen bells, thick with dripping verdigris tolled, Doom! Doom! Doom!

Dante was surrounded on all sides. Overhead a giant face manifested, leering down at him with the certainty of triumph.

'Horus!' gasped Dante.

A giant, clawed hand reached down to pluck him up and crush him.

'My lord.' Arafeo's voice was muffled by the hellish tumult.

'My lord!' Small hands shook his arm.

Dante came awake all of a sudden. Still ensnared in the horrors of his dream, his hand shot out and grabbed Arafeo by the throat. His teeth bared, his face flushed. His gifts pushed his system into battle readiness.

'My lord! Please, it is I!' Arafeo's arthritic fingers pried unsuccessfully at Dante's crushing grip.

Dante's fangs pricked at his lips. The blood thrall's pulse thrilled under his fingertips.

'My lord, please!'

The crushing pressure at Arafeo's throat released. The lord commander's face cleared. Arafeo staggered back. Dante leapt out of his bed and went to his equerry's side, steadying Arafeo with hands that moments before had tried to choke him to death.

'My servant!' Remorse choked Dante. 'I... I am sorry. Have I harmed you? My dreams have been dark of late. Are you hurt? Look at me!'

Arafeo sagged against a couch. Dante grasped his face gently and turned it from side to side. The wrinkled skin of Arafeo's neck was discolouring.

'How long did I sleep?' demanded Dante.

'You have slept not seven hours, my lord. I obey your command as you asked.'

'Then we are not free of the Aegis Diamondo. Forgive me. You have done your duty well. I am out of sorts.'

'I understand, my lord.'

The rebuke that Arafeo could never understand fought to be free of Dante's throat. 'I could have broken your neck. You were seconds from death.'

'But I am not dead. I am well, my lord,' Arafeo gasped hoarsely. 'It was I who asked that you rest. I should be more careful in my care in future.'

Dante smiled a little. 'Your spirits are unharmed, at least, my friend.'

'There is a messenger here for you from the astropathicum. Adept Koschin?'

Dante shook his head. He had no knowledge of the man. The servants of his Chapter numbered in the thousands, all told, and they lived and died so quickly the lesser of them did not register on his notice.

'Alert my arming thralls. Send refreshment to this Koschin. I will greet the adept in my armour.' He turned his face further away from Arafeo, into the shadows.

'Of course, my lord. It shall be done,' said the aged thrall.

Dante came to his audience chamber garbed and masked for war. The room was sized appropriately for its purpose and decorated to emphasise the majesty of the Blood Angels. The adept, a mortal servant of the astropaths, looked lost under the painted dome. The servants of the Adeptus Astra Telepathica rarely had cause to leave their quarters, and he eyed the statues ringing the chamber as if they would smite him. His posture became submissive when Dante strode in.

The adept quaked under Dante's inscrutable red-glass gaze and averted his eyes, his expression a mix of awe and terror.

'I do not know you.'

'I am Adept Koschin, my lord, translator extraordinary to Lord Astropath Prime Jareth.'

'You are blessed. Jareth has served me well for two centuries. He is a good man.'

Koschin nodded too fervidly. 'It is an honour to serve him. My post is a new one. I have never had the pleasure of making your acquaintance.'

The man was terrified. Dante took a step back and moderated his tone, mindful of his effect on mortal minds.

'I am sure you will also give my Chapter many good years of devotion, adept. You have a message for me?'

'I have. It is here, my lord.' He held out a parchment. 'It is from High Chaplain Astorath the Grim.'

'I was told communications would not be possible until we were further from the mind shadow of the Great Devourer, and that would not be until we were free of the Aegis Diamondo.'

'The shadow in the warp lessens, my lord. This message was sent at extreme boost through astropathic lensing stations at the highest priority grade, and so we knew immediately that it was of the gravest import. Astropath Prime Jareth received it an hour ago. We expedited its translation and have been processing the message for you since its arrival.'

'Text or image encoding?'

'Text only, my lord. There are image components, but the transliteration of the astropath's reading into finished picts will take time.' He held out the scroll with shaking hands. 'It was highly encrypted, iambic hexameter duo-coding. The metaphors were of the rarest kind and required three shifts of translation.'

Dante took the message delicately in his gold-armoured fingers, searching for something positive to say to this cowering man.

'The ink is still wet,' he said. 'You did well to bring it to me with such dispatch. You have my thanks.'

The adept bowed but tensed as Dante opened the seal and unrolled the scroll. Koschin knew the content and feared the reaction it would produce.

Dante read the message in one glance. His gauntlet clenched, rumpling the parchment.

'Thank you, adept. You are dismissed.'

The cold anger in Dante's voice shook the mortal to the core. He left bowing, turning to hurry off as soon as he thought he was out of sight.

Although he had memorised the message, Dante read it once more, scarcely believing it to be true.

Framed between the humdrum information of the astrotele-pathic process – the heraldic coding of the Fifth Company, Astorath, signum data of relay stations, the names of the astropaths involved and every paragraph signifier rendered in exquisite calligraphy – was news of such import that Dante was at a loss for the first time in centuries.

Lord Commander,

Grave tidings from the Cadian Gate. Abaddon has emerged from the Eye of Terror at the head of a Black Crusade of unprecedented size. Auguries are unclear but ill portent is everywhere to be seen. The daemon primarchs are abroad. Thousands of ships essay into real space. Cadia is attacked. I have reports that the thrice-damned Skarbrand has emerged once more into the material realm, and comes in the van of the traitor's hordes. The Diamor System is assailed. The priests of Mars have been conducting excavations there, and I cannot think it by chance that the arch-traitor leads his forces against the system now. Whatever the tech-priests have uncovered cannot be allowed to fall into the hands of the enemy.

I have instructed Captain Sendini to accompany me to Diamor, along with the full strength of the Daemonbanes. I petition you to directly send as many warriors to me as can be spared to aid in the defence of Diamor. Should the Great Enemy break free of the Gate, Abaddon has enough vessels and warriors to drive for Terra.

I realise this puts the Baal System at risk. However, I judge that the presence of our Chapter will have a large beneficial effect upon the morale of Imperial forces gathering to repel the traitors. This war was begun by our forebears. We should finish it.

The decision is yours alone to make, my lord, yet I hope you trust my counsel, and have faith enough in the wider brotherhood of Sanguinius that they might keep Baal from harm.

I await your reply as soon as it may be delivered.

Your obedient servant,
High Chaplain Astorath

Dante's soul withered in him. Another choice between two evils. He had thought his earlier years full of hard-won victories. The difficulties of those times were nothing compared to the dilemmas that tormented him daily.

As he read and reread the missive his composure broke. Dante howled in fury, ran at the wall and slammed his perfect golden fist into the mosaic there, destroying a portion of ancient artwork a yard square and denting the metal beneath. Shattered tesserae tinkled to the floor.

The doors burst inwards. A pair of Dante's Sanguinary Guard came in, weapons raised. Arafeo came after them.

'My lord!' said Arafeo.

'Commander?' asked one of the Sanguinary Guard.

Dante swayed back from the wall, his hand up. 'It is nothing, Brother Dontoriel. Return to your post.'

'As you command it.' The Sanguinary Guard scanned the room a last time and left.

Arafeo did not leave, but approached carefully. 'What is it, my lord?'

'Dire news from Astorath. A new threat as bad as the Devourer.' Dante's armour felt unbearably claustrophobic, and he sank into a crouch. He had a fleeting memory of a boy who had sat like that habitually, but he could not remember his name.

'Will you convene your brothers, my lord? You have but to ask and I shall pass on your summons.'

Behind Sanguinius' mask, Dante closed his eyes and bowed his head in reflection. The purring whine of his armour systems irritated him. He longed for the dry silences of Baal.

'I must think on this a while. I shall speak with them after we are free of the Aegis. We can do nothing for the time being but fret at the problem, and I need to consider this carefully before I make any decision.'

CHAPTER SIXTEEN

RED THIRST

471.M40
Lost colony
Ereus V
Ereus System

Jet turbines roared upon Dante's back, arcing him over the rough barricades surrounding the orreti camp. Dante crashed through leafless trees and came down firing. His bolt pistol kicked satisfyingly in his hand. Every shot ended the life of a scavenger. Dante slammed into the ground at the centre of the camp, denting the packed earth. The orreti brandished their odd-looking guns at him. In return he gunned his chainsword. The small xenos scattered shrieking. Gathering their weapons under them in their mismatched belly appendages, they loped away at surprising speed, knuckling along on their long forelimbs, powerful thrusts from their single back limbs accelerating them away. Dust puffed up from the dry ground behind their hoofs. Long grasses rattled frantically as they sped through then fell still.

Dante scanned the sparse woodlands. The xenos had supposedly overrun the colony of Ereus, but they seemed too few in number to have done so, and the planet looked undisturbed for decades. His helm overlays revealed nothing. The orreti had gone.

Jump packs howled as Lorenz landed next to him, Ristan coming next. Giacomus, Arvin and Sergeant Basileus completed their squad. They spread out, peering into the dirty tents of the orreti. Arvin lifted piles of rags with the end of his chainsword distastefully.

'Filthy xenos,' he said. 'Look at this place. Worse than animals.'

'The area is clear,' said Giacomus from one end of the camp.

Dante knocked down a hut roofed with fabric. Besides a few bones around a dead fire, it was empty. 'Nothing here either, sergeant,' he said.

Their jump engines whined down. Chainswords purred to a stop. An unnatural quiet fell. The myriad animals of the bush held their silence.

'We should not be here. These things are no threat,' growled Lorenz, toeing the shredded remains of an orreti. There wasn't much left but a few jointed, insectile limbs and rag. Its blood stained the ground. The sight made Dante's lips tingle.

'They are pathetic foes. One bolt-round and there is nothing left of them,' said Giacomus.

'Quiet,' said Sergeant Basileus, holding up his hand irritably. He pulled his auspex from his belt and bent his head to the screen. Far off a beast roared. The Space Marines fanned out into a defensive circle without thinking. Arvin lifted his pistol to cover the shadows. Dante shifted his grip on his chainsword.

'Sounds big,' said Giacomus.

'Sounds angry,' said Lorenz. 'Let us go and fight that instead. There is more honour there than exterminating these weaklings.'

'I will kill them all, weak or not!' said Arvin fiercely. Dante and Lorenz turned to look at him, such was his vehemence.

'I said silence!' said Basileus. Lorenz made a dismissive noise, but obeyed. Arvin growled. The quiet chirruping of the auspex filled the clearing. The camp was small, three interlinked circles around campfires, fenced by barricades of scavenged metal.

'The colonia is that way,' said Basileus, gesturing to the north with his auspex. 'Spread out. Stay low to the ground.'

'We should be fighting a better war,' Lorenz voxed Dante. 'This scale of action is beneath us. How many colonists were there here? Two thousand? Send more, is what I say.'

'We are obliged to defend every world of the Emperor, brother,' said Dante. 'No matter how small. If they send more people and there is insufficient military presence, they will die.'

'Commander Milonus should be more selective in responding to requests for aid,' grumbled Lorenz. He kicked over a charred log in a fit of pique, scattering ashes.

'Dante, Lorenz, concentrate.' Basileus cut into their private conversation. 'No talking, anyone. You're not so long into your black carapace that I can't knock you down, and I will if you don't stay alert.'

Basileus' suit was artfully decorated where the others' plate was plain. The style suggested a considered artist. In truth, Basileus was, but he was also an exceptionally angry man. He had to be, to keep the impetuous young Space Marines in check. There had been one older brother in their squad, acting as battle squad leader when the unit split, but as their campaign had proceeded he had been reassigned to other duties, leaving Basileus with a band of hotheads to chaperone alone.

'I don't see why we can't fly,' muttered Ristan. All of them yearned to. Flight was in their blood, a legacy of Sanguinius' gene-seed.

Basileus halted. With swift battlesign, he sent his squad out wide either side of him, Lorenz with Dante and Ristan on the right, Giacomus with Arvin on the left. Arvin ran forwards brashly.

'Easy,' voxed Basileus.

Runes blinked up on Dante's faceplate as Basileus took temporary control of the display. A cartograph overlaid the view through his lenses.

The colonia, Basileus communicated via vox-text reinforced with battlesign. *Expect resistance. Dante and Lorenz, scout ahead. Provide suitable attack point. Stealth, brothers. Do not alert the enemy.*

Dante and Lorenz signalled their affirmatives and stole forwards, sharp orange grasses rasping on their power armour. Despite their heavy armour, their stealth was commendable, the Blood Angels dropping their shoulders so that their jump packs did not knock on the branches of the dwarf trees, the footfalls of their heavy boots close to silent.

A wall of creepers appeared between the trees. Leaves rustled in the warm wind, flashing glimpses of crumbling plascrete.

'The colonia wall,' said Dante.

Dante signalled he would take the primary position. Lorenz nodded, took shelter by the earthen spires of some communal creature's nest and covered his brother with his pistol. Dante approached the covered wall, pulling away the vines. Chunks of plascrete came away with it; the roots had penetrated deeply. The metal fence that would have continued the barrier another five metres upwards had fallen, rusted strands of it providing a framework for plants to climb. Dante crumbled the decaying material between his fingers. On Baal Secundus, structures that had been ruined twelve thousand years were periodically uncovered by the sand, perfectly preserved at the moment of their destruction. Less than twenty years had passed on Ereus V since the colony had gone quiet. Already the stamp of man upon the world was melting away. The power of vital worlds fascinated him. Life was potent.

He looked back to Lorenz and signed that he should shadow him, then proceeded along the wall. Through gaps in the fortification's length he saw tumbled ruins similarly covered in vegetation.

It was quiet. The landscape lived gently. The sounds of growth and small animals rustling in the undergrowth were crisp in his ear beads. His breathing mask was open, admitting the healthy scents of a vibrant ecosystem. Soft wind played over his armour; the temperature was forty-two degrees. He saw all of this as read-out runes, but felt none of it. Caution forbade him from taking off his helmet. The energy weapons the orreti carried were too weak to penetrate Adeptus Astartes power armour, but they would easily hollow out a bare head.

They came to the gates. A road, made of prefabricated rockcrete sections, led away into the scrub, its flat surface broken up by the actions of tree roots and crowded with waving grasses. Finding the road's position without the reference to the gates would have been impossible.

Lorenz joined Dante.

'We have reached the gates, sergeant,' voxed Dante. 'We proceed.'

'*Understood,*' said Basileus. '*Keep vox to a minimum. I am detecting no electromagnetic informational traffic, but prudence is the ward of life.*'

The vox clicked out.

'Basileus doesn't like us,' said Lorenz. He kept his voice low, but there was an edge to it through his suit vox-grille that helped it carry.

'Do you think?' said Dante. 'It's nothing personal. I hear he's been a sergeant to Assault Marines for a century and a half. If his humours were better balanced, he would have been promoted to captain.'

'I'll be a captain one day,' said Lorenz.

'We've been full brothers for less than four years. You're getting ahead of yourself,' said Dante.

They skirted the overgrown road. Avians cawed from their roosts in the wrecked colonia buildings. The rusting hull of a Taurox military transport blocked the road. Dante pointed to blast damage in its side.

'That's heavy projectile weaponry damage. The orreti didn't do that.'

'How do you know?' said Lorenz, leaning around the tank and tracking his pistol across the terrain. 'Nobody knows anything about them. They're not in the Chapter records.'

'Because all we've seen them wield are weak particle beams.'

'Maybe they've got something stronger.'

'You were the one that said they were feeble,' said Dante.

'That they are,' said Lorenz. 'Lord Milonus knew that, otherwise he would have sent more than two squads to deal with them. They're just another beggar race, picking over the rubbish of better species. This is a waste of our time.'

'Doesn't their lifestyle remind you of anything?' said Dante. They jogged down the street. The purr of their armour blended into the hush of the day.

'They're not like the Baalites,' said Lorenz. 'Our life made us hard. It made us fit to be angels. These things are weak. We'll kill them all, and it will be as if they never were.'

The colonia was laid out to a standard settlement pattern dredged out of an STC. A grid of streets with designated areas for industry, governance and habitation. Neatness was inherent to its conception.

'Hard to believe a hive world can spring from a seed like this,' said Dante.

'Maybe they all start out like this. Some must. But this seed died on stony ground. There will be no human domination here for some time,' said Lorenz.

Dante took a deep breath of the fragrant air. Such clean atmosphere, free of the taint of chemicals. He had recently visited his first hive world and, beneath inculcated indifference, found it profoundly shocking. He struggled to regret the colony's failure.

'The centre.' With his bolt pistol. Dante gestured to the crumbling edifices of Administratum buildings.

'I see something!' said Lorenz. 'There!'

Dante caught a flash of movement darting across the street.

Lorenz raised his gun and sent a spray of bolts shooting after it.

'By the wings of our lord, I missed the little kreck,' said Lorenz angrily. Without warning he wrenched his chainsword from his belt, ignited his jump pack and flew down the street. The silence of the ruined town shattered.

'Wait!' shouted Dante. But Lorenz was frustrated and his blood was up. He landed, sending up a spray of powdery rockcrete from the road, and charged around the corner firing. The fizzing pop of orreti weapons welcomed him.

Dante opened full vox-channels. 'Basileus, this is Dante. I have found the rest of the orreti crew. They're in the colonia centre, these coordinates.' He sent a datasquirt from his suit's cogitator.

'Hold and wait for reinforcement,' voxed Basileus back.

'Negative, sergeant. Lorenz is engaged. I am following.'

Not wishing to receive the inevitable order to wait, Dante ignited his jump engines. He welcomed the push of them as they lifted him from the ground. So powerful, the thrust tugging at his shoulders and waist. His annoyance at Lorenz vanished in the roar of turbines. Both his hearts pumped hard; the anticipation of combat fired the gifts of the Emperor, flooding his system with synthetic hormones. The flight from Angel's Leap ten years ago was nothing to jumping into combat. By the time he landed his teeth were clamped hard together in a wild grin. He jumped again, daring to burn the pack's limited fuel reserves to attain something close to true flight. With consummate skill, he swerved around the moss-draped statuary of a building shell and landed in the town centre.

The orreti had laid out large sheets of fabric in the square. Upon them the components of deconstructed machines were set out neatly. Such work suggested the creatures were not aware of the destruction of their scows in orbit, or maybe they were, and this salvage had been intended for a defensive purpose he could not divine. It was pointless trying to second-guess xenos. They were by their nature unknowable, and contemptible.

Lorenz was embattled on the plaza. Dozens of orreti were firing on him from windows. Their energy slashes scorched his armour around his head, turning the yellow of his helmet brown and black. There were larger things in combat with him, three beings twice the height of a Space Marine. They had the same overall shape as the lesser orreti – two long forearms, a stumpy limb-tail and an array of specialised limbs on the chest – but where the lesser things were covered by loose robes, the larger creatures wore plates of iridescent armour. Helmets covered their long heads. They brandished a variety of pistol-type weapons with their chest arms that discharged particle beams. These were as inoffensive to battleplate as the fusils carried by the lesser orreti, but the creatures' powerful forelimbs were tipped with gleaming blades that did pose a threat.

The aliens reared up on their thrusting limb-tails to drive down and strike at Lorenz. He dodged between their blades. A pair of swords slashed at him and he caught them on the edge of his chainsword. Sparks flew from the weapon. With a grunt he threw the creature back, and was immediately set upon by the other two larger creatures before he could finish the first.

Dante thundered down among them, bolt pistol blazing. Five bolts hammered into the side of one of the creatures, punching through its gleaming armour as if it were paper. Multiple explosions blew out craters the length of its body. Subsidiary arms flew everywhere. It rocked back on its muscular limb-tail, exposing pulsing organs within its ruined torso, threw its head back and died.

Loosing bolts in every direction, Dante slammed into the melee.

'Brother!' shouted Lorenz. 'I may have been hasty.'

'We should have waited!' said Dante, aiming a blow at an alien leg. The Space Marines twisted around each other until they were back to back, facing one creature each. He meant to chastise his squad mate, but he was joyous. He did not mean what he said. Who would want to wait when battle beckoned?

'What by the pits of Baal are these things?' said Lorenz.

'Warrior forms? The little ones could be the males and the big females, or vice versa. Does it matter? They're all trying to kill us.' Dante raised his gun. A knock from a limb-blade sent his shots wide and jarred it from his hand. Anger seized him at the affront to his wargear. Taking up his chainsword, he roared and threw himself forwards, beating back the alien with a flurry of violent blows.

Lorenz ducked a blade that hummed as it parted the air.

'These are the females?' he shouted. 'Ha! I like this better – their women fight properly!'

Jump packs roared. Arvin slammed into the middle of the fight. If Dante felt fury, it was nothing to Arvin's rage.

'Kill them! Kill them!' he shouted. Dante advanced on the retreating alien, but Arvin knocked him aside. 'This is my kill! I will deliver the killing blow!' he shouted. Though furious that his prize had been stolen, Dante was wary at Arvin's tone and stood back.

The others landed around the melee, peeling off into the buildings. Roofless halls echoed to the reports of boltguns, the squealing of aliens and chainsword song. The volleys of particle beams decreased dramatically. In less than three minutes the aliens were dead. Lorenz had dropped his female. Arvin's was dead, but he would not stop hitting it over and over again, flinging sprays of blood and ground-up meat up the walls.

'It is dead, brother, come away.' Dante touched Arvin's shoulder. Arvin rounded on him and punched him in the face with the spiked guard of his sword, cracking his helm lens. Dante staggered back. Arvin raised his weapon over his head and roared incoherently.

He wants to kill me, thought Dante.

'Stop him! Pin him down!' Basileus was shouting. His brothers joined their cries of alarm to the sergeant's, but their voices sounded distant, something from a fading memory. Dante was preoccupied by Arvin's sword swinging down in a heavy, overarm blow. Time seemed to slow. Dazed, he raised his weapon to meet Arvin's.

Their blades met, teeth shattering, and time resumed its normal pace. The force of the blow staggered Dante. Arvin had the strength of a man possessed.

'Stop him! Stop him!' shouted Basileus.

Another blow hammered down on Dante. The chains of both blades ground together again. Arvin's unspooled onto the floor, Dante's jammed up the drive unit, causing the motor to ignite. Dante threw the weapon aside in time to catch Arvin as he jumped. Dante grabbed him, bringing them both to the ground.

'How dare you! You take me away from my prize, my kill, my soul tally!' Arvin's combat discipline had gone, and he scrabbled at Dante's head like a madman. Dante could not retaliate effectively; he was struggling to stop his helmet being torn off.

'Get off him!' shouted Lorenz. He locked his arm around Arvin's shoulder, but was thrown back. He returned. Ristan grabbed Arvin's other arm, Giacomus grasping the stabilisation vents on his backpack. Together, they hauled Arvin off Dante and threw him down. Arvin lumbered to his feet, ready to attack again. Lorenz tackled him around the midriff and they both crashed to the floor again.

Dante got up. He was physically shaking inside his armour. In part this was due to the shock of his brother's attack, but largely he wrestled with his own desire to fight Arvin. The kill had rightly been his, not Arvin's. His brother's temerity infuriated him. His hearts pounded, his vision tunnelled. Arvin bucked and shouted under the weight of Lorenz and Giacomus.

Reeling, Dante turned away, battling his rising bloodlust. He made himself concentrate on his suit, running through the post-battle checklist.

'Focus, focus, the first grace,' he whispered. 'Be respectful of your battlegear,' he said. His breath was hot in his helmet. 'Be mindful of your armour. Restraint, restraint, restraint!'

A shudder ran through him, so powerful his armour whined oddly as it sought to match the movement, and his neural jacks tugged in their sockets.

'My weapons,' he said. He had lost his bolt pistol and his sword. He went to retrieve both, whispering calming mantras as he did so.

As he picked up his wrecked sword, he noticed one of the orreti females lived. Its back stump leg was twisted back on itself. One of its forelimbs was broken, the other hacked off at the elbow, leaking purple vitae. The nest of lesser limbs around its chest moved weakly. Dante levelled his gun at its long face. Multiple eyes blinked at him.

'Peace, peace!' it said in musical Gothic. 'Take our salvage. We save for you these things!' said the orreti, gesturing with bleeding manipulators at the neatly arrayed machinery. 'We leave. No harm. This dead world we think. But not dead. Is yours. We mistake. We go.'

'Why did you attack us?' said Dante, and was surprised at the snarl in his voice.

'We not attack. You attack.'

Dante's gun wavered. Feelings of disgust and hot rage battled with those of pity. This was a xenos, an implacable enemy of man by its very nature, and yet it pleaded for mercy. Mercy was the third grace. He stared it in the eye. It held its arms up pleadingly.

It was terrified.

Dante dropped his weapon a fraction.

The rest of his brothers were occupied with their raging comrade, but Arvin saw Dante hesitate. 'Kill it! I will kill it! Let me slay it! Let me drink its blood!' raged Arvin. He attempted to get at the wounded alien, dragging Lorenz and Giacomus after him. Basileus slammed Arvin in the chest, knocking him off balance so that Lorenz and the others could subdue him. The sergeant ripped off his helmet.

'Arvin! Calm yourself!' he ordered. 'All of you, focus!'

'Sergeant, this one lives. It calls for clemency,' said Dante.

Basileus looked back. Savagery had replaced dignity on his face, contorting it into something wild. His eyes were bloodshot, and his fangs extended. 'What are you doing, Dante? Kill it. It is xenos. It does not deserve to live. Do not hesitate.'

Dante levelled his gun at the thing's head. The eyes arrayed on its long face widened. He couldn't stand the sight of its fear. Before he knew what he had done, he had obliterated its face with a shot from his gun to save himself from looking at it. The remaining few eyes shut slowly, and the corpse curled in on itself.

'Keep him down!' ordered Basileus. He walked away from the ranting Arvin, and activated the vox-pickup at his neck. 'This is Basileus. The orreti are dead. I have no indication of any more nearby. I doubt they were responsible for the disappearance of the colonists, but they have stripped the colonia of all useful materials. By their profaning of the Emperor's world with their unclean tread they earned death. Send extraction for us now. I declare this world cleansed. I will append the report to the Departmento Colonia, suggesting a heavier military presence for the next settlement attempt.'

Arvin was still raging, his strength taxing the three Space Marines trying to hold him in place. 'Arvin! Brother! It is us! Why do you fight?' shouted Lorenz. He was panicking. A warrior fearless in the face of the foe, he was frightened by Arvin's loss of control.

'Let me go!' bellowed Arvin. 'I shall crush their corpses, set their maimed bodies about this place! They will know fear! I will destroy them all!'

'Emperor's Throne!' snarled Basileus. 'He will not calm. Hold him still!' he said. Basileus took out his combat knife and went to the dead orreti.

'What ails him?' said Lorenz.

'It is the rage – the Black Rage has him!' said Giacomus.

'It is not the rage. It is the Red Thirst,' said Basileus thickly, his control steadying the others. 'It has him in its grip as it has me in its grip. I have the measure of my own passions, that is all.'

'We have all experienced the thirst!' shouted Giacomus. 'It has never been like this. I don't understand.'

'Then you have much to learn. There is only one medicine for this ailment. Get his helmet off.' With evident disgust he searched around an alien neck, then bent and cut once with his knife. He cupped his hand under the wound, filling it with the purple blood. Lorenz and Giacomo pinned Arvin's arms while Ristan grappled with his thrashing head. Finally, Ristan got his fingers into the release catches at the top of the soft seal and yanked off Arvin's helm.

Their brother had gone. A monster had taken his place. The veins throbbed on Arvin's neck and face. His alabaster skin had turned crimson, his eyes bulged, and their whites had reddened. His bared teeth snapped at the arms of his brothers, his fangs fully extended.

'Hold him!' said Basileus. Careful not to spill the precious liquid, the sergeant brought his hand close to Arvin's mouth.

'Drink! Drink the vitae. Let it slake your thirst, brother,' said Basileus.

Arvin let out a strangled howl. Basileus jammed the blade of his palm into Arvin's mouth, forcing his teeth wide. Arvin's fangs squeaked on ceramite.

'Drink!' commanded Basileus.

Blood slopped into Arvin's mouth. His thrashing calmed. With desperate laps he licked up the blood from Basileus' hand. Lorenz, Ristan and Giacomus stepped cautiously back.

Arvin's face had lost its horrible red colour. He licked frantically at the alien blood, eyes dilated.

'He is blood drunk,' said Giacomus.

'He will calm now,' said Basileus, his face and voice hardly less savage than Arvin's.

The young Space Marines looked hungrily on the blood, their own thirsts stirring.

Basileus looked at them. 'It is affecting you too. It is the way of our Chapter that when one falls to the thirst, many follow. All of you, drink, quickly! Drink for the victory you have achieved. Drink for the glory of the Imperium! Drink for the memory of Sanguinius! Partake of the communion of blood. Wash away your savagery. Rediscover restraint, and through it seek forgiveness for this lapse.'

They had never partaken of such a libation, not in these circumstances. Blood and the drinking of blood were sacred to their Chapter, but it was always done under the watchful eyes of the Sanguinary Priests. Gingerly at first, they knelt by the alien body and removed their helms. Lorenz was first to kiss the alien's hide. His face wrinkled with disgust at the touch of it on his lips even as his skin reddened in anticipation. Dante followed. The leathery flesh was still warm. Despite his abhorrence, his mouth watered. His fangs extruded themselves fully from his gums, piercing the skin. Spiced, xenos blood trickled into his mouth, spurring his appetite. With increasing need, he sucked at the wound, dragging in mouthfuls of the stuff. Fragments of alien memory spilt through his mind as he drank of its soul, his omophagea snagging bits of the dead creature's life.

He knew the orreti then. They were wanderers, their world dead. They had never been numerous, and were in the twilight of their kind. He felt their sadness, and their pain. They were not aggressive creatures, but carrion feeders, living off the leavings of the galaxy. Dante did not care. Blood was all there was. Their sorrow-ful story was submerged in a tide of red.

He tasted the creature's death. Its fear broke the hold of the thirst over him, and he snatched his head back.

Dante took a long, shuddering breath. He blinked, back in him-self again. The stolen life of the alien coursed through his body, and he saw his fellows with clear eyes. Giacomus lapped blood from the ground. Lorenz sucked at its arm. Ristan had his face buried in the creature's chest like a beast-pup at the teat.

What have we become? he wondered. But the thought was fleeting in the face of the thirst. The smell of vitae had his mouth watering. His reason retreated, and he returned to the corpse.

There was blood to be drunk; mercy be damned.

CHAPTER SEVENTEEN

BLACK RAGE

518.M40

Holywell Hive

Tobias Halt

Halt System

'This is Dante! Requesting urgent support! We're cut off!' Laziel was a dead weight on his arm, his armour streaked a wetter red from his brother's wounds. Dante pushed him on. His brother stumbled, his ragged breathing amplified by his vox-grille.

A power-armoured figure stepped into the end of the corridor, its defaced iconography streaked with rust and undercity filth. Dante fired one-handed and shot its hearts full of bolt-rounds. The mass-reactives blew, their explosions contained by the renegade's armour plating, and he fell down dead.

'This is Dante, can anyone hear me?' He moved on, dragging Laziel to his feet, glancing back over his shoulder. More traitors were filling the corridor. Bolt-rounds crackled off broken sheets of plasteel hanging off the walls.

Several whined off his armour. One exploded on his plastron, the detonation making the battleplate shiver.

'Laziel, get up!' shouted Dante. He fired back at the traitors, emptying his bolter at them.

'I... I... can't,' he said. 'I'm... I...' He sagged against the wall.

The renegades advanced, guns up, through the cramped corridor. Their pauldrons scraped rust from the decaying walls. Small flies swarmed around yellow lumens set into the ceiling. A sense of dankness prevailed, though they were high in the atmosphere of Tobias Halt, well above the oceans.

Dante braced himself, but the traitors did not fire. 'They want our gene-seed,' Dante snarled. Anger rose up in him. The pounding of his hearts became war drums. Before he could consider his actions, he was running at them, chainsword growling. He slammed into the first, rocking the fallen angel back on his feet.

'Traitor! Traitor!' he yelled in the Space Marine's face.

The warrior was knocked back, contacting with his fellows. A combat knife scraped a bright furrow across Dante's chest eagle. Dante elbowed his foe hard in the face, cracking his retinal lenses and staggering him further. The Purge, they called themselves – once loyal, now filthy acolytes of the god of plague. Their armour was painted green around the greaves and shoulders, black elsewhere. He reversed his chainsword and drove it point first through the traitor's chest. Blood fountained over him as the warrior died. Dante wrenched his weapon free.

The traitor following the slain renegade fired at Dante. Bolts exploded on his armour. Warning runes flashed all over his display, but he paid them no heed. The Traitor Space Marine continued firing at Dante until his chainsword took the warrior's hand and gun off at the wrist. He took his blade and sawed up lengthways through the enemy's helm. Black blood spurted from his ruined respirator grille.

Dante sprang forwards off the corpse, kicking a second foe hard in the leg, denting his armour and sending him off balance. Then he decapitated him. His sword snagged in the traitor's armour, and so he threw himself at the third warrior, screaming incoherently. The Red Thirst rose up through him, drowning his soul in a tide of bloody rage. His weight bore the traitor down, his hands locked about his neck. He buried his fingers in the vulnerable joint, pushing so hard his hands pierced metal softseal and flesh alike. The traitor smashed at Dante, making his faceplate display fizz, but he did not relent. With a final, crushing grip, he choked the life from the traitor, and tore his helmet off.

The warrior looked not so different to Dante, his face distorted in the same transhuman way, although he lacked Sanguinius' beauty. Dante wondered what primarch had given this creature its gifts. It enraged him that supposedly loyal Adeptus Astartes would turn to Chaos. His fangs slid from his gums. He wished to feast on this thing, and steal the secrets of its mind.

He opened his filters preparatory to removing his helmet. The rotten stink of the traitor's blood stopped him. It smelt rancid.

Dante stood back, his thirst receding but not quenched. It could never be quenched.

He went to the struggling Laziel and dragged him up again. 'Come on,' he said. 'We have to keep moving.'

Dante helped his brother through the network of tunnels. Everywhere there were the emaciated corpses of citizenry. The Purge had occupied Tobias Halt and begun to systematically starve the inhabitants to death. Millions had died. Some of the bones they saw bore signs of butchery, inflicted as the desperate inhabitants resorted to cannibalism.

The hive shook to explosions, hivequakes following in their wake as the mountain-sized city shifted. At any moment he expected the whole edifice to collapse on them, but it held. His calls for aid went unheard.

'We have gone too deep,' Laziel gasped. 'They cannot hear us.'

'Then we must get nearer to the hive skin,' said Dante. They were on the brink of a shaft that disappeared into darkness a thousand metres below them. Distant gunfire rattled down towards them from above. Dante struggled to orient himself. Holywell Hive was six kilometres wide.

'Which way is it?' he said.

Laziel leaned against the wall. His armour leaked blood and machine fluids in equal amounts. The breaks in his armour were sticky with foaming shock gels. He wheezed painfully. Dante suspected at least one of his lungs had been punctured. 'Ask her,' said Laziel. He pointed.

Dante spun around. His bolter came up to aim at a wraith-thin girl in a dirty grey smock.

He lowered his gun. 'Little one, we are the angels of the Emperor. We seek a way out. Can you help us?'

She came forwards fearlessly. She was around twelve Terran years old. Dante hoped that was old enough for her to tell the difference between loyalist and traitor.

'Food,' she said.

Dante nodded and knelt. Slowly, so as not to scare her, he took a ration biscuit from his belt. 'We were given these to give to you, so you would not starve,' he said.

She snatched it from his hand, tearing its plastek package open with her teeth. She wolfed it down. Her threadbare dress blew against her, showing ribs made prominent by hunger.

'You know we are here to save you? We are not like the others.'

She nodded. 'You are the red angels. Father says you are good. Come this way,' she said.

Dante stood in relief. Still his thirst surged, but for now it was under control. He suffered thoughts of him ripping the girl's throat open and drinking her dry, but he discarded them and they had no effect on his comportment.

'See?' said Laziel, as Dante grabbed his arm. 'We must trust to those we protect to help us. With her aid we will rejoin the Legion.'

Dante froze. 'Legion, brother?'

'Our Chapter,' said Laziel muzzily. 'Our Chapter.'

Laziel's voice slurred. Dante hoped from pain. The alternative was too terrible to consider.

They went up obliquely through manufactory districts emptied by deliberate starvation. Factory dormitories stood silent, the bones of the dead shrouded by dust. They were moving away from the sounds of battle, and a deep quiet fell on the hive.

Laziel became stronger and needed Dante's aid less and less, but his confusion grew. Dante faced a dilemma: he needed to signal his comrades, but if Laziel was succumbing to the Black Rage then disaster beckoned.

The girl darted into a crack. Dante peered after her. She had gone into the fabric of the hive via a fault line in its wall. Stalactites orange with ferric compounds hung from the ceiling. She stopped and beckoned to him. He examined the passage; although tall, it was only just big enough for him to get into. He pushed Laziel in first.

'The Palace will hold,' said Laziel. 'You will see.'

'Laziel! Stay with me. Please, remember who you are.'

'I am Brother Laziel, and you are Brother Dante,' he slurred.

'That's right, I am Dante. Now crawl. Stay focused on the present. The memories of our father reach for you. Resist them.'

'Yes,' he muttered. 'I see them. I know, Dante. I will not fall. I swear.'

The passage cut into a proper access way, although one long disused. The girl led them down this to a recently patched door. Two sentries waited outside, stick-thin from starvation, clothes filthy and threadbare. Nevertheless, they were vigilant, and fell to their knees when they saw the Blood Angels emerge from the dark.

'My lords!' one said.

'On your feet, please. Do not bow,' said Dante. 'My brother needs urgent help. I have to contact my Chapter.'

The men nodded. One rapped on the gate.

'Open! Open!' he called.

The gates swung wide. Another corridor, broken by barricades, led a short way before turning sharply right into another set of gates. Ragged men stood up from their firing positions to gape at the demigods in their midst. Dante ignored them, dragging the semi-conscious Laziel with him. The second gates opened into a large, galleried factory filled with people. They lay on makeshift beds and crammed every square inch between giant steel presses. They crowded the catwalks running across the width of the hall, and sat in groups on balconies. Everywhere he looked, there were people.

The warm fug of close human life hit the Space Marines. So much life. So much blood. Laziel stirred. Dante's worry grew. Saliva filled his mouth.

'Who is in charge here?' Dante said.

Many of the crowd knelt in supplication and made the sign of the aquila, but they parted wide to let the Space Marines through.

'Father!' said the girl, running to a heavily bearded man. Like all of them, his cheeks were hollow and eyes sunken from the lack of food. He embraced his daughter and approached the Space Marines.

'I am Segelyes, factory headman. I am in charge, by the assent of my citizens. We are grateful to see you. The Emperor truly protects – we see that now, eh brothers and sisters?'

He shouted out to the room. A chorus of tired 'Ayes!' came back.

'The war is not done yet,' Dante said. 'Do you have a room where I might lay my brother? He is sorely wounded.'

'Yes, of course.' Segelyes led them to a small office. He ushered out the two families inside.

Dante lowered Laziel to the ground, glad to be free of his weight.

'Horus comes, brother,' whispered Laziel.

'What is he saying?' said Segelyes curiously.

'He is delirious,' said Dante, more sharply than he intended. 'Please, a moment. I have to signal my brothers.'

'Of course.' Segelyes bowed and withdrew, closing the door after him. Too flimsy to hold a brother. Dante cursed inwardly.

'Laziel, listen to me. You must remember.'

'Remember?'

'The Five Graces. Remember.'

'What graces?' he said feverishly.

'The Rule, Laziel. The Five Graces and the Five Virtues.'

'Rule? I impose no such thing on my sons.'

Dante's pulse rose with his anguish. He opened his vox-channels. 'This is Dante. Respond. We are separated from Squad Ophid. Please respond.'

A tense second followed. Dante nearly shouted in relief when the vox crackled in response.

'*Dante, this is Lorenz. We thought you were dead. The enemy is retreating. Victory approaches. Stay where you are and we will come to retrieve you. Captain Avernis has located your suit signum. I warn you, it might take a while. There is a knot of resistance between us and you. Somehow, you have pushed your way through The Purge's lines.*'

'How long?' said Dante. He was whispering.

'*What is wrong?*'

'Lorenz, we have been taken in by a group of civilians. There are a thousand or more of them.'

'*It is good that someone has survived this horror.*'

Dante's mouth went dry. 'Laziel is badly wounded. Lorenz. He's falling.'

'*Black or red?*'

'The black. The Black Rage. He's gibbering about Legions and the Imperial Palace.'

The vox snapped. Avernis' voice replaced Lorenz's. '*Dante, you must leave immediately. Get Laziel away from the citizens. Head for this rendezvous point here.*'

A cartograph flashed across Dante's faceplate. A red dot pulsed upon it.

'*I will send someone to get you now. The route is harder, and you will be at risk, but you have to leave. Be ready for extraction in one hour.*'

'Yes, captain,' said Dante. 'Stay here,' he said to Laziel.

Laziel moaned. Dante stopped by the door. Know no fear. He felt no fear for himself – that part of the legend was true – but he feared greatly for the fate of the people in the machine hall.

'Segelyes, I need your help,' he said, as evenly as he could. 'My brothers are coming to evacuate my injured comrade. I need to get to here.' Quickly, he sketched the map on the floor with the tip of an armoured finger, scratching it into the rockcrete floor. The mortals glanced at each other, amazed at the skill the rendition exhibited.

'I recognise it – it is half a mile from here. An external port in the hive skin. Maintenance.'

The hive shook to a faint rumble.

'Can you point me in the correct direction?'

'It would be easier to show you,' said Segelyes.

'It is not necessary.'

A cry came from Laziel. Dante weighed his options. He could probably get there on his own. But if he didn't...

'Very well. Take me, but only a few of you. We cannot risk attracting the enemy's attention.' That was not the reason. Dante could not tell them of the risk Laziel posed to them. Better a few die than many.

'We shall leave immediately. Zelger, Bozots! Get your guns and your crews.' He spoke again to Dante, face bright with pride. 'I will lead you out personally.'

On reflection, Dante was glad of his guides. They took him through a tangled labyrinth of neglected passageways that would have confounded him had he attempted the trip alone. Laziel moaned every so often, but was quiescent, and Dante dared to hope.

In half an hour they stood in the antechamber to an airlock leading outside. Segelyes looked at it thoughtfully.

'I have never seen beyond this place.'

'You would need breathing apparatus to survive outside,' said Dante. 'The air is thin so far above your world's seas.'

Segelyes nodded. 'So it is said. It is good to know for certain.'

Dante glanced at Laziel, who was slumped against the wall.

'You must go.'

Segelyes' men gathered up their guns. The sentry at the door held up a hand. The rest fell instantly silent.

'Bootsteps,' he said. 'Heavy. Adeptus Astartes.'

'Your brethren?' asked Segelyes.

Dante shook his head. He unslung his boltgun and moved alongside the sentry.

The burning glow of helm lenses shone down the passageway. A bolt-round slammed into the wall by the door and exploded.

'The Purge!' he shouted. He fired back. They were trapped. The civilians would be slaughtered. Segelyes' men were prising cabinets from the walls and taking shelter behind them. Such barricades would be next to useless against mass-reactives, and the militia would last seconds in combat with renegades.

Dante's fury rose. So close, and here innocent men would lose their lives because of him. He emptied his boltgun, filling the approach to the antechamber with streaking micromissiles. They exploded loudly around his enemy. One gave out a metallic cry and fell dead. They retreated a step.

'Are they falling back?' asked the sentry. More men joined them around the door.

'Get back!' said Dante. Too late. A rocket streaked down the corridor, exploding on the outside of the door. Dante was flung backwards. He slammed down and tumbled over, crushing a man under the weight of his armour.

The men who had guarded the door with him were splashed all around the entrance. The smell of burned meat and blood flooded Dante's nostrils. He tried to seal his helm, but it was malfunctioning. His ears rang. He glanced round at scared faces, at men firing guns that could not hope to penetrate Space Marine armour. They had come there for him, to aid him and his brother.

Figures moved down the corridor.

Unreasoning fury overpowered Dante's reason. He surged to his feet, sword in hand, and ran howling at The Purge. Bolt-rounds blew all over his armour. The insistent peeping of warning runes became a clamour. He crashed into the traitors, sword hewing the first down. His bolt pistol ended the next. Knives jabbed at him, hammered by transhuman strength into the ceramite of his battleplate. Swords bounced from his pauldrons. Hands grappled with him, but Dante could not be stopped. He slew them, smashing their treacherous bodies down. His helmet was wrenched away, and his senses were flooded with blood – its colour, its smell. His rage built until he was a killing machine. From there it was a short step to a warm, wet world, rich with the scent of iron. The thing that was Dante receded, leaving an unguided weapon in its stead. His last foe fell, and he pounded back into the antechamber.

'Lord Dante?' asked Segelyes. He took a step backwards, horrified by the bloodshot eyes and extended fangs of the Blood Angel.

Howling incoherently, Dante attacked. The world became a confusion of screams and hot, red blood pouring down his throat.

There was a flash of gold. A mightier angel than he stood before him. With a single blow the Sanguinor sent him reeling backwards. A second banished him deep into unconsciousness.

'Dante? Brother Dante? Can you hear me?'

A bright light flashed in his eyes.

'He's awake, captain.'

'Is he cogent?'

'Captain Avernis?' said Dante. 'Where am I?'

It took a moment for Dante to place himself in the airlock adjoining the antechamber. His brothers stood around him, weapons ready. Both interior and exterior doors were open. A Stormhawk hovered in the dirty sky outside. A humid decompression wind blew out from the hive.

'The Purge,' said Dante.

'You killed them all,' said Avernis. 'Six of them, by yourself. Impressive. You display the Warrior's Virtues strongly.'

Dante got to his feet.

'What of Laziel?'

'He is unconscious. We shall heal his hurts. Then we will know soon enough if he has fallen too far.'

'Unconscious? I remember blood, and screams...' he said in sudden dismay. Dante looked down at his hands. They were drenched in blood. The salty iron of vitae coated his throat. Not Laziel. Him. 'The civilians.'

Two of Avernis' command squad caught his arms. 'Let me go! Let me see!'

'Stop, brother!' commanded Avernis.

Dante yanked free and stumbled back into the antechamber.

The natives were dead, their throats torn out, skin pale from exsanguination. Dante looked around himself in horror. Segelyes yet lived. He was propped dazed against a wall, his stomach bleeding from a ragged wound. He stared ahead blankly. 'The golden angel, the golden angel,' he said repeatedly.

Avernis took Dante's arm, and drew his hand into both of his own, gripping it tightly. 'Dante. The thirst took you. You are not responsible. You would have been dead if it had not. You have saved hundreds of civilians like these. This is the price we pay.'

'I cannot...' said Dante. He could not deny what he saw. He could not deny the flavour of vitae on his lips. Against his horror, his appetite rose again and he turned away in shame.

'What of this one?' asked Veteran-Brother Strollo, one of Avernis' warriors. He pointed at Segelyes.

'No one can know of this,' said Avernis. 'Our shame must remain secret.' Gently, he shepherded Dante from the room into the airlock chamber.

Dante was climbing into the Stormraven when a single bolt shot banged from inside. He made to go back across the shifting assault ramp of the gunship, but Avernis pushed him inside.

The ramp closed, and the Stormraven bore Dante away.

Appalled, Dante henceforth resolved he would take no blood from a living host ever again.

CHAPTER EIGHTEEN

THE GRACE OF MERCY

998.M41
The Aegis Diamondo
Cryptus System

The lord commander's private librarium aboard the *Blade of Vengeance* held thousands of volumes. Many had been painstakingly copied by hand from data-retrieval devices broken long ago, and as such were unique. Of these treasures, none were as precious as the Scrolls of Sanguinius, ninety-nine rolls penned by the hand of the primarch himself, recording his innermost thoughts. The originals were interred deep in the Vaults of Marest in the Librarium, protected from decay by powerful stasis fields. There were only five other copies. In his long life, Dante had handled the originals only three times.

Dante sat in day robes of red and gold at his oversized desk. Though the copy exhibited little wear, Dante had read Sanguinius' words on countless occasions. One passage in particular he returned to more than any other. His fingers traced the words now, smooth velvet gloves protecting the vellum from the secretions of his skin.

I fear what I have seen, the primarch wrote. *My visions plague me with darkness. So little of comfort can be gleaned from them. The consequences of our victory are dire indeed, as I have described in these writings, and yet there are some things I cannot bring myself to record, visions so dark that they fill my heart with despair.*

The dreams of my father are dead, that is certain. Long aeons await of war and suffering that would break the heart of the Emperor to perceive. He never showed any sign that He saw the dark future advancing towards us. Does He know? I cannot credit that He does not. My gift of foresight – if gift it can truly be named – descends from His, and His is more potent than I can conceive. Time and again I have asked myself, did He always know, and did He foresee all that has come to pass? Or was He, like me, taken unawares? The brighter future I once saw has been burned to ashes and a second, rotten potentiality raised in its place. I curse you, Horus, I curse you to the end of days.

I have written too often on these matters. I still cannot divine the answer. I shall instead write down my dream of last night. This brought some comfort to me when no comfort ought to be expected, and is thus worthy of record.

Dante unrolled the scroll, exposing the next page.

There shall come to pass days of great darkness, when mankind is diminished and all the lights of the world shall be extinguished, and the final scraps of hope torn away. I dreamed I was upon a plain of black sand studded with diamond stars. In the dream there was a great hunger that pervaded all time and space, a more terrible and consuming appetite than the thirst that dogs my sons. It rose from the east of the night, and swallowed the moons of Baal that coursed across the unfamiliar sky. Before Baal Secundus was consumed, a bright light flashed upon it and sped away, outpacing the shadows.

The hunger spread rapidly, bloated by its meal of my home. Fortified by the blood of Baal, the formless hunger took shape, becoming a ravenous dragon that consumed the stars in great mouthfuls, until the only light was the memory of their glory, trapped in the diamonds on the sand. As the last star was eaten, the hellish Octed of the traitors burned through the western sky, writ in fire on the starless void. Then this too went out, and I was alone in the dark.

Shadows swirled and parted. The vision lost its disguise of metaphor, and I looked upon a scene that may be a true echo of the future. I saw my father. Ruined. Broken. I knew it was Him, though His body was little more than a corpse, for I could feel His mind. His power was much reduced in potency, and I could feel no sense of consciousness there, merely raging, ungoverned power that threatened to obliterate my sleeping mind. This living corpse of my father was trapped in machinery that fed His soul the essence of others. I do not know if I should commit this to paper, even in my private writings. He cannot ever know of this fate, if He does not already. Or is He aware, and makes this choice between that life in death and the utter destruction of mankind? If so, my respect for my father grows.

As the guns of the Warmaster pound at the walls of the Palace, perhaps this miserable reality is the best that can be hoped for. Perhaps this is what I must die to ensure.

The hunger came for my father. The puppets of the Dark Gods clashed with the hunger for the pleasure of killing Him. There was a warrior in gold before the throne, surrounded by my father's Custodians and other heroes who, mighty though they were, paled next to the lords of our days. There they fought, and there they died. The vision ended as the devourer of flesh and the devourers of souls closed in on my lord and creator. There was despair only, despair and more despair. But before I woke something more. I sensed stirring in the warp, and the touch of my father, His mind made anew, and the knowledge that all might be well.

As I am fated to, so too did this golden warrior lay down his life to protect my father. The precious seconds he bought with his blood could change everything, or they could change nothing. Maybe the vision is false. I pray the future is mutable, and so it has proved in the past. All but the moment that draws near, the reckoning when I must face my brother. That I cannot avoid.

I do not know who this golden warrior was. He appeared similar to my Herald, and I saw my own face depicted upon his mask, but he was not me, and he wore a form of armour I do not know. It is certain that he was one of my sons, and whether his sacrifice will prove to be in vain or not, I know this: that he was a noble warrior, true and purer than any of his age, and I love him for that, for it means that my works for the Emperor, at least, have not been undertaken in vain, and that my unavoidable death might also prove fruitful.

The entry ended.

The commander sat back in his chair, the ancient rosewood creaking with the shift in his weight. He did not recall the first time he had the notion that the warrior was him. Others assumed it was the Sanguinor, but Dante was convinced it was not. He had dismissed his thoughts as vainglory, and sought penance.

His discomfort at casting himself as this great saviour grew every time he read the scroll. The compulsion to read it only grew in tandem with his conviction that Sanguinius had been describing he, Dante, nine thousand years before he had been born.

Maybe he was like Sanguinius, facing his own certain end, searching for hope in a cruel future. But even that comparison was arrogant.

He let his eyes wander over the priceless volumes of his librarium. Could it be that the primarch had foresight of the Devourer? That passage had mystified and worried Dante for centuries before the tyranid threat emerged. When the scale of the threat became apparent, he had known what the primarch saw. And now Abaddon struck out from the Eye of Terror. The likelihood that he was the warrior in gold increased.

He fretted over what he should do. Should he emulate his gene-father and rush to face his fate, or should he try to defy it? Would seeking to hasten the event lead to disaster? Was it only resistance to the bitter end that would make Sanguinius' vision come true?

There was only one answer to that question. He let his mind wander. He imagined himself dying in the face of impossible odds.

Such daydreaming was his only indulgence, and more restful than sleep. The relief death would bring to him... How he anticipated it more eagerly every year.

He must wait. He must fight. Dante would never allow himself to give up to any enemy, least of all despair.

'My lord?'

Arafeo stood at the far end of the room, bearing a rattling tray of food and drink in his gnarled hands.

'Approach, my servant,' Dante said. He was relieved his dark reverie was broken. Arafeo's presence anchored him to the present and reminded him who he was, and of his appointed task.

'I thought you might need refreshment, my lord.'

Dante made an equivocal gesture. Arafeo set the tray down. 'You are troubled, my lord,' said Arafeo.

Dante almost shouted at his servant for presuming to know his mind. He subdued his anger and laid a hand flat on the scroll, seeking to draw comfort from Sanguinius' words by physical contact.

'Who could not be troubled, Arafeo? The galaxy burns. I have led this Chapter for over a thousand years. I served as captain for three hundred, and before that I was a line trooper and sergeant for two hundred more.' He looked into the rheumy eyes of his servant. 'I have fought every foe that mankind must face, from the overt aggression of the orks to the grinding of unthinking bureaucracy.'

'You have triumphed over them all, my lord,' said Arafeo. His face lit up. 'You are the greatest hero of the Imperium! Who can claim to have lived so long or achieved so much?'

'I am an outcome of probability,' said Dante. 'There is nothing particularly special about me. It has often been said of my kind that we are functionally immortal, but we rarely survive long enough to test the theory. When I see the lines on my face, I begin to understand what that means. I am not immortal. I have become old. I wonder often how many years are left in me. And it is not my skill at arms or my skills in leadership that have preserved my life, Arafeo, but chance. Someone, from the thousands of Space

Marines of Sanguinius' line, had to reach so advanced an age. It just happened to be me.'

'You are more than a product of chance, my lord! You are a being of will, and power. A warrior saint.'

'Arafeo, I am no saint,' warned Dante.

His servant continued to speak, his words rushing out. 'Before I attempted the trial on Baal Primus, I used to listen every night to stories of your heroism. It was your example that made me dream of the stars, of ascending in the sky chariots to Baal itself and serving in the Emperor's wars.' He spoke rapturously, carried away to some other place.

'I am sorry you were not chosen.'

Arafeo smiled, exposing teeth made long by age. He bent forwards and gripped Dante's hand in his cold, gnarled fingers. 'My lord, serving you has been my great pleasure. When I was denied entrance to the Chapter, my heart was broken. If I could go back to that day when I was taken from the chosen ones, I would whisper in my younger self's ear, be glad! Sanguinius smiles upon you, for you shall serve Lord Dante himself.' Arafeo gave Dante's hand a fatherly pat. Although Dante was fourteen centuries his senior, Arafeo's paternal attitude comforted the commander.

Dante withdrew his hand. 'I read these scrolls looking for meaning in my life. I am afraid to admit it, but I must to someone. I apologise for what I am to share with you, Arafeo, you who have served me so well.' He paused. The gravity of what he wished to say was unbearable. He had to share his fears with someone. He spoke measuredly, without emotion. 'The Imperium will fall – not today, but soon. I search for a way out but all I see are the black walls of dead ends. Great victories were once mine, and confidence and a certainty in a better future. How like Sanguinius I must have been!' he said ruefully. 'My triumphs have become tarnished with the knowledge of certain defeat. Has all I have done been for naught? I have slain creatures that are not of this reality, Arafeo. I have faced the curse of the Chapter and kept my soul free of its taint. All my life I have striven to serve not only the Imperium, but humanity.

To be a Blood Angel is to immerse oneself in blood and death. My salvation is to defy it, to turn death upon itself in the name of life.

'This Chapter has come close to total destruction three times in the last three thousand years. During the Ghost War, at Kallius, at Secoris. Every time, we come back. Every time, the winged blood drop has flown from the standards of ten full companies again.'

Arafeo nodded in mute sympathy.

'I understand, Arafeo, that I must be a hero for humanity. They must look on the golden mask of Sanguinius and know he is there with them as they die or worse in the name of Terra. This is my role in life – to pretend to be something I am not. I allow my legend to grow beyond all measure of truthfulness. I allow men to think me infallible and potent beyond my means. I embrace it gladly for the service it gives mankind. But although I am mighty and wise, and of the Adeptus Astartes, I am just a man. Under my armour beats a human heart alongside the one gifted me by the Emperor. No man is isolate – all need company and companionship. This is why I share my thoughts with you. I apologise for my indiscretion, but I cannot keep my own concerns hidden from everyone. They will crush me.'

'I understand,' he said softly. 'I am sorry to have raised these fears in you while you are at rest, but know you are never alone.'

'I am never at rest,' said Dante bitterly. 'And I am forever alone.'

Cowed, Arafeo departed. Dante barely noticed him leave.

The Chapter Master returned to his reading. Confessing his fears to his equerry had done nothing to lessen them. He felt ashamed. He should not burden a mortal with such knowledge. By naming an evil, he had given it strength. The words of the scroll seemed to swim, and he bowed his head.

A cry sounded deep in the stacks. Dante leapt to his feet.

'Arafeo? Arafeo, are you all right?'

A soft moan answered him. Dante strode past book stacks and scroll cases, went by towering crystal racks.

The scent of blood reached his nostrils before he found Arafeo, hot and vital in the dusty atmosphere of ancient knowledge.

Arafeo was kneeling on the ground, holding his wrist. The librarium was so quiet that Dante's enhanced hearing had no trouble picking up the weak, erratic beat of his servant's heart. Blood dripped onto the carpet.

Dante hurried to him. Arafeo smiled. The smell of blood flooded Dante's nostrils, arousing his thirst. He grabbed his servant's hands and held them up. He had cut his wrists, his life fluid flooding from long vertical slits running from his hands to elbows.

'Arafeo! Arafeo!' he cried. 'What have you done?'

A smile slow as spilt blood spread across the equerry's face. 'Master, it is time I left you.'

'Not now! Hold on, my friend. I am sorry. I should never have burdened you with my woes. It was not right. I did not mean to frighten you. I shall summon Corbulo himself to tend to you.'

Dante reached for the vox-bead embedded in his collar, but Arafeo pawed at his arm with a feeble, paper-skinned hand until his weak fingers snagged themselves around Dante's thick wrist. Dante was horribly conscious of the thick blood slipping around between their skins.

'My lord, please do not. I am not frightened. You did no wrong. The Emperor is calling me to His side. My time is done in this world.'

Dante reached for his button again. Arafeo gripped with surprising strength.

'You are my master, but I beg you, allow me this one decision. My heart is old, and I am weary in my own way.'

'You do not have to die,' said Dante.

Arafeo shook his head, so painfully slowly. His neat grey hair had come undone from its fastenings and hung about his head in a curtain. 'We all have to die. Except you, my lord. You cannot.'

'That is not true. I can die, and I will.'

'Yes, my lord,' breathed Arafeo. 'But you must not yet. While you live, while the golden mask of Sanguinius is seen on the battlefields of this awful era, you can make a difference. My lord, do not give up.'

Arafeo swooned. Dante caught him. Cradling his servant, he smoothed the old man's hair. 'I am weary, Arafeo, and worn down by ennui, but I cannot give up. I never shall. I swear. While I breathe, I shall fight, and no man shall know what troubles me again.'

Arafeo closed his eyes happily. 'That is good. You are hope, even if you feel little yourself.'

'But why kill yourself? I do not understand.'

'You do, my lord, though you say you do not. I have one last request.'

'Name it, and it shall be yours, Arafeo.'

'Take my life, my lord. Drink my blood. Grant me one last boon. Give me the angel's kiss. This is why I have chosen to die now, so that you can take on the strength in my blood, so much greater than that in my body, and rise anew. Let me die knowing I have served you one final time. I offer my life, to you, so that so many others might live.'

Weakly, he held up his bleeding wrist towards Dante's face.

'I will not.' Dante moved back. Blood ran in rivulets and soaked into the carpet.

'I have served you a long time. You have not known the taste of vitae from a living vessel for as long as I have known you.'

'Longer,' said Dante. His teeth were extruding from his gums against his will. His blood rushed around his skull. 'I made an oath to myself never again to drink living blood.'

'Then you must break it. To drink the stuff of life is the curse of the angels, but you need it. You are weak without blood – you are so old. I am dying anyway. Take it from me. Become strong.'

'This should not be,' said Dante. 'I refuse.' He recoiled. Arafeo's blood covered his hands. He wanted more than anything to lick it off his skin.

'Then you go back on your word.'

'You use my honour as a weapon against me,' said Dante. His resolve was dying. His fangs dug into his jaw. His face flushed.

'There is no other weapon that might harm you,' said Arafeo with a dry chuckle. He grimaced. His hands clenched. 'Please. I do not have time. This blood of mine I bequeath to you. Drink your fill. Restore your strength for the wars to come.' He stared into Dante's eyes fiercely. 'Now!'

Again, Arafeo held his wrists up to his lord. Against his will, Dante opened his mouth wide. Saliva flooded his mouth as his lips brushed against Arafeo's blood-slippery skin. Arafeo gave a little moan as Dante's needle-sharp teeth slid into his wrists.

Dante gulped greedily at the man's blood, feeling its warmth flood his body, a rich, raw tingling that spread from his hearts to the tips of his limbs. With the flow of vitae came a rush of emotion from the dying man. Dante's omophagea engorged itself with fragments of the man's genetic lifecode, teasing his memory from the engrams graven upon their metaphysical fabric. A hard childhood, like his own. A brief moment of glory in making his way to the Place of Challenge. Crushing disappointment as the Sanguinary Priest's testing device chimed angrily and flashed red. A ray of hope as he was sent to join the blood thralls. A moment of indecision when he was given the choice to return home or go to Baal – a choice revisited thousands of times in a life of grinding servitude.

Arafeo swooned and toppled over. Dante followed, his mouth fixed to his servant's arm.

Arafeo's life was tedious and short, and wholly lacking in glory. But his memories were suffused throughout with his sense of privilege at working for the Chapter, a satisfaction that what he did was necessary and appreciated, a service to the Emperor as important as wielding blade and bolter, and a genuine love for his master. Dante wept as he drained the man of life. In the last iron drops of blood to slide down his gullet came Arafeo's gratitude.

Arafeo's heart fluttered under Dante's hand and stilled. The lord commander sat back on his heels, leaving one hand on his dead servant's chest. With the other he wiped the mixture of blood and tears from his face. Arafeo's eyes were open, and though the soul-light had gone from them, his final expression was one of happiness.

A complex mix of emotion coursed through Dante: satisfaction from his feeding, sorrow for his servant, revulsion at his thirst, and, most difficult to quantify, shame that he could not live up to the way Arafeo had seen him.

He was calmer. The weight of years sat more lightly on his shoulders. He felt his skin tighten and the lines that marred his face shallow. He got to his feet, heavy with his meal, yet already feeling the first sting of renewed vitality. He depressed the tiny emerald that served as his vox-switch.

'Grennius,' he said, summoning his master of household. 'Arafeo has left us. Send a mortuary team to my private librarium. And summon my armourium thralls. I need my armour.'

Dante knew what he must do. The time for thought was done.

CHAPTER NINETEEN

THE PIRATE KING

752.M40

Odrius Freeport

Mas

Tivian System

'Everyone down!' ordered Dante.

Squad Dante threw themselves into the heaved earth. Ceramite scraped on buried masonry. The booming chug of heavy bolter fire sent shrieking munitions past them.

Dante took shelter in the corner of a wrecked building. Blue paint still clung to the plaster in the angle of the walls, bizarrely bright in the grey-and-brown dust of the shattered city. A large-calibre mass-reactive blew a chunk from his cover, and he leaned back and reached for his auspex.

The device supplemented his suit's sensorium, projecting fine detail scans on its screen and into his faceplate simultaneously. His squad took opportunistic shots at the shadows flitting through the buildings on the other side of the street as he scanned the pirate strongpoint.

'Heavy bunker emplacement at the crossroads,' he said. 'Anti-tank cannon, threat extremis. Keep the armour back.'

'Let me take it, brother-sergeant,' said Gallimus.

Dante risked another look across the rubble-strewn road. The city had been so heavily bombarded it had become a wasteland of bricks and toppled blocks. The roads were evident as valleys amid hillocks of ruination. The bunker guarded a crossroads on the route to the palace, but the roads were choked with rubble and the bunker was buried to the vision slits in a plain of loose stone. Dante looked from Gallimus' position to the bunker. The heavy-weapon trooper was in a poor position.

'Stay where you are. They will bring you down before you have a chance to fire.'

Gallimus nodded at him and slid back a little on his knees, the green glow of his plasma cannon lighting the wreckage around him.

'Squad Dante! Stand ready for assault,' ordered Dante.

A cry sounded over the squad vox-net. Brother Thorael's signum rune flickered.

'Thorael?'

'*I have a crack in my armour, sergeant. It is sealing. I will be fine,*' said the warrior.

It was not unknown for his men to fight on when they should head back for treatment, so Dante checked the truth of Thorael's statement, bringing his status runes to the top level of his layered datascreed. Thorael's vital signs held steady. His armour blinked from amber to green again as its sealant systems closed the breach, sealing it from the environment.

'Lorenz!' he called.

'*Dante,*' replied his friend.

'You are in charge. I need to call in an artillery strike.' Dante switched channels to the company vox. 'This is Brother Dante. Captain Avernis?'

There was pause. The vox jumped as another responded.

'*This is Duvallai, Dante. No one's heard anything from the captain for ten minutes. There is an interference pattern over the western quadrant where he led the third and fourth squads. The Freeborn are jamming his communications.*'

'Then they are more stupid than we thought if they think that will stop us. I am going to push forwards. I could do with some support. Are you with me?'

The crackle of weapons fire heard through the thick plating of Space Marine armour was Dante's answer. Duvallai's bolter coughed through the vox.

'*Sorry. Busy. I am with you. I am about a hundred and fifty yards behind your position. Let me clear these irritants out. We are nearly done.*'

Dante peered out from the ruin. He snatched his head back when his movements drew another burst of fire from the heavy bolters of the bunker. 'Advance along the left,' he said, forced to shout. Gravel pinged off his armour. 'There's a large rubble mound round the stump of the bell tower.'

'*I see it, brother.*'

'Stand ready to provide covering fire. I cannot discern if there is anything beyond the bunker, so this might be all we have to deal with here, but it will be good to have you watching our backs.'

Another crackling eruption of fire. Shouts of triumph echoed in Duvallai's helmet. His vox cut out for a second. Dante waited for him to return.

'*Sorry, sorry – taken by surprise. That is the last of them. We are moving up in support. Sanguinius guide us.*'

Duvallai's feed went dead. Dante ran through his vox-codes for the Armoury net.

'Brother Havrael? Can you hear me?'

'*The Armoury listens, brother-sergeant.*'

'I need a Whirlwind strike on this position.' He adjusted the knobs of his auspex, homing its targeting matrix onto the bunker. 'You will not be able to bring up the armour unless we deal with it. They have some kind of large-bore cannon in there.'

'*I am able to oblige immediately. Whirlwind strike incoming.*'

A fraction of a second later Whirlwind rockets screamed into the ground from the smoky sky. Multiple explosions detonated yards from their position. Dante huddled back into the isolated corner until they were done. He poked his head out. Smoke billowed from the bunker's vision slits. The cannon barrel jutted impotently at the sky. No bolt-rounds responded to his appearance.

'Duvallai?'

'*I am in position,*' voxed Duvallai. '*Brother Damiano has a fine shot lined up on the bunker.*'

'Very well. Let us finish this. Squad Dante!' bellowed Dante. 'Forward!'

'For the Emperor! For Sanguinius!' his warriors responded.

They rushed up from their cover, blood-red armour shedding sheets of dust. They roared through their vox-grilles. From the stump of the bell tower came a storm of bolt shots. The ruby stab of a lascannon blasted through the air, vitrifying the dust swirling through the ruins into a glittering fall.

Dante was at the bunker first, bounding powerfully forwards. He kicked open the door, sending an avalanche of brick shards inside. He ducked within. A Freeborn corsair came out of the rear firing room, blood running down his dust-caked face. Dante shot him before he could bring his autogun up, blasting his viscera all over the wall. Dante sealed his suit mask, shutting himself off from the enticing smell of blood.

Brother Emanuele slid down the bricks into the bunker. Dante strode forwards, flinging a frag grenade into the rear room. The entrance to the front was sealed tight. Dante plucked his melta bomb from his thigh. It was a waste to use the munition – the Freeborn in the firing chamber were probably all dead – but his patience was frayed from the delay and he wished to be done.

He signalled Emanuele back and remotely detonated the bomb. It hissed as its fusion reactor went off and burned out, taking the door to the floor as a sheet of orange liquid metal.

Dante approached along the wall. He had not seen the Freeborn wield much in the way of personal weaponry that could penetrate Adeptus Astartes battleplate – not the human ones, anyway– but his natural caution had never left him. He plucked another frag grenade from his belt and tossed it around the door. It banged loudly and he followed, bolter up.

Wisps of blue fyceline smoke curled up from the floor. There were four pirates, three human and a reptilian sslyth. All of them were dead, their bodies opened up by shrapnel from the rocket strike. The vision slits were ragged with chunks of metal.

'Clear,' said Dante.

'No enemy here,' said Emanuele.

'Duvallai, brother, any more trouble?'

'*Negative, the Freeborn are dead or fled. I count about fifteen – mostly men, a handful of eldar.*'

'There's a sslyth here.'

'*A sslyth?*' cut in Lorenz. '*I have not seen one of those for* years. *Make sure you get its skin. It is a pleasure to work with.*'

'You're welcome to it, brother. Havrael filled it with holes.'

'*A pity,*' said Lorenz.

Dante strode out. Emanuele stepped aside. When he exited the bunker, he put up his back banner. The pole emerged from his powerplant, the crossbeam opened out and the cloth unfurled into the dust-clogged breeze. 'Squad Dante, form up on my position. Duvallai, are you joining us?'

'*Brother, you are senior sergeant of the Fifth. While Captain Avernis is absent, I will gladly follow you.*'

'Brother Havrael, this quadrant is secure. You are safe to bring up the armour.' Dante walked up the shifting slopes of rubble. The strike cruiser had done a thorough job of flattening the city. He reached a ridge formed by a tower that had fallen across the street. It had come down whole, the masonry separating only as it laid itself across the road. The stone and brick parted slightly in a way that gave it the appearance of a great skeleton.

From his new vantage point, Dante had a clear view to the Pirate King's palace. All of the freeport was cast down. The smell of corpses rotting under the broken buildings grew stronger every day. Only the palace stood, protected by its shimmering void shield. Beyond, green oceans glimmered.

'This world will make a fine addition to the Imperium,' said Lorenz as he joined Dante on the pile of rubble. 'Once it is pacified.'

'This nest of pirates has had its day. The time of the Freeborn is done,' said Dante. 'So shall all suffer who defy the Emperor of Mankind.'

'Well said,' said Lorenz. 'A shame we had to devote a demi-company to clearing it out.'

The howling thrum of grav motors overhead made them look to the sky. Three light eldar support vehicles zoomed past, weapons pointing backwards, firing rapidly at the Stormhawk pursuing them. Tracer fire blazed from the interceptor's assault cannons, shattering one of the eldar skiffs. They raced away, lost to sight.

The squeal of tank tracks on stone echoed up the street. Two Baal Predators, a Land Raider, a Vindicator and the Whirlwind advanced upon the crossroads.

'The forces of the Armoury approach,' said Dante. 'We shall wait for the captain. He will most likely order a frontal assault.'

'That is his way,' said Lorenz. 'What would you do?'

'I would order a full frontal assault, brother,' said Dante.

Lorenz chuckled.

'*Brother-Sergeant Dante.*' The urgent voice of Veteran-Brother Strollo cut into their conversation.

'Brother,' said Dante. 'You have dealt with the pirate's jamming devices?'

'*We have, but that's the only good news I have. We need you here, now. Captain Avernis is slain.*'

Avernis lay twisted on the rubble, his battleplate gaping with ugly, half-melted breaches, his neck bloody where his progenoids had been removed.

'Eldar?' said Dante. The five sergeants of the demi-company were gathered together around their fallen leader.

'Eldar,' said Strollo. He pointed to a collection of bloody rags in the corner. 'I killed it the second it shot the captain. Multi-shot melta weapon, burned him from the inside out. Cursed luck.' Strollo was a phlegmatic man. If he sorrowed, he did not let it show.

Techmarine Havrael knelt at the captain's side. Sanguinary

Initiate Viscomi stepped away to allow him space to work. He slid out the reductor pod carrying Avernis' gene-seed and placed it into an armoured case. 'I have salvaged his progenoid glands,' he said. 'His line will live on.'

'But his armour is ruined,' said Havrael. 'Where is the rest of his wargear?'

Strollo pointed back to his squad mates. Havrael went to them and took the captain's weapons.

'The Pirate King is looking to behead us,' said Duvallai.

'He has succeeded,' said Sergeant Horael.

'No, no, he has not,' said Sergeant Malthus. 'They think removing our leader will stop us. I do not think they have fought Space Marines before.' His blue helmet looked around the circle of Space Marines. 'They are wrong, are they not, brothers?'

'They could not be more wrong,' agreed Sergeant Kalael. 'Victory is within our grasp. Who shall lead us?'

'We should ask Chaplain Fernibus to come down from the ship,' said Horael.

'He is injured, and waiting would delay our attack,' said Malthus.

'Dante is senior in the demi-company,' said Duvallai.

'Then I shall lead,' said Dante. 'Do any of you object?'

'No,' said Horael.

'Nor I,' said Kalael.

'We shall verify this with Fernibus,' said Malthus. 'But as far as I am concerned, you are our captain for now, brother. Congratulations. I can think of none better.'

Dante nodded curtly and looked to the archaic stone castellum of the palace. A modest structure by Imperial standards.

'Then let us plan our attack,' said Dante. 'We shall add vengeance to our mission objectives.'

The corridors of the castellum echoed with the sound of boltgun fire. They were narrow, wide enough for only one Space Marine to walk, so Dante went at the forefront of his squad, his bolter spewing explosive death at anything that dared show itself. Humans, eldar and aliens of lesser races died at his hand. They went into a long gallery. Shurikens hissed through the air, spat by the guns of bounding aliens. Humans fought alongside them, firing from behind barricades made of toppled statuary.

The Blood Angels fanned out, their armour shrugging off the worst of the enemy fire.

'Remarkable,' said Lorenz. 'I have never seen eldar working with humans.'

'It is a wonder we could do without,' said Dante. Three shurikens thunked into his armour, their monomolecular edges protruding from his chest. He blasted apart a pirate lurking behind a pillar in reply. He ran into a storm of las-bolts and shurikens, his squad with him. Brother Cherael went down. The rest of them thundered into the barricades, kicking them over and making short work of the men behind. They caught a handful of the eldar, but several raced away, disappearing deeper into the palace. Lorenz made to chase them.

'Leave them. This place is small. They will not go far.' Dante reached down and hauled a dying man to his feet. 'The Pirate King, where is he?'

The man gurgled, choking on his own blood. 'The Freeborn will never submit.'

'As you wish,' said Dante. He broke the man's neck with a twist of his hand and dropped the corpse. 'We'll try the throne-room. These xenos are arrogant enough that he's probably sitting in there waiting for us. Brother Gallimus!'

The squad heavy-weapon trooper moved to the front.

'Sergeant.'

'Stand by me. Prime your weapon.'

'Yes, sergeant' said Gallimus.

'Ortiel! Bring your flamer up. Cleanse the rooms as we pass. Do not stint on your fuel. I do not care if we burn this place to the ground. This ends today.'

The Pirate King was indeed in the throne-room. He lounged in his throne, sipping at a tall glass full of purple wine. His angular alien face teetered between boredom and anticipation. When Dante entered he unhooked his legs from a throne arm and saluted with his glass.

'Hail to you, angel of blood!' he said in mellifluous Gothic. 'I am Prince Hellaineth, the so-called Pirate King. Welcome to the heart of my kingdom, all that is left, alas.'

The eldar made no move. Dante scanned the room for hidden threats. His helm outlined possible hiding places for weaponry. False colour highlighting flickered off as it discounted them one by one.

'Oh, there's no need for that,' said Hellaineth, guessing what Dante was doing. 'I didn't bother fortifying this room. It didn't really seem necessary. I reasoned, and I do like to think quite a lot – and, excuse my conceit, I am rather good at it – that by the time anyone got this far, a laser array or lance hidden behind the paintings wouldn't do me much good. Besides, such alterations would destroy the character of this castle. It is so delightfully... crude.' He waved his arm at the dark stone walls, showing them off.

Squad Dante filed into the chamber, crowding it with their blood-red forms. At a command from Dante, they levelled their guns at the alien, their slides racked back in mechanical unison.

'Xenos! You have enslaved the human populace of this world and used it as a base to commit gross crimes against the Imperium of Man. Do you have anything to say for yourself before I kill you?'

'I enslaved nobody. All were freeborn here. My people were free of the path of my kind, your people liberated from your soul-sucking Emperor. I doubt you can understand the concept of freedom, though. No more than a sword of dull iron could. You are a tool. Tools are not free. What a pity. You destroy that which you cannot understand.'

'Very well,' said Dante, not interested in the least in the eldar's words. 'Squad!'

Hellaineth stood, his face darkening. 'You think you can kill me? Your arrogance almost matches that of the eldar! They could not contain my ambition. You will fare no better. This world was a haven! Look at how many kinds of creature lived here in har-mony. Do you not think before you destroy?'

'They were all thieves,' said Dante.

'And why should they not be? The galaxy gave them nothing.' The eldar smiled wickedly. 'It is the duty of the weak to take from the strong, so they themselves may be strong. The strong dislike to be dispossessed, so? It is good to make people see things from the other side. Life is too precious to experience from one standpoint alone.' He looked at Squad Dante. 'Though I suppose my philoso-phy falls on deaf ears here. You engineered creatures were never particularly flexible of thought.' He took another sip of his wine.

'Your ships are taken, your city is levelled,' said Dante. 'Your fol-lowers are dead. You do not appear overly concerned. I know your kind, xenos. You do not care. This is a game to you.'

Prince Hellaineth shrugged. 'Perhaps. These last fifty years as ruler have been a distraction from despair. This galaxy was once so bright and vital – now horror walks where joy danced. I do need a distraction from all that. What's your distraction, adept of the stars?' His face lit up. 'Isn't it drinking blood then feeling sorry for yourselves?'

'Enough!' shouted Dante. He drew his chainsword and thumbed it to life.

'Ah well,' said the eldar. He drew no weapon. 'I tell you what – if you can kill me, we'll say you win. That's a fair wager.'

'Silence!' Dante said. He advanced on the prince and swung his sword at him. Hellaineth made no move to block it, but stepped around the blow liquidly.

'You must try better,' he said.

Dante attacked in earnest, directing a flurry of blows at the eldar. The prince slid around them, pulling mocking faces at the sergeant, until Dante tricked him with a complicated reversed attack. His sword cleaved through the eldar, chopping him from shoulder to hip. There was no resistance. He cursed as the teeth of the blade jarred on the flagstones with a spray of sparks. Hellaineth shat-tered into a thousand dancing pieces of light that recoalesced.

The eldar mimed a choking death and swooned to the floor, then sprang to his feet and bowed.

'This has been most edifying, but I must bid you farewell, Sergeant Dante.'

'Fire!' roared Dante.

His men opened up on fully automatic fire. Dozens of bolt-rounds streaked past him, the frantic candles of rocket-burn lighting up the dim chamber. The bolts smashed into the walls, blasting rock splinters everywhere. Hellaineth stood in the middle of the firestorm, his laughing outline breaking apart and reforming as bolts rushed through him.

The Space Marines' magazines ran out. They clattered on the floor as the warriors ejected them from their guns and slammed fresh ammunition home. Dante held up his hand.

'Cease fire!' He stormed over to the throne and kicked it over. The wood broke on the floor. He kicked it to splinters as he hunted for a projection device, but found none. 'Search the chamber!' he commanded. 'Short-range hololith doppelganger. He can't be far away.' The Space Marines ripped tattered tapestries from the floor, prised stones from the wall, smashed out the windows and ripped up the floor. In minutes, the chamber looked as if it had taken a direct hit from heavy artillery.

'Spread out! Check every chamber!' Dante said. He ran for the roof, scraping his stabilisation jets on the walls of a narrow spiral staircase. He emerged onto a primitive roof sheathed with lead. Isolated gunfire crackled in the ruins, but the battle was over.

'*There's no sign of him,*' voxed Lorenz.

Dante growled deep in his throat. Later, after the company standard was raised on the parapet of the ancient keep and victory proclaimed, Dante searched one final time, but no trace of the prince was to be found.

Before they left, they demolished the keep.

CHAPTER TWENTY

LORD OF THE FIFTH HOST

753.M40

The Arx Angelicum

Baal

Baal System

The Council of Bone and Blood met to choose Avernis' replacement. A convocation of the Chaplains and the Sanguinary Priests, only they had the right to select the captains of the Chapter.

Dante waited on their judgement. He stood upon the high parapets of the Arx Angelicum, looking out over the desert. Both moons were in the sky; Baal Primus waxed full, Baal Secundus at half. A chain of black craters marred the surface of Baal Primus. Every time Dante saw that, he was reminded of his father and the stories he used to tell of the taking of Baalind's necklace. His recollections of life before were fading, three hundred years on, but those that remained were precious to him.

The dunes of Baal receded to the limit of his vision, timeless in their ever-changing movements. They were always different, but forever the same. He learned early in his life as a Blood Angel that Baal had always been a world of deserts, with precious little life. The moons, though... They were a different story. Lush, paradises – before the Dark Age of Technology had ended and night descended across mankind's first empire. War between them had reduced their landscapes to ashen desert and toxic waste.

Home, he thought. What is home? As a boy it was Baal Secundus; as a man it is the Arx Angelicum; as a human being it is Terra. He wondered if all men felt the shiftless sense of dislocation he felt, and if men were ever meant to travel the stars at all.

His encounter with the Pirate King made him thoughtful. The eldar had ruled a large part of the galaxy for millions of years; their technology was strange but advanced. They had a highly developed sense of the aesthetic, and yet there was one living in comparative squalor for amusement, surrounded by creatures most of its kind despised. He had seen the eldar's worlds. He could appreciate the beauty of the things they made.

He drew strength from mankind's superiority. The eldar had not recovered from their fall. The Emperor had lifted men high again. They were the true masters of the galaxy.

Unbidden, his eyes rose to the moons. If mankind is so wise, a treacherous voice whispered, why did Sanguinius leave the moons as wastelands, when he could have restored them? Leaving one's own people to suffer so that their strife-hardened children might be recruited. Is that the action of an angel?

Dante shook the thought away. It was the way it was, because it had to be that way.

A cool wind blew over the dunes. Streamers of sand undulated from the crests of each, the banners to the desert's imperceptible march. Four hundred miles to the north was the remains of the greatest city on Baal, buried in the sand. A colony of the moons in the era of mankind's supremacy, it had died when Secundus and Primus had turned on each other. On buried streets preserved under impacted sands were the bones of millions of people. He had seen them, where the indecisive movements of the dunes covered and recovered them.

He bowed his head.

Sanguinius, he thought. Guide me. Through the link I share with you. Help me be the best that I can be.

Thoughts blank, head bowed, he let the wind tug at his robes and carry his sense of time away, until he felt a presence beside him.

He looked up with a start. Staring at him, his golden mask carved with sorrow, was the Sanguinor. Dante blinked furiously, but the golden figure remained. It reached out a golden hand and rested it upon Dante's shoulder. Wellbeing flowed from the Herald of Sanguinius into Dante. Heavy with melancholy though it was, it steadied him.

'Sergeant.'

Reality blinked. The Sanguinor was gone. Another figure in gold stood behind him, Brother Demetrean of the Sanguinary Guard.

'The council has gone into recess, brother.'

'Have they reached a decision?' said Dante.

Demetrean shook his head. 'I have not come to deliver their verdict to you. Chaplain Malafael wishes to see you.'

As Malafael received Dante in his private chapel, Dante tried to guess, not for the first time, what he looked like. The brothers of the Chaplaincy never removed their helms in front of any but the captains, Chapter Master and Sanguinary Priests. To the brothers-of-the-line, they were aloof, mysterious figures. And yet Malafael had taken it on himself to mentor Dante, and Dante had come to regard him as a friend.

'Brother Dante,' said Malafael. He occupied the skull throne before the chapel altar.

'Lord Malafael.' Dante bowed.

Malafael gestured to a ewer of wine and silver goblets, beautifully engraved by the Chaplain's own hand. Surprisingly, the images on them were all of life, not of death.

'Take wine. You probably need it. Waiting is taxing on the nerves.'

Dante gratefully poured the wine and drank it down. 'It would be good to share this with you,' he said.

'Perhaps you will soon. The Council of Bone and Blood will make their decision tomorrow,' said Malafael. 'I am permitted to reveal my face to a captain. But we shall see. I have voted for you, Dante.

You are a good commander. Your men find you inspirational. Your strategies are sound, and you exhibit the Five Graces and Five Virtues in much of what you do. I believe you to be suitable.'

'Thank you.' Dante sipped the bitter wine. The grapes of Baal seemed to draw on the tragedy of the system. Little sweetness was found there.

'Do not thank me. My judgement is founded on fact, not affection.'

'I saw the Sanguinor again,' Dante said.

Malafael sat forwards.

'When?'

'Bare minutes before I came here.'

'Where?'

'Upon the Sanguis Wall.'

'And what were you doing there?'

'Taking the air. Thinking,' said Dante.

'Did anyone else see him?'

Dante shook his head.

'Then how can you be sure it was there? The Sanguinor is a material being. If it was not seen, it was not there.'

'I saw it,' said Dante. 'I have seen the Sanguinor four times now, my lord Chaplain. Each time it has appeared at some important point in my life. It saved my life on Baal Secundus. Sergeant Gallileon, I am sure, more closely paid attention to my leadership training after Rora. It pulled me from the depths of the Red Thirst on Tobias Halt. And now, today, it came to me on the wall.'

Malafael dipped his skull helm and took hold of his throne's armrests.

'Dante, do not speak of this before the judgement is delivered.'

'But why? Should not this manifestation be recorded in the Days of the Herald?'

'It should, but you must be careful. We are noble servants of the Emperor, but our blessed status does not make us immune to envy. There will be those among the higher ranks who see your claims of these visions...'

'But they are real!' protested Dante.

'All solo experiences are claims, Dante, because subjective experience cannot be verified by anyone other than the observer,' said Malafael patiently. 'Our Chapter above others must be especially circumspect. Every brother has his visions. We cannot make decisions based on every one – we would tear ourselves apart.'

'This is different.'

'I believe you, but not everyone will. I advise caution, that is all. If you are to speak of your visitations, then in all other areas of your life you must be above suspicion.'

'Suspicion of what?' demanded Dante angrily.

'We are an order of warriors, Dante. Do not be so naive as to think that others do not covet the position of captain, or would not resent you for taking it.'

'But the choice of the Council of Bone and Blood is final,' said Dante.

'Yes, and men's minds will be bound by that, but their hearts are another matter. We Blood Angels are creatures of great and terrible choler. Anger is too easily sparked from our souls. If you look like you are setting yourself above others–'

'I am not!'

'Do not interrupt me again,' said Malafael firmly. Dante clenched his fists and breathed through his teeth. 'I am not impugning your honour,' continued the Chaplain. 'Others will not see this relationship you appear to have with the Sanguinor the same way I do. They will see an ambitious brother who is desirous of high office.'

Dante began to speak, but Malafael spoke over his objection.

'There have been many examples throughout man's long history of people claiming divine intervention in order to grow their own power, often for what seemed like noble reasons. The Sanguinor is not divine, but it is mysterious, and it is dangerous. Be wary, that is all.'

Dante breathed, fighting his anger. He let his mind go blank, reaching for elusive restraint.

'I understand,' he said eventually.

'You show great control. That is good. I advise you to rest, Dante. If you are chosen, the Blessing of the Host will tax you. You will need your strength.' He stood from his throne and rested his armoured hand on Dante's shoulder.

'Who knows, after tomorrow we may be able to share a drink, after all.'

All lights were extinguished within the Arx Angelicum. The strength of the Chapter present on Baal gathered in the Basilica Sanguinarum, mortal and Space Marine both. A thousand blood thralls, two hundred brothers, all the Chapter's unassigned neo-phytes. They were helmless but armed for battle. Dante felt naked among them, standing by the sealed door in naught but a pair of three-quarter-length breeches. Bowls of glowing coals gave off pillars of red smoke. Red glass screened the windows of the basil-ica, so that the cathedral appeared drenched in blood. Serf choirs sang low, repetitive hymns that quickened and shushed like the thrum of blood in veins, while others chanted a wordless heartbeat. Blood scent was thick and coppery. The sound of blood, the scent of blood. Dante's mouth watered, and he became lightheaded.

A semicircle of thrones were arrayed in front of Sanguinius' statue. In them sat those Chaplains and Sanguinary Priests cur-rently on the home world. Their armour gleamed redly. Their helm lenses glowed in the low, ruddy light.

High Chaplain Bephael stood. Of all his brethren only he went unhelmeted, as was his right as their leader.

'Brother-Sergeant Dante!' he called down the length of the basil-ica's aisle. His pale skin glistened. His teeth flashed, eerily bright. 'The Council of Blood and Bone has sat these long hours in delib-eration. You have been judged worthy to lead your brothers in battle. Do you accept our judgement?'

'I do!' Dante shouted down the length of the basilica.

'Will you undertake the pains of the Blessing of the Host?'

Dante spoke clearly. 'I will!'

'If you falter, you will return to your squad. If you pass, you shall be made captain. Is this simple term acceptable to you, o brother of the blood?'

'It is!' shouted Dante.

'Then come forward, and face the kiss of steel.'

One member of every squad turned on the spot to face the aisle. With a single movement, all of them drew their combat knives. The oiled rasp was as delicate as a breath.

Dante walked forwards. He passed through the ranks of servitors, then by the hooded blood thralls singing their heartbeat song. A pair of cyber-cherubim swept down from their eyrie in the vaulting, trailing his banner between them on chains. A herald seraph flew before them, chanting his name. 'Dante, Dante, Dante.'

As he passed the first of his battle-brothers, the one chosen for the honour of the blessing stepped out.

'Accept this blessing of steel, in the name of the host,' he said. His knife flashed brightly in the red light, as if it were covered already in wet blood. The edge slashed across Dante's chest, opening up a long cut. Blood welled from it, and ran down his body. The Space Marine stepped back and licked his knife clean.

Another stepped out. 'Accept this blessing of steel, in the name of the host,' he said. His cut was shallower, slicing into Dante's upper arm.

Dante continued, his footsteps falling in time to the heartbeat chant.

'Accept this blessing of steel, in the name of the host,' said another, and slashed at him. This blow bit deep, and Dante gritted his teeth at the pain.

Despite the rapid clotting of his wounds, dripping blood left a trail behind him. It ran from his fingers and gathered between his toes, making the stone floor slick. Still he measured his pace. Cut after cut came. The feeling of light-headedness intensified. His thirst was aroused by the scent of his own fluids.

He approached the Council of Bone and Blood.

'Kneel!' commanded Bephael.

Dante knelt in a puddle of his own blood. Already the last of the cuts were closing, and the blood ceasing its flow. His banner cherubim fluttered overhead. The herald seraph flew down to head height.

'Lord High Chaplain Bephael,' it said in a piping voice. 'We present Brother-Supplicant Dante, of Squad Dante, of the Fifth Battle Company, the Daemonbanes, for your judgement.' It bowed its head and flew back to its roost.

Bephael raised both his hands like wings. Sanguinary High Priest Tazael stood and unveiled the Red Grail, the most holy relic of the Blood Angels. The other Sanguinary Priests rose and undid their gauntlets. Tazael handed the grail to an acolyte and cut his wrist, allowing nine drops of blood to fall into the chalice. He went to each of the Priests in turn, and they did the same, opening their veins with a small, curved knife the shape of a claw. As the grail was filled, Bephael put both hands atop Dante's head and spoke.

'Brother-Sergeant Dante!' he intoned. 'As you have not faltered today, do you swear never to falter in battle?'

'I do so swear,' said Dante.

'As you have bled today, do you swear to bleed for our Chapter, in the name of the Emperor of Mankind, and His Imperium?'

'I do so swear.'

'As you have suffered the blessing of our brothers, do you suffer the blessing of command?'

'I do so swear.'

'Do you swear to protect the weak and smite down their oppressors, to resist the thirst and the rage so long as you are able?'

'I do so swear.'

'And do you accept the judgement of the Council of Bone and Blood?'

'I do.' Dante's words echoed over the pulse-hymn.

The grail was brought forwards. Dante tilted his head to the side. A nick was made in his throat. Nine drops of blood were added to the mingled vitae inside. The cup was full.

'Then drink!'

The grail was held to Dante's lips. He sipped at first, then gulped as the blood touched his tongue. His thirst swelled and his fangs slid from his gums, scraping on the metal of the grail. He grabbed the cup and upended it, draining it dry. He blinked. The blood filled him with borrowed life; his senses sang. Never did he feel so alive as after sharing the sacrament.

Quickly as it came, it ebbed. The blood began dying as soon as it left the veins of its hosts, and its refreshment was fleeting. Tazael took the grail away, wiped it clean with fresh white cloth, and covered it over again.

'My Brother-Chaplains.' Bephael turned to the grim, skull-faced figures still sitting to his left. 'Do you uphold the judgement of the Council of Bone and Blood, and the Chapter Council, of which it is part and ruler of? Do you deem Brother Dante worthy of the direction of the Red Council in war?'

'I, Chaplain Fernibus, so uphold the judgement,' said the first, and stood.

'I, Chaplain Verimus, so uphold the judgement,' said the second, and stood.

So it went on.

'I, Chaplain Malafael, so uphold the judgement,' said Dante's mentor. Then the last, until seven Chaplains and nine Sanguinary Priests stood in a semi-circle in front of their chairs.

'It is done,' said Bephael. 'Stand, Dante, Lord of the Fifth Host, captain of the Daemonbanes!'

Dante stood and turned. The heartbeat chant ceased.

'Hail Dante, Fifth Captain of the Blood Angels!' his brothers shouted, and went to their knees.

Dante's hearts filled with pride. The council came to him one by one and took his hand, and offered their congratulations.

The ritual was over, and the feasting began.

CHAPTER TWENTY-ONE

THE PROMISE OF HOPE

998.M41
Mandeville point
Outside the Aegis Diamondo
Cryptus System

From one of the *Blade of Vengeance*'s observation domes, Commander Dante watched the ships of the First, Second and Fifth Companies peel away from the fleet. They accelerated hard, their engine stacks blazing brighter than suns. He watched for an hour, Sanguinius' death mask under his arm, wishing to see the sight of his men with his own senses, not those of his suit. The stack shine of the vessels dwindled into the wider starscape of the Red Scar and was lost in the slow undulations of the cosmic landscape.

A flash came from their position. A purple globe enveloped them. The light hurt Dante's eyes, bored through his optic nerves and scratched his brain. Still he watched as the warp enfolded his warriors.

The globe blinked out. The ships were gone.

The dome's angel of address swivelled on its podium. Its mechanical mouth opened. '*The task force has departed, my lord,*' said Asante. '*We are making preparations to enter the warp ourselves.*

I note you are in observation dome upsilon. I will be ordering the external shutters closed soon, my lord.'

'Thank you, Asante. I am done here.'

Dante felt better. The crushing sense of futility had been alleviated by Arafeo's sacrifice. He thanked his equerry in his heart. He could not grow used to this state of mind. His weariness would return, and he dare not take more blood for fear of where the red road led. But for now, at this crucial juncture, he could think clearly, and a plan was forming in his mind.

He turned away from the giant armourglass panels. The segments of their shutters rose up point first from their housings outside. The dome shook as they crawled up their tracks to meet at the apex.

The door opened and Corbulo entered. He looked more drawn and haunted than ever.

'My lord,' said Corbulo.

'What can I do for you, brother?'

The dome shutters clanged together, sealing the dome against the void and the coming storms of the warp.

'I have tested the small amounts of Satryx elixir we managed to recover from the Cryptus System.' He was despondent. The chemical had been used by the inhabitants of the Cryptus worlds to stave off madness. Corbulo had hoped it would similarly alleviate the thirst and rage. 'I believe it would have treated the flaw. It was not a cure, but it was a start, and now it is all gone. Satryx is devoured, and the stocks at Cryptus lost.'

'Can you synthesise it?'

Corbulo shook his head. 'No. Its structure is too specific. I apologise, my lord.'

'No one should bear his burden alone, not while he has a brother. The search must go on, Sanguinary High Priest. We can never falter, never stop. It is a setback, that is all.'

'I was sure this would be it. I do not know how many more near successes I can bear. I should put the darkness from me and concentrate on my duty.'

'Your visions?'

Corbulo nodded. 'They grow worse. I… I cannot speak of them. But I will submit myself for penance to Ordamael for my doubt. The Sanguinor itself said there was hope. We live in an age of wonder.'

Dante lifted his helmet onto his head. The seals locked, replacing his face with Sanguinius'.

'Hope is not always enough, Corbulo, but while there is blood, there is strength.'

CHAPTER TWENTY-TWO

HOMECOMING

764.M40
The Great Salt Waste
Baal Secundus
Baal System

The Thunderhawk banked. The Great Salt Waste slipped by, an endless tract of white, flat as paper, tinted a barely perceptible pink by the glow of Baal's parent star. It was hard to credit now, but until Dante had experienced artificial illumination and the colours of other stars, he had never seen true white. Every colour in the system, and everything in the Red Scar beyond its bounds, was polluted by the shades of blood.

Something as big as the waste could not fail to impress, but its featureless nature undid the spectacle of its size, making it inconsequential. Human experience gave scale to all things. Without it, the enormousness of the universe, the size of its stars, the sweep of its oceans, the number of suns and of worlds and of men, were incomprehensible. So it was with the Great Salt Waste. It was both magnificent and nothing from the air.

Dante watched the waste through the ship's auguries, sampled it through his sophisticated sensorium. He understood it now like he could not before, but he could never know it. No man could.

299

Black shapes on the salt drew his attention, crawling beetle-slow over the land.

'Brother Vulastin,' he said. The servant of the Armoury piloting the ship turned to look at Dante, his rust-coloured armour a subtly different shade to the blood-red of Dante's own.

'Put down there, by the nomads,' he said.

'We are not due to stop here, brother-captain,' said the Techmarine. 'Our schedule demands we pass on to Selltown and edify the locals there.'

'All must hear the call of the Trial. There are youths in those roamers. They have as much right as any to be informed of their chance.'

'The Salt Clans are small and scattered,' said Vulastin. 'Few recruits will be found among them.'

In the communications station behind the pilot and co-pilot's seat, Lorenz laughed.

'You evince the independence of the Armoury too strongly, brother. Do as the captain says.'

'He may be assigned herald, and captain. But he has not ordered me to set down,' said Vulastin. 'I follow the direction of the Master of the Blade, and the schedule I have tells me to head next for Selltown.' The Techmarine looked to Dante to see if he would be ordered. Dante remained silent.

'Do it for the graces, you damn fool,' said Lorenz. 'The captain wishes to go home. He *was* one of those few recruits.'

Vulastin glanced at Dante. 'As you wish, sergeant. Captain.' He pushed the flightstick forwards. Engines howling, the Thunderhawk sped towards the caravan.

They came in fast, landing before the lead vehicle. The caravan stopped abruptly. It was so similar to his own clan, Dante thought. There was the great hauler in the centre, not so impressive now he had seen voidships and the Arx Angelicum, and three dozen roamers. They looked like the one he had been born in. One could have been, for all he knew.

The population spilled out of their homes, pointing at the ship.

The men organised themselves into a loose phalanx, fingers ready on spring gun triggers. They were waiting when Dante strode out of the front of the Thunderhawk. The whole clan stood in nervous silence. Dante halted. The wind made his cloak and banner snap. Now he was there, he realised he had no clear reason for coming down and speaking. Was it nostalgia? Kinship? The people were so malnourished, stunted by hard living. They were dirty, the few parts of their exposed skin blistered with chemical and radiation poisoning. He was an angel, perfect. He felt no connection to them. He was disappointed, and regretted his impulsive decision.

Still, he had a task to perform. He would see it done.

'Let it be known that the time of the Duplus Lunaris is nigh upon us,' said Dante, his amplified voice roaring across the salt flats. 'Fifty youths will be chosen and taken to the Arx Angelicum upon Baal, there to dwell with us in brotherhood and fight the wars that must be fought against the foes of man. If there be any here with the guile and the courage to attempt our testing, let him make his way to us at Angel's Fall, so that he might be judged among the rest.'

'Angel's Fall is a long way from here,' someone muttered in the crowd. He had his voice pitched very low, not knowing Dante's enhanced senses could hear.

Dante rested his hand upon the pommel of his sword and surveyed the silent crowd again. There was nothing, no feeling. No sign of any kin. He scolded himself. What had he expected – to see his father come out to beg his forgiveness and protest his love? The man was long dead. Dante had no kin but his battle-brothers.

He turned to go, but a boy burst from the crowd and ran towards him. His mother gasped and called him back. The men shifted unsurely. So, this was what happened when you were confronted by your legends. Fear.

But the boy was not afraid. He came right up to Dante, staring at him with wonder. Hesitantly Dante turned again and looked down at him. Other children came forwards a little, shrugging off the protective hands of their parents, but no other dared come so close.

'You are an angel, a servant of the Great Angel?' said the boy.

'I am,' said Dante.

'There are stories of one boy from our clan, who ran away to join them more than a hundred years ago. Do you know him? Are the stories true?'

'I know a man who was a boy,' said Dante. 'He ceased to believe in stories the day his mother was buried in the salt along with his brother who never had the chance to take a single breath in this life.'

'You know him?' The boy's eyes widened. 'Is it true he sailed the seas of the void, and battled dragons? Did his gifts give him wings, and the power to run through the stars? Is it true that he became the lord of angels?'

'Most stories are not true,' said Dante. 'But what this boy failed to grasp, when he lost his belief, is that in stories lies the essence of truth. In that way, a fiction can sometimes be truer than fact.'

'Are you him?'

Dante did not reply. The boy was undaunted.

'They say I am brave. Could I become an angel like you, my lord? Is that possible?'

Dante stared down at this wretched youth. He seemed far away, barely reaching Dante's waist. But there, yes. Perhaps, there was the kinship he sought. In this boy, he saw himself.

'Anything is possible, boy. If one has determination, and will, and courage, there can be no failure. I am living proof of that, and as my word is my bond, I shall ever remain to be so.'

He looked to the crowd. 'The trial begins in four moons' time. By the blood of the Great Angel, spread the word.'

Leaving the boy to stare after him, Dante returned across the deserts of his childhood and re-entered the Thunderhawk, his thoughts already turning to his next war.

ABOUT THE AUTHOR

Guy Haley is the author of the Horus Heresy novel
Pharos and the Warhammer 40,000 novels *Dante,*
Baneblade, Shadowsword, Valedor and *Death of*
Integrity. He has also written *Throneworld* and *The*
Beheading for The Beast Arises series. His enthusiasm
for all things greenskin has also led him to pen the
eponymous Warhammer novel *Skarsnik,* as well as the
End Times novel *The Rise of the Horned Rat*. He has
also written stories set in the Age of Sigmar, included
in *Warstorm, Ghal Maraz* and *Call of Archaon*. He
lives in Yorkshire with his wife and son.

WARHAMMER
40,000

Darius Hinks

MEPHISTON
Blood of Sanguinius